ECHO IN TIME

ECHO TRILOGY, BOOK ONE

LINDSEY FAIRLEIGH

RUBUS PRESS

Editing by Sarah Kolb-Williams
www.kolbwilliams.com

Cover by We Got You Covered Book Design
www.wegotyoucoveredbookdesign.com

ISBN: 9781480075269

ALSO BY LINDSEY FAIRLEIGH

ECHO TRILOGY

Echo in Time

Resonance

Time Anomaly

Dissonance

Ricochet Through Time

KAT DUBOIS CHRONICLES

Ink Witch

Outcast

Underground

Soul Eater

Judgement

Afterlife

ATLANTIS LEGACY

Sacrifice of the Sinners

Legacy of the Lost

Fate of the Fallen

Dreams of the Damned

Song of the Soulless

THE ENDING SERIES

Beginnings: The Ending Series Origin Stories

After The Ending

Into The Fire

Out Of The Ashes

Before The Dawn

World Before

World After

FOR MORE INFORMATION ON LINDSEY FAIRLEIGH & THE ECHO TRILOGY:

www.lindseyfairleigh.com

For my beta readers—
you're each worth your weight in gold.

For Jim, who encouraged my love of the ancient world.

PROLOGUE

"Meswett, know yourself and you shall know the gods.
Meswett, trust yourself and you shall trust the gods.
So it ends, from start to finish,
as found in writing."
—taken from the Prophecy of Nuin, Old Kingdom, c. 2180 BCE

I thought I knew people. I didn't.

I thought I could trust my family and my friends. I couldn't.

I thought I at least had some idea of who I am. Wrong.

But here's the real kicker: I never thought I'd be in the heart of an ancient temple, driven by desperation and hatred, ready to kill my own father.

Screaming, I launch myself at him. My rage and sorrow are so great that I no longer have room for any other emotions. Coherent thought is foreign to me. I have one purpose—to destroy *him*.

He doesn't see me coming. He *can't* see me coming. I'm

moving too quickly, bending time to my will. It's impossible, but that doesn't make it any less real.

"How—?"

My father doesn't have time to finish the question. I've already torn the gun from his grasp and pressed the muzzle against the side of his head.

I flex my index finger.

Click.

PART I

University of Washington
Seattle, Washington

UNREAL & REAL

"NO!" I screamed as a speeding, moss-green station wagon slammed into my graduate advisor, who had been running across the street.

Dr. Ramirez's body rolled up onto the hood, his head hitting the windshield with a sickening crack, before sliding back down and settling on the asphalt. His arm flopped out to the side, landing in one of the many puddles created by the morning's incessant drizzle.

"Oh my God! Dr. Ramirez!" I sprinted the rest of the way down the paved path, across the sidewalk, and onto the university's main drag. As I knelt beside Dr. Ramirez, I dropped the copy of the Journal of Mediterranean Archaeology I'd been carrying—I'd been intending to show him an article on the discovery of a new Iliad manuscript, but the journal's pages lay askew, dirty and collecting droplets of rain.

My hands hovered over Dr. Ramirez, but I was too afraid of injuring him further to touch him. He was wearing his usual, casual professor's garb—medium-wash jeans and a heavy, navy-blue raincoat—but it hadn't protected him during the collision. The hair on the left side of his head was matted with blood, and his forehead looked slightly misshapen.

"I'm so sorry!" the driver cried as she lurched out of the car, leaving the driver's side door open. "I didn't see him . . . He just ran out . . . Oh my God . . . I . . ."

I ignored her and the flurry of activity taking place around us, instead reaching for Dr. Ramirez's limp hand, which still lay in a puddle. Trembling, I placed two fingers on his wrist to check his pulse, but I felt nothing.

"You killed him," I said hollowly.

The driver looked at me—into me—her eyes filled with horror.

Gasping, I jerked upright. My right leg was curled under me, numb. I'd fallen asleep in one of the wooden torture devices that doubled as desk chairs in the Anthropology graduate office, and according to my stiff joints, it hadn't been a wise decision. My beloved monstrosity of a desk—a battered, oak rolltop that might have been worth something if it wasn't covered with as many dents and dings as carvings—had been an equally foolish place to rest my head. *Damn,* I thought as I took in the disarray under my elbows. A chaotic jumble of open books, photos, and papers was scattered across the desk's surface, some with brand-new folds and wrinkles, and one with an unfortunate drool spot.

"Fabulous," I muttered, wiping away the wet stain with a tissue.

Once again, I'd been attempting to decipher the ancient, oh-so-frustrating puzzle that had been driving me nuts all quarter. A combination of ancient Egyptian hieroglyphs—two parallel, vertical lines, one with a flag-like protrusion, the profile of a lion's head, a filled-in half circle, and a full circle with a smaller circle cut out of the center—that seemed perfectly content to remain undecipherable.

Shaking with adrenaline lingering from the awful dream, I sighed, shifted my leg from under me, and lowered my head to rest my cheek on the desk. I stared at the end of my coffee-brown ponytail, unbelievably glad that I'd been asleep and that Dr. Ramirez hadn't been hit by a car. It had been a dream . . . just a stupid, freakishly realistic dream.

"Hey, Lex!"

"Gah!" I exclaimed, jumping slightly and causing the invisible pins and needles poking into my reawakening leg to jab with renewed gusto. At seeing the short, excited man standing beside my desk, I shook my head and laughed. It was almost impossible to be irritated at Carson, whose diminutive build, artfully mussed brown hair, and bright blue eyes made him look more like a member of a boy band than a fellow grad student. "Seriously, Carson? Was that absolutely necessary?"

He slapped his hand down on one of the open books, lifting it a few seconds later to reveal a folded hundred-dollar bill. "You win," he said grudgingly. "I still think my article was *far* superior, but apparently my opinion doesn't count." He tossed an academic journal onto the desk beside the money. It was opened to an article titled "Fact From Myth: Cross-Referencing Texts Across Ancient Cultures to Decipher Unknown Symbols"—my article.

With a smug smile, I crossed my arms and sat back in my chair. We'd made a bet several months back—a Benjamin to whichever of us was published by a major academic journal first. Though we'd both been co-authors or contributors to other people's articles, neither Carson nor I had been published for our individual work. Until now.

"I'm surprised they didn't take one look at that monstrous title and toss your article into the trash," Carson said.

"Ouch! You wound me with your pointy words!" I exclaimed, clutching my chest dramatically.

Carson flopped down in a chair beside my desk and let his head fall backward with a groan. "It's not fair, Lex," he whined, only amplifying his pubescent image.

"You're ridiculous," I told him, laughing. I patted his knee, happily noting that my own leg was back to normal. "Maybe you'll be in the next one . . . doesn't *Mediterranean Archaeology* come out tomorrow? I thought you submitted a few things to them?" Remembering my dream, the *Journal of Mediterranean Archaeology* discarded on the grimy road, I stifled a shiver.

Carson raised his head and stared at me with annoyance. "That's the latest issue of *Mediterranean Archaeology*," he said, pointing to my article.

My blood instantly chilled, and this time I couldn't repress a shiver. It was Thursday, and that particular journal was *always* delivered on Fridays. *It's just a coincidence*, I told myself.

Pointing to the open journal, I asked, "So, other than my *amazing* article, is there anything else in there worth noting?"

Carson shrugged. "Mostly it's just the usual . . . retranslations of this or that text, an update on Pompeii and the volcanic activity at Mount Vesuvius, an explanation of some new techniques for underwater excavating"—suddenly excited, he leaned forward and rubbed his hands together—"and, an analysis of a new Iliad manuscript. It's fragmented, but it's also the oldest version ever found."

Something in my chest tightened, and my lungs felt too weak to draw in enough air.

When I didn't say anything, Carson added, "Awesome, right?" He specialized in the classics—Homer, Plato, Catullus—practically worshipping the long-dead poets and philosophers.

"Uh . . . yeah." I snatched my iPhone off the desk and checked the time—half past eleven. In fifteen minutes, I was scheduled to meet with Dr. Ramirez in his office downstairs for my final advisory meeting of the quarter. He'd barely been able to squeeze me in between appointments with professors and other students, so there was no reason for him to be crossing the road as he'd been doing in the dream . . . even if it did pass right by our building.

Suddenly, my phone vibrated, and a blue text message alert box appeared in the middle of the screen. The message was from Dr. Ramirez.

Running out for coffee. Will try to be back in time for our meeting.

"No effing way!" I hissed, standing so quickly my chair nearly fell over backward. I grabbed the journal, then shook my head and tossed it back onto the desk before speeding through the maze of desks and cubicles honeycombing the communal graduate office.

"Lex? Where are you going?" Carson called after me.

"Be right back," I said, not even glancing over my shoulder. I raced down the dim, narrow third-floor hallway and shoved the heavy stairwell door open. It slammed against the wall with a loud, metallic thud. In a matter of seconds, I descended the two flights of stairs and exploded into the main hall of the first floor. I bumped into someone, receiving a masculine grunt as we both crashed to the linoleum floor. My knee and elbow hit the floor so hard that bruising was inevitable.

"I'm *so* sorry!" I exclaimed, extricating myself from beneath the legs of . . . Dr. Ramirez. "Oh my God . . . are you okay?"

Dr. Ramirez—tall, dark, middle-aged, and dignified—stood and made a bit of a show of dusting himself off. He studied me, holding back a smile. I was still sprawled on the floor.

"I'm going to assume your rush was caused by excitement about the recent publication of your work," he said.

Blushing, I stood. "I . . . yes," I lied.

"Well, since you're here, Alexandra, do you want to come with me to get coffee?" Dr. Ramirez checked his watch. "I don't think I'll have another chance all day." *But then he might cross a street, and there might be a moss-green station wagon, and . . .*

"No!" I blurted, thrusting my hands out in front of me. When his eyebrows rose, I added, "I'll go get coffee for us both. I'm sure you have better things to do." Spinning away from him, I jogged to the main doors. From the ache in my knee, I could tell the bruise was going to be a beauty. "You just stay here," I said over my shoulder.

It wasn't until I was through the glass doors and halfway down the steep, slippery stone steps that I realized I had no clue what kind of coffee Dr. Ramirez liked. I turned around and, when I poked the upper half of my body through the open door, was only half-surprised to find my advisor standing exactly where I'd left him, his face utterly bemused. "I forgot to ask what you wanted," I said breathlessly.

Chuckling, Dr. Ramirez said, "Just black coffee. Large, please."

"Okay. Great! Sorry about . . . you know. I'll be right back!" Again I hurried down the stairs, not caring that it was raining and that I was wearing only a thin sweater, jeans, and slouchy suede boots. I paused when I reached the sidewalk and road that had featured so prominently in my midday nightmare. Looking up the street toward the campus gatehouse, I spotted a single car approaching, but it was too far away to distinguish any details. I squashed my curiosity and changed direction, heading for the coffee stand in Suzzallo Library instead of the cafe in the Burke Museum, which was closer but across the main road. My psyche wouldn't be able to handle passing a moss-green station wagon, coincidence or not.

My phone buzzed as I was walking back up Denny's steep front steps, one to-go cup of piping hot coffee in each hand. I set both on the campus newspaper stand beside the glass doors and pulled my phone out of my back pocket. Dr. Ramirez had texted me again.

Check your email.

Intrigued, I opened my inbox and quickly scanned through the newest messages. Three were from students and were utterly predictable—two of my undergrads were asking for extensions on their final papers and one wondered how much it would affect his grade if he skipped it altogether. Shaking my head, I snorted and muttered, "Too much."

The fourth message also had a University of Washington domain, but it wasn't from anyone I knew.

Hello Ms. Larson,

I am a visiting professor in the Classics department here at UW. I contacted your department head, and he directed me to you. I need an on-site ancient languages specialist at an upcoming excavation in Egypt, preferably someone with a background deciphering unfamiliar symbols. Please let me know if you are interested, and I will send you the specifics. If you agree to participate, you will be abroad during the latter half of spring quarter and most of summer. Please let me know if you have any questions. I hope to hear from you soon.

Marcus Bahur
Professor of Classical Archaeology
University of Washington
University of Oxford

I studied the email, rereading it several times. A professor visiting from Oxford wanted me, specifically, to accompany him on a dig in Egypt . . . as an ancient languages specialist. I'd worked on a half-dozen excavations all around the Mediterranean, but mostly just as a grunt—a field school student. Being a specialist would give me the chance to pursue my own research along with that of Professor Bahur. The opportunity sounded too good to be true. It also sounded too expensive, and there wasn't enough time to apply for grants to cover room, board, and travel expenses. If it cost anything on my end, I'd have to pass.

Rushing, I replied, vaguely proclaiming interest and requesting more details. As I typed, I thought, *please be free . . . please be free . . . please be free . . .*

Again with coffees in hand, I headed back into majestic Denny Hall. Built late in the nineteenth century, it was the university's first building. Accordingly, the exterior was stunning—a combination of stone and archways and small-pane windows that befit a French chateau far more than a university building—but aside from the first-floor professor's offices, the interior was laughably mundane.

After squeaking my way down the wide hall, I knocked loudly on the heavy wooden door to Dr. Ramirez's office.

"Come in," he called, his voice rumbling.

As I entered, Dr. Ramirez was placing a book on the top shelf of the built-in bookcase beside his desk. "Ah, I see the coffee has arrived," he said, his eyes laughing though he wore no smile. After taking in my appearance, he asked, "Did you take a dip in the fountain on your way?"

I glanced down at myself, unsurprised to see that my clothes were more than a little damp, clinging to me like plastic wrap to ceramic, which was pretty much how they felt. "I forgot my coat," I said lamely. I set the two cups of coffee on his well-organized desk but didn't sit in either of the wooden visitors' chairs. I didn't want to be rude and drip all over them.

Noticing my internal predicament, Dr. Ramirez said, "Please, Alexandra, sit."

For the thousandth time, I noted how lucky I was to have landed him as my graduate advisor. A sturdy, former college football player, he was like a towering, slightly intimidating father figure to everyone in the archaeology department. He was both stoic and sage, and tended to hand out criticism far more often than praise, but the criticism was always of the constructive variety.

I sat in the chair on the right, unable to repress my desire to examine the cluttered bookshelves lining the walls on either side of the office. They were filled with volumes of every color and size. Many of the spines were faded with age, some even flaking, making them stand out next to their younger brethren. Beside books on many of the shelves lay little trinkets and photographs from all over the world. Like always, I felt the overwhelming urge to examine each item, to discover its meaning, origin, and personal value to Dr. Ramirez.

"So, Alexandra," Dr. Ramirez said, interrupting my visual reverie. He'd seated himself in his old-fashioned, brown leather executive chair. "How do you think this quarter went?"

Unashamed, I said, "Really well."

Dr. Ramirez smiled. "Specifically, what do you think your top achievements were?"

I crossed my legs, pursed my lips, and thought for a moment. Finally, I said, "My dissertation proposal was accepted several weeks ago, as you know. I'm really excited to move forward with it next quarter. My ability to translate hieroglyphic, hieratic, and demotic texts has progressed really well . . . and I started learning Coptic, too." I wiggled my foot. "Umm . . . I won't know for sure until after I've graded their final papers, but I think my undergrads did really well this quarter." I paused, knowing I was forgetting something. "Oh, and I was published in a major archaeology journal," I added proudly.

Leaning back, Dr. Ramirez intertwined his fingers and rested his hands on his belly. For a moment he merely studied me, and I tried not to fidget under his pondering gaze. "You know, I don't usually take on graduate students . . . but I have to admit, accepting you was a very good decision on my part," he stated, giving himself a verbal pat on the back. I half-expected him to physically do it, reaching his arm over his shoulder. He didn't.

"Thank you," I responded, stifling the sudden urge to giggle. I glanced down at my hands.

"I've spoken with all of your professors. They're all very impressed with your progress. And your proposal—I'm really quite excited to see where this project ends up taking you. I'm expecting great things from you, Alexandra."

At the moment, all I could do was smile . . . and blush. Dr. Ramirez's overt praise stunned me.

"Now, unless you have any questions, I believe we're done for the quarter. Grade your students' papers early and make sure you enjoy your break—and get some well-deserved rest," he ordered with mock severity.

Hearing the dismissal, I stood. "I will. Thank you, Dr. Ramirez," I said before heading for the door.

"Oh, and Alexandra . . ."

Pausing with my hand on the doorknob, I looked back at him over my shoulder.

"I hope the excavation works out—I know you're perfect for the job," he told me, grinning before turning his attention to some papers on his desk.

"Thanks," I replied quietly. "Have a nice break, professor." I slipped out of his office, gently pulling the door shut behind me.

An hour later, I was unlocking my apartment door. I was more than ready to begin winter break—even if it was as low-key as hanging out with my cat in my seventh-floor apartment, grading mind-numbingly boring final papers and overindulging on pop culture via the television. The only thing to break up the glorious couch time would be a three-day Christmas visit with my family in Central Washington.

My little brown tabby, Thora—I'd named her after the adored Egyptian goddess, Hathor—greeted me with a soft meow from her perch on her favorite windowsill. The building was nearly one hundred years old, and it had the single-pane windows, scuffed hardwood floors, and steam radiators to prove it. It worked out well for Thora—the windows made the cars, busses, and pedestrians who trafficked the street below sound like they were *in* the apartment and thus provided her ample entertainment—but it was more of a bummer for me. I liked quiet . . . and sleep.

"Hey, Thora. Are you ready for break?" I sang, crossing the cramped living room to scratch under her chin. I earned a loud purr in response and watched her bright green eyes narrow to happy slits.

My apartment was pretty standard to a century-old building —the kitchen was tiny, with ceramic tile countertops, a deep, porcelain sink, and absolutely no dishwasher; the living room was cramped, with barely enough room for a sienna microsuede couch, an antique walnut steamer trunk that doubled as a coffee table, a pair of tall, matching bookcases finished to resemble walnut, and a small, flat-screen television; and beyond the living room, the small bedroom, adjoining bathroom, and closet were equally as spacious—as in, not at all. The place was cozy, and I loved it.

I dropped my messenger bag on the couch and headed straight for my room to change into comfy, dry clothes—a plain white T-shirt, a zip-up hoodie displaying the name of my favorite band, Johnny Stopwatch, and some black sweatpants that had long since faded to gray. Finally feeling more like a human than a swamp monster, I sat on the couch, pulled out my thin, steel-gray laptop, tapped the power button, and waited. As the slender machine hummed to life, I stared through the rain-streaked window. I had a view of the university campus, an artful arrangement of graceful brick buildings and emerald-green grass and pines. People hurried along crisscrossing paths like ants in an ant farm, eager to get to their next class, if only to be out of the incessant drizzle.

Unexpected anticipation fluttered in my stomach as my attention returned to the computer screen. The email window was open—it almost always was—and there was a new message from Professor Bahur. Hesitantly, I opened it and began to read.

Ms. Larson,

I am excited to hear of your interest in participating in my excavation. Attached you will find a document containing further details of this project and your potential position. I would like to set up a time to meet so we can solidify your participation. I also want to make sure you know what you are getting into and that you have time to prepare—it will be quite the adventure. Are you available to meet up the Thursday or Friday before the start of the new quarter? Please let me know what time is good for you, and I will rearrange my schedule accordingly.

I am looking forward to meeting you, Ms. Larson, as you come very highly recommended.

Marcus Bahur
Professor of Classical Archaeology
University of Washington
University of Oxford

For the first time, I wondered what the mysterious, visiting professor looked like. His permanent position was at Oxford, so I figured he was British, and his formal language patterns indicated someone older and gentlemanly . . . possibly with a crazy mustache or overgrown eyebrows. Shaking the frivolous thoughts away, I opened the attachment and scanned it, looking for dollar signs. I found them.

Oh. My. God. I sat back on the couch, staring at the screen. I could more than afford to participate in the dig. Housing and food would be provided, and along with a stipend for leisure and travel expenses, I'd get paid a sizable commission for my finds. The bigger the discovery, the more money in my pocket. It was, in a word, unbelievable.

Without hesitation, I sent a quick reply to Professor Bahur, informing him that I was eager to participate and that I was available to meet with him on either that Thursday or Friday, whenever worked best for him. Despite my curiosity about the professor and his extravagant excavation, I could wait the three weeks . . . barely.

Just as I clicked send, my phone vibrated. I plucked it out of the little pocket on the side of my bag, and seeing the caller's name, answered. "Hi, Mom."

"Hi, honey," my mom, Alice, replied. Disappointment was heavy in her voice.

"What's wrong?" I asked, instantly concerned. "Is Grandma okay?"

"Oh, it's nothing like that. I was hoping to surprise you by showing up at your place tonight, but the darn pass is closed. But . . . I should be able to make it over there by tomorrow afternoon."

"Oh . . . well . . . I didn't know you were coming! That's so sweet, Mom!" I said, genuinely excited. It had been more than six months since I'd seen my mom, and I missed her. Besides, I could barely wait to tell her the great news about the excavation. "I'm excited to see you!"

"Me too, sweetie. Let's just hope the weather behaves."

"My fingers are crossed," I said, actually crossing my left index and middle fingers. "Will you call me when you leave?"

"Of course!" she exclaimed, laughing. "I want to make sure you have time to clean up all the piles on your floor."

I rolled my eyes, avoiding looking at the various mounds of books, clothes, and mail strewn haphazardly around the apartment. "Thanks, Mom, that's so thoughtful of you," I said dryly.

"I'm just being your mom, Lex . . . trying to take care of you," she stated with mock concern.

"Yeah, yeah. I'll talk to you tomorrow." I paused, then added, "And Mom?"

"Hmm?"

"I'm glad you're coming."

"Me too. Bye, sweetie."

"Bye, Mom." I tapped the screen to end the call. After only a few seconds of thought, the phone was back up to my ear.

In the middle of the third ring, I was greeted by the voice of Cara, a young, prosperous businesswoman and one of my best friends. "Hey, Lex."

"So . . . I just found out something *amazing*," I said, leading her with my excitement.

"What?"

"Guess," I ordered.

"Umm . . . you're a princess?"

I laughed out loud. "Definitely not."

"Didn't think so. You won a Caribbean cruise?"

"Nope."

"You dropped out of grad school and decided to pursue life as a nun?"

I choked on nothing. "You've got to be kidding me. That's ridiculous."

"Alright, I give up," she sighed, and I could hear a smile in her voice.

After listening to me tell her about the two emails from Professor Bahur and that I would almost certainly be working as one of the leaders of an excavation in Egypt—my dream—Cara squealed. Very, very loudly.

Unfortunately, I pulled the phone away too late, and my ear rang from her high pitch and volume. Even Thora stirred from her study of the pedestrians far below to glare at the phone.

With obvious urgency, Cara blurted, "This calls for immediate, emergency celebrating! I'll call Annie right now, okay? We'll be over in a couple hours for dinner before we go out."

"Umm . . . I don't really have anything to make . . ."

"No problem. Annie and I'll stop by the store on our way—we'll surprise you!" she said, her words bursting with enthusiasm.

"Sounds good," I replied.

"Great! See you soon!" She hung up before I could say goodbye.

Glancing at my laptop screen, I noticed there was a new message in the inbox. It was from the professor—I couldn't believe how quickly he'd replied.

Ms. Larson,

Very well. How about Friday at 3:30 in the afternoon at the café in the Burke Museum? Please let me know if either the time or location is unsuitable to you.

Until then,

Marcus Bahur
Professor of Classical Archaeology
University of Washington
University of Oxford

"If nothing else, Thora, this should be interesting," I

muttered, reaching over the arm of the couch to rub the top of the tabby's head.

I'd been waiting at the bar, shoulder-to-shoulder with dozens of other patrons, for about ten minutes. Finally, a harried bartender finished making the three drinks I'd ordered—all vodka cranberries—and set them on the bar. I paid in cash and reached for the drinks just as the woman on my right lurched against me. In my attempt to grab the bar for support, I knocked two of the glasses over, and bright red liquid splashed directly onto the man beside me.

"Oh!" he exclaimed, leaning away too late.

"Oh no!" I stared at the blaring crimson stain marring the lower half of his formerly pristine, pale gray shirt. "Oh God! I'm *so* sorry! I didn't mean to . . ." I trailed off, losing all sense of coherency when I glanced up.

Eyes the color of Baltic amber held my gaze, too vibrant and rich to be considered brown. I couldn't help but wonder if they were an artifice. Strong, straight, and defined, his bronze features were equally as striking, especially when paired with the hint of dark-as-night hair covering his shaved head. He was absolutely stunning.

As he watched me, frustration seemed to blanket his face. "It's not a problem," he assured me in a deep, smooth-as-milk-chocolate voice. It was slightly accented, sounding Middle Eastern with a sprinkling of French and maybe a touch of German or Swedish.

"But . . . but . . ." was all I could say.

The corners of the stranger's mouth turned down in a partial frown and he shook his head. "Really, it's fine. Don't worry about it."

"Are—are you sure?" I asked quietly, incapable of breaking eye contact but desperately needing to. I blamed my awkwardness on the wine I'd consumed during dinner. *He's just a guy in a bar*, I told myself. *Get a grip!*

"Yes, perfectly," he assured me again. "I believe your friends are waiting for you—if those"—he smirked as his eyes flicked to the table where Cara and my other best friend, Annie, were sitting—"are your friends?"

Following his eyes, I found Annie and Cara, watching us in awe. Their wide-eyed expressions mirrored mine perfectly. "Um, yeah . . . those are my friends," I admitted, and then I remembered that they had been two-thirds of the reason I'd been at the bar. "Damn! Their drinks . . . now I'll have to wait for another ten minutes," I muttered.

Within seconds, the enthralling stranger had snagged a bartender and ordered replacements for my spilled beverages. "I'll help you carry them . . . to make sure they actually make it to their destination this time," he teased.

I didn't know how to reply to that, and he didn't wait, so I just followed him to the table where Cara, a blue-eyed goldilocks, and Annie, a half-Japanese beauty, sat and stared. They gaped at my new acquaintance as he set the drinks on the table.

"I hope you ladies have a nice night," he said, flashing us a tight-lipped smile. He met my eyes one last time, then turned and walked away.

"Whoa!" Cara nearly shouted.

"Uh . . . yeah," Annie added.

"I know," I agreed. Wishing the gorgeous stranger had joined us, I searched the crowd for him, but he'd already disappeared.

2

MOM & DAD

I sat down beside my mom, curling my legs under me and relaxing into the couch with a satisfied sigh. My belly was full of the most delicious take-out Thai food the University District had to offer, my mom was with me and nearly as excited about the upcoming excavation as I was, and I had nothing but free time for weeks to come. *Damn, life is good.*

"Sweetie," my mom began in a voice that instantly told me something was wrong. "I came out here for a reason . . . not just to surprise you." She took a deep breath, either to calm her nerves or strengthen her resolve. "Your dad and I were talking the other night, and we decided that, well . . . Lex, haven't you ever wondered why you don't really look like your dad?" she asked, gazing intently at the empty wine glass in her hand. Sickly yellow light from the kitchen reflected off its convex, crystalline surface.

What's that supposed to mean? Tons of people don't look much like their parents. Why would she ask me that? Unless . . . she can't mean that . . . Dad's not my . . .

My mom had asked me a question. But her words . . . I couldn't figure out what they meant. Deciphering the true, hidden meaning behind words was what I was best at, but I couldn't decipher *these* words. They implied that there was something I should have noticed before, something that should have been obvious. *But she can't mean that Dad's not my . . . not my . . .*

Suddenly, I was more aware of the bite-sized living room than ever before. The bookcases set against the opposite wall were in serious need of dusting, and I had the urge to reorganize the hefty collection of historical fiction and romance books packed onto the shelves. The framed prints on the wall between the bookcases captivated me more than ever before. Dali's *Persistence of Memory* stood out beyond all others. I felt a strange kinship with the melting pocket watches, like I, too, was losing form.

On my right hand, my grandpa's ring became hypnotizing. Grandma Suse, his widow, gave it to me on my sixteenth birthday, and I'd had the wide, silver band resized to fit my slender ring finger. Its inky obsidian stone seemed to suck in the light rather than reflect it back to the waiting world. Was my greedy ring sucking in all of the air too? I couldn't seem to draw a full breath.

Haven't you ever wondered why you don't really look like your dad?

It was true—I didn't really resemble my dad. Had I noticed before? I looked so much like my mom that I'd figured I'd inherited less obvious characteristics from my dad—his laugh, the way he walked, his single-minded determination. But now, I realized those characteristics were undefinable as well. Truth stared me in the face, forcing me to *see. She really means that Dad's not my real dad.*

But why tell me now? How did this happen? Possibilities, vile and corrosive, swirled around in my mind. Had my parents separated and been with other people before I was born? Had my mom had an affair? Had I been adopted? The last, I knew without a doubt, was wrong—other than differences in coloring,

I was practically a physical clone of my mom. But an affair or separation was still a possibility. *Is my happy family a lie?*

Carefully, I reached for my wine glass with a trembling hand, hoping to numb myself with its contents. As my fingers touched the smooth stem, fear cleared my thoughts. Fear, and unexpected anger. If I was someone else's daughter because my mom cheated on my dad . . .

"What do you mean, exactly?" I asked, voice sharp and eyes narrowed. It felt like eons had passed since my mom initially asked the question, but my chaotic thought process had borne conclusions in less than a minute.

Hesitantly, my mom raised her warm brown eyes to search mine, and then she shifted them to focus on the wall behind the couch. "Grandma Betsy had a really hard time having kids. She was given certain drugs. At the time, doctors were giving specific hormones to women who were at risk of miscarrying. Betsy, well, she was one of the women treated that way."

"So . . . ?" I prompted, impatient.

Suddenly my mom was looking at me, weariness in her eyes. She sighed. "The treatment had an unforeseen side effect on the children. They were sterile, Lex. Your dad couldn't have children."

Dad couldn't have kids? That meant Mom never had an affair . . . they never separated . . .

Relief flooded my body. It began in my lungs as I involuntarily inhaled a delicious breath of air, and it flowed out toward my nerve endings. *Mom and Dad were never separated . . . my family is real!* I was ecstatic.

My mom furrowed her brow.

Abruptly, relief fled from my body. *If Dad couldn't have kids . . .*

"Then who's my father?" *This can't be happening.*

"We went to the best place, where the donors were all guaranteed to be intelligent, talented men with a healthy family history."

But none of those intelligent, talented men were Joe Larson, my dad—or rather, the man I'd believed to be my dad until two minutes ago. Despite my best efforts to hold it together, my chin began to tremble. The quivering spread to my cheeks and then throughout my entire body, but I didn't cry. I was too stunned to cry.

Watching my devastation, my mom said, "Maybe I shouldn't have told you, but your dad thought . . ." Again, she sighed.

I pulled my legs up to my chest and fit my head between my knees. My mom tried to comfort me by rubbing my back, but I flinched at her touch. I stared down at the hardwood floor, trying to focus . . . trying to breathe.

Me, the very essence of my being, retreated inside, seeking the only haven available: solitude.

Thud-THUMP. Thud-THUMP. Thud-THUMP.

I focused on my heartbeat. It was still the same. It hadn't changed in the last few minutes, unlike everything else I knew about myself . . . or thought I'd known.

I'm still me.

Right?

3

NIGHTMARES & DREAMS

"Are you sure you—"

"Let's just go already, Mom," I interrupted. I knew I was being a brat in the worst way—my mom felt awful for lying to me about my parentage for twenty-four years, and I was taking out my inner turmoil on her, but . . . she'd *lied* to me. So had my dad. And it wasn't just a little, I-broke-your-favorite-vase-and-told-you-it-was-the-cat lie, oh no. It was a whopper of a lie, requiring me to do a complete identity overhaul. I couldn't just pretend that everything was hunky-dory. I'd never been a good liar.

Searching for a safe place in my mind, I focused on the beads of rain clinging to the passenger window of my mom's dark red sedan. As the car picked up speed, the droplets seemed reluctant to stream across the glass, moving in a stuttering rhythm.

Part of me worried about leaving Thora alone so abruptly, but I knew Annie would take good care of her. I'd sent her a text in the wee hours of the morning, asking her to cat-sit for the next three weeks, and she'd agreed immediately. She hadn't asked a single question. Annie had the kind heart of a saint, and I loved her for it.

As I felt myself falling asleep, a small sense of relief washed over me.

"Haven't you ever wondered why you don't really look like your dad?" my mom asked, her voice echoing all around me.

I was standing in front of a wood-framed mirror hung at eye level on a seemingly endless wall. A picture of my dad's face was pinned to the mirror's frame. I examined his features closely, and then did the same with my own, attempting to reconcile their many differences.

Maybe his lips, *I thought* . . . those could look a little like mine. *But after cross-referencing the reflection of my own narrow, rosy mouth with his, I realized they weren't a match.*

Horrified, I stared at the photo of my dad, watching his mouth disappear completely. When I tried to scream, there was only silence. I looked into the mirror, and with gut-wrenching terror, realized that my own mouth had vanished as well.

My ears were next, as were my dad's in his picture. And then my long, dark brown hair.

I brought my hands up to my face, attempting to hold the remaining features in place. As my nose vanished, so did my ability to breathe. I panicked, trying to suck air through a smooth expanse of unbroken skin.

I watched my frantic brown eyes until the lack of oxygen caused dark spots to wash over my vision. I glanced one last time at the picture of my dad before my world faded to black.

All I could think was, I am nothing.

I woke with my head resting against the chilly car window. Involuntarily, I brought my hand up to feel my face. Everything was right where it belonged, including the salty tears streaming down my cheeks.

Glancing out the window, I realized the rain had turned to light snow and we were nearing my hometown. Yakima, the central Washington city where I'd grown up, was really quite demonstrative in terms of the stereotypical seasons. There are four distinct times of the year: sweat-inducing summers, reddish-gold falls, snowy winters, and flowery springs. I was always amazed by the way the fruit trees in the countless orchards accentuated the seasons. Nothing screamed winter like bare branches sheathed in ice, or heralded spring like apple and cherry blossoms.

As the familiar, mostly barren landscape of the high desert glided past, I wondered if coming home and seeing my dad was going to make the realignment of my identity any easier. Or, would it become infinitely more difficult?

Silently, each unique, beautiful snowflake found a home on the deck around me. In the back of my mind I felt envious of the moonlit flakes—each was well-defined and individual. I, on the other hand, was vague, undefined. They didn't have to worry about where they might fit in, let alone where they came from. They would just . . . land. *Where am I supposed to land?*

I'd been home for two weeks, and so far, the frigid Yakima winter had proven to be the only thing that could bring me peace. The falling snow offered a distraction from my morose thoughts. And because it rarely snowed in Seattle, sitting outside in below-freezing weather didn't belie my sanity too much. It *was* snowing, after all.

At a knock on the sliding glass door, I jumped. I heard it open partially. "Lex?" It was my mom.

"Yeah?"

"Cara's on the phone, sweetie. She said she tried your cell but it went straight to voicemail. She sounds really worried—you should talk to her." My mom had always been a master guilt-tripper.

I took a deep breath, closed my eyes, and surrendered. "Fine." I could only avoid talking to people for so long. And if I was being honest with myself, even I was getting sick of the moping, sullen woman I'd become. I needed to rejoin the world, bask in the sunshine, seize the day, and . . . you know, all that bullshit.

As I entered the house, my mom handed me the phone with a sympathetic smile. I wandered upstairs to my old bedroom and shut the door, sitting cross-legged on the burgundy duvet. I focused on taking long, deep breaths, then closed my eyes and raised the phone to my ear.

"Hey, Cara," I said in a reluctant, slightly hoarse voice. Not speaking for days tended to do that to a voice.

"Oh my God, Lex! It's *so* good to hear your voice," she said enthusiastically. "So, are you going to let me know what the hell's going on? Why'd you just take off? I mean, weren't you planning on staying in the Yak with your fam for only a few days during Christmas? How much family time can you really stand? Aren't things still bad with your sister?"

I really didn't want to lie to Cara—at least, not outright. After searching for the courage to respond to her barrage of questions, I spoke carefully. "Uh, yeah . . . I was planning on only being here for a few days." *True.* "But when my mom was about to leave, I suddenly felt like I needed more time with her." *Also true.* "So, on a whim, I just sort of decided to ride back to Yakima with her and stay until after Christmas." *True-ish . . . success!* But I couldn't ignore the sick feeling churning in my stomach.

"So . . . you're not, like, dying or anything?" she joked.

"Nope . . . not that I'm aware of. I guess I've just been really distracted here. It's been a long time since I've been home." The partial truth was coming more easily.

"Don't worry, darling. I'll see you when you get back," Cara said, and I smiled sorrowfully at her usual term of endearment.

29

"Definitely," I replied.

"Love ya, Lex. Don't be a phone stranger. I mean, you can only expect me to survive for so long with Lex deprivation . . ."

Surprising myself, I laughed. "Got it. Love ya, too."

After goodbyes were said and the call was disconnected, I stood and stretched. Still clad in my winter deck-wear, I was extremely overheated and a little sweaty. I tore off my mittens, unzipped and removed my navy-blue down jacket, and slid my feet out of my waterproof, fur-lined boots. I traded my jeans for some purple and blue plaid pajama bottoms before curling up on a bed that had always been mine, in a room that had always been mine, with the odd sense that neither belonged to me anymore. *That* Lex no longer existed.

Unsure of how I'd fallen asleep so early in the evening, I awoke. Night had fallen completely, darkening the room. My first thought was of being cold, so I quickly maneuvered myself under the covers. My second thought was one of relief—for the first time in two weeks, I had slept without having the nightmare. My *third* thought was about the strangely vivid dream I'd just awoken from. It had taken place in my parents' house, and it could easily have been real, except that the dream switched back and forth between two time periods. The more I thought about it, the clearer my memory of it became.

Standing in the doorway between the kitchen and dining room, I saw my mom sitting at her brand-new, oak dining room table, her hands clasped together on the surface. My dad was sitting across from her.

Shaking her head, she said, "I just think it's too late. We've gone such a long time with this secret . . . it just seems easier to keep it."

"But Alice, don't you see? The girls have a right to know who they are . . . where they come from." My dad reached across the table and covered her hands with his. "It's just not fair to keep hiding it from them. It's nothing to be ashamed of."

Suddenly, the scene shifted—I was still in the dining room, but the table was our old, battered one. My mom and dad, who seemed to have lost a couple decades, still sat in relatively the same places.

"I just don't know, Joe," my mom said, shaking her head. "I think we should wait until they're old enough to understand why we had to do it."

My dad sighed. "I wish we wouldn't ever need to have this conversation with our little girls. I just . . . okay, I guess a couple more years couldn't hurt. But we will tell them eventually, Alice."

Closing her eyes, my mom nodded.

In the blink of an eye, the scene shifted back to my mom and dad sitting at the new table, his hands covering hers.

"Alright, Joe . . . this weekend, I guess I'll visit Lex and tell her. If she doesn't take it well, I'll just bring her back with me. But, if it's too hard for her, then we're not telling Jenny—she's just not as, well . . . as strong." When my mom glanced up at my dad, her eyes were as fierce as those of a lioness.

My dad scooted his chair back, stood, and walked around the table to her. As I followed him with my eyes, I noticed a flicker of movement just beyond the wide, arched doorway leading into the living room.

Lying in bed, I couldn't shake the feeling that I'd really been present during my parents' conversations. A sense that a dream was more real than, well, *just* a dream was something I'd experienced before. But it had only happened when I'd awakened from a dream that was really a memory.

Once, when I was a freshman in high school, I forgot my locker combination. It happened near the beginning of the school year, but I'd already stashed a couple of books inside. After sharing a friend's locker for more than half the year, I had a sudden need to get into mine—the library was going to send a bill home for the books I'd "lost" in my locker, and I really didn't want to pay the fee to reset the combo. The day before the library fine was due, I went home, resolved to pay the reset fee the following morning. That night, I had a vivid dream. In it, I was sitting on my bed after the first day of school, going through my backpack. In my hand was the card displaying the elusive combination to my locker. When I woke from that dream, I hastily jotted down the locker combination, absolutely positive of its accuracy. Later that morning, I opened my locker for the first time in months, saving myself a hearty sum of money. *That* dream had felt the same as the one I just had: absolutely real.

But, so had the dream of Dr. Ramirez getting hit by a car, and *that* never actually happened. I couldn't possibly have "remembered" the conversations between my parents in my dream because I hadn't been there. *It's nothing*, I told myself. *I'm just being obsessive.*

For the second time in two weeks, I laughed out loud. If I mentioned anything about my crazy dreams to my mom, all of her worried looks and concern over my mental stability would quickly give way to a leather couch in a psychiatrist's office. *No, thank you.*

Regardless, I couldn't ask my mom or dad if they'd had any conversations like the ones in my dream . . . for their sake. I was pretty sure I'd been making the past few weeks fairly hellish on them, and I wasn't about to make it worse.

I eventually chalked up the dream to my overactive obsession with understanding who I was . . . where I came from . . . who my father was . . .

Gradually, like a dimmer switch lighting up my thoughts, I knew where I could get more information—from Grandma Suse. My indecisive mom discussed nearly everything with her mother. *Tomorrow*, I told myself, *I'll drive over to Grandma Suse's house and hopefully get some much-needed answers.*

4

ANSWERS & QUESTIONS

When I cracked my eyes open, the glowing green numbers on the clock on the nightstand read 7:43. For the first time since I'd been home, my cheeks and pillow were dry of tears, and even with the odd dream earlier in the night, it had been the best night of sleep I'd had in weeks. Groaning, I stretched languorously and tossed the covers to the foot of the bed. I pulled on a sweatshirt and some socks, arranged my hair in a loose ponytail, and padded downstairs to the kitchen.

The coffeemaker was my first stop. My delightfully over-prepared mom had already loaded the filter with fresh grounds and the machine with water, so I just had to push the start button and wait. My favorite mug, covered in cheesy, cartoony Egyptian images, was already set out on the counter beside two other, far more grown-up mugs.

Catching my reflection in the window above the sink, I raised my eyebrows. I'd been smiling . . . for no apparent reason. *Maybe I really* am *still me,* I thought with wonder.

To distract myself from too much pre-coffee psychological analysis, I decided to make a big, fancy breakfast for my parents. I still had about a half hour before they came downstairs for their oddly rigid morning routine—plenty of time to make a Christmas Eve breakfast feast. After filling my mug with coffee, a splash of milk, and a spoon of sugar, I gathered some necessary ingredients on the counter. I was going to whip up a scrumptious batch of French toast.

As I cooked, the sound of footsteps on the stairs forewarned me of my mom's arrival. I turned from the stove to see her watching me from the doorway, smiling.

"Smells great, Lex," she said cautiously. "What brought this on?" Translation: *Why are you acting normal?*

"Oh, I don't know. Consider it a 'thanks for putting up with me' breakfast," I replied, returning my attention to the bacon popping and crackling in a large frying pan.

Just as my dad entered the kitchen, I set a platter of food on the table. Joe Larson was a big man—a little over six feet tall and thicker around the middle than was probably healthy. His face had gained wrinkles and a certain middle-aged plumpness, but his crinkled eyes and easy smile still bespoke his gentle, friendly nature. His light brown hair was damp from his morning shower, and his face was freshly shaven. I smiled, thinking his morning routine hadn't changed over the years.

Although he'd probably been attempting something resembling stealth, I caught the questioning look he aimed at my mom, as well as her answering grin. By the time I sat down across from him, my dad's expression had changed to a self-satisfied smile that glowed with a silent "I told you so." I refused to focus on the fact that, in the dream, he'd expressed confidence in my ability to handle the information about my paternity.

It's not real! The thought was closely followed by another: *I need to talk to Grandma.*

"Mom?" I asked, drizzling syrup over my French toast.

She was chewing, so she only looked at me and mumbled, "Hmm?"

"Well, I know how you have a lot of cooking and whatnot to do today, so I was thinking I might do something to make it a little easier for you," I said, my eyes wide in an attempt to look innocent.

"You want to help me cook?"

Forcing a smile, I replied, "Um . . . I'd love to when I get back. I was actually thinking I could go pick up Grandma for you. That way, you guys won't have to leave at all. You won't have to drive in the snow . . ."

My mom frowned slightly. "I don't know, Lex. You aren't on the insurance for our cars anymore. What if . . . ?"

Seeing my eager expression falter, my dad stepped in on a fatherly rescue mission. "Come on, Alice," he said. "It's not really that far, and Lex hasn't seen Grandma Suse in a while. Let her go. I'll help you cook while she's gone . . . if you want . . ."

I gave my dad a huge, grateful grin before glancing at my mom, eyebrows raised in hope.

She blew out a breath. "Okay . . . but you have to promise to be careful."

"Of course, Mom."

Attempting to not appear in too much of a hurry, I excitedly told my dad everything I knew about the excavation—which wasn't very much—and the supervisory role I would be playing. My mom had already heard it all back in Seattle, but she didn't seem to mind. Eventually, I finished my breakfast and offered to help with the dishes. After all, I'd created most of them.

"Don't worry about it," my dad told me. "Why don't you just go get ready and then head over to Grandma Suse's?"

Surprised, but not wanting to waste my escape route, I rushed out of the kitchen to prepare for the day. I got ready in record time.

Sitting in my mom's parked, ruby-red sedan, I stared out the windshield at my grandma's home. A true product of its time, the house was all bricks, winter-barren ivy, white trim, and huge windows, with a large arched porch that led to the front door. Its street was filled with other brick Tudors that looked just like it and yet were completely different at the same time, all remnants of the early 1900s.

After a few contemplative moments, I abandoned the warmth of the car and crunched across the de-iced driveway and pathway that spanned the front yard. I walked through Grandma Suse's unlocked front door, shut it loudly to let her know someone was there, and hung my coat and mittens on the antique coatrack set off to one side in the narrow entryway. The house wasn't small—it held enough bedrooms that each of Grandma Suse's three children had grown up with their own room—but it had been built before the "bigger is always better" ideal truly took over. Throughout the house, the floor was a dark hardwood, and the rooms were smaller, the hallways narrower, and the doors just a little bit shorter than those in a modern home.

Making my way down the hallway toward the family room, I could hear the quiet chatter of the TV. "Hi, Grandma," I chirped, poking my head around the doorway into the cozy room.

Susan Ivanov, otherwise known as Grandma Suse, was lounging in her favorite blue suede armchair with a fuzzy yellow blanket draped over her legs. Her hair was perfectly arranged in a gray halo and her sparkly red and green sweater screamed *Christmas!*

"Lex?" she asked, evidently surprised that I wasn't my mom, who she'd expected to pick her up. Before she could stand, I rushed over to hug her. Tiny bells jingled on her sleeves as she wrapped arms that were more frail than I remembered around me.

"Well, this is a surprise! What are you doing here, honey? Not that I mind . . ."

Her bright, hazel eyes stayed locked on me as I flopped into an oversized, brown leather chair a few feet from hers. It had been my late grandpa's chair and was by far my favorite place to lounge in the entire house.

"I convinced Mom to let me pick you up. She had so much stuff to do and I haven't seen you in, I don't know, a year . . . so I thought, you know . . ." I shrugged.

Grandma Suse watched me as I spoke, her eyes keen. "Oh, and how are you, honey? Your mom said she told you about your dad—said you've been having a tough time. Sweetheart, is there anything I can do?" she asked, radiating grandmotherly warmth.

I hesitated, a little surprised at her directness. "I don't know, Grandma. I guess . . . I just wish there was a way for me to know who my real father is."

"Honey, Joe Larson will always be your real father. Whether or not you share his genes, he's still a part of who you are. Nothing will change that," she said, her eyes glittering with moisture.

I clenched my jaw as the crushing weight of a handful of emotions momentarily overwhelmed me. In my heart, I knew Grandma Suse was right—my dad really *was* my dad. He'd always been there to pick me up when I fell, and he'd fostered my love of both history and reading. He'd helped shape me into the person I'd become. In every way that mattered, he was my dad, but I didn't feel the same assuredness in my own identity. I didn't feel like I was still his little girl . . . still *me*. Part of me was lost, and I didn't know where—or how—to find it again.

I sighed. "You know what I mean . . . I'm not trying to replace Dad. I just want to know who my biological father is because, you know, what if some freaky disease runs in his family and I don't know to watch out for it?" I'd voiced a reason, but not *the* reason for my curiosity. What I really wanted to know was what kind of a person he was. I wanted to know if I was like him, even the tiniest bit. I wanted to know *something* . . . anything.

"Well, sweetheart . . . I don't know who he is. The clinic your parents used was very careful about keeping that information confidential." She suddenly looked frustrated. "They said it was 'to protect the donor.'"

An idea formed in my head—*what if the information was confidential* then, *but isn't anymore?* "I don't suppose you know the name of the clinic, do you?" I asked.

She paused before answering. "Maybe."

"Will you *please* tell me, Grandma? Please? Nothing has ever been so important to me," I pleaded, desperate.

Grandma Suse held my eyes for a moment, wariness adding new creases to her wrinkled face. "It was in Seattle," she finally said. "But I don't know if it's still there. If I remember right—which really would be amazing—it was called Emerald City Fertility."

I let out the breath I'd been holding. "Thank you *so* so much, Grandma!" *Emerald City Fertility*, I repeated silently. I quickly made a note in my iPhone. With my history of random acts of forgetfulness, not writing it down somewhere was far too risky.

"Do your parents know you're looking into this?" Grandma Suse asked, her eyes sharp behind her thick, rosy-rimmed glasses.

The question took me by surprise. In my haste to dig up answers, I hadn't considered the possibility that Grandma Suse might tell my parents about my sleuthing. I bit my bottom lip as my stomach grumbled.

"I didn't think so," Grandma Suse said with a frown. "Well, maybe it's best if we just keep this between you, me, and the lamppost for now, dear." She rose and shuffled across the several feet separating us to pat my knee, then said, "Let me go finish getting my things together and we can be on our way. I'll be quick as a bunny."

"Take your time, Grandma," I said, grateful she would keep my inquisitive secret . . . at least for a little while.

Suddenly exhausted, I rested my head against the back of the cushy leather chair. Years ago, when Grandma Suse's mobility had dwindled to the point that going up and down the stairs was akin to playing Russian roulette, my mom and I had moved her into the single downstairs bedroom. Currently, I could hear my grandma's soft voice as she puttered around in her room, but I couldn't keep my eyes open long enough to register her words.

My grandma was sitting on the left arm of the same chair where I'd fallen asleep. She looked younger than I'd ever seen her. A very handsome man sat in the chair, his hand resting on Grandma Suse's lower back. With his dirty blond hair and strong, chiseled features, he was easily recognizable from photographs—my grandpa. On the couch opposite my grandparents sat my mom and dad, holding hands. Judging by my mom's hairstyle, I figured she was around twenty-five years old. Before she had kids . . . before she had me.

From my position in the doorway between the family room and the hallway to the front door, I observed their conversation, watching . . . listening. Everything about the room was wrong. Where are all the knickknacks? *And the pictures on the walls didn't belong in my grandma's house—they were supposed to be at my parents' house. In fact, the painting hanging on the wall above my grandparents' heads—of a dusky, sunlit forest—was currently in my old bedroom.*

An unfamiliar male voice interrupted my confused examination of the room. Strong and clear, it was faintly accented with Italian. It belonged to my grandpa. "I asked around," *he said.* "I think I found a good place for you kids to go. The doctor is very reliable. I know another family he helped."

At hearing his voice, my confusion tripled. I'd never heard anything about him being from Italy, and I never would have guessed based on his appearance; he was so fair. In fact, I was pretty sure my mom had told me his ancestors fought in the American Revolution.

"We're ready to try anything, Dad," *my mom said, and beside her, my dad nodded.* "So, where's this place?"

"It's called Emerald City Fertility in Seattle. It's run by a Dr. James Lee. He is one of the best in his field."

"Do you know if they're accepting new patients?" *my dad asked.*

My grandpa glanced down sheepishly before meeting my parents' eyes. "Well . . . yes. In fact, I may have already set up an appointment for you." *He rushed his next words.* "I know you were planning on spending the afternoon here, but I thought you'd want to meet the doctor as soon as possible. They're expecting you in about four hours, so . . ."

"Oh! Um . . . thanks?" *My mom said, giggling nervously.* "I guess we should hit the road."

My parents quickly said their goodbyes and departed, slamming the front door in their excitement. After they were gone, Grandma Suse twisted on the arm of the chair to gaze down at my grandpa.

"Are you sure this is safe, Alex?" *she asked, more than a hint of anxiety straining her voice.* "You know what could happen if he . . ." *She trailed off, pressing her lips into a thin line.*

"I've seen all of the possibilities, Suse. He won't interfere in this generation. The child will be fine. It will be normal," *he assured her.*

What the hell does any of that mean? This generation? Interfere? He, who? Normal?

"He's right, Susan," *a man said from the living room's other doorway, the one leading to the dining room.* "We've kept the two lines separate for more than four thousand years. Nothing he's tried has worked so far, and that's not going to change in the next twenty-five years. The prophecy will be invalidated and all will be right."

My confusion increased with every additional word. What does he mean by "prophecy"? And there's that "he" again. I abruptly realized there was something familiar about the hidden man's voice. Slowly, I crossed the room toward it, toward him, but something *stopped me . . . someone. Long, golden-brown fingers were gripping my shoulder.*

I turned my head and started to raise my eyes . . .

I awoke to Grandma Suse shaking me by the shoulder. With a rush, realization dawned on me. The dream I'd just had felt the same as the one the previous night . . . and the one with Dr. Ramirez. It felt too real, too much like a memory. *Oh my God . . . I'm losing it,* I thought.

"I made us a snack before we hit the road," Grandma Suse said, setting a plate of food on the wide chair arm.

Eyeing a delicious-looking sandwich piled high with sliced turkey, cheddar, lettuce, and tomatoes, I said, "Aw, Grandma, you didn't have to do that. It's only fifteen minutes back to Mom and Dad's, and . . . I would've helped if—"

"Nonsense, dear. You looked so peaceful . . . I wanted to let you rest for a while longer," she said as she carried a second plate to her usual chair.

"Thanks, Grandma." I took a bite and savored the flavors that only she could coax into something as generic as a turkey and cheese sandwich. I was pretty sure it was the combination of toasted bread and real mayonnaise, but my sandwiches never tasted as good, even when I did my best to mimic her methods.

"Yum," I mumbled as I swallowed. "So, Mom told me the painting in my room—the one of the forest—used to be here," I lied. "Where was it?"

Chewing, Grandma Suse pointed to the exact location where I'd seen the painting in my dream—on the wall behind the chair I was sitting in. My blood seemed to transform into liquid nitrogen, giving me chills as it circulated throughout my body. *How'd I know that . . . dream that?* It was one hell of an odd coincidence.

In archaeology, all claims must be substantiated by hard evidence, usually in the form of artifacts, ruins, or historical texts. The methodology was ingrained in my bones. I needed to dig deeper—to find more evidence—so I could know what was going on. Was I losing my mind? I just needed to know.

Thinking of another, relatively safe piece of information from the dream—the doctor's name—I asked, "So, this Dr. Lee, did you ever meet him?" I was surprised that my voice didn't tremble as I spoke.

Grandma Suse nodded, watching me while she finished her bite. "Yes, honey. I went with your mom to a few of her appointments. He was a very competent doctor. He was a little young, but . . ." As she trailed off, her thoughtful smile disappeared and worry temporarily shadowed her face, but she quickly masked her features with a pleasant, placid expression.

I took another bite, feigning obliviousness. *How did I know the doctor's name?* The painting's location could have been a coincidence, but the doctor's name . . . ? It just didn't seem possible. *What the hell is going on?* My heart was pounding so hard that I feared my grandma would be able to hear it. I finished my sandwich, playing at normalcy, though I'd lost my appetite somewhere between *maybe I'm losing it* and *I'm definitely losing it.*

After minutes passed with only the low sounds of a tennis match intruding on our silence, I picked up Grandma Suse's empty plate. "I'll take care of the dishes, then we can head over to Mom and Dad's. I know Mom would love some help in the kitchen."

"Sounds good, sweetheart." Grandma Suse smiled, but it didn't reach her eyes.

While I rinsed our plates in the kitchen sink, I thought about my grandma's reaction to my knowing Dr. Lee's name. She'd been worried—or afraid. Why? *Because I'm clearly acting like a crazy person,* I told myself.

"I think the dishes are rinsed," Grandma Suse said from behind me, her voice gentle.

Startled, I laughed before turning off the water and gathering my things to leave. I slipped my hands into my mittens as I followed my grandma to the front door, sparing a glance back up the hallway. My mind was filled with questions. *Who was the hidden man in my dream? Who grabbed my shoulder? What had my grandparents been talking about after my parents left? And most importantly, why are my dreams becoming so . . . real?*

A single word kept replaying in my mind: *impossible.*

5

SISTERS & FRIENDS

It was a short, pleasant drive from Grandma Suse's to my parents' house. In less than fifteen minutes, I learned everything that had happened to my aunts, uncles, and cousins over the past year. Grandma Suse had always been a font of knowledge when it came to matters of the family.

As I pulled into the slick driveway of my family's firmly middle-class home, I stopped beside my sister's sky-blue hybrid. Evidently Jenny had arrived while I was out and had parked directly in front of the garage door I needed. Irritated, I rolled my eyes and inched my mom's car as close to the garage as possible.

"Sorry, Grandma . . . looks like we're going to have to walk on the ice for a few feet," I said as I pushed the little gray button on the garage door opener. When my frail, elderly grandma opened the passenger side door, I quickly added, "Wait a second and I'll come help you, okay?"

"Alright, dear," she agreed, sitting back in her seat.

I rushed around the front bumper and gripped her arm to steady her as she emerged from the car. Slowly, we traversed the ice to the safety of the garage floor.

My mom greeted us from the glowing doorway leading into the house. "You didn't slip at all, did you, Mom?" she asked, concerned.

"No, no, Alice. Lex and I skated our way to the garage quite gracefully." She caught my eye, and I spotted hints of a suppressed smile glittering behind her glasses.

I grinned. "Yeah, Mom. I think we earned a nine-point-five for balance and a ten for our expert spins."

"You two!" my mom said, throwing her hands up. "You act more like sisters than Lex and Jenny do!"

"We look like sisters, too. I only have a few more wrinkles than Lex," Grandma Suse claimed.

My mom rolled her eyes expertly. "Please, Mom. Don't kid yourself."

"Oh, that's my Alice . . . such a sweet girl," Grandma Suse responded, reaching up to pat my mom's cheek as she ascended the three wooden stairs to the doorway.

With an exasperated smile, my mom held the door open so we could enter the warm laundry room. Grandma Suse was through the doorway leading into the living room before me, issuing cheerful greetings to my dad and sister. From the sound of the television, they were watching *A Christmas Story* for the eight-thousandth time.

"Grandma!" Jenny practically screamed as she bounced up off the couch and flew toward us. She slowed in time to give Grandma Suse a gentle hug and lead her to the cushy recliner next to the couch.

"Nice to see you too, J," I muttered. In the back of my mind I was thinking about what I'd recently learned regarding my paternity. I couldn't help but wonder if we even shared the same biological father. It was a legitimate question, considering the many differences between Jenny and me—she was creative where I was logical, she was sincere where I was sarcastic, and she seemed to spend half of her life sick with the flu, strep throat, or chronic allergies while I couldn't remember having more than a hint of sniffles.

"Good to see you, Suse," my dad said. "Would you like something to drink?" He raised his dark brown beer bottle. It appeared to be some sort of winter ale that no doubt resembled motor oil.

Grandma Suse smiled. "Yes, thank you, Joe. I'd love some tea."

"Oh . . . I, um, don't really know . . ." he stuttered.

"Don't worry, Dad. I'll take care of it," I said, chuckling.

He laughed and shook his head. "Thanks, Lelee."

Lelee. The old nickname nearly brought tears to my eyes, and Grandma Suse's earlier words replayed in my head. *Joe Larson will always be your real father.* No matter what, I would always be his little girl . . . his Lelee. Close to tears—the happy variety for once—I joined my mom in the kitchen.

Her face was etched with worry when she looked up from the ham she was doctoring. "We need to talk, Lex."

Freezing in the middle of the kitchen, I eyed her warily. I wasn't ready for any more enormous family revelations —not yet.

"Oh, don't worry, sweetie. It's nothing like *that*," she said, placing the ham in a roasting pan. "It's your sister—I just . . . I don't want you to tell her."

Relieved, I continued on my tea-making mission. "I know, Mom. You don't think she's strong enough to handle it."

"You—how did you . . . did you talk to your dad?" she asked, bristling. "He shouldn't be telling you . . ."

Oh, crap. I nearly dropped the mug I'd just pulled from the cabinet. Where *had* I heard that? It came to me all of a sudden —*the dream from last night.* "Um . . . no? I mean, Dad and I haven't really talked much about this at all. I've just been thinking about it a lot and . . . I guess I came to the same conclusion. About Jenny, I mean." *Can she tell that I'm lying?*

My mom raised her eyebrows. "Really? I'm surprised in you. I sort of thought you'd demand we tell her the truth as soon as possible." She skewered me with her sharpest "mom look," apparently doubting my sincerity.

Nonchalantly, I shrugged. "Dunno. I guess it just makes sense to me." I quickly turned away to fill the yellow enamel teapot. "I'm just gonna make Grandma some tea and then I'll help you with dinner," I said, hoping to divert her thoughts.

"Oh? That's wonderful! I'm a little behind schedule," she confessed, hoisting the roasting pan into the oven.

After I delivered the tea and fitted myself with a burgundy apron proclaiming "I cook with wine; sometimes I even add it to the food," I was directed toward a multitude of duties. I chopped, mixed, boiled, stirred, and mashed without a moment between each task. Every year, my mom felt the need to try to outdo her previous holiday feasts.

At least I know where I get my love of cooking, I thought contentedly.

That night, belly stuffed with ham, potatoes, and way too many frosted Christmas cookies, I fell asleep . . . and dreamed. Again, I watched my parents discuss whether or not to tell Jenny and me the truth. Again, I witnessed my grandpa directing my parents to Dr. Lee's practice. Again, the hand jerked me from the dream before I could uncover the identity of the hidden man who'd been speaking to my grandparents.

In the early hours of the morning, a new scene played out in my dreams.

47

My family was eating the previous year's Christmas Eve dinner. My mom's failed sweet potato soufflé sat, deflated, on the edge of the table.

I inhaled in surprise—another version of me was entering the room, carrying a full bottle of wine.

"I just don't know what I want to do yet . . . I guess I'm not ready to commit," Jenny said.

Setting the bottle on the table next to my dad, the past version of me said, "You still haven't picked your major?" She scoffed. "You're in the middle of your third year, J. You're sort of running out of time."

"Gee, thanks for the heads up. I hadn't noticed!" My sister glared at the other me. "Damn it, Lex, I can survive in the world without you reminding me of things I already know!"

She'd always had a hair-trigger temper, but I remembered how shocked I'd been at the severity of her reaction.

"J, c'mon," the other me said. "I just meant that it's an important decision, and unless you plan to stay in school forever, you—"

"No, Lex. Just stop talking for once. God, sometimes I can't even stand to be in the same house with you!" She threw her napkin onto her full plate and stormed out of the room, leaving our parents and Grandma Suse gaping.

The other me rushed after her.

I followed.

"J, c'mon. What's wrong?" the other me called through Jenny's closed bedroom door.

Watching the past, I leaned against the upstairs hallway wall, cringing at what I knew was about to happen.

The door flung open, and my sister huffed out, pushing past the other me and dragging her suitcase. "It's you!" she screamed as she marched down the hallway. "It's always you! Lex this, Lex that! 'Lex knew her major before she started college.' 'Lex got a full ride to grad school.' 'Lex is so perfect.' 'Why can't you be more like your self-centered, stuck-up, know-it-all sister?' God, I wish we weren't sisters. Then I wouldn't have to pretend to like you!" She heaved her suitcase down the stairs and out to her car.

The other version of me was crying, but I left her in the hallway to follow my sister outside. I found her in our mother's consoling embrace beside her car. Their words became clear as I moved closer.

". . . what's best for you, sweetie. You are both special, intelligent young women, just in different ways."

My sister pulled out of the hug and wiped her eyes. "Sometimes it's just too much, Mom. Sometimes I just want her to accept me as I am. What if I don't want to be just like her? What if I want to drop out of school and become an artist? What if . . ."

"She'll love you no matter what, sweetie. You just have to give her a little time to understand. You know how stubborn she can be."

My sister glared back at the open front door. "She's had twenty-one years to understand me. How much more time could she possibly need?" She took a deep breath and sighed. "I'm sorry, Mom . . . I just can't be around her right now. She's just so . . . judgey. Can you tell Dad and Grandma I . . . I don't know. Just tell them that I'm sorry and that I love them. Oh, and tell them Merry Christmas."

My mom shook her head. "You don't need to leave, sweetie."

"Yeah, Mom, I do."

"What about your presents?" our mom asked, a thread of desperation twining through her words.

"I don't know . . . I'll pick them up after she leaves." She kissed our mom on the cheek, slid into her car, and drove away.

When I woke, my cheeks were sticky with partially-dried tears. *Did J really say those things to Mom? If she did, is she right about me?*

I dragged myself out of bed and tiptoed to my sister's room. Her door was cracked open, allowing me to slip into her bedroom without waking her.

"J," I whispered, sitting on the unoccupied side of the bed.

Blinking, she stared at me from her pillow. "Umph . . . Lex? What are you . . . ?"

"Can I sleep in here with you?" I asked timidly.

Jenny snorted. "Did you have a bad dream?"

"Sort of," I admitted. "But . . . mostly I just wanted to apologize. For last Christmas . . . for everything."

She sat up abruptly, tugging at the multi-hued comforter beneath me. "I'm sorry—what?"

Taking a deep breath, I dove in. "I'm really sorry. I *did* want you to be like me. I wanted to be able to relate to you, which would've been so much easier if we had more in common. And . . . you're right, I'm self-centered. I never considered trying to be more like you. I just wanted you to be like me. Which is *so* stupid of me, because you're an amazing, talented person, and I *never* want you to change. And I'm proud to call you my sister."

"Oh," she said, staring at me wide-eyed. "Um . . . thanks." After a moment's pause, she added, "Well, are you getting in, or not?"

As I crawled under the covers on the left side of the bed, I felt one of the flailing, broken strands of my life begin to mend. Whoever I was, whoever my biological father was, I would always be sure of one thing—Jenny was my sister, and she always would be.

6

IGNORANCE & STUPIDITY

"But really, thanks for the ride, Mike," I said to the man sitting in the driver's seat. Jenny had known I needed a ride back to Seattle, and when she overheard that her best friend's brother, Mike, had plans to return to Seattle before New Year's Eve, she'd asked if I could ride along with him.

Mike smiled as we exited the freeway and entered the U District, an area of the city famous for its excellent selection of budget-priced ethnic food, endless rows of apartments and turn-of-the-century bungalows, and of course, the University of Washington. "No problem," he said. "I'm still surprised you're living here too. Don't know how I missed that. Suppose it shouldn't be a surprise—half our high school has migrated over here."

"I know! It was a mass exodus," I said, laughing. "Though technically I wasn't part of it since I did my undergrad in Montana."

"True," Mike said, nodding thoughtfully.

As I stared out the window, I found comfort in the familiar surroundings. Nature, lush and green, seemed to be at war with the cold, man-made structures . . . with nature always on the

51

verge of winning. Yakima had been home for most of my life, but Seattle had supplanted it two and a half years ago, when I started my graduate studies at UW.

"You said you live on Fifteenth, right?"

"Yep," I said, eager to see Thora and to just be home.

Mike adjusted his baseball cap, then glanced at me. "So Lex, we should do something sometime."

"Oh?" Studying him briefly, I took in his warm, brown eyes and handsome, if not slightly youthful, face.

Mike Hernandez had been one of *the* guys as a teenager. Every girl in our grade at Eisenhower High School had fantasized about him at least once, including me. I'd had a short phase of Mike-obsession during our sophomore year, but nothing had ever come of it. Until a couple hours ago, I hadn't seen Mike since high school graduation.

Smirking, he said, "Yeah. We should get drinks or something." When he smiled, he had adorably faint dimples.

"That sounds great." I pointed to a large, brick apartment building on the left side of the street. "That's me."

Mike deftly navigated the busy road and parked by the curb near the main entrance. "It's lucky our sisters are still friends, so we could, you know, do this," he said, gesturing to me and around the interior of the car.

"Yeah, it is," I agreed, and I meant it. Mike was definitely attractive, and he seemed to have grown up a lot over the past six years, leaving his party boy reputation behind. Besides, I hadn't been having much luck in the man department—every guy I met on campus was either too absorbed in his research, or overly enthusiastic about the college social scene. I was looking for a balance.

"I have this thing I have to go to on New Year's Eve—a work party. It could be fun . . . but I'd have a *much* better time if you came with me." He removed his hat and watched me, his eyes glittering.

"Sure, yeah," I said, trying to hide some of my eagerness.

His answering smile was radiant. "Great! I'll pick you up at eight. Oh, and it's cocktail attire."

"It's a date," I said, blushing as I scooted out of the passenger seat and retrieved my bag from the backseat of the silver Audi.

"See you in two days, Lex," Mike said before I shut the car door.

I walked up to the building's main entrance and fit the key in the lock. By the time I looked back, Mike's car was nowhere in sight. I felt giddy with excitement . . . and I really, *really* needed to talk to Cara and Annie.

Once I was in my apartment, I tossed my bag onto the bed, snuggled on the couch with Thora, and pulled my phone out of my pocket to call Cara.

"Lex? Is it really you? Are you *alive?*" was Cara's greeting.

"Yes, yes, and yes. And I have news. When can you get over here?"

She paused. "If I leave the office early . . . maybe four-ish?"

"Okay, great!" I said excitedly. "I'm going to call Annie. See you la—"

"Lex, wait," Cara blurted before I could hang up. "Is it good news or bad news? I want to be prepared."

I considered holding back the info about my parentage and only focusing on the date with Mike, but thought better of it. "Both," I told her, unsure if I would go so far as to fill them in on the weird, way-too-real dreams.

"Okay. See you later!"

"Bye." I quickly called Annie and had a nearly identical conversation. Both women would be over in three hours, and I had some thinking to do.

Disturbing Thora from her euphoric cuddling, I rose from the couch and retrieved a yellow notepad and pen from atop the coffee table. I kept both items generously scattered about the apartment as a general rule—I couldn't predict when research inspiration or insight would strike. When I reclaimed my comfortable position on the couch, my cat simply glared at me from the windowsill, stretching and lying down with her feet curled primly under her.

"Have it your way, Thora," I said, clicking the pen open.

I drew a line down the center of the page, dividing it into two columns. At the top of one, I wrote THE DREAMS AREN'T REAL. Atop the other, THE DREAMS ARE REAL. Quickly, I began listing items in the AREN'T REAL column, like, "impossible," but I ran out of ideas almost as soon as I started. Switching to the ARE REAL column, I marked up the page with furious starts and stops. After five minutes, I compared the lists, shocked.

AREN'T REAL
—Impossible
—Wasn't even alive for the Grandma/Grandpa scene
—~~Impossible~~
—I might be in shock

ARE REAL
—The painting
—Dr. Lee
—Dr. Ramirez???
—Grandpa's voice—he's Italian?
—Convo between Mom and Jenny
—Knowing Mom thinks Jenny isn't strong enough for the truth
—Mom's fashion is way too ridiculous for even me to dream up
—Feels just like the memory dreams I've had since high school
—I can remember the dreams too well when I wake up—unnatural
—I'm fully aware in the dreams—also unnatural

"Well, shit," I said, copying my mom's signature profane exclamation. It was the one she used when she realized she'd forgotten an essential item at the grocery store or when she received a notice from school notifying her of Jenny's skipped classes. For her, it meant, "Huh, I guess I should've seen that coming, but it still sucks!"

I flipped the page up over the top of the notepad and started a new list, cataloging all of my recent dreams. As I wrote, I started to notice several common characteristics.

First, I had to be asleep—but that one was pretty obvious, seeing as they were dreams. However, I did find it a little odd that I'd fallen asleep at Grandma Suse's right after I'd had a great night's sleep. Tiredness had crept up on me, then wrestled me into submission.

Second, location seemed to be important. Each dream first played out in my mind while I slept in the same place as the scene had actually happened. I'd been at my parents' house when I'd dreamed of their conversations about telling Jenny and me the truth, and when I dreamed of the blowup during the previous Christmas Eve dinner. After dozing off at Grandma Suse's, I'd dreamed of the discussion about the clinic and Dr. Lee. The Dr. Ramirez nightmare hadn't technically been in the same location—the accident had taken place just outside of Denny Hall, where I'd fallen asleep—but I still wasn't one hundred percent convinced *that* dream had really been like the others.

Third, I'd been experiencing extreme emotion each time I'd fallen asleep. I'd felt overwhelmingly eager for winter break before the nap in Denny Hall, lost before the first dream at my house, desperate before the one at Grandma Suse's, and regretful before I'd dreamed of Jenny. *Eager . . . Lost . . . Desperate . . . Regretful . . .*

As I thought about the emotions, I realized that other than the Dr. Ramirez nightmare, the dreams shared a common thread —they seemed to pop up out of need. I'd needed to understand where I came from, to figure out where I could learn more about my paternity, and to make things right with my sister. The dreams of my parents, my grandparents, and my sister had met those needs respectively.

With that realization came another thought. *Can I control this?* If I could focus on something I needed at the moment, maybe I could force another one of the too-real dreams . . . maybe I could learn to use them to help me discover other useful bits of information. I ignored the part of my brain screaming about delusions and straitjackets and padded rooms.

Checking the clock on the wall, I saw that I still had two hours before Cara and Annie arrived—plenty of time to test my insane theory. I was tired enough to nap, so I stretched out on the couch and covered myself with a blanket. Thora, apparently forgiving me for displacing her, hopped down from her perch to curl up next to me. I thought about what I needed, what was making me feel extreme emotions at the moment, and eventually drifted off to sleep.

My apartment door opened, admitting a stumbling, laughing couple. The man was wearing a black suit, his jacket unbuttoned and metallic blue tie undone around his neck. The woman was wearing a silky black dress that skimmed the bottoms of her knees, and her feet were bare. Her gleaming, dark hair was falling out of its loose updo. I was watching . . . me.

The man, Mike, pressed the other version of me against the wide, polished wood post separating the kitchen from the living room. She giggled. He kissed her hungrily, pressing his whole body against hers and running his hands over every reachable part of her. She twined her fingers in his soft black hair and groaned.

I moved closer, equally curious and disturbed by the scene playing out in front of me. I couldn't imagine myself ever being as inebriated as the other version of me seemed. Part of my mind whispered that what I was watching wasn't real. Another part wondered if it was, but it just hadn't happened yet.

"God, I want you, Lex . . . can you feel it?" Mike groaned, grinding his hips harder against hers. *"Can you feel how hard you made me?"* He slipped one hand up her skirt while the other fumbled with his belt buckle.

"Wait . . . wait," the other me whispered, trying to push Mike's groping hand out from under her dress. *"I'm . . . dizzy. I don't feel—"*

"No, it's good. You're beautiful," Mike said hoarsely, unbuttoning his pants and lowering the zipper.

"Mike, wait," she demanded. *She turned her head away and made an effort to push him back.*

He ignored her, using both hands to raise the skirt of her dress and pull down her black lace boy shorts.

"No! Stop, Mike!" she repeated, her protests growing shrill as Mike became more forceful.

I couldn't stand it anymore. I lurched forward, intending to push him away from her, but I bounced off an invisible barrier. "STOP!" *I shouted.* "LEAVE HER ALONE!"

Mike glanced at the couch, then shoved the other version of me into the living room.

She screamed, tripping on the underwear tangled around her ankles. As she fell to the floor, her head smashed against the corner of the steamer trunk coffee table. Within seconds, she was still.

Mike stared down at her, mouth hanging open in shock, and the front door crashed open.

I lurched to a sitting position and immediately felt nauseated. *It was just a dream, just a regular, meaningless dream.* But I couldn't get over the way it had felt, like a memory . . . like the others. *But how could it be real? Mike wouldn't—*

Before I could dwell further, there was a knock at the door. Cara and Annie had arrived. Still a little shaken, I quickly finger-combed my hair and stretched before letting my friends in.

"We brought wine!" Cara exclaimed, hugging three beautiful bottles of the nerve-calming libation.

"And cheese!" Annie sang immediately after her. She offered

up a canvas shopping bag filled with cheeses and, knowing her penchant for decadence, some other tasty goodies.

"Amazing! Splendid! Genius!" I said, bowing as I showered them with praises.

"I wasn't sure how much we'd need," Cara said, using a corkscrew to point at the bottles lined up on the counter.

Without hesitation, I replied, "Probably all of them."

After laying a half-dozen varieties of cheese along with strawberries, sliced apples and pears, crackers, and olives out on the coffee table like an offering to the divine, we settled in the living room with glasses full of wine. My friends perched on the couch, and I settled on a floor cushion on the opposite side of our little feast. Taking frequent sips of wine, I listened to their soothing, inane chatter. It was nice to be surrounded by silliness for a few moments.

"So . . . spill," Cara demanded, her bright blue eyes focusing on me.

"Cara!" Annie admonished, slapping Cara's leg. "She'll tell us when she's ready."

"No, it's fine," I said. "Good news, or bad news first?"

"Um . . . bad," Cara said, doing her best to contain her curiosity and appear supportive.

"So, it all started with my mom's surprise visit . . ." I began. It was surprisingly easy to tell them the story of my mysterious paternity. However, though I tried, I couldn't bring myself to spill about the too-real dreams. I ended my enormously long monologue with the good news—a replay of the ride home with Mike and the resulting planned date. "But, I'm not really sure about it," I said, feeling my eyebrows draw together.

"Why?" Annie asked.

"Yeah, why? If he's such a stud, why would you possibly consider backing out?" Cara asked, clearly confounded.

Blushing, I shook my head. "Well, it's weird. I, um, took a

nap this afternoon and the dream I had was just"—I shivered
—"unnerving."

"And why would that change your mind about going out
with Studly Martinez?" Cara asked, emptying the remaining
contents of the first wine bottle into her glass.

"Hernandez," Annie corrected.

"Whatever. You know what I mean."

I rolled my eyes and took a deep breath before explaining.
"In the dream, Mike came back here with me after the party and
. . . and he sort of tried to force me to have sex. I mean, I wanted
to . . . I think . . . or at least at first I did, but not like that."

Cara held up her hand like a traffic officer. "Wait. He dream-
raped you?"

"No . . . at least, not all the way. I woke up before it was
over," I said and let my friends ponder the information for a few
seconds.

"Kinky!" Cara exclaimed.

"Cara, you're horrible!" Annie accused, glaring at the blonde
sitting beside her. "It's creepy, not kinky!"

"What? It was a *dream*. As in, *not real*. Come on, Lex. You
have to go out with him. You haven't been on a decent date in at
least six months. You're just nervous. When was the last time
you even had sex?" Cara asked, crass as usual.

"A while," I mumbled, hiding behind my hands. *She's probably
right—it was just a dream, and I am nervous.*

When I lowered my hands, I found Annie and Cara studying
me with identical expressions: eyebrows raised and mouths
pinched. I immediately burst into giggles, and upon seeing each
other, they joined me.

As soon as the laughter died down, I expressed one of my
several anxieties about the impending date. *Anxieties,* I told
myself, *not excuses.* "I don't have anything to wear, and I can't
really afford to splurge on a new dress," I said, moping.

"Oh my God, shut up! You are so ridiculous! I have the

perfect dress," Cara said, bouncing on the couch again. "I haven't actually worn it yet, so you *cannot* get *anything* on it. But, because I love you so much, I'll let you borrow it."

"Oh!" clapped Annie. "And I can come over and get you fixed up. You are *not* going on a date to a fancy New Year's Eve party with a ponytail!" She waggled her finger at me sternly.

"Okay, okay," I said, holding up my hands in submission.

"Good!" they exclaimed and began plotting and laughing and hiccupping. The night went downhill from there.

"Okay, you're done," Annie stated, finally allowing me access to the full-length mirror hanging on the back of my bedroom door.

I examined her handiwork, noting the classiness of the loose, low bun. "Annie, you're a genius!"

She blushed and shrugged, gathering her various salon-grade tools into a bag with seemingly infinite compartments. I had just experienced one of the very amazing perks of having a hair stylist as one of my closest friends.

Finished packing up, Annie studied me. "Hair, check. Makeup, check. Nails, check," she said, accenting each statement with a flick of her raised finger. "You, my dear, are ready to get dressed."

I unzipped the garment bag hanging on the closet door. "Are you sure it's not too much? What if I'm overdressed?"

"Better overdressed than under," she said.

I removed a silky black dress from the hanger and unzipped the back. "If you say so," I muttered. I stepped into the dress and let Annie zip it up, glad my bruises from the collision with Dr. Ramirez had healed in a matter of days. At least I didn't have to cover the ugly marks with tights. When I turned to face the mirror, my heart nearly stopped.

I was wearing *the* dress, the same one I'd been wearing in the nightmare. *This can't be happening,* I thought, terrified by the beautiful dress. It was simplicity at its best, with thin straps crisscrossing my back and flowing black silk draping over my hips and reaching just past my knees. It fit snugly around my chest and waist, emphasizing my slender curves. Against the inky fabric, my skin looked like smooth, flawless alabaster.

"Oh, wow," Annie said in a hushed tone. "Maybe you should just buy it from Cara. It looks *amazing* on you."

When I didn't respond, she studied the reflection of my face. It had blanched from creamy alabaster to bone-white. "Lex? Are you okay? You're shaking. Sit down." She guided me to the edge of the bed.

"I'm fine," I responded hollowly. *It's just a dress . . . a common, black dress. This whole thing is a stupid coincidence.* "I just haven't eaten much today. I think I'll make some toast." I stood and hurried from the room, shrugging into a light robe to keep the dress clean . . . and to hide it.

A few minutes later, Annie emerged from my bedroom carrying her bag and some strappy silver heels. "You have to wear these. I found them buried in the back of your closet." She placed the shoes on the table.

"Those? I don't know if I can even walk in those!"

"Then you'll just have to lean on Mike," she suggested, her face slack with mock innocence. Having been in the same relationship for nearly six years, Annie liked to date vicariously through her friends. Usually she was limited to Cara, whose love life was both varied and active, but for once, I was included.

I snorted and buttered the toast.

"I should go. Mike'll be here any minute, and I don't want to get in the way," Annie said, raising her eyebrows suggestively.

"Come on, Annie, it's the first date. We'll at least go to the party first!"

She fixed an unusually stern gaze on me. "Fine, but don't be a nun. You need this."

"Yeah, yeah." I gave her a quick hug and thanked her for all her help, and then she was gone.

I finished the toast quickly and was in the process of strapping on one of the silver death traps when there was a knock at the door. "Be there in a sec!" I called, trying to keep my balance as I strapped on the other shoe.

Dropping my robe off in the bedroom, I took a quick peek in the mirror to make sure everything was still in place, frowned at the dress one last time, and hurried to open the door.

"Hi!" I said, a little breathless.

For several seconds, Mike just stared, his eyes wide and childlike before crinkling with a smile. He looked quite handsome in a black suit with a blue tie, and I was relieved it wasn't a *metallic blue* tie like he'd worn in the dream. *It was just a dream*, I reminded myself again.

"You look gorgeous," he said.

"Thanks," I replied with a slight shrug. "You look nice too. Do you want to come in?"

"Well, we should probably go. We're already late. My fault," he said, holding out his arm.

Slightly relieved, I smiled. Part of me was convinced that if I let him into my apartment, the horrible nightmare would play out, but if I kept him out . . .

"Let me grab my coat real quick." I plucked my favorite coat —a nearly knee-length, plum-colored pea coat—out of the pint-sized coat closet, grabbed my keys and handbag, and locked the door on my way out.

Nearly four hours and way too much Champagne later, we broke apart from a very enthusiastic New Year's kiss. Mike had been a charming gentleman all evening, and the wine had settled my unnecessarily jumpy nerves. Caught up in the excitement of the holiday, I was on the verge of pulling Studly Hernandez into the nearest coat closet for a little seven minutes in heaven. Perhaps being on a date with someone from my high school was making me feel a little bit like a teenager again.

Luckily, Mike was way ahead of me. He leaned closer, bringing his lips to my ear. "So, is that offer to come into your apartment still open?" My eyes wandered to the back of his neck, mere inches away. Because he was a few inches taller than me, I could just barely see the edge of a black tattoo peeking above his collar.

"Absolutely," I said, smiling. Though I was twenty-four and had slept with several different men, I'd yet to have a very enjoyable experience. If that kiss was any indication of Mike's bedroom manner, my luck was about to change.

"Great, let's get out of here," he said, capturing my hand and leading the way. We gathered my coat, hopped into his Audi, and arrived at my apartment in record time.

While I was attempting to unlock my apartment door, Mike was occupying himself by using his lips to do pleasant things to my neck and shoulders. A nagging feeling in the pit of my stomach—a sensation that I was forgetting something important—was washed away by twin torrents of desire and drunkenness. It was so bad that I couldn't focus on the lock long enough to slip the key in.

Mike chuckled against my shoulder, making me shiver, and said, "Here, allow me." He ran his right hand down my arm until he held the keys. The door was open in seconds, and laughing, we stumbled inside.

I giggled as Mike backed me against the wide, polished

wooden post that separated the kitchen from the living room. Oddly, I couldn't remember walking the ten steps from the door to the post.

Mike kissed me hungrily, pressing his whole body against mine and running his hands up and down my sides. I twined my fingers in his soft, black hair to anchor my swaying body. *How did we get here?*

Mike's hands became greedy, grabbing at my breasts and hips and butt a little too roughly, but my wine-muddled mind couldn't hold onto any thought long enough to care.

"God, I want you, Lex. Can you feel it?" He groaned, grinding his hips harder against me. His erection jabbed against my hip bone. "Can you feel how hard you made me?" After another groan, he breathed, "I'll come so hard for you."

As I felt one of his hands slip up my dress, the world suddenly became liquid. It seemed to heave and dip randomly, like the swells of a stormy sea. It was nauseating.

I heard the clink of metal and looked down to see several identical belt buckles being undone. "Wait . . . wait," I whispered, trying to push his groping hand away. It had made it past my lacey underwear, and his fingers were rubbing some area that wasn't the least bit pleasurable. *This is wrong.* "I'm dizzy. I don't feel—"

"No, it's good. You're so beautiful," Mike interrupted. He continued his misdirected rubbing of my groin while he used his free hand to lower the zipper on his pants. Fumbling with his boxers, he exposed himself.

"Mike, wait," I said more forcefully. On the verge of vomiting, I turned my head away and made an effort to push him back. He didn't budge.

With both hands, he raised my dress and pulled down my underwear. Nausea and panic battled for control inside me. *I have to get away. Why won't the world hold still? Why won't he stop? What's happening?*

"No! Stop, Mike, please!" I yelled, but he only pulled his pants down further. "Please, Mike, no!" I said, my voice shrill. I squeezed my legs together as he tried to wedge himself between them.

"Mike, stop!"

He pressed against me, his erection pushing between my thighs.

"Easier on the couch," he muttered, his words barely audible. Without warning, he pulled away and shoved me into the living room.

I screamed, tripping on the underwear tangled around my ankles. My head hit the corner of the coffee table. The last thing I heard was the apartment door crashing open.

This can't be real.

Blackness.

7

EXPLANATIONS & OMISSIONS

I opened my eyes, only to be blinded by bright, florescent light. I yearned for the glorious golden fire that had been in my dreams. It had been beautiful and soothing, nothing like the awful luminescence currently boring through my eyeballs into my brain. From all directions, beeps and hums and voices pounded against my head like jackhammers. Squeezing my eyes shut, I attempted to cover my ears with my hands, but I couldn't seem to move my arms. I moaned, or possibly grunted.

"Hey . . . guys, she's awake," a familiar voice murmured.

My inability to move my arms was making me panic, and I started to squirm from side to side.

"Lex, it's okay. Lex . . . it's Annie and Cara. You're okay," Annie stated calmly as she pressed her arm across my shoulders to hold me down. It didn't take much effort on her part—I was weak and groggy.

I opened my eyes and was instantly caught in her warm, earnest gaze. "Rick, can you get a nurse?" she asked her long-time boyfriend, not looking away from me.

"Lex?" Cara poked her head around Annie's shoulder. "Do you know who we are? We won't hurt you. I . . . I'm so sorry!"

She burst into tears, collapsing over my stomach and splaying her unusually limp blonde hair over the bed.

I tried to pat her head, but my damn arms were tucked under the blankets. "My . . . arms," I whispered.

"Cara, get up. She wants to be able to move," Annie said briskly.

Cara sat up and wiped her eyes. "Oh. Sorry."

Gently, Annie withdrew each of my arms from its cotton prison and rested it on top of the thin, blue blanket. "There. Is that better?"

I smiled at her and nodded. "Thanks. And I do know who you are." I paused, trying to remember how I'd ended up in the world's brightest hospital. "What happened? How long have I been here? And why do I have the mother of all headaches?"

My two best friends exchanged worried glances, and then looked down at the thin hospital blanket.

Unease swelled in my chest. "Guys?"

"You came in early this morning," Annie said slowly. Glancing at the clock on the opposite wall, she added, "It's almost midnight, now."

"I see our patient is awake," a plump nurse chirped from the doorway. Rick entered the room behind her, offering me a little wave.

"Um . . . yeah?"

"Alexandra—"

"Lex," Cara interrupted, frowning. "We told you—her name is Lex."

The nurse scowled at Cara for a moment, but turned an indulgent look on me. "*Lex*, we need to talk to you about some personal medical matters. Your friends will need to leave when the doctor arrives." She looked at the door as it opened again and admitted a pretty, petite woman wearing a white lab coat. "Ah . . . here she is now. Time to go, friends of *Lex*." The nurse said my name as if acquiescing to a completely ridiculous whim.

Cara, Annie, and Rick vacated the room, but not without scornful looks at the nurse. Apparently they hadn't formed the best relationship while I'd been unconscious. Before shutting the door, Annie said, "We'll be right outside if you need us, okay, Lex?"

I nodded at her, grateful for her steady support.

"Thank you, Nurse Roctenberg, but I can handle it from here," the doctor said, dismissing the nurse.

Bristling, Nurse Roctenberg also left the room.

"Ms. Larson, the police would like to speak with you when we're done. For a statement about the assault," the doctor told me. I couldn't get over how attractive she was—of Mid-eastern descent, she had chocolate-brown, almond-shaped eyes, smooth, symmetrical features, and perfect, bronze skin. She was by far the prettiest doctor I'd ever met.

"A statement about . . . about wh—" Without warning, a montage of images tumbled through my mind, coalescing into a horrid memory.

Stumbling through the door with Mike. The wooden post at my back. The world spinning. His hands everywhere. Begging him to stop. Mike refusing. Mike shoving me. Hitting my head. The door crashing open. Golden fire.

I burst into instantaneous and uncontrollable sobs.

"Ms. Larson—"

"Lex," I corrected through heaving breaths.

"Lex, I'm Dr. Isa," she said grasping my nearest hand. "What that man did to you—and what he tried to do—is horrible . . . unforgivable. But," she continued, "it could've been worse."

I looked into her sure, brown eyes, entranced.

"He could have succeeded. He could have raped or even killed you, instead of simply assaulting you."

A bitter laugh escaped from my lips. "Simply?"

"Yes, Lex, simply. Some women haven't been as lucky as you. *I* wasn't as lucky as you," she explained calmly, releasing my hand.

"You . . . you were raped?" I asked, suddenly abashed.

"Yes. It was a long time ago, and it no longer has a hold over my life, but I understand the terror. Okay?"

I wondered if she was the most honest person I'd ever met. I nodded, ignoring the pain in my head. "Okay."

"You were very lucky to have had someone nearby who responded so quickly. For many women, it's the inaction of those around them that enables their rape . . . or murder."

"Who? The door . . . I heard the door crash open, but I don't remember anything afterward. What happened?" I asked, completely confused. *Who saved me?*

Smiling, Dr. Isa shook her head. "It's quite amazing, actually. Almost like a superhero story. The nurses who were on duty when he brought you in said he was the most striking man they'd ever seen." She sighed wistfully. "I wish I'd seen him. The police found the alleged assailant, Mike Hernandez, tied up in your apartment. He was in pretty bad shape when they arrived." After only a brief hesitation, she added, "You should know, he's on a different floor, but he *is* in the hospital."

I flinched and did my best to huddle into a ball.

"Please don't worry, Lex. He's under guard. A police officer is watching his room at all times."

Slowly, I relaxed, stretching back out.

Dr. Isa reached for my hand again, gripping it almost painfully. "There is something you must know . . ." She hesitated for the briefest moment. "Soon, other doctors in this hospital will begin approaching you with very intense questions about your medical history. You must not, under any circumstances, tell them of your unknown paternity."

I eyed her, taken aback. "How do you—"

"It doesn't matter. What's important is your safety. They will

69

ask you about your parentage, and you *must* say that Alice and Joe Larson are your parents . . . your *biological* parents. If you stay here too long, they will eventually ask you questions about your genetics and any differences or abnormalities you've noticed about yourself. You *must* tell them that everything is normal and as it has always been. If you don't, your life and others will be at great risk. Do you understand?"

I swallowed, shocked and confused by her words. "I think so . . . yes." *How does she know anything about me . . . about any of the weirdness that's been going on in my life?*

Dr. Isa let out a relieved breath. "Good. There is one more thing. We found a very rare and little-known compound in both your and Mr. Hernandez's systems. It doesn't affect the average person—like Mr. Hernandez—but for a very few, unique people, it acts similar to Rohypnol, which you may know as the date-rape drug. If you hadn't hit your head, you probably would have passed out within minutes anyway. I'm assuming you felt its effects before you lost consciousness?"

Is she saying that Mike drugged me? Feeling numb, I nodded.

Tilting her head to the side, Dr. Isa frowned. "This will be difficult, but you must not tell anyone about your reaction to the compound. Nobody else here knows about it, and it's safest to keep it that way. Unfortunately, withholding that information may or may not affect the charges against Mr. Hernandez, since nobody else will be aware that you were drugged, but it *will* be essential to your well-being. Again, do you understand?"

I licked my lips before responding. *She is saying that Mike drugged me.* My mind was whirling with questions. "Yes, I think so. How do you know all of this? You know things about me that *I* don't even know."

She looked away. "I'm so sorry. I'm not permitted to answer any questions like that."

"Permitted by whom? I need more information!" I persisted.

She looked conflicted, but the door opened, cutting her indecision short.

"Lex? Are you okay, sweetie?" my mom asked, oozing gallons of concern. "When they called me . . . I'm sorry it took me so long to get here . . . the pass . . . I called your friends . . . I didn't want you to be alone . . . I just . . ."

I sighed, my frustration at being interrupted giving way to immense relief. *I love you, Mom.* "I'm okay."

She studied my blanket-covered body for a few seconds before turning to the doctor. Sniffling, she asked, "Well, what's wrong? What happened?" Based on my mom's tone, Dr. Isa might as well have been my attacker.

"Mom," I said, answering for the doctor. "Dr. Isa was just conferring with me about some of the less family-friendly details. I love you, but there are some things I don't want you to hear, at least not from a doctor. I'll fill you in later, okay?" I desperately hoped she would give me a few more minutes alone with the doctor.

My mom frowned before she answered. "Dad will be here soon, he's just parking the car. I'll be right outside with your friends, okay, Lex?"

I nodded. "Thanks, Mom."

While we'd been talking, another doctor had joined Dr. Isa in my room. He politely shut the door as my Mom left. Dr. Isa gave me an apologetic smile before he began his questions. Once he began, it was a relentless waterfall.

"Ms. Larson, are you aware that your body heals at an unheard-of rate?"

"Have you noticed anything exceptionally different between you and your peers?"

"Do you have any knowledge of allergies or an allergic history in your family?

"Are you very similar to your parents?"

And on. And on. And on.

I listened to each of the questions carefully and answered based on the advice from Dr. Isa, leading the other doctor to believe there was nothing unusual about me and that I'd been unaware of the strange compound in my blood. More than an hour after the barrage began, Dr. Isa proclaimed that her patient needed rest and that I was to be left alone until breakfast.

After the other doctor exited the room, Dr. Isa used the pretense of adjusting my blankets to whisper a few enlightening pieces of information. "You hit your head *very* hard. You *should* be in a coma, and nobody understands why you're not. Your recovery is astounding. You must tell anyone who asks that you've always been a quick healer." She glanced at the clock. "Make sure you leave before breakfast. It's served between seven and nine, so you have a few hours. Your release orders are already signed." She reached down to squeeze my hand. "I wish you luck, Alexandra Ivanov," she said, using my mother's maiden name.

"That's not my—"

The door opened suddenly, cutting me off. As my parents and friends poured into the room, Dr. Isa checked my papers one last time and removed my IV. My head was reeling from her unbelievable revelations—not to mention her cryptic instructions—and a multitude of questions were sprouting in my thoughts. I vowed to return to the hospital for one specific reason: to talk to Dr. Isa.

Putting on my cheeriest grin, I exclaimed, "They said I can go home! Who's driving?"

Everyone but Dr. Isa looked utterly confused as I hopped out of bed. The doctors had been correct about my body's ability to heal quickly—I felt a hundred times better than I had when I first woke. I'd always been a fast healer, a trait I attributed to having a strong immune system, but this was unbelievable.

"Did someone bring me some clothes?" I asked, holding my peek-a-boo hospital gown closed as I checked the empty closet.

"Lelee, I don't know if you should be going home yet," my dad said, concern etching his kindly face.

My mom set a half-full duffel bag on the bed. "I brought you some clothes, Lex, but we didn't expect you to be released so soon. When the hospital called, they made it sound like . . . like . . . well, like you might not . . ." Her chin quivered and tears welled in her eyes.

"Just a little mistake, Mom," I said, reaching out to squeeze her shoulder. I couldn't hug her—if I did, I'd break down. *The hospital didn't think I would make it?* It explained why they were all staring at me like I'd sprouted an extra head.

Rifling through the bag, I found a couple pairs of old sweatpants and a few T-shirts from high school. Not that I minded—anything was better than the drafty hospital gown. I pulled out a worn, gray T-shirt, some cotton boy shorts, and faded blue sweatpants, and disappeared into the bathroom. Again, everyone but Dr. Isa watched me with confused expressions; the good doctor simply smiled.

Almost two hours later and after a lengthy chat with the Seattle police, I arrived home to find a brand-new door barring the entrance to my apartment. *Man, my apartment manager works fast*, I thought. Its pristine, polished wood looked odd next to the nicked door frame and smudged walls. One-hundred-year-old apartment buildings tended to accumulate more than their share of wear and tear.

Using a shiny new key that had been stashed in my mailbox, I unlocked the door and let it swing open. My parents and friends stood behind me, holding their collective breath.

Straight ahead was the wooden post Mike had held me

against . . . had shoved me away from. I shuddered at the memory, practically able to feel his greedy, groping hands, but I refused to let my fear of something that happened in the past keep me out of my own home. With a shaky breath, I closed my eyes and stepped through the doorway. When I opened them again, I found that everything in the apartment was perfectly arranged . . . too perfectly, like the whole nightmarish encounter with Mike had never happened. *But it* did *happen!*

I'd been gone for little more than a day, but it felt like weeks. Time wasn't settling right with me, just like the pristine state of my apartment.

Needing a distraction, I dropped my keys in an engraved metal bowl on the kitchen table and called out, "Thora? Where are you, little girl?" *What if she got out while the door was broken?* My breaths started coming faster as I imagined her wandering around outside, scared and alone. *Oh God . . . she has to be here!*

My small entourage milled around in the kitchen and living room while I frantically searched the apartment, calling out Thora's name. I retrieved a crinkly bag of cat treats and shook it, hoping the sound would draw her out. Finally, after minutes of searching, I heard a faint squeak come from under the bed. Kneeling on the floor, I lifted the bed skirt and peered into the darkness. Two glowing, green orbs floated just out of arm's reach. Letting out a sigh, I righted myself and quieted my frantic thoughts. *It's okay . . . Thora's okay . . . everything's okay.*

When I emerged from my bedroom, I felt as though I was standing before a firing squad. Five pairs of eyes were lined up, each watching me attentively.

"I'm fine," I reassured them, my voice a little too high, and their expressions intensified. "Cara, Annie, Rick—thank you so much for everything you did at the hospital. I really, *really* mean it." I bit my lip, feeling bad for completely hijacking the past twenty-six hours with the insanity that had become my life.

"You guys must be exhausted. Why don't you go home and get some rest?"

Annie took a step forward, opened her mouth, and closed it again without saying anything. She studied me closely before nodding. "Okay, Lex. If you need us, just call. Any time, okay?" Her eyes seemed to add, *but this isn't over.*

I watched my three friends leave before turning my attention to my parents.

My mom cut me off before I had the chance to open my mouth. "Don't even think about it, Lex."

"But—"

"No buts. I'm staying here until the quarter starts," she said, steamrolling my unsaid protests.

"But—"

She interrupted me again, somehow responding to my unspoken thoughts. "Dad can't stay, so you don't need to worry about where we'll sleep. It's just me, and I'll make myself at home on the couch. He'll pick me up when he's here on business next week."

Though I'd planned to convince them to leave, a huge weight lifted from me at knowing my mom wouldn't be budged. I really didn't want to be alone. Even if having her stay with me postponed my intentions to question Dr. Isa further, I wanted my mom around, at least for a little while.

I sighed. "Okay."

With two big steps, my dad wrapped me in a comforting bear hug. "Thank you, Lelee," he whispered. "It's as much for her as it is for you."

I squeezed him in response, then pulled away. With a yawn, I said, "I think I'm going to take a nap."

My parents both nodded encouragingly. It seemed that after attempted sexual assault and hospitalization, naps were a parent-approved coping mechanism. Marching out of the hospital, on the other hand, was not.

Feeling far too exhausted for someone who'd spent most of the past day asleep, I smiled at my parents and trudged into my bedroom. After I shut the door, I collapsed onto the bed. I only had a few seconds to wonder about the man who'd crashed through my apartment door to save me before sleep whisked me away to the land of dreams.

8

RECOLLECTION & RECUPERATION

My apartment door opened, admitting a familiar couple, stumbling and laughing.

I was standing in the middle of the cramped living room, watching, helpless to stop what I knew would happen. Panic made my heart race and my breathing quicken. I closed my eyes, incapable of watching—experiencing—the horrible incident again. But I could still hear *Mike whispering to me . . . the other me. Desperately, I wished for it to be over. I heard the other me scream, closely followed by the crack of her head striking the steamer trunk and the thud of her body hitting the floor.*

There was a crash, an explosive splintering and cracking of wood, and my eyes sprang open. A figure stood in the doorway, silhouetted into obscurity by the light from the hallway. The man who saved me, I realized. *As he stepped out of the light and into my apartment, I noticed that the darkness surrounding him hadn't only been due to backlighting. Shadows darker than the night cloaked him, seeming to emanate from him. To my eyes, he was a man composed of nothing but those impenetrable, pitch-black shadows.* What the hell?

The shadowed man paused after a few long strides, looking at the other, unconscious version of me before turning toward the shocked man cowering before him. At least, I thought he looked at the other me; I

77

couldn't actually see his face through the shadows he seemed to be wearing like a disguise.

"You!" Mike howled in terror. Shocked, I realized that Mike knew my rescuer. "No, no, no—" Mike dropped to his knees, groveling. "She fell, I swear. I didn't do anything."

Confusion and frustration displaced my earlier panic. Who is he? Why can't I see him? It was pretty obvious that he didn't walk around like that—all shadows and menace—outside of the dream, or memory, or whatever it was. Mike had seen him, as had the hospital staff. So why can't I?

The shadowed man's steps devoured the distance to Mike in two long strides. His midnight-coated arm backhanded Mike, and the smaller man fell to the floor in a limp heap. Swiftly, the stranger moved to the sprawled form of the other me, hovering over her. His hands flew over her body.

"Hey!" I shouted, forgetting that I was only watching something that had already happened . . . forgetting that I couldn't change it. "Keep your hands off her!"

His hands gently pulled up her underwear, and from the way the shadows cloaking his face shifted, I thought he must have looked away as he did it. He arranged her black silk dress so she was decently covered before gently rolling her onto her back and touching her wrists. Abruptly, he leaned over her face like he was listening for something. When he sat back on his heels, he brushed a lock of hair out of her face and simply watched her.

I moved closer, circling around the man. I searched for a crack in the dense blackness surrounding him but could find none.

From the kitchen floor, Mike groaned, and the shadowed man glanced at him. Gracefully, my rescuer rose. He lurked toward my fallen attacker, spitting vicious, incomprehensible syllables along the way. But . . . something about the words, the language, sounded familiar.

I hovered over the other, unconscious me while the shadowed man attended to Mike with sharp jabs and swift kicks. I despised Mike— thought I'd lost the capacity to feel pity for him completely—but seeing him being beaten so brutally awoke a sliver of sympathy in me. Did he really drug me? *Part of me couldn't accept Dr. Isa's claim, and I was pretty sure it was the same part of me that felt bad for Mike as I watched.*

Eventually the shadowed man's need for violence was expended. He sat Mike, head lolling forward, with his back against the wood post and quickly arranged him so his arms extended behind him. I moved closer. At some point, the shadowed man had produced a zip tie and secured it around Mike's wrists, effectively binding him to the post. Both Dr. Isa and the police had mentioned that Mike had been tied up and in pretty bad shape when he'd been found, alone, in my apartment. In fact, I was pretty sure the police wanted to find my rescuer . . . to arrest him for what he'd done to Mike. The severity of his actions hadn't really sunk in until now. He saved me—but he's definitely dangerous.

I returned my attention to the shadowed man, watching as he again approached the wounded version of me. Why had he been so enraged? Why had he beaten Mike into unconsciousness? His reaction seemed personal, like he knew me—cared for me—and couldn't let Mike go unpunished for what he'd done . . . and for what he'd intended to do. But if that were true, why was he hiding from me? Why hadn't he stayed at the hospital, or at least left contact information so I could thank him for rescuing me?

While I wondered about him, the shadowed man picked the other me up easily, like she weighed no more than a child, and carried her through the broken apartment door.

Rooted in place, I watched Mike's limp form until the police arrived. According to the wall clock, it took only a matter of minutes.

In bed, I felt awareness tug on my consciousness, but I wasn't ready to wake up. I had other plans. A new need was growing—a need to never fall victim to someone like Mike again, a need to never again be drugged into oblivion. I focused on that need as I slid back into the dream.

I was standing in the middle of a wide-open, tech-friendly office space filled with cubicles and decorated in blues and grays. I was at the New Year's Eve party. A few feet to my right, the other version of me was locked in an embarrassingly brazen kiss with Mike. Ugh.

Watching them, I grew so disgusted that I wanted to slap the other me. I felt the urge to tear her away from Mike and shake her and scream, "Open your eyes, you idiot! He's going to hurt you! Run away!" But I couldn't do any of that, and it wasn't for lack of trying. I attempted to pull her away, just as I'd attempted to push Mike off her the first time I'd dreamed of the incident in my apartment, but she was separated by the same impenetrable barrier I'd encountered before. I couldn't touch her . . . I couldn't touch him . . . I couldn't touch anything but that damn barrier.

I slapped my palm against the barrier separating me from Mike's shoulder. "I hate you!" I hissed. For some reason, seeing him before the night devolved into violence was more frustrating than anything I'd seen in the other dream.

"Happy New Year!" Mike's colleagues hollered from all around me while they kissed and pawed at each other.

Mike was leading the other me away. At most, she was tipsy. While he waited for her to retrieve her coat, Mike took out his phone and tapped his thumbs against the screen.

I hurried over to him, nearly gagging at his overly-cologned stench. I couldn't understand how I'd ever been attracted to him. Pushing past the nauseating reaction, I peered over his shoulder at the screen.

He was reading a text message from someone named Seth.

Use the lip balm to make her compliant, then complete the mission.

Suddenly awake, I lurched upright in bed, panting. Thora glanced up at me from her cozy position near my hip and meowed quietly. I stroked her soft fur absentmindedly, thinking about the last dream. Memories of what had happened between leaving the party and stumbling through my apartment door flashed through my mind.

Mike kissing my wrist . . . pulling over to kiss me before resuming the drive . . . slobbering all over my neck as I tried to open the door to my apartment . . . obsessively putting on lip balm every few minutes.

Use the lip balm to make her compliant, then complete the mission. Based on the text, I realized that Mike's lip balm must have been the source of the substance Dr. Isa had told me about. She'd said it only affected a few, unique people. *Why am I one of those people?*

Use the lip balm to make her compliant . . .

How had the sender of the text, Seth, known the substance would work on me? And why had he wanted Mike to use it in the first place? My stomach tied into knots as questions swam around my mind. Had some person I didn't know—someone named Seth—instructed Mike to drug me and do whatever "completing the mission" entailed? Had Mike been instructed to drug me into unconsciousness and rape me? It was too horrible to consider. It was also too preposterous.

"I'm losing it," I muttered.

Laughing at myself for my wild, slightly twisted imagination, I rose from the bed, shuffled to the adjoining bathroom, and examined my reflection in the mirror. "Holy crap," I breathed, barely recognizing myself. My brown eyes looked different, like they'd gained a reddish tinge, and my face was washed-out and gaunt. Simply based on my appearance, I looked like I was suffering from some ghastly illness, like I was two steps away from death's door and already had my hand raised to knock. But I felt fine, if a little weak . . . and hungry.

I squeezed my eyes shut. "It's fine. It's just all the stress," I told myself, thinking not only about Mike and my physical injury, but also about the identity crisis and the strange dreams I'd been dealing with over the past few weeks. "Everything is just fine." The words were confident, but my voice was breathy.

Turning on the faucet and rinsing my face with cool water, I felt some steadiness return. Eyes still closed, I focused on the delicious smells invading from the kitchen and just breathed. I opened my eyes and stared at my hands. My fingers clutched either side of the rim of the pedestal sink, the tendons standing out sharply on the backs of my hands. I took a deep breath. Again. Finally, I turned and left the bathroom, avoiding looking at the stranger in the mirror.

I traded the worn sneakers I'd been too tired to remove for fuzzy, purple slippers. I added a gray University of Washington sweatshirt to my scrubby ensemble and opened the bedroom door.

My mom stood in front of the stove, humming and swaying from side to side. The little kitchen radio played a generic soft rock song. It was the perfect background music to the pops and sizzles coming from the pans on the stove. A junkie of mothering people, my mom was more in her element than I'd seen her in years. She almost glowed with purpose.

Quietly, I slipped out of the bedroom and crossed the living room to the small, rectangular kitchen table. I pulled out my usual chair—the one nearest the bedroom—and sank onto its flattened cushion.

"Smells yummy, Mom. I'm starving," I said enthusiastically.

Startled, my mom spun with her spatula hand extended in front of her. "Lex! You scared me! I didn't know you were up. How are you feeling?" An odd combination of accusation, concern, and contentment filled her face.

"Better, I think," I said, scanning the living room and kitchen. "Where's Dad?"

She sighed. "He left about an hour ago. He'll call when he gets home."

"Oh," I said, disappointment radiating from the single word. Knowing he wasn't my biological father made me second-guess all of my dad's actions. Did he really care as much as I thought he did? Did he really love me?

"Stop that, Lex," my mom chided.

I looked up at her, wondering for the thousandth time if she could read my mind.

"He thought you'd feel more comfortable with just me for the time being, considering . . . you know . . ."

I nodded as her words trailed off. Drumming my fingertips on the table, I wondered how much my parents actually knew about the incident with Mike. *I* had yet to explain to them what happened, so they'd gathered whatever information they had from my friends, the hospital staff, and the police. I took a huge, steadying breath and asked, "Aren't you, um, curious? About what happened, I mean."

My mom studied me closely before turning back to her stovetop ministrations. "Sweetie, you take your time. Wait until you're ready, and not a minute sooner." She resumed her faint humming.

Sighing, I felt both relief and stress. The story had to come out of me eventually, and I dreaded telling it. The longer I waited, the larger the heaping, stinking pile of dread would grow.

"Is there coffee?" I asked as I watched my mom's movements. Judging by her arm motions, there were pancakes in one of the skillets on the stove. If there was one thing I truly loved, it was my mom's pancakes . . . with syrup . . . and butter . . . and bacon.

"I made tea," she said over her shoulder. "I thought it'd be better for you. More relaxing." Carefully, she removed crispy strips of bacon and perfectly browned sausage links from two pans, leaving only popping grease behind, and set them on a stack of paper towels on the counter.

My stomach growled audibly. I didn't think I'd ever been so hungry.

"Almost ready, sweetie," my mom said as she transferred the mouthwatering meats to a plate. She brought it to the table, along with another plate piled high with golden-brown pancakes, and went back to the kitchen for round two. When she returned, she carried two more dishes, one loaded with a mountain of scrambled eggs with onions, peppers, and cheese, and the other with oven-fried potatoes. After one final trip, she settled in the chair perpendicular to mine and placed a steaming mug of tea at both of our place settings.

"What are you waiting for, Lex?" She gestured to the feast before us. "Dig in."

I ogled the mounds of deliciousness. "Um, Mom . . . there's absolutely no way that you and I are going to be able to eat all of this."

After scooping some of the scramble onto her plate, my mom looked me square in the eye and said, "Have you seen yourself? You're skin and bones. If I didn't know any better, I'd think you've lost at least twenty pounds since I saw you four days ago. And your face—it's nearly colorless." She shook her head. "Now eat."

And eat I did. By the time I sat back in my chair, my stomach was painfully full, and my mom wore a smug expression. All of the eggs were gone, as were the sausage links and strips of bacon. Several pancakes remained, and the potato dish was barely half-full. Without realizing it, I'd eaten enough for several burly lumberjacks after a hard day's work.

My mom smiled, looking as content as a sunbathing kitten. "See, Lex? Your coloring looks better already. A good, home-cooked meal can fix almost anything." She gave me a pointed look. "A little sun wouldn't hurt you either."

Rolling my eyes, I laughed. "Right, Mom, 'cause there are so many chances to get some sun in Seattle in January."

"You could go to a tanning salon."

I scoffed. "I will not go to a cancer factory! I'd rather keep my skin smooth and healthy and nicely pasty until I'm Grandma's age."

With a long-suffering sigh, my mom raised her hands in front of her in defeat. "Your dad ran some errands for me before he headed back home. He's supplied us with quite a few movies to keep us occupied while you recuperate. Why don't you pick one out? They're over there," she said, pointing to the coffee table behind her.

"Really?" I asked, perking up from my food-induced lethargy. If there was one thing I loved as much as pancakes, it was movies. For the most part, I really was a simple soul to please.

So, with all the excitement of a child on Christmas morning, I settled on the couch and rifled through a stack of DVD cases. Silently, I thanked my dad for picking movies from nearly every genre: romantic comedy to action, science fiction to period drama. There was a flick for every mood. At the moment, I was in the mood for some rigid chivalry and modest ball gowns. The latest Jane Austen adaptation shimmered in my hand as I placed it in the tray of the DVD player.

I lost myself in the music and language of another time, my mom curled up beside me. I slid down, resting my head on a pillow in her lap, and sighed as she started combing through my hair with her fingers. Breathing in her familiar scent of floral perfume and hand lotion, I felt some of the tension seep out of my body.

I was so incredibly glad she'd stayed.

9

DETAILS & ARRANGEMENTS

As I strolled along a wet concrete path, I thought back on the last three days, savoring the chance to finally get out of my apartment . . . alone. My wonderful, caring mom had spent every waking moment stuffing me with her culinary creations and enticing me into watching movies or playing board games. I'd barely had time to grade my students' final essays. I loved my mom dearly and appreciated all of the effort she was channeling into my recovery, but I was getting a little stir-crazy.

As I passed well-trimmed expanses of grass and mini-forests of large evergreens, overgrown blackberry bushes, and abundant ferns, I felt a piece of me—one I hadn't even realized was missing—return.

It felt like an eternity since we'd set up the meeting, but I was finally on my way to meet Professor Bahur, mysterious archaeologist and user of archaic speech patterns, at the Burke Café. I almost couldn't contain my anticipation. I wanted to know everything about the dig and what my exact role would be. I still didn't even know the location of the excavation site. I'd left my apartment early, taking the opportunity to turn the half-mile straight shot into a three-mile zigzag across the

86

university's familiar grounds in hopes that the fresh air might help settle my nerves.

Entering the quad from the southeast, I ascended gradual brick stairs, thanking my luck that the morning's frost had worn off by midday. I paused on the top step, taking deep breaths of chilly, humid air. I was still weak, recovering from the unforeseen aftereffects of the incident with Mike. While my brain had fully healed during the hours spent in the hospital, the rest of my body still looked as if it had been starved for weeks. All of my clothes were noticeably loose, and as I hadn't had much spare bulk to begin with, the weight loss definitely wasn't an improvement to my appearance. At least my mom's dietary plan of continual force-feeding seemed to be helping.

Breath caught, I resumed my stately pace down one of the brick walkways crisscrossing the quad's lawn. If I were a soaring bird looking down at the rectangular, open space with its border of brick buildings, I imagined the sight would resemble an enormous stained-glass window with emerald panes cut into symmetrical, geometric shapes. The usually crowded area was devoid of people, leaving barren cherry blossom trees and the towering brick-and-stone buildings as my only companions. Their beautiful, classic architecture appeased the part of me that yearned to replace modern, impersonal structures with those rich in character from earlier centuries.

Lost as I'd been in my wandering thoughts, I had a sudden moment of panic, fearing that I would be late for my meeting with Professor Bahur . . . or that I already was. I checked my phone; it was a quarter past three. Thankfully, I wasn't late . . . yet. If I hurried, I might have time to order a vanilla latte before meeting up with him.

Ten minutes later, I reached the Burke Museum, heading for the entrance to the café in the basement. I sighed appreciatively as I opened the narrow glass door. If I ignored the electric bulbs and the scatter of laptop-focused patrons, I could almost imagine that I'd stepped back in time. The carved wooden wall panels and the small, dark-stained tables with their sturdy, matching chairs belonged in a world gone a hundred years.

I scanned the café, and upon finding that all three patrons were women and therefore not Marcus Bahur, stepped up to the counter.

"What would you like?" the petite young barista asked.

"A tall vanilla latte, please," I said without thinking. "Actually, can you make it a grande? And I'll have a blueberry scone."

"That'll be five sixty-three," she told me.

I handed her the money. "Do you know if there's a Professor Marcus Bahur here right now?"

Her eyes went wide and her cheeks flushed. "Oh, um . . . no, I haven't seen him."

I lowered my eyebrows, confused by her reaction. "But you know him?"

"Oh, yes! He's been a regular since summer," she explained. Suddenly her eyes narrowed and she asked, "Why? Are you looking for him? What for?" She glanced at the door, then back at me.

I put on a friendly smile. "I'm meeting him for an academic project. Would you mind describing him to me? I'm not sure who I'm looking for."

Her mouth transformed from pouty to pretty, and she giggled. She didn't speak for a few moments while she retrieved my scone and started making my drink. Finally, she said, "He's . . . um . . . sort of hard to describe." She blushed again while she steamed milk.

"Okay . . . well, is he tall?"

"Yes," she replied with a nod.

"Does he have gray hair?"

She giggled again. "Definitely not."

I was growing impatient with her witless inability to simply describe a person. "Well, what color is his hair, then? Or is he bald?"

Her eyes squinted in thought. "Nope, he's got hair."

As she handed me my coffee, I grabbed the scone off the counter and muttered, "Thanks." I started to turn away from her, but paused. "How old do you think he is?"

As I'd been speaking, her face had grown redder and her barely-contained giggling seemed ready to explode out of her. "Oh, you'll have to ask him," she said.

"And how am I supposed to do that if I can't find him because all I know is that he's tall and has hair?" I asked, irritation clipping my words. *Is she even old enough to work?*

She managed to squeak, "Because he's right behind you," before doubling over in laughter.

Squeezing my eyes shut, I took a deep, calming breath before turning around. He was standing several feet away, wearing gray trousers and a heavy, black wool coat and was, in fact, tall with black hair. My breath caught in my throat as I realized just how minimal that description had been. I'd been expecting an older gentleman, but this was a man in his prime, in his early thirties at most and strikingly handsome. His face was composed of strong lines and sharp angles, his full lower lip the only hint of softness.

He'd been looking at his phone when I faced him, leaving my embarrassing reaction—blushing and staring—mercifully unnoticed. When his eyes raised and latched onto mine, I nearly dropped my coffee. His irises were an amber so rich they practically glowed. It was an eye color I'd seen before, only once. Professor Marcus Bahur was the guy I'd spilled vodka and cranberry juice on at the bar. *You've got to be kidding me.*

As recognition registered on my face, the faintest smirk pulled up one corner of his mouth. I groaned and closed my eyes momentarily. "I am *so* sorry . . . about the drinks and your shirt, I mean. God, this is embarrassing."

His mouth widened into a tight-lipped smile.

This isn't awkward or anything, I thought. *Time for some damage control*. I closed the distance between us in two short steps and held out my hand, very businesslike. "I'm Alexandra Larson."

Reaching out, he grasped my hand and shook it firmly. "A pleasure, Ms. Larson." His accent was as rich and beautiful as I remembered from our brief encounter at the bar.

"Yes, it is, Professor Bahur." I forced myself not to stare at him like a moon-eyed teenager, which was exactly how I'd acted at the bar.

As he released my hand, he flicked his eyes to the barista and said, "The usual, please. Thank you, Cassandra." To me, he said, "Well then, Ms. Larson. Why don't you pick a table and get settled. I'll join you shortly."

"Sure."

Pleasantly disturbed and highly confused, I wound through the haphazard clusters of tables and chairs to an unoccupied corner. I sat on a bench against the wall, hoping to catch a glimpse of the intriguing professor's interaction with the barista.

Cassandra bubbled and chirped nonstop while Professor Bahur waited for his order. He rarely spoke, only providing one-word answers when required, but she was unperturbed. At every shift of his body she giggled or simpered or sighed. *Such a little girl*, I thought blandly. I ignored the fact that my body had wanted to respond in an unfortunately similar fashion during both of our brief encounters.

"Get a grip," I muttered. The director of the greatest excavation opportunity I'd ever been offered was a no-flirt zone. I needed to get my ridiculous, unprofessional reactions to him under control.

But damn, even though he was still wearing his heavy wool coat, I could tell he was well built. When he moved, every inch of him seemed utterly sure of its placement, like a dancer or a master of the martial arts. I couldn't help but imagine what his body would look like without clothing, unintentionally leading me to think about it pressed against mine . . . covering mine . . . moving against mine. Unbidden, Mike's body replaced the professor's in my lewd thoughts. My heart rate increased dramatically, and my breaths grew short.

"Ms. Larson? Are you alright?" Professor Bahur asked from across the table. He sat, placing a cappuccino cup and saucer on the wooden surface.

"Hmm?" I snapped my mind back to the here and now, shoving away all lust or panic-inducing thoughts. Under the professor's steady gaze, I said, "Yes . . . yes, I'm fine. Thank you. I was just thinking . . ."

Like a falcon, he cocked his head to the side and scrutinized me. "Sometimes, I find that stray thoughts can be quite troublesome. A curse of the intelligent, I suppose." He included me in his undefined "intelligent" group with a flick of his hand on the table.

"I suppose," I said. "Or a curse of the cursed."

"Are you cursed, Ms. Larson?" His amber eyes were penetrating.

I shook my head and laughed softly, thinking of all that had happened during the last month. "Maybe."

Professor Bahur's expression turned serious. "Well, that can be quite an inconvenience when bounding around on excavations and such, don't you think? One might accumulate more curses than one can bear."

"I've been on several excavations over the past five years and the curses have yet to interfere with my life. What about you, Professor?"

He lowered his eyes and studied his cappuccino. "Some people are more cursed than others."

I coughed, choking on the sip of coffee I'd just taken. "I . . . I'm sorry. I didn't mean to—"

He waved away my concern with his hand. "Please, don't worry about me. I've had a long time to learn how to live with my curses."

Unsure of how to respond, I took another sip of frothy latte, this time cough-free.

"I'm very eager to work with you, Ms. Larson. I've been reading up on your work. Your piece in the *Journal of Mediterranean Archaeology* was exceptionally enlightening."

I brightened, happy to veer toward a less-personal topic of conversation. The article he spoke of focused on my unconventional method for deciphering unknown or unclear symbols across dozens of ancient languages using similar, but technically unrelated texts; it formed the basis for my dissertation as well.

"Thank you, Professor. Honestly, I'm hoping your excavation will provide an opportunity for me to test some of my theories. I think it'll really increase the methodology's validity."

"I'm certain it will," he agreed, taking a sip of his coffee, which also appeared to be a latte. "Now, I'm sure you'd like the specifics of the excavation."

"Yes, I really would."

He nodded absentmindedly. "Several years ago, I discovered a couple of stone tablets referring to a temple in Deir el-Bahri. A temple that, as far as we know, doesn't exist."

"Or just hasn't been discovered yet," I added. Deir el-Bahri, located on the west bank of the Nile in southern Egypt, was world-famous, mostly because the mortuary temple of one of the most famous female pharaohs—Hatchepsut—was located there. The idea that there might be an undiscovered temple somewhere among Deir el-Bahri's steep, limestone cliffs was astounding . . . and so incredibly intriguing.

"Precisely," he agreed.

"Professor, if you've discovered an entirely unknown temple *there*, you've made the find of a lifetime!" I was in complete and utter awe of the beautiful creature sharing a café table with me, not for his looks, but for his unquestionable intellect.

Eyes sparkling, he continued, "It gets better, Ms. Larson. The temple has remained hidden for so long because of its unique construction. Unlike the three main temples at Deir el-Bahri, *ours* was designed without majestic colonnades and ramps—the entire structure is supposedly carved into the cliffs."

I nodded, trying to comprehend the enormity of the potential find. "So it's supposed to be more like the tombs in Valley of the Kings?" I asked, referring to the cluster of tombs located on the other side of Deir el-Bahri's cliffs.

He nodded. "Based on recent geologic studies, we are fairly certain of the location of the temple's buried main entrance."

"Main entrance? As in, not the *only* entrance?"

The professor's mouth quirked into a mysterious smile, an expression I was quickly growing fond of. "You're quick, Ms. Larson. Dr. Ramirez warned me about that aspect of your character."

"Warned you? Last I checked, being quick wasn't a bad thing." Damn, my tongue was going to get me into trouble with him.

He acquiesced with a dignified nod. "You're correct, of course. I must remember not to underestimate you, though your youth and . . . other attributes may lead me in that direction."

I kept my face blank, pretty sure my new boss had just insulted and complimented me at the same time.

His lips quirked again. "Back to the issue of multiple entrances—you see, the tablets indicate that our undiscovered temple connects to Djeser-Djeseru."

My mouth fell open and I held up a hand. Djeser-Djeseru—roughly meaning "holiest of holies"—was the ancient name of Queen Hatchepsut's mortuary temple. I couldn't believe that the most famous, visited, and explored temple in Deir el-Bahri contained an as-yet-undiscovered secret passage that led to an as-yet-undiscovered secret temple. "You're kidding, right? That's impossible!"

Professor Bahur stared into my wide, stunned eyes with a complete lack of humor.

"You're not kidding? Oh my God . . . you're serious?"

He raised one eyebrow at my shocked redundancy.

Placing both of my hands flat on the tabletop, I said, "Let me get this straight. You think you can find a previously unknown temple that connects to Hatchepsut's mortuary temple?"

He gave a single, minute nod.

"But that would mean there's an undiscovered *secret* passageway in Haty's temple. That site's been scoured by . . . I don't know—*everyone*—over the past century! It must draw more than a million visitors every year! How is this even possible?"

"It would appear, Ms. Larson, that *Haty*"—the corner of his mouth twitched in amusement at my nickname for the famous female pharaoh—"was a woman of many secrets. Her stepson and her architect did a very good job of covering them up. Your main role on this excavation is to uncover those secrets—particularly the exact location of the entrance in *her* temple—as I've yet to have much luck."

Oh my God . . . Oh my God . . . Oh my God, I thought, and my nerves hummed with excitement. Professor Bahur had just handed me a task that pretty much every archaeologist would kill for.

He made a low, knowing sound. It was annoyingly attractive. "Yes, I thought you might enjoy that bit of information."

"This is unbelievable. Thank you so much!" I practically laughed.

"You are quite welcome. It just so happens that your skill set is precisely what might crack the final riddle. You specialize in deciphering difficult, ancient texts . . . we have difficult, ancient texts to decipher," he said cheerily. "Do keep in mind that you will need to do a fair amount of research in preparation for our departure."

I nodded, brimming with anticipation. I would do almost anything to participate in his excavation.

Professor Bahur continued, "The university has been kind enough to set aside a classroom on the top floor of Denny Hall for the excavation team to plan and prep. I expect you'll spend most of the winter term there. I'd like you to come by on Monday morning so I can give you a key and introduce you to the rest of the team."

"Sure. What time?"

"Half past eight should work nicely. Additionally, I've made arrangements with Dr. Ramirez for your graduate duties to be pushed aside. You won't need to teach students or complete any unrelated research projects. This excavation will function as your entire course of study for the next year. I need your focus uninterrupted. Is that acceptable?"

I was stunned. This enigmatic, visiting professor had spoken with *my* advisor and completely altered the next year of *my* life before he'd even met me . . . at least, officially. I felt a twinge of irritation that he hadn't consulted with me before rearranging the next year of my life, but the results were amazing enough that I ignored it. "Yes, I think so. Thank you . . . again, Professor Bahur."

"You're welcome . . . again, Ms. Larson. I expect your participation will invigorate the excavation."

Invigorate the excavation—what the hell does that mean? Along with uncovering the secrets of a long-dead queen, I anticipated uncovering the mysteries behind the confounding man sitting across from me.

We discussed some of the more technical details of the excavation over the next several hours. During a lull in our conversation, Professor Bahur glanced around and then said, "I'm afraid our meeting lasted longer than I'd anticipated and night has fallen. I'd hate for you to have to walk home alone in the dark. Might I walk with you?"

Gazing through the narrow, floor-to-ceiling windows on the opposite wall, I found that the sun had indeed set and twilight had come and gone. "Oh, I hadn't noticed." Although the idea of a companion on my trip home was tempting, I didn't want to impinge on Professor Bahur's undoubtedly valuable time. "You really don't need to walk me home," I told him, but for a reason I didn't understand *at all*, I wanted him to. I should have been running for the hills after what happened with Mike, but I felt an overwhelming amount of trust for the professor. I shook my head the barest amount. *Yep, I've officially lost it.*

Professor Bahur lifted his coat from the back of his chair and shrugged into it. "Really, Ms. Larson, there is a great deal of difference between want and need. I'd expect someone of your advanced academic experience to be familiar with the disparity."

Standing, I blushed at the idea of him wanting anything non-academic from me and used arranging my coat and scarf as a shield. "Alright, but only if you *want* to," I said, attempting to keep the teasing tone in the friendly range.

"I assume, then, that a combination of want and need are acceptable," he said with a severely polite air, the sharp sparkle in his eyes the only hint of playfulness. "One must always keep a watchful eye on those he needs in matters of business, and I couldn't possibly turn down the chance to spend more time in the company of such a lovely, knowledgeable colleague." He indicated the crooked path toward the door with a negligent gesture. "After you, Ms. Larson."

Baffled again by his strange behavior, I slipped between the tables and headed for the door. I made sure to smile at Cassandra as I passed the counter.

She glared back, her sour expression turning to honey as she looked at the man following me. "Goodnight, Professor Bahur," she chirped.

"Cassandra," came his emotionless response, and though I wasn't looking at him, I pictured him giving her the slightest nod of acknowledgement.

Once the door closed behind us, I smiled and glanced at the professor. "You know, I think you might have just broken her heart with a single word."

"Yes, well . . ." he said as he looked up into the cloudy night sky, a tired smile playing across his lips. "I can't waste time and effort on every woman who desires my attention, Ms. Larson."

"A curse of the beautiful, I suppose." As soon as the words left my mouth, I wished for them back. I was sure I'd just crossed a line in our newly-established, mostly professional relationship.

Professor Bahur chuckled and casually placed his hands in his coat pockets. "A curse whose effects you must suffer from every day," he said before turning to walk toward the nearest concrete path.

I stood in place, dumbfounded. *Does* that *man really think* I'm *beautiful?* I was more of a shrug and a "Yeah, she's pretty" kind of woman, and I was perfectly comfortable with the fact that I would never turn many heads or stand out in a room full of people. And then I remembered my current appearance, that I looked like I was suffering from some ghastly wasting sickness. *He's just being nice*, I realized.

"Ms. Larson, are you coming? It is most difficult to walk you home when I neither know the way nor have you beside me," he called over his shoulder.

I caught up quickly, noticing he'd been heading in the correct direction without my assistance. "You seem to be doing just fine on your own. I live in the Malloy—do you know it?"

"Ah, yes. How nice that you're able to reside in such a lovely building."

I snorted. "I don't know about that. I think it lost most of its loveliness half a century ago." After a moment, I said, "Professor Bahur, how—"

"Please, call me Marcus," he interrupted. "It seems inappropriate for such an accomplished scholar to address me as a student would a teacher."

"But that's what we are," I countered.

"Ms. Larson, your status as a graduate student is a flaw that I'm certain will be corrected by the end of our excavation."

Bristling, I recalled how neatly he'd rearranged the next year of my graduate career and stopped in my tracks. "You know, I can *earn* my PhD, just like everyone else—with hard work and years of research. I don't need you to do me any favors, and I'd never accept a degree I haven't earned."

When he turned to face me, his lips were parted in surprise. He retraced his steps until he stood so close that the condensation in his breath nearly touched me. "You misunderstand me," he said evenly. "I merely meant that I have great belief in your ability to use the excavation to finalize your degree. After the discoveries we'll make over the next twelve months, I can't imagine the university could hold back on granting your doctorate of philosophy." His nearness and height were slightly intimidating when paired with the chill in his voice.

"Oh."

"Might we continue on?" he asked.

Embarrassed and worried that I'd damaged any possibility of friendship, I blurted, "I'm so sorry . . . I overreacted. I shouldn't have, Profess—"

"Marcus," he corrected. "And it's already forgotten."

"Marcus," I agreed with a shy smile. "You'll have to call me Lex, then."

"Very well, Lex. Now, I believe you were going to ask me something," he reminded me as we continued along the path.

"Oh, yeah . . . I'm sure you already have a plan for this, but how are you going to clear Hatchepsut's mortuary temple of visitors for *months*? The SCA will lose a ton of money." The SCA, short for the Supreme Council of Antiquities, was the organization in charge of pretty much everything relating to ancient Egypt. "I can't imagine them agreeing to give us exclusive access for the sake of scholarly discoveries."

For the first time, Marcus smiled fully, and the beauty of his joy nearly made me stumble. "Well, Lex, let's just say that I have friends in high places."

"Of course you do."

Across the street from my building, we stopped, waiting for the crosswalk light to change. "You don't need to cross with me. I'll be safe inside in less than a minute."

Marcus turned to me, searching my face for something only he would recognize. "Need and want, Ms. Larson. Need and want." No hint of humor pervaded his words. *He's certainly an odd one*, I thought, but the sense of safety—of trust—had only increased during our walk.

Seconds later, as we crossed the street, I grew increasingly curious about the man beside me. *Who is he, besides an archaeologist? How did he make friends in such high places? How have I never heard of him?* It was as though he'd simply appeared on the archaeology scene last month. *That just doesn't happen.*

We stopped in front of my building's glass door, and Marcus waited while I fished through my bag for my keys. I felt a flash of anxiety as I remembered the last time I'd been standing in front of the same door. Seeming to sense my unease, Marcus took a few steps away. Miraculously, with the breathing space, calm returned.

I unlocked the door and held it open with my body, half in and half out of the building. "Thanks for keeping me company . . ."

"Anytime," he replied with a quick bow of his head. "I'll see you bright and early on Monday."

I smiled and nodded, retreating into the warmth of the building. For the briefest moment, I wondered what Marcus would have done if I'd invited him inside. My mom was still there, so the thought was purely hypothetical. Unfortunately, it triggered more memories of Mike, of being helpless to him, and I shuddered.

Silently, I vowed never to date again.

10

ASLEEP & AWAKE

Marcus lurked in my thoughts throughout my mom's delicious dinner of roast beef and mashed potatoes, as well as our evening screening of a covert ops action flick. Though I'd only been out of the apartment for a few hours, the exercise and excitement had exhausted me. From the looks my mom kept flashing me, my weariness was poorly hidden.

"Why don't you go to bed, sweetie?" she suggested after she turned off the TV. "You look like you're about to fall asleep, and you'll be more comfy in your room."

Stretching on the couch, I yawned. "Good idea." It didn't really matter that it was only nine o'clock. I gave her a hug, stood, and headed to my room. "Goodnight, Mom," I said before closing the door.

I had just enough energy to wash off the light makeup I'd donned for the meeting with Marcus, brush my teeth, and change into flannel pajama pants and a lavender T-shirt displaying a cuddly cartoon version of the UW Husky. I slipped under the covers and fell asleep almost instantly.

I was standing in a dark study filled with mahogany tables, built-in bookshelves, and rich, leather furniture. I was surrounded by the spicy scent of cigars and Cognac mixed with the musk of aged books. In the soft glow of a Tiffany lamp, a dark-haired man was leaning over a desk, his back to me. I moved closer, suspicion growing with each step.

As I rounded the desk, my instinct proved true. Marcus Bahur. His face was taut with concentration as he studied photographs of hieroglyphs. I recognized most of them, but one specific set stood out beyond the others—the lion's head above a half-circle paired with a full circle and two vertical parallel lines, one with a flag-like protrusion. It was the same set of symbols that had been evading my deciphering abilities for months.

"Makes sense," I mumbled, dismissing the pictures. My brain was just mashing together a bunch of the things that had been occupying my mind lately.

Marcus leaned closer to one of the images, his expression changing. Two fine lines creased the space between his eyebrows, and his lips puckered minutely. For a moment, all I could think about was how much I wanted to truly know the mesmerizing man sitting before me—the same man who was handing me the career opportunity of a lifetime.

Without preamble, the scene shifted in a dizzying swirl of colors. Marcus was the only constant in the chaos, remaining seated as the frenzied colors surrounded us. I became nauseated and had to close my eyes as I waited, hoping the endless swirling would stop. When I opened them again, I gasped.

Marcus was still sitting in front of me, but on a short, gilded stool instead of an oversized desk chair . . . and he was shirtless. His golden-brown skin glowed in soft firelight. Smooth lines of muscle led from his shoulders down to an intricately woven belt, which was holding up some sort of white linen garment.

He stood suddenly, displaying his odd attire—a calf-length skirt. After seconds of confusion, I realized it was the Middle Kingdom royal kilt. I laughed out loud, accepting that my imagination was getting the best of me, combining my new fascination with the professor and all of the recent excitement about the excavation.

I took one last, lingering look at the immaculate physique my mind assigned to Marcus, then closed my eyes for a long moment, willing my consciousness to move on to another dream.

Again, when I opened my eyes, the scene around me had transformed. I was in a long, arched stone corridor. Narrow, glassless windows lined the left side, letting in silvery moonlight. I almost screamed when I looked down at the floor. In the square of light coming through the nearest window lay a man, eyes open and sightless. There was a very deep gash cutting across his throat, and blood soaked the front of what could only be called a once-pale doublet.

I looked up, away, anywhere but at the dead man. My eyes landed on a second body further down the corridor . . . then another, and another. Shadows and moonlight had tricked my eyes at first, but once I started seeing them—the dead—I couldn't look away. There were so many. A dozen? More?

Behind me, there was a masculine shout, closely followed by a grunt and a loud thump. It sounded like a fight. Is it whoever killed these people? *I took several hasty steps in the opposite direction and promptly tripped, sprawling on the uneven stone floor. At first I thought I'd caught my toe on one of the stones, but when I looked back, I realized it had been the dead man—the one with the cut throat. "Ugh!" I exclaimed, skin crawling.*

Carefully, I stood and started picking my way down the hallway, away from the sounds of men fighting. I'd just stepped over the sixth body —a beautiful, dark-haired woman in a burgundy and gold gown whose neck was bent at a very unnatural angle—when I heard a guttural gasp, and the sounds of fighting stopped. I froze.

The sound of rusty hinges preceded footsteps and two low, whispering voices. They were behind me, and getting louder. I found the alcove of a door a little further down on the right side of the corridor, and hid in its shadows, pressing myself into rough planks of wood. As the voices drew closer, I realized that one of the whisperers was male, the other female. I held my breath as they neared my hiding place.

" . . . too quick. I don't know how he keeps finding me," the woman whispered. She let out a harsh sob. "Oh God . . . Jane." I could just see

the top half of her cloaked and hooded body as she dropped to her knees and bent over the woman with the broken neck. Her shoulders shook and she rocked back and forth, murmuring something to the dead woman.

"No, it's his fault, not yours," the man said fiercely, and I suddenly recognized his voice. Marcus. He gripped the woman's shoulders and raised her back up to her feet, then wrapped his arms around her middle, drawing my attention to her swollen belly. She was incredibly pregnant, which was pretty much the only thing I could tell about her under the cloak.

She placed her hands over his on her belly and whispered. "I don't know where to go. I thought this would be my last stop, but—" Again, her body shook with the strength of her sorrow. "I don't want to leave you again."

"Shhh . . ." Marcus's voice was soft, soothing. "You must trust that you will find me."

The woman turned in his arms and reached up a pale hand to cup the side of his face. "I will always find you, my falcon, but for now, you must forget." As she said, "forget," the look of adoration slipped off Marcus's face, and the woman withdrew her hand.

A door banged open further down the corridor, and I turned my head to look. When I glanced back at Marcus and the cloaked woman, she was gone. There was only Marcus and a hallway filled with dead bodies.

It was barely seven in the morning when I woke, well-rested from a long night's sleep. I spent a few minutes lazily thinking back on my dreams, unsurprised that nearly all had featured Marcus. He was such a beautiful conundrum . . . my mind had been bound to latch onto him.

Moving on to more practical matters, I stretched, dislodging Thora from her cozy position by my thigh. I had tired too quickly the previous day, and I needed to get back into active scholar mode by Monday—only two days away. My worthiness as a team member on Marcus's excavation was at stake. As I rose from bed and readied myself for the day, I set out a plan, fully aware that the first part would be the hardest.

"Morning sweetheart," my mom said when I emerged from my room. She didn't turn away from the stove as she spoke. "Breakfast's just about ready."

"Is there coffee?" I asked, giving her a hug from behind.

She patted my forearm. "Yep. In the pot."

I kissed her cheek and pulled away, saying, "Thanks, Mom. You're the best ever!"

"Oh, stop it, Lex. You'll make me blush."

Smiling, I fixed myself a cup of coffee with milk and sugar and shuffled to the table.

"Hold on, sweetie. Come carry these plates over."

Acquiescing, I helped my mom load the table with our fourth breakfast of way too much food. I'd pretty much accepted that my ability to gauge my own appetite had gone wonky, and I was content to let my mom fatten me up like a Thanksgiving turkey. The current layout included blueberry muffins and a small mountain of breakfast burritos, most of which I would probably end up consuming.

"Are you going somewhere?" my mom asked, setting her coffee on the table and sitting in her usual spot.

"What? How'd you know?"

"Your clothes, Lex—you're already dressed. Usually that doesn't happen until at least noon, if ever."

Laughing, I shook my head. "Yeah, I have some errands I need to run on campus. Some books to renew at the library, a little research to do . . . you know, the usual," I lied.

"I thought the quarter hadn't started yet."

My heartbeat sped up, and I felt guilty for the coming lies . . . necessary lies. "No, you're right, but that's the life of a grad student—working on research projects even though the rest of the school's on break. Plus, with the excavation . . ."

She sighed, clearly preferring that I stay on the couch for

another day of mom-monitored relaxation and recuperation. "Do you want me to come with you?"

"While I'd love your company, Mom, you'd be bored to death. Plus, I'll be able to do everything faster on my own."

"You'll just be on campus?"

"Yeah," I said, cringing on the inside. *Damn, I hate lying to her!*

"Well, I know I can't tell you no. You're an adult. But promise me you'll come home right away if you feel yourself getting worn out."

I smiled, feeling like a worthless piece of donkey crap. "Of course, Mom."

After breakfast, I gathered a few necessary items into my messenger bag, including my wallet and bus pass, a black spiral-bound journal, and my hospital release papers, and then left the apartment. I crossed the street to the Burke–Gilman Trail, which circumscribes the southeast edges of the university, and followed it straight to the hospital at the south end of campus— Dr. Isa owed me some answers.

Unfortunately, when I reached the hospital's info desk and asked the stick-thin nurse manning it where I could find Dr. Isa, the results were anticlimactic.

"Dr. Isa? Do you know the doctor's first name?" she asked.

"Um, no. But she was my doctor in ICU last week."

The receptionist narrowed her eyes, scrutinizing me. "Are you sure you were in ICU last week?"

Glad I'd come prepared, I pulled the release papers out of my bag and set them on the counter. "I was. See." I pointed to the release date just in case she missed it.

"Hmmm . . ." She turned to her computer screen, her skeletal fingers clacking the keys rhythmically as she searched the database for my records. "Ah, yes, I see your Dr. Isa. What do you need?"

Barely suppressing my excitement, I said, "I need to ask her some questions. About some personal medical diagnoses she made."

The nurse tapped her keyboard a few more times before responding. "Well, she's not here. Your records show you had another doctor assigned to you. He is in the hospital right now. Do you want me to page him?"

I frowned. "Er . . . no. I really just need to talk to Dr. Isa. Do you know when she'll be working again?"

The nurse's smile was condescending. "I'm sorry, but she's not here anymore. I mean, at the hospital . . . she no longer works here."

Instantly, the hope-filled balloon that had been expanding inside my chest started to deflate as frustration and despair poked little holes in its surface. *What about my answers?*

Trying not to sound too defeated, I thanked the nurse and left through the automatic sliding doors, hurrying to the bus stop. I had one more lead, and I wasn't ready to give up all my hope.

Miraculously, one of the many buses heading to Capitol Hill, my current destination, was just opening its doors as I reached the stop. I waited in line behind a bearded man who desperately needed a shower, a tired-looking woman in blue scrubs, and a young punk-rocker with spiked, electric-blue hair, multiple facial piercings, and heavy black eyeliner.

The last smiled at me while nodding to the beat of whatever music blared through his earbuds. I assessed my reflection in one of the bus's windows, wondering what exactly had endeared the young man to me, and found a surprisingly flushed version of myself staring back. The rosiness in my cheeks and lips paired with my dark mahogany hair and alabaster skin made me resemble a modern-day Snow White. I hadn't really *looked* at my reflection in days, and this was a vast improvement from the skeletal stranger I'd seen the last time.

Smiling slightly, I stepped onto the bus, showed the driver

my pass, and found a solitary seat in the middle. Astonishing me further, my eye-catching admirer sat beside me and removed his black and purple earbuds.

"Hey," he said, his voice unexpectedly deep.

"Hi?"

"Your eyes are really cool. Are they, like, contacts or something?"

"Uh . . . no. They're just my eyes," I said, confused.

He laughed, his smile wide and his pale eyes earnest. He was really quite adorable, if I looked past the many holes and markings modifying his appearance. "They're practically red . . . and they're like that naturally? That's way more awesome than contacts. Natural's cool."

I nearly snorted, thinking my new friend and natural didn't belong in the same room . . . or even the same country. I thought back to the reddish tint to my brown eyes I'd noticed several days earlier, and wondered if the red had become even more prominent. *Can a person's eye color even change like that? Why hasn't Mom said anything?*

"Yours aren't too bad," I said, wanting to take the attention off myself. "They're so pale."

He leaned in conspiratorially and whispered, "They're fake."

"Oh!" I said, laughing. "What's their natural color?"

"Hazel. Boring."

I nudged his shoulder with my own. "Hazel's not boring—it's multicolored. Besides, I read that it makes people seem more approachable because hazel's a warm eye color."

He barked a laugh. "Oh, you're funny. I doubt changing my eye color would do much to improve my approachability." He stood and flashed another brilliant smile as the bus slowed to a halt. "This is me. See you around, red-eyed girl."

"Sure." I watched him disembark, his demeanor reverting to the expected—sullen and angry—but I knew better.

After three more stops, we reached mine at Broadway and

Thomas. I pulled the cord and waited for the bus to stop, then exited through the rear door. *Emerald City Fertility* sat tucked inconspicuously between *Harold's Body Art* and an adorable Irish pub aptly named *The End O' The Rainbow*. Depending on my luck in the clinic, I thought I might end up sitting on a stool in *The Rainbow* in an hour or two.

Taking a deep breath, I approached a glass door stenciled with *Emerald City Fertility* in clean, white lettering and pulled it open. I had to climb a narrow set of stairs to reach the fertility clinic's nearly empty, second-floor waiting room. Only a young couple occupied two of the cushioned chairs, holding hands as they nervously examined their surroundings.

"Can I help you?" a young, blonde receptionist asked. I wondered if she ever had issues with her hair sticking to the pink lip gloss smothered on her lips.

"I hope so," I said, approaching the desk. "I'd like to talk to Dr. Lee. I don't have an appointment, but I can wait if he can squeeze me in between patients."

She smiled indulgently, looking like an all-American cheerleader, and explained, "Dr. Lee doesn't usually see anyone without an appointment. If you'd like to make an appointment for a later date, we can schedule that now. We usually start with a two-hour consultation that includes both partners."

Partners? Consultation? "Oh! I'm not here as a patient," I clarified. "My mom was. I guess you could say I wouldn't be alive without Dr. Lee. I've been meaning to stop by for years, and I was in the neighborhood, so . . . I guess I thought I'd just come in and thank him." Lying was becoming as natural to me as breathing. It disgusted me.

The receptionist's expression transformed as I spoke, turning from fake warmth to genuine excitement. "Really? We rarely get to see the children as adults. I'm sure he'd be delighted. Can you wait here while I check with him?"

"Sure."

She hurried down the hallway and disappeared around a corner, returning less than a minute later. "If you'll follow me, Ms. . . . ?"

"Larson. Alexandra Larson."

"Ms. Larson. I'm going to put you in the consultation room. Dr. Lee will join you in a few minutes."

"Thank you."

I sat on a comfortable couch set against the wall on the left side of the room and took out my journal. I started writing down questions that might give me some hints about my biological father. I had nearly a dozen listed when the door opened, admitting a dignified, middle-aged man with gray-winged hair and a kind face. His slacks and dress shirt made him appear more like a lawyer than a doctor.

"Alexandra Larson. I'm Dr. Lee." His tone was friendly, his voice deep.

Standing, I accepted his outstretched hand, noting its dry warmth, and smiled. "Hello, Dr. Lee. It's so nice to meet you."

"Well, we've actually met, but it was a long time ago and you were about this tall," he said, holding his hand less than two feet above the blue carpet.

I laughed and sat back down. "Oh, I didn't know."

"Of course not. I remember your parents well . . . lovely people." He sat down in a leather chair across from me, a medical file resting on his lap. "So, what can I do for you, Alexandra?"

"Well, I wanted to thank you for helping my parents and . . . I guess . . . helping me."

He smiled modestly. "You're more than welcome. Helping young families is my passion."

I hesitated, holding my breath, and then expelled it in one long question. "Dr. Lee, is it possible for you to tell me anything about my biological father even though, you know, there are privacy agreements and whatnot?"

His smile widened a little. "I have yet to meet a child created through artificial methods who didn't wonder that very thing. Unfortunately, as you've already pointed out, there are privacy and confidentiality issues."

I slumped against the back of the couch.

The doctor held up a hand with his index finger extended. "However, I can tell you a little bit about him, just not his identifying information." He opened the file and began reading. "Twenty-five at the time his sample was collected. He had light brown hair, hazel eyes, and a pale complexion. He was six feet tall and had a lean body type."

My eyes were wide with surprise at the sudden flow of information, but I still felt unfulfilled. "He sounds just like my dad . . ." . . . *who I don't resemble at all.*

"Yes, that's the point. We try to match the surrogate with the legal father. I can also tell you . . ." I could hear the doctor's voice continuing on as he further described my supposed biological father's attributes, but I was distracted by a sudden blurring of my vision.

The man in that folder is not *my father,* I thought. I knew it with absolute certainty, like I knew the sound of my mom's voice before she started crying or the smell in the air before it snowed.

For several nauseating seconds, the world disappeared into a swirl of colors before resettling.

I was standing in the center of the fertility clinic's dark waiting room. It must've been the middle of the night, as the only illumination came from the glitter of city lights through the windows. I was pretty sure I was having another one of the weird dreams . . . but I was also fairly certain that I hadn't fallen asleep. Did I faint? *I had no idea what the hell was going on.*

A click sounded, and the door from the stairs to the clinic creaked open. A tall, sleek man with pale skin and black hair entered the room.

I rushed to the receptionist's desk, searching for anything with a date. A calendar taped to a lower cupboard caught my eye. The office staff, bless their little administrative hearts, crossed off the days as they passed. It was almost exactly nine months before I was born.

The intruder headed down the hall to the furthest door. Its polished wooden surface bore a golden placard with DR. JAMES LEE etched in black. The man entered the office and headed straight for the doctor's desk. Remaining standing, he looked through a short stack of files, pulled one out, opened it, and ran his finger down the top page.

Joining him at the desk, I was baffled by his ability to see well enough to read in the darkness. I took out my phone and flashed its light on the file. It was labeled LARSON, ALICE—my mom's name. I frowned.

Having evidently found what he was searching for, the man replaced the folder and snuck out of the room.

Following him, I couldn't help but wonder how common alarm systems had been two and a half decades ago. Obviously the clinic hadn't been equipped with one.

The man approached another door, this one designated LABORA-TORY. After he entered, he turned on the lights and headed for two glass-doored freezers on the opposite side of the lab.

I peeked over his shoulder as he opened one and searched its contents. He removed a small, round glass container and replaced it with an exact replica. On the side, there was a white sticker with "F.C.M. 08-12 for Alice Larson" written on it in black permanent marker.

I was getting the uncomfortable feeling that the sample-swapping man was my actual biological father. I was really trying not to acknowledge that I was staring at his semen in the replacement container. Gross . . .

Abruptly, the man turned, and nearly black eyes stared out from strikingly familiar features. My eyes—aside from the color—high cheekbones, and square jaw were reflected on the stranger's face. Oh my God . . . I was absolutely certain that the breaking-and-entering semen-replacer was my father.

Within seconds, he was trotting out the lab door. He hurried back to the waiting room, out through the clinic door, and was down the stairs and vanishing into the night before I could fully process what had just happened.

" . . . and I can tell you with certainty that he's successful in what he does now. You most definitely received the best genes available. You're a lucky woman, Alexandra," the doctor stated, finishing his description of a man I wasn't remotely related to.

I blinked, clearing the remnants of the vision and steadying my shock. "Dr. Lee, thank you so much," I said, hoping my gratitude was appropriate for the words I hadn't heard. "I really didn't expect you to be so generous with your information. You're a very kind man. Thank you."

"Oh . . . well, thank you, and you're welcome!" he said, sounding a little flustered.

I smiled, hoping he couldn't tell my heart wasn't in it. "I should go. You have a sweet young couple waiting for your help, and I don't want to keep you from them any longer." *Did I really just see my biological father in a dream? While I was* awake? *I need to get the hell out of here!*

"Well, you're right." *His* smile was genuine as he stood. "I'm glad you stopped by. It's nice to know one's work is appreciated."

"Oh, believe me doctor, your work is appreciated as much as any can be."

"You're too kind."

He escorted me out of the clinic, shaking my hand again at the top of the stairs. My heart rate was nearing Olympic sprinter levels by the time I stepped out into the damp midday air. Adrenaline was coursing through my bloodstream, fueled by the excitement and insanity of what I'd just seen—my biological father . . . breaking into a fertility clinic . . . replacing sperm samples . . . in a goddamn vision.

It can't be real, I thought. But the dreams—visions—had

proven true multiple times before. *It can't be real, but it has to be real.* People believed contradictory, even hypocritical things every day, but this was really pushing the boundaries. *I wish I could talk to Dr. Isa. She knows something, I know she does!*

Feeling like a crazy person, I headed for the bus stop across the street. A painted shop sign behind the stop caught my attention: *The Goddess's Blessing.* Based on the items displayed in the wide front window, it specialized in the unexplainable—from the mysterious to the magical—and of course, fortunes. Well, it just so happened that I was dealing with something pretty unexplainable at the moment.

Maybe someone in there can explain it, I thought as I veered around the bus stop, determination lengthening my strides. It was either that, or accept that I'd flown so far over the cuckoo's nest that I'd mistaken it for a rainbow. After all, the dreams that I dared to dream really were coming true.

DISCOVERY & ACQUISITION

A crystalline chiming punctuated my entrance into the cluttered shop. I'd been expecting a dark and mysterious space with shadowed nooks overflowing with eerie objects and ancient leather tomes . . . but I was surprised by its warm, welcoming atmosphere. Bookshelves lined the walls, many filled with shiny new paperbacks. A rainbow of crystals and tiny glass bottles decorated several bookcases from floor to ceiling, each item with its own sign proclaiming this or that mystical property. Tables were arranged close together throughout the shop, displaying spicy incense, aromatic candles, and a variety of odd items I would have been hard-pressed to identify. The cheerful atmosphere was somewhat of a letdown for my first venture into an occult shop. *Is it too much to ask for a few shrunken heads and some eye of newt?*

"Can I help you, Miss?" a woman asked, her voice husky.

I nearly dropped the statuette I'd picked up—a beautiful, carved representation of Thora's namesake, the powerful Egyptian goddess, Hathor. "Um, yes," I said, gently placing the pale, beautiful woman back on her pedestal.

"Are you a practitioner?" the shopkeeper asked as I turned to face her. She fit the shop perfectly with her flowy, ankle-length skirt, layers of clattering gold bracelets, and wavy, black hair that nearly reached her waist. She wasn't overtly attractive, but her curves in all the right places paired with her rich voice and graceful movements gave her an air of sensuality and mystery.

Am I a practitioner? Of what? Witchcraft? "Not exactly. I'm here on research . . . for a graduate project. I'm a PhD student in the archaeology department over at the U."

She studied me with eyes so dark they were nearly black before saying, "Mostly true, but I don't think you're here for a project."

I frowned, wondering how she had guessed that.

"Many people come here under the guise of some other purpose," she said, seeming to answer my thoughts. "I'll answer your questions to the best of my ability if you tell me why you're really in my shop."

I weighed my options and decided it wouldn't hurt me to divulge my story. Or at least *some* of my story. After all, it was the reason I'd entered in the first place. With a heavy sigh, I nodded.

"Alright," she purred. "Follow me."

Swaying, she led me through a curtain of multi-hued glass beads and into a cramped back room that had clearly been decorated with fortune-telling in mind; there was a small, square table of polished oak, several dim antique lamps, and a short bookshelf filled with tarot cards, leather-bound books, and other tools of the trade. A teenage version of the shop owner was sitting at the table, rapt attention on her phone. She cocked her head inquisitively at our arrival but didn't look up.

"Kat, go watch the counter. I have some business with this customer."

The teenager—Kat—rolled her eyes before standing and exiting the room with a huff.

"Your daughter?" I asked, amused.

"Do you have children?"

I shook my head, surprised by her question.

"I'd advise that you spend some time remembering your teenage self before reproducing. If you can't stand the idea of being around that version of yourself for more than a few hours, you're not ready," the shopkeeper replied.

"I heard that, Mom!" Kat called from the front of the store.

My hostess pointedly raised one artful eyebrow. "Please, have a seat." She took her daughter's place while I sat in the wooden chair opposite her.

"Thanks for agreeing to speak with me," I said after a long silent moment. It wasn't much of a conversation starter, but it was the best I could come up with under pressure.

With a knowing smile, she said, "I'm sure it will be enlightening for us both. Now, what brought you here?"

I pursed my lips, considering the best way to start. "I guess you could say I'm looking for answers . . . or an explanation. You see, I've been experiencing something sort of . . . odd."

"Odd how?" she asked, resting her clasped hands on the table.

"Well . . . it's these dreams I've been having. Except, I just had one and I was awake, which doesn't really make sense, does it? And they're not dreams exactly, but more like visions. I mean, some are things I've witnessed in my life, but some happened before I was born, and—this is going to sound totally nuts—some haven't even happened yet. But they're *all* real."

As I spoke, my companion sat up straighter, evidently intrigued. "What makes you think it's anything beyond an active imagination? What makes it 'real'?"

I leaned forward, intent on making the woman—a stranger— believe me. If *she* believed me without thinking I was crazy, maybe I could too. "Because I *know* things." I said. "Things I shouldn't know . . . things I *couldn't* know. I dreamed something bad would happen to me, and it happened *exactly* as I saw it."

"If you knew it would happen, why didn't you try to change it?"

I laughed bitterly. "I thought I was just anxious. It didn't seem possible that I could see the future in my dreams."

"You said it's not always a dream, that you've been awake for these 'visions'?"

"Yeah . . . just once, about fifteen minutes ago."

She leaned back in her chair, studying me, her generous lips pressed together in a flat line. After a protracted silence, she asked, "You want to know what's happening to you, correct?"

"Yes." Eager, I licked my lips. *She knows something . . . she has to.*

"I've heard of people with abilities like this. Usually it's genetic." She paused. "Have you spoken with your parents about it?"

Frustrated, I shook my head. "My mom doesn't know about any of it. She'd tell me if she did. And . . . I don't know who my father is."

"Mom!" Kat called from the front of the shop.

"Just a minute!" the woman across the table from me yelled back. To me, she said, "Your situation is odd, like you said, but there are others like you out there. It's standard for your kind to learn about such things from their families. I'm amazed you've slipped through the cracks for so long."

"My *kind*? What are you talking about?" My hands gripped the edge of the table so firmly that my nail beds were turning white.

The muffled sound of Kat's voice, along with a deeper, male voice, grew louder from beyond the beaded curtain.

"Yes, your kind." The woman seemed to be struggling with something as she stared into my eyes. Her head turned toward the doorway, and almost inaudibly, she whispered, "I'm truly sorry, but I can't tell you more. Just know there *are* others like you and they *will* find you."

"But you—"

Kat's pleading whine sounded from just outside the back room. "But she's busy right now!"

"My dear girl, your mother is never too busy for me. You know that. I must see her immediately," a familiar, faintly-accented voice said. *Oh, you have* got *to be kidding me!*

"Hey!" Kat's outraged admonition came just before a well-dressed man walked through the beaded curtain, making the pieces of glass clack excitedly. His eyes widened when they met mine, then narrowed slightly as he turned to my hostess.

"Marcus?" I asked, stunned. He was the last person I would've expected to run into at a quirky magic shop, and seeing him triggered a deluge of the images from the previous night's dreams. *Oh God . . . those* were *just dreams, right?* I shook my head, suddenly afraid I would start to suspect all of my dreams were visions. I cleared my throat. "What are you doing here?"

Kat and her mother wore identical expressions of surprise.

"I could ask you the same thing." The corner of Marcus's mouth quirked slightly. "Is Genevieve reading your cards . . . or perhaps your palm? She's earned quite the reputation as a reader of fortunes. She specializes in past lives, you know."

Irked that he'd avoided my question, I responded in kind. "Is that why you're here? Want to peek into a crystal ball?"

Marcus laughed out loud, finding unexpected humor in the question. "No, definitely not. Genevieve, here, is quite skilled at acquiring certain rare, moderately illicit antiquities."

Slowly, I stood and backed into a corner, looking from Marcus to Genevieve and back. "You deal in black-market arti-facts? Both of you? That's . . . that's . . ." I couldn't finish the statement, my mind reeling at the implications. Over the past two millennia, innumerable pieces of archaeological evidence had been destroyed or stolen as a result of the antiquities black market. So much of the ancient world had been lost because of it—because of people like Marcus and Genevieve. "I don't think I can . . . can do . . ."

Marcus strode around the table, stopped an arm's length away from me, and placed his hands on my upper arms. I didn't know when we'd become touching friends, and I wasn't sure how I felt about the new development. In his present, looming state, I was leaning toward not-so-great. The memories of Mike attempting to force himself on me were still too fresh.

Marcus leaned down so his eyes were closer to my level, and his expression changed from haughtiness to concern. "Lex, the black market is a necessary evil. You have to understand that if you want to make it in our field. It already exists, and the only way to save bits and pieces of the artifacts floating around in its torrent is to join in. I promise you, I only rescue artifacts from greedy hands—I never give them any."

The intensity of his words chipped away at my anger and fear. "And her," I whispered, flicking my eyes to the woman still sitting at the small table. "What does she do?"

He smiled wolfishly, but his tone matched mine in softness. "She's like me, rescuing the most important pieces." Shaking his head, he added, "The disparity between value and importance has always amused me."

"What do you—"

"Later," he interrupted and dropped his hands, turning to face Genevieve and Kat. "I need to take care of some quick business with Gen, then I'll explain everything."

Genevieve raised her delicate eyebrows.

"Well, maybe not everything," Marcus corrected, smirking. Unintentionally, I wondered if Marcus and Genevieve were more than business acquaintances. If he felt comfortable enough to barge in on one of her private meetings with a customer and she could ask him a question by simply raising her eyebrows, surely there was something else between them. The thought caused an unexpected vise to squeeze my heart, making it throb with an emotion I wasn't used to: jealousy. *Where did that come from?*

Looking at the floor, I said, "I'll wait out front," and rushed out of the room.

Kat followed me, retreating to a stool behind the checkout counter. As I perused the shop, I could practically feel her laser-like glare piercing my skin.

"Something wrong?" I asked pointedly. I found the small, grayish-white Hathor carving again and held it up, examining its exquisite detail. I would've guessed it really *was* over four thousand years old, if any Old Kingdom Egyptian alabaster pieces had ever been carved with so much detail. The goddess's lithe, feminine body, carved so she was eternally standing with one foot stepping forward, fit perfectly in the palm of my hand. Her exquisite face stared back at me with such determination, I almost expected her to open her mouth and make some godly demand.

Still glaring, Kat grumbled, "Are you, like, going out with him or something?"

It took me a few seconds to shift all of my attention to her. "Am I dating Marcus?" I asked, incredulous.

"Yeah," Kat said, rolling her eyes and sighing dramatically.

I snorted. "Definitely not. We work together."

"Oh." She brightened noticeably, straightening from her slouched position.

I hesitated, worried I wouldn't be able to conceal my unreasonable jealousy if I asked the question I wanted to ask, but I couldn't resist. "Your mom seems to have a, uh, connection with him. Is there something between them?"

Giggling, Kat hopped off her stool and skipped around the counter to join me. She was built like her mom—curves everywhere they should be—just not quite so filled out. If it weren't for her outfit, she easily could have passed as an undergrad. As it was, her white, neon-splashed t-shirt, black skinny jeans, and bright green Chucks placed her in high school, maybe as a junior or senior. Her long, nearly black hair was twisted up into a high, messy bun, and the multiple piercings in her ears were filled with a variety of gemstone studs.

"No," she whispered, "but Mom totally wishes there was. I mean, damn, who wouldn't? He's totally, like, the hottest guy I've ever seen . . . *ever*. It doesn't even matter that he's so old."

I laughed—I couldn't help it. There was no way Marcus was beyond his mid-thirties, but to a teen, I knew that could seem ancient.

"How much is this?" I asked, holding up the carving. I'd come to the highly improbable conclusion that the little goddess wasn't a reproduction, but was actually the real deal. What she was doing in the shop, on a table of artful junk, was beyond me.

Kat bit her glossed lip. "Um . . . that's one of the special items. I have to ask my mom." *So it really is authentic . . . I knew it!*

"Ask me what?" Genevieve asked, her rich voice startling us both as she walked through the beaded curtain and joined us in the front of the shop. I was surprised Marcus hadn't followed her out. *Maybe he's busy buttoning his pants*, I thought snidely. And then I mentally slapped myself. *Not mine . . . off-limits . . . get a goddamn grip!*

"The cost of this statuette," I explained, holding up the small carving for her to see.

Genevieve pursed her lips and squinted before coming to a decision. "Take it, no cost."

Kat's mouth fell open. "But . . . Mom—"

A firm hand gesture from her mother quieted the teenager. "Consider it an apology gift, since I can't give you the information you seek. It seems to want to be with you anyway. It's fitting."

By the time Marcus emerged from the back room, my newly acquired artifact was wrapped in a soft, pale green cloth, fitted into a gift box, and tucked into a small, dark purple bag.

"Thank you," I said to Kat and Genevieve, briefly raising the little paper sack.

"Of course," the mother replied while her daughter ogled Marcus.

He approached me, amusement tugging at the corners of his mouth. "Did you purchase something? Perhaps a good luck charm . . . or a love potion?"

"Not exactly," I replied coyly. "I'll show you later . . . maybe." My nonchalance was all a bluff—there was no way I could withstand bragging about my little Hathor carving, but I could drag it out for a little while . . . make him wait.

What had been only a hint of a smile turned into a full-blown grin. "Ah, Lex, I am *so* looking forward to the coming year."

I blinked. That most certainly had not been the reaction I'd expected.

Before I could respond, Marcus turned to Genevieve and her daughter. "A pleasure, as always. Genevieve, Katarina." He gave each a slight nod and placed his hand against the small of my back, ushering me toward the door. Even through my pea coat and sweater, the contact felt extremely intimate.

"Goodbye! It was nice to meet you both!" I called over my shoulder.

"And you," Genevieve said. Oddly, she sounded relieved.

Once outside, Marcus and I had to huddle together in the entrance's alcove to avoid the rain. It had been drizzling earlier, but that had turned into a rare winter tempest.

"You said you'd tell me more about your forays into the illegal artifact trade," I said loudly, snuggling deeper into my scarf.

Marcus leaned in, negating the need to shout. "Yes, of course, Lex. But not here . . . unless you prefer huddling together in this god-forsaken portion of the city."

I wouldn't say I dislike it, exactly . . . "You'd better not say 'I'll tell you later,'" I said, deepening my voice and attempting—poorly—to mimic his accent. "You seem like an 'I'll tell you later' kind of guy."

He scowled slightly, confirming my suspicion. Leaning in a little closer, Marcus said, "Might I suggest we take refuge in my car?"

Who the hell talks like that? I wondered but nodded with enthusiasm anyway. I was equally as excited about the prospect of dryness as the promise of answers. "Where'd you park?"

He pointed to an unbelievably suave, gunmetal-gray coupe parked three cars away on our side of the street. Staring at it, I tried, with all of my mental power, to make the thing turn into something more realistic, like a Toyota or a Ford. "Who the hell are you? James Bond?"

Marcus held his arm out toward the car, pressing a button on a tiny remote. "Not quite. Shall we?" The car's lights blinked once, and Marcus strolled into the rain. Based solely on his walk, I would've assumed it was a sunny summer day.

I waited until he had almost reached the car, then burst out of hiding and hustled toward its promised dryness. Much to my surprise, Marcus headed straight for the passenger door and held it open for me.

"What are you doing? It's pouring . . . you're getting soaked . . . go get in!" I shouted, making a shooing motion as I neared the car. Against my commands, he waited until my soggy self was safely nestled in the dark gray interior. It was the most monochromatic car I'd ever seen. From the paint to the leather to the dash—everything was the darkest of grays.

Sliding into the driver's side a moment later, Marcus shrugged and smiled knowingly. "It's only a little rain, nothing to get so worked up over. Now, show me what you procured from our mistress witch."

Hugging the damp bag against my stomach, I bargained, "Only after you tell me about this black-market stuff. I don't want to get involved in anything that'll ruin my career before it even starts."

Marcus studied me for a moment, then sighed and settled in his seat, resting the back of his head against the headrest. With closed eyes, he explained, "It's really more of a gray market than black. Many of the participants are trying to help save artifacts that would otherwise be lost to know-nothings or thieves, or that would be destroyed by a lack of proper care. All successful archaeologists have some dealings with the antiquities black market, so you'll need to get over this little moral dilemma of yours. Millions of priceless artifacts are already out there in the hands of people who can only harm them. Part of our job is to protect any evidence left from the past, and sometimes that includes searching through illicit streams." He sounded like he was lecturing a dimwitted pupil.

"And you've *never* sold any of your findings to the highest illegal bidder?" I asked.

He scowled, keeping his eyes closed, and I used the moment to study the clean lines of his profile. To my eyes, it was proportioned to masculine perfection with a strong nose, full lower lip, and broad chin. The contours of his stubbled jaw and prominent cheekbone were emphasized by the slight hollowing of his cheek. There was nothing pretty about him, but rugged or handsome weren't the right words to describe him either. He was . . . striking, and sexy as all hell. *And off-limits*, I reminded myself.

Without warning, he opened his eyes and turned his face to me, catching me staring. I blushed, hoping the storm's darkness masked my embarrassment. Marcus's eyes, black-rimmed amber, seemed to blaze in the car's dim interior. I couldn't look away.

"No," he said.

"No? No, what?" I asked, confused.

Smiling faintly, he held my eyes. "No, I've never sold any pieces to the highest bidder. I don't deal, Lex. I buy."

"Oh . . . that's good." Looking into his eyes for too long was like staring at a solar eclipse—sure to cause blindness . . . or at least it felt that way. I blinked, slowly, seeking a respite from their natural intensity. When I fixed my gaze on him again, the corners of his mouth were turned down in the faintest of frowns. For some reason, he was frustrated.

I cleared my throat. "You said something earlier, in the store, that I didn't quite understand."

"What did I say?" he asked, the tension in his face easing.

"You said the difference between value and importance amuses you. What'd you mean?" I really was curious, but the true motive behind my question was to distract him from whatever I'd done to trigger such frustration.

"Ah, yes. You see, many of the wealthy love to collect antiquuities because they want to impress their friends. For the most part, as you know, they haven't the faintest clue as to how to preserve what they acquire. Fortunately for you and I, most of them don't really know anything about their illegally gained pieces, other than that they came from some famous excavation or they're made of precious materials. But people like us—*we* desire the items of importance, those that tell us some vital piece of information about the past. The artifacts *we* usually hunt on the black market are rarely the most valuable in the eyes of collectors."

I listened closely and nodded when he finished. "That makes sense . . . kind of like people who buy a really expensive bottle of wine for the brand, not realizing that the actual wine might not be as good as the wine in a much cheaper bottle," I said, using some of the knowledge my winemaker dad had instilled in me growing up.

"Precisely," Marcus agreed.

"Okay . . ." The rain had decreased to the usual, soft drizzle, and I reached for the door handle.

"Lex?" Marcus said before I opened the door. "Where are you going?"

"To the bus stop. I thought I'd head home." When I saw the confusion wrinkling his brow, I added, "I'm kind of tired . . . it's been a long morning."

"Ah. I'm on my way back to campus. I'll give you a ride."

"Oh? Thanks. I'd appreciate that," I said, truly grateful. I really hadn't been looking forward to heading back out into the rain.

Marcus's responding smile was mischievous as he started the car. "Besides, we have to finish our game of show and tell. I told you about the *black market*," he said the last two words like they were the name of a scary monster. "Now it's your turn to show me what's in the bag."

I laughed. "I almost forgot!"

The look he gave me as he pulled away from the curb seemed to say, *I'm sure*, with heavy sarcasm.

As he drove, I pulled the little box out of the bag and lifted its lid. The carving was swaddled like a mummy in layer after layer of soft cloth, but I managed to unwrap it eventually. I studied the miniature goddess in the dim midday light. She was unusual for a Hathor depiction; though the traditional ankh was dangling from her fingers at her side and her head was crowned with the usual graceful cow horns cradling a sun disk, she was also holding a Wedjat—an Eye of Horus—in front of her stomach.

I'd been examining the statuette so intently that I hadn't noticed the car stop. Looking up, I saw the bright red light of a stoplight and could feel Marcus's eyes on me. "See," I said, holding Hathor up for his inspection.

He breathed in sharply. "Lex, where did you get that?" His voice held a chill I didn't understand.

"Uh . . . you're kidding, right? From Genevieve's shop . . ."

He waved my obvious explanation away. "I know that. I

meant, where in her store was she keeping it? This is the type of thing she usually reserves for me."

I puffed up, excited that I'd found something Marcus wanted . . . and I'd found it *first*. "It was on one of the tables. Isn't she beautiful?"

"Yes, quite," he said softly. We were moving again, the road drawing his attention away from the carving in my hand.

"Can you tell what the stone is?" I asked, testing him.

"Alabaster—true Egyptian alabaster." *Damn.*

"And what's unusual about it? Aside from the amazing detail, I mean."

"Her accessories." *Double damn.*

"What period is it from?"

"Old Kingdom, Sixth Dynasty."

"You got all of that from a ten-second glance?" I asked, dumfounded . . . again. If those were the observation skills of a truly talented archaeologist, then I had no business in the discipline.

"No."

I scoffed. "So . . . what? You've seen it before?"

"Yes."

Which, much to my annoyance, meant I hadn't found it first. "Where? When? That's not fair!"

He rolled over my indignation as if it were nonexistent. "She belonged to my sister."

Again, I was stunned. "Your sister? Where'd she get it? And why the heck did she give it away?"

"She acquired the statuette a long time ago, though I don't know from where. And she didn't give it away." He paused, frowning. "She, ah . . . many of her things were shuffled around and many were lost after she died."

"Oh, Marcus, I—" I swallowed several times, unsure of what to say. I wanted to know where Marcus's sister had obtained the statuette, but it *really* wasn't the time to ask. "I'm sorry. I didn't know."

Bringing the car to a stop, Marcus said, "I never expected you would." He looked at me, a small, sad smile on his face. "It was a *very* long time ago. Don't waste your sympathy on me."

"But—"

"Enough, Lex. I'm not fond of talking about her." He shifted his eyes to stare out the windshield. "We're here."

Surprised, I looked around and found my brick apartment building just beyond the passenger side window. I'd been so focused on Marcus and the carving that I probably wouldn't have noticed if we'd run over someone during the drive.

I turned back to him, holding up the statuette. "You should take this. It was your sister's, and—"

He reached over, plucked Hathor out of my grasp, and began rewrapping her in the pale green cloth. He tucked the bundle in the gift box, and that in the bag, then set it on my lap. "No. She belongs to you now." Finally, he met my eyes again. "Just take good care of her."

I nodded, my mouth dry. "I, um . . ." I cleared my throat. "Okay. Thank you. And thanks for the ride."

"You're quite welcome."

As I exited his car, I thought back on the eventful day.

"Lex?" Marcus called out before I could shut the door.

I poked my head back into the car. "Yeah?"

"See you on Monday."

I smiled. "Bye, Marcus."

AH-HA! & AGH!

After a tearful goodbye hug, I left my mom in my apartment, knowing she would be gone by the time I returned. The farewell was bittersweet—my eagerness to begin working with the excavation team mixed with a longing for the days when my mom was always waiting for me when I got home. She'd always been a safe place—a comforting embrace—and having her stay with me after the Mike incident had been exceptionally therapeutic. Unfortunately, it also seemed to have reverted my emotional state to that of a twelve-year-old.

In my morning prep, I had been surprised by my reflection. My face had abandoned the gauntness of several days past, but retained the almost feverish coloring—my cheeks were still noticeably rosy, and my lips were so pink that they contrasted starkly with my pale, blemish-free skin. And my eyes . . . they still teetered on the precipice between brown and red, a far more conspicuous color than they'd been a week earlier. For the most part, I credited the changes to excitement. However, my eyes still troubled me.

On the walk to Denny Hall, I did nothing to suppress the cheerful bounce in my step. Before I bounded up the three flights of stairs to the top floor, I considered stopping by Dr. Ramirez's office for a quick hello, but I opted not to. I *needed* to start working on the excavation like I needed air.

When I reached the rarely used fourth floor, I peeked into each consecutive darkened classroom and a few of the smaller offices. The narrow, windowless hallway zigzagged around the floor like a well-planned maze, giving the odd impression that the building was larger on the inside than it had seemed from the outside.

When I approached the second-to-last classroom door, I noticed a laminated sign taped to the front with *THE PIT* written in bold over a Wedjat. Since the well-known symbol of Horus's eye was second only to an ankh in representing all things ancient Egyptian to the masses, I was pretty sure I'd found excavation central.

Opening the door and stepping inside, I nearly collided with Marcus. "Oh!" I exclaimed.

"Lex," he said, seeming to hold back a laugh. "I thought you might have become lost."

I chuckled nervously, very aware of the three other sets of eyes examining me from further in the classroom. "Not exactly. I didn't know the room number . . . had to guess and check. You probably heard me banging around."

His lips curved into a faint smile. "Perhaps a little. My apologies for the oversight." He stepped aside. "Please, come in."

Without his sleek, towering form blocking my view, I could see the layout of the room. It was larger than I'd expected, and much wider than it was long. Mismatched, wooden bookshelves lined every available space along the walls, only absent in those spots already occupied by one of a half-dozen desks. Each shelf had a small bronze placard attached to its front. Tables of various sizes and materials were arranged around the room, and nearly every surface was covered with cardboard boxes or antique chests.

I'd never been in the room before, and was excited by the prospect of discovering all the goodies it contained. *Are the tablets Marcus mentioned here? What's in the chests? Which texts are lining the shelves?* I had no doubt the collection would prove to be filled with rare items. *And who are the people staring at me?*

As I walked through the doorway, Marcus again placed his hand on the small of my back and guided me away from the prying eyes to a very familiar, battered desk. Its presence was enough to shake my focus from the pressure of his hand.

"That's my desk from downstairs!" I exclaimed happily. Just seeing it made me feel oddly at home.

"Yes, well, I thought it might help you settle in. I'm afraid I've shaken up your world a bit."

"Thank you, Marcus," I said earnestly, grinning at him. For a moment, I forgot my new surroundings and lost myself in his amber eyes.

At the other end of the room, someone cleared a throat, and Marcus's mouth thinned, transforming him from friendly colleague to annoyed businessman.

"Come, Lex, I'll introduce you to the team," he said, leading me across the room. Three notably attractive people watched our approach with differing expressions. I briefly wondered if, along with antiques, Marcus made it a habit of collecting beautiful people.

"This is Dominic l'Aragne, the excavation's Project Manager," Marcus said, indicating the man on the left. He was pale and trim, and he studied me with exceptionally dark eyes. His features were sharp, almost pointy, an effect made more severe by the way his dark brown, jaw-length hair was swept back.

"Hello, Ms. Larson," Dominic said, a thick French accent making the simple greeting sound remarkably elegant.

"Hi," I said, smiling shyly, and his severe expression softened a little.

"If you need anything, just let Dom know and he'll make the

arrangements. And this young lad is Josh Claymore, my research assistant," Marcus told me, introducing the man on the right. He was blond and slightly burly, but he had an open, youthful face. His short hair stuck out haphazardly, making him appear slightly unkempt.

Nearly bouncing with excitement, Josh extended his hand. "It's nice to finally meet you! We've heard a lot about you."

His enthusiasm surprised me. "Um . . . it's nice to meet you too," I said, shaking his hand.

The last of the three people, quite possibly the most breathtakingly gorgeous woman I'd ever seen, was glaring at Marcus.

Indicating her with a sweep of his hand, Marcus said, "And this is Neffe, my second-in-command."

"Ms. Larson," she said, meeting my eyes and pursing her full lips. The perfect, sultry features on her heart-shaped face hardened.

"Hello," I said, more than a little intimidated.

Josh leaned forward and, loud enough for everyone to hear, whispered, "Don't mind her, she's always like that. Must've been how she was raised or something."

To my complete shock, Dominic barked a raucous laugh. Neffe transferred her glare from me to Josh and Dominic, and I took the opportunity to send a questioning glance to Marcus.

He shrugged, his eyes opened wide in the most ridiculous imitation of innocence.

Backing away from the potentially insane group of people, I mumbled, "I think I'll just get situated at my desk." My retreat was complete within seconds.

Sitting down, I was grateful that my torturous wooden chair hadn't been relocated along with my desk. Instead, I had a cushy new leather office chair. *Better to encourage long nights of intense concentration and research*, I supposed. I was surprised to find that everything on and in my desk was exactly as it had been in the graduate office, which meant it was a mess. A slight pang of sadness twanged in my chest at the realization that, with the abrupt change, I'd rarely see the few graduate students I'd befriended over the past two and a half years.

"I thought you might like to see this," Marcus said softly as he set a flat, wooden box on top of the papers scattered on my desk. Through the glass top, I could see an impeccable, hiero-glyph-covered stone tablet.

"Marcus," I said without taking my eyes from the object in front of me. "Is this—"

"Yes."

"But where's the other one? You said there were two." I was leaning closer to the glass, trying to get a better look at the box's contents.

"It's unrelated to our present work."

I barely heard his words, entranced as I was by the slab of smooth, gray-green schist.

"Lex—"

"Can I open it?" I interrupted, eagerness evident in my voice. I looked up at him, pleading with my eyes.

Marcus grinned and nodded.

"Oh. Wow." With the glass lid removed, the artifact was even more amazing. Shaped like a closed parabola, the dark stone tablet looked like it could have been carved only a few days earlier. Every inch was untouched by the usual rigors of time. "Where'd you say you found this?" I whispered.

"I didn't," Marcus said, avoiding the question.

I gently closed the glass lid and faced him. "Okay, he-who-can't-answer-an-implied-question, then where *did* you find it? And when?"

Across the room, one of the other men coughed in a way that sounded suspiciously like an attempt to cover up a laugh.

The corner of Marcus's mouth quirked, but I couldn't tell if he was hiding a smile or a frown. "I can't remember the exact date, but it was years ago. It was hidden in a secret compartment at the foot of Hatnofer's coffin."

"Hatnofer? As in, Senenmut's mother?" I clarified.

Ever since I'd first learned about the many mysteries surrounding Hatchepsut and her relationship with her chief advisor and architect, Senenmut, years ago, I'd been enamored with the subject. Had they been lovers? Had Senenmut betrayed the female pharaoh, and had she banished him as a result? His body wasn't in either of the tombs he'd carefully prepared for himself, so where was it? And what happened to Neferure, Hatchepsut's daughter and Senenmut's one-time pupil? As far as history was concerned, she simply disappeared as a young woman. My mind whirled with the possible implications of the tablet having been hidden with Senenmut's mother's mummy, especially because Senenmut had been the architect of Hatchepsut's mortuary temple, Djeser-Djeseru, which apparently contained the hidden entrance to a secret, underground temple. It was just ... *wow*.

"Marcus," I said, my voice low and trembling. "If this was concealed in Hatnofer's coffin, isn't it logical to deduce that Senenmut put it there?"

"It is."

"And if he put it there, then he probably *made* it?"

"One would think."

My heart started beating faster. "Then, wouldn't the next logical deduction be that this hidden temple, *linked* to Djeser-Djeseru, might actually be Senenmut's elusive final resting place?" People—treasure hunters and archaeologists alike—had been searching for his body for centuries.

"Quite possible," Marcus said in his infuriatingly calm way.

"How are you *not* exploding with excitement over this? This is unreal! We may end up solving one of the greatest historical mysteries *ever!*" My chest heaved with each breath as I tried to calm myself down.

Finally showing some emotion, Marcus smiled devilishly. "I assure you, Lex, I'm quite excited. I'm just . . . practiced . . . at keeping my *excitement* hidden." From his deep, velvety tone, I had the distinct impression that we were talking about two entirely different things. "Would you like the translation?" he asked smoothly.

Translation? Of his innuendo? I was pretty sure I could guess what he meant by his 'excitement.' Briefly, my eyes flicked down to the front of his pants. "Uh . . . what?" I asked, totally befuddled.

Eyes sparkling like singed topaz, Marcus widened his smile. "Senenmut's tablet. Shall I tell you what it says?"

Embarrassed at my reaction, I felt the need to prove my academic worth. Marcus had told me my youth and "other attributes" might distract him from remembering my quick wit. It was time for a not-so-gentle reminder.

"Thank you, no. I prefer to translate it myself. Besides, you might've missed something," I proclaimed. I smirked, wondering which of my "other attributes" distracted him the most. The thought that anything about me distracted him was exciting, causing a warm flutter low inside me, which I quickly quelled. *He was probably just being charming. He probably makes a habit of flirting with every remotely attractive woman he crosses paths with. He* probably *had a dozen girlfriends, all models . . . and geniuses . . . and humanitarians . . . and—*

"I wouldn't be so sure," Marcus said. For a moment I thought I'd accidentally voiced my inappropriate analysis of him, but then I recalled what I'd said about him missing something in the translation. *A challenge!*

Before leaving me to my work, Marcus pointed to one of the nearby bookcases, which was filled with the various reference texts commonly used for translating Egyptian hieroglyphs. I politely informed him they wouldn't be necessary.

The first thing I noticed in my examination of the tablet was that the infuriating combination of hieroglyphs I'd been struggling with was present . . . in several places. I wondered if the tablet was the subject of the photo Marcus had been studying in my first dream of him—the one that *had* been a "vision"—because the symbols had been there as well. I also wondered if I finally had the last puzzle piece I would need to decipher those infernal hieroglyphs.

As I stared through the glass for several hours, Senenmut's tablet came to life. It revealed elements of his final years that, though previously unknown, didn't shed much light on the historical mysteries surrounding him. I learned he'd spent nearly a decade on a secret building project at Deir el-Bahri—the location of Djeser-Djeseru—under the direction of Hatchepsut, and of all the ridiculous claims, Set, the Egyptian god of the desert and chaos.

The previously undecipherable combination of a lion's head, a half-circle, a whole circle, and two vertical, parallel lines was included near both Set's and Senenmut's names, and I had a sudden epiphany. It had been speculated that the combination of symbols was adverbial, meaning "god's time" or "eternal," as in "eternal Senenmut" or "eternal Set." But I started playing with the part of speech, finally settling on reading them as a title —*god of time*. Thinking back on the other texts I'd been analyzing that contained the hieroglyphs—including papyri, tablets, and reliefs—I realized that "god of time" was a viable alternate translation to "infinite" or "eternal." After recording my findings in a spiral notebook and giving myself a *very* enthusiastic mental high five, I continued translating the tablet.

Indeed, as Marcus had claimed, one set of symbols suggested that the mysterious temple or tomb was physically connected to Djeser-Djeseru. According to the scribe, there was an even more secret portion of the hidden temple, containing the power of Nun—which was *really* odd. Nun was generally known as the god ancient Egyptians attributed with creation, specifically the creation of mankind. The ancient people had believed him to be the primordial waters, the chaos, from which everything had begun. Never had I heard of the ancients referencing any way to access his power . . . or even wanting to do so.

The tablet closed with two equally befuddling statements before the usual "So it ends, from start to finish, as found in writing." I translated the preceding statements as "The power and domain of Hathor is life, the power and domain of Anubis is the afterlife. Under Hathor we are created, above Anubis we are changed by the power of creation." I retranslated the symbols three times, looking for alternate meanings, then read through the translation again and again . . . and again. Abruptly, it clicked.

"No," I whispered. "It can't be that simple."

From across the room, Josh called out jovially, "She's talking to herself—she's really one of us now!"

"Quiet, Josh," Dominic told his colleague. "Let her do her work and pay more attention to your own."

"Right, because reading through undergrad field school applications requires so much—"

"Quiet, Josh," Marcus said softly, repeating Dominic's words, and Josh fell silent.

Smiling like a fool, I stood and hurried over to Marcus. He sat comfortably at a desk set flush against the wall opposite mine.

Without looking away from his laptop, Marcus asked, "Can I help you with something, Lex?"

"Yes." I mimicked his infuriatingly secretive tone.

"And what exactly would that be?"

"Oh, I just need a pen and a piece of paper."

"Really, Lex, you have plenty of paper and writing instruments at your own desk," he chided, finally turning his attention on me. His eyes widened at my barely contained exhilaration.

I held out my hand, and he supplied me with a ballpoint pen and a blank sheet of printer paper. I promptly set it on his desk and began sketching the floor plan of Djeser-Djeseru. It was a complex temple, with multiple levels, courtyards, chapels, colonnades, and shrines. "Why would Senenmut include that weird bit near the end about Hathor and Anubis and two stages of creation? There's no reason, it's complete nonsense," I said as I worked.

"I'm aware," Marcus replied dryly.

"Which means it's not actually nonsense . . . it's there for a reason. Earlier, Senenmut mentions that 'the power of Nun' is in the secret temple. For whatever reason, he's saying that Nun's power—creation—is hidden away, correct?"

"Yes."

"He's probably just using this reference as a key to guide us toward the correct location of the hidden entrance. Obviously Nun's power isn't really there."

"Obviously," Marcus mused, his eyes lighting with interest.

"If we think about creation being locked away in the temple, then Senenmut's statements about Hathor and Anubis become relevant."

Marcus leaned over the sketch I was just completing, labeling Hathor's chapel on the left side of the rough floor plan and the two Anubis chapels on the right.

"It makes no sense for there to be two Anubis chapels—we all know that. But they're there anyway. The upper chapel fell into disrepair because of its redundancy. It was purposeless . . . or so we thought. But on Senenmut's tablet, he tells us that 'above Anubis we will be changed by creation.' The part about Hathor is junk, just meant to disguise the trail, but the bit about 'above Anubis' tells us to look in Anubis's *upper* chapel . . . upper . . . above . . . ." I pointed to the upper chapel on my map. "You see, in order to be 'changed by creation,' or by Nun's power, we first must find it. And, to do that, we have to enter the secret temple. So—"

"The hidden entrance should be in the upper chapel to Anubis," Marcus said, finishing my statement. "Dear gods . . . I can't believe I missed this." He tore his eyes from my drawing and gazed up at me wondrously.

I squirmed under his intensity. "It's not *that* big of a deal. I only figured out the general area."

"Don't belittle yourself, Lex. If you knew how long . . . this is unbelievable." He glanced down at the sketch of the temple again, and then back up at me. "You . . . *unbelievable*," he whispered. His expression had altered minutely to one of reverence.

Overwhelmed, I took two steps back . . . and ran into a warm, firm body. I would've fallen to the side if strong hands hadn't grasped my arms, keeping me upright.

"Careful, *ma fille*," Dominic cautioned, stabilizing me.

"Thank you," I whispered. I was surprised to discover that Dominic, Josh, and Neffe were standing shoulder-to-shoulder behind me. *How long have they been standing there?* I wondered.

"I'm sure you all heard . . . you're so very talented at listening when you choose. The Djeser-Djeseru entrance would appear to be in the upper Anubis chapel." Marcus shook his head slowly. "This, my friends, is a much-needed breakthrough. Congratulations, Lex."

As he finished, my three new colleagues huddled around me, each murmuring a different exclamation or form of praise at the discovery.

"Thank you," I said, my neck and cheeks flaming.

Needing a break from the Lex worship, I excused myself and spent the afternoon examining various other texts and artifacts strewn about the room. Each item was fascinating in its own right, from pressed scrolls I'd believed to have been lost, to heavy manuscripts darkened with age. The afternoon passed quickly, and soon I was bidding the team goodbye and heading home . . . alone.

I strolled along familiar paths, taking the long way home. I used the solitary time to think, to process everything that had happened in that elongated, top-floor room. Beyond that, I considered everything that had happened lately, and realized the past month had unquestionably been the most eventful of my twenty-four-year life . . . with a big, fat exclamation point.

As I neared my apartment building in the falling darkness, I checked my phone—one new voice mail. I quickly accessed my mailbox and was greeted by my grandma's age-roughened voice.

"Hi sweetheart, it's Grandma. I'm sorry to do this on such short notice, but there's someone who needs to meet you. We'll be stopping by this evening between six and seven. Traffic, you know . . . Anyway, you might consider making a little dinner. I think you'll want to make a good first impression. See you tonight, honey!"

Wait, so does Grandma have a boyfriend? Utterly confused, I picked up the pace; it was five o'clock, and I had absolutely no idea what I was going to cook for dinner.

By the time I'd made it home and whipped up something presentable, if not memorable, from the ingredients my mom had left behind, I was bouncing with excitement. I'd convinced myself that Grandma Suse had been swept up into an adorable, old-person love affair and wanted me to meet her new sweetie.

My heart skipped an excited beat when I heard the knock at the door. It skipped a few more beats after I opened the door and saw the couple standing in the hallway. My elderly grandma had her arm linked with that of a very handsome, familiar man. He was taller than me by a handful of inches, wore his dusty blond hair long enough to show its loose curl, and looked to be in the prime of his life. And he was smiling. *Impossible!*

"Grandpa?" I asked before my vision spotted over with blackness.

13

THE BEGINNING & THE END

"Suse, my darling, do you think perhaps we should have done this another way? I've startled the poor girl half to death." The deep voice was barely accented with Italian.

"Oh, hush, Alex," my sweet grandma admonished. "I know Lex a little better than you, if you'll recall. *I've* been around. And I am *not* your 'darling.'" I'd never heard Grandma Suse sound so spiteful.

"If *you'll* recall, Suse, you're the one who told me to 'get the hell out or risk everyone discovering the truth.' I was fully prepared to risk it."

Opening my eyes, I sat up on the couch and stared at the unbelievable couple sitting at my kitchen table. "Um . . . hi. If you guys could stop word-stabbing each other for a minute and explain why my *thirty-year-old grandfather just walked into my apartment*? It'd be peachy," I declared with an unpleasant smile.

Grandma Suse gasped. "Alexandra Marie Larson! You wipe that look off your face right this instant!"

I grimaced and sat up straighter. "Sorry, Grandma."

"That's better!" She reverted back to my kindly grandma. "Now, honey, your grandpa's going to explain some important things to you. Things he *should* have explained weeks ago, but he was conveniently out of town."

"I was in Antarctica! How could I have known . . . there are zero reasons why she should have manifested. Alice never showed any signs of being a carrier and I even peeked into the future—which you know is all but forbidden—and I saw nothing of this. Not everything shows up, you know," he said a little sulkily. "Besides, I had Heru watching over her . . . just in case. He owed me."

Some guy named Heru had been watching over me? Remotely, I wondered if it had been the same man who had broken down my apartment door, pummeled Mike, and whisked me to the hospital. If so, I owed him . . . and was a little afraid of him.

"Well he obviously wasn't trying hard enough," my suddenly furious grandma spat. Her body was visibly trembling. "I assume he told you what happened . . ."

"Yes, but he said—"

"*Enough!*" I yelled, slapping my palm on the steamer trunk coffee table. "Will someone please explain why I feel like I'm losing my mind?"

Ignoring my outburst, Grandma Suse stood and said to her not-so-late husband, "I'm feeling a bit tired. I think I'll just go lie down in Lex's room while you two chat." As she hobbled toward my bedroom, she gave me a pointed look that seemed to say "behave yourself" and "give him hell" at the same time.

"So . . . Grandpa," I said after the bedroom door shut, thinking I'd never had a more surrealistic, awkward experience. "Sorry about the whole fainting thing."

He shrugged. "I've had worse reactions. A few people even tried to stab me, and dozens have run away shrieking about ghosts." Smiling roguishly, he added, "You should call me Alexander—or Alex. 'Grandpa' doesn't really fit with my appearance. People will talk."

"Okay . . . Alexander." Saying his name hammered the final, rusty nail in the this-feels-so-wrong coffin.

"Don't worry, you'll get used to it . . . and to me." He patted the kitchen table in front of my grandma's abandoned chair. "Come join me, Alexandra. We have some catching up to do."

"I'll say." I was feeling a bit irked, a lot crazy, and insanely curious. If I hadn't been experiencing all of the weird dream-visions lately, I would've been totally freaked out. As it was, I was moderately freaked out, but I shoved the feeling away. Answers were finally throwing themselves at me . . . I couldn't turn them away just because I didn't understand them. I joined my grandpa, Alexander, at the table.

He stared at me with midnight-blue eyes. "You look so much like my little Alice. I almost feel like I'm sitting here with her instead of her grown daughter. We gods of time suffer far worse from its passing than those who age and die. *We* have to go on."

We gods of time? Is that from a poem? I was utterly baffled. "What?"

A crease formed between my grandpa's eyebrows, and he grabbed my nearest hand. "My dear child, Suse always says I have a way of circumventing the truth. An occupational hazard, I suppose. Shall I just dive right in?"

I nodded, hoping his words would somehow translate into something coherent. My mind was too numb for anything cryptic to get through, and I was usually *really* good with cryptic.

"Very well. You and I, and the others like us, are not human . . . not exactly."

My mouth fell open. "Not . . . human? You're kidding, right?" *He has to be kidding! Of course I'm human!*

Alexander shook his head. "Many thousands of years ago, a human woman bore a son who became the most talented spiritual leader his clan ever had. He was able to guide his people away from the dangers of the desert and other clans until they settled near a fertile river. He was a very powerful seer of the past, present, and future. Some said he could alter the very fabric of time." He shrugged, as if he was saying, "I'm not so sure about that . . ."

"Through recent developments in the understanding of evolution and genetics, we now know he was the first to be born with a unique and beneficial genetic mutation, which he then passed on to some of his descendants. In his time, power came with many . . . consequences. One being that he had many wives and consorts, which led to many children. Those children had children and so on. Over time, as the bloodlines intermixed, his mutation was passed on. He is, in essence, the father of our species."

Alexander held up a hand, cutting off the words threatening to explode from my open mouth. "Wait—all will become clear. This man's name was Nuin, and his people became the rulers and aristocracy of Upper Egypt, while he—the most powerful of his people—became known as the creator of mankind. You know of him as the god, Nun. Like him, many of his descendants became deified by the people of their times, such as Heru, Set, and Aset," he said, listing the ancient names of the Egyptian gods more commonly known as Horus, Seth, and Isis to the modern world. "I'm sure you see the big picture. Nuin's descendants became known as the Netjer-At, which means . . . ?"

I cleared my throat, unprepared to participate in the conversation. "Roughly, 'gods of time.'" It was the exact translation I'd settled on earlier that day for the hieroglyphs that had been driving me mad for months. It could have been a coincidence, but I doubted it was.

Alexander nodded, clearly pleased. His eyes crinkled faintly at the outer corners when he smiled, making him appear endearingly kind. "Over the past millennium, with the rise of lingua franca, the name simplified into Nejerette or Nejeret, for women or men, respectively. I am Nejeret, and you, Alexandra, are Nejerette. As a whole, our people are Nejerets. Our kind, the descendants of Nuin, are able to step out of time to see its various threads. As you hone your skills, you'll be able to view the past and the present, and maybe even the future possibilities to some degree. It's different for each of us."

His words were pure impossibility, but it also sort of made sense, what with the too-real dreams I'd all but accepted as real. "So you're saying we're *time travelers?*" I asked, skepticism coating my words.

Alexander laughed. "Everyone asks that. But no, we don't travel through time. We're only able to *see* time, to see what has happened and some of what may be. We cannot actually interact with any time other than the present." He paused, frowning thoughtfully. "Think of time as a vast cavern, and of our visions as the echoes of every sound that has been, is being, or might ever be made. Many Nejerets have actually started calling what we see 'echoes.'"

"How is this real?" I whispered to one of the empty spots at the table.

Alexander squeezed my hand. "The how is irrelevant. That it *is* matters."

As he spoke his final words, the world melted into a swirl of colors, writhing all around us like a psychedelic hallucination. "Whatever you do, don't let go of my hand until it stops. We could easily get separated, and I don't have the talent to track you if that happens."

"Um, okay." When the world finally righted itself, I muttered, "You've got to be kidding me." I spun around in a circle, taking in my surroundings. "What is this—ancient Rome?"

Hand in hand, Alexander and I stood off to the side of a high-ceilinged room. The walls were painted in a rich red and black, and several dining couches, each draped in lustrous fabrics, were arranged artfully around a small, wooden table.

"Not exactly," Alexander said. "We're in Herculaneum." He released my hand and held both of his arms out wide. "Welcome to my childhood home."

"No," I breathed, stunned. I gaped at everything around me—it all looked new, not like it had been buried under volcanic ash for thousands of years, which meant it hadn't been buried yet. Suddenly fearful, I exclaimed, "Herculaneum—but Mount Vesuvius!"

"That's not for another seventy years, and even if Vesuvius were erupting right now, we would be safe enough. No need to worry. Remember, we're not really here—we're only witnessing an echo of the past."

My unusually sluggish mind finally caught up, screaming about what was important, and it wasn't the impending volcanic eruption. "Your childhood home?! You grew up in Herculaneum before Mount Vesuvius erupted? That's . . . that's impossible! You'd have to be over two thousand years old! This can't be real!"

It's not real . . . it's not real . . . it's not real . . . Scrunching my eyes closed, I repeated the mantra for a long moment. When I reopened them, I hoped to find myself standing in my apartment, my impossibly ancient grandpa gone, and sanity and reality firmly reestablished around me. I was sorely disappointed.

"Alexandra, calm down." My grandpa's fingers regained their strong grasp on my hand, acting like an anchor to something tangible, to something real. But touching him was almost as disconcerting as considering the possibility that everything he'd told me was true. He wasn't the steadiest of anchors.

Wide-eyed, I stared at Alexander, taking dozens of deep, slow breaths.

"I know your Nejerette traits have been manifesting. You must feel like you're losing your mind, noticing physical changes with your body—possibly heightened senses—and seeing things that happened in the past. You're having dreams that feel like memories, but they couldn't be your memories because you were never there, correct?"

Incapable of forming words, I nodded.

"This is all real, Alexandra. You aren't human . . . you're Nejerette."

As much as my mind wanted to disagree, the logical part of me assessed every piece of evidence—the dreams and visions, the healing, my eyes—and drew the only possible conclusion. Alexander Ivanov, my thirty-looking two-thousand-year-old grandfather, was telling the truth. Nuin, the Nejerets, the "echoes"—it was all real.

Decisively, I nodded. I still felt queasy and a bit crazy, yet at the same time, I felt more stable than I had in weeks. I had the explanation I'd been seeking . . . and I had people. I belonged.

Alexander let out a relieved breath. "Wonderful! You wouldn't believe how long it takes some people to accept the truth."

I cleared my throat. "So, um . . . what now?"

He smiled. "Now, we watch, and eventually, you learn. Look." He spun me around, leading me to a wide doorway. Beyond, the geometric pattern on the tiled marble floor changed as it led out to a manicured garden filled with shrubs, brightly colored flowers, and waving palm trees. Past a carved stone banister at least thirty yards away, the tiled ground dropped off, revealing an undulating, rich, blue mass—the Bay of Naples.

I took a deep breath, inhaling the tangy sea air. It seemed so pure compared to the polluted air of my time. "So we can smell, too? Not just see and hear things in these . . . these 'echoes'?"

Alexander looked at me with surprise. "Not everyone can. Many talents that used to be common have faded from our gene pool. Being able to smell in the At is almost nonexistent among those born during the last several centuries." From the way he said "At," I wondered if it was the official term for the echoes. In Middle Egyptian, it meant "time," so it made sense.

"Well . . . I can." I felt pride at excelling, but it was tinged with sadness; even among my own people, I was doomed to be a little different. I glanced away, uncomfortable with Alexander's measuring look.

Before I could point out that it wasn't polite to stare, the sound of sandaled feet slapping against marble tiles drew my attention. Two small boys, one with brown hair and one with blond, squealed and clattered onto the patio. They tried not to giggle as they struck at each other with wooden swords. After a particularly deadly fake stab from the blond boy, the brown-haired boy staggered to the ground with melodramatic gasps.

"The victor . . . is that . . . ?"

My grandpa responded wistfully, "Me? Yes. My brother and I were playing our equivalent of 'cops and robbers.' It was more like 'Alexander the Great and the Persian Heathens.' They terrified us more than modern human scholars understand. Ah . . . but looking back, I think we could have focused less on the Persian threat and more on the religious strife within our own society. But I suppose no civilization, no matter how grand, is meant to last forever."

It was my turn to stare at him. "You miss it."

Gently, he squeezed my hand. "It was home. It's part of who I am—I'll always miss it. Someday you'll understand."

"I can accept the visions or echoes or whatever . . . I get it, I've seen enough to know this isn't just a hallucination. But what's with the really great aging perks?" I asked, unable to hold in my curiosity any longer. Alexander looked amazing *for a guy who'd lived through two millennia.*

Alexander tightened one side of his mouth as he thought. "I'm much more a philosopher than scientist, but as far as I understand it, some other genetic traits are linked to the Netjer-At chromosome. First, and inconsequentially, our dentition patterns are two-one-two-two."

I recalled from my undergraduate anthropology classes that the standard pattern for humans was two-one-two-three: two incisors, a canine, a couple of premolars, and three molars. "So, no wisdom teeth?" I asked.

"Correct. It generally holds true among carriers as well, though for you to be Nejerette, Alice must have been a carrier, and she had wisdom teeth on the bottom. Poor girl had to have them removed when she was a teenager." He shook his head at the memory. "Ah . . . but more importantly, we exhibit exceptionally enhanced cellular regeneration. This suspends the aging process and dramatically increases both our senses— seeing, hearing, etcetera—and our ability to heal. I believe you've recently experienced this?"

I nodded, recalling that Dr. Isa had been aware of my remarkable healing ability and hadn't been surprised. Is she Nejerette, too? I wondered.

"You must've been starved afterward? Lost weight? Possibly looked ill

or older for a number of days?" At my responding nod and frown, he continued, "Have you noticed any other physical changes?"

"Yeah, my skin is lighter, if that's even possible, and pretty much perfect. I mean, I have no blemishes, no moles, no scars—nothing. And my eyes have become . . . I guess 'brighter' would be the right word. Now they look reddish-brown instead of just brown."

"Yes," he said. "That's all normal. Your appearance may change as the years pass and your body continues to renew and heal, though, for the most part, you should stay the same. You might get a little taller, or stronger, or a number of other things. Also . . ." He hesitated before adding, "Alexandra . . . the women of our kind, Nejerettes, can't bear children."

My stomach dropped, like a plane abruptly losing altitude. The reaction was unexpected. I'd pretty much written off having kids when I'd committed to a life of gallivanting around the globe from excavation to excavation, but hearing it was a definite impossibility saddened me.

"Why not?" I asked.

"The regenerative abilities interfere with the growth of the fetus, inevitably leading to spontaneous abortion. Usually the fertilized egg never even attaches to the Nejerette's uterine wall," he explained, equally scientific and sympathetic.

I shook my head. Something wasn't adding up. "Then how do we reproduce?"

"Through the men. It's always been through the men. Usually our children are normal humans, either carriers or non-carriers—but if a Nejeret mates with a female carrier, the child has a small chance of manifesting, of becoming Nejeret or Nejerette. Between a male carrier and a female carrier, producing a child capable of manifestation is very rare, but possible. The last must have been the case with you. I really didn't expect you to manifest."

I frowned. "Couldn't you, you know, test people's DNA for the Nejeret chromosome? Then you'd know for sure and could prepare people so the change would be less"—I paused, searching for the right word—"traumatic."

Alexander's eyes filled with sorrow. "Your situation is unusual, Alexandra. It's unfair, I know. For certain political reasons, I was allowed to search the future At to see if there was any chance of Alice's children manifesting. There was absolutely no sign that either you or Jennifer would become Nejerette." He shook his head, clearly frustrated. "I'm sorry, I'm not answering your question very well. You see, the mutation isn't genetically traceable until an individual comes of age, until they manifest, so it's impossible to predict, even with modern technology. There was no way to know this would happen, and no clear explanation for why it did."

"Hmm . . ." *I said, thinking about the man—my biological father—I'd watched break into the fertility clinic.* Is it possible that he's Nejeret? Is that why he swapped the sperm samples? Did he know Mom was a carrier? *I considered telling Alexander about what I'd seen, but it didn't seem like the right time. Not that I thought any time would seem like the right time to relay such weird information, but still . . . this wasn't it.*

"Come, I'll show you something you'll enjoy," *Alexander said, misinterpreting my thoughtful silence as sadness.*

The swirling colors surrounded us again, and after a short time, we were standing in a very familiar backyard—Grandma Suse's. Seven flowering apple trees were scattered near the edge of an expansive lawn. A young girl, maybe eight or nine years old, giggled gleefully in the middle of the vibrant, green grass. Barefoot, she danced around with a slender branch, pretending to fence with an alternate version of the man holding my hand. Her long, brown hair flew around her as she twirled and lunged, and her cheeks were flushed from exertion. "I'll get you, Persian beast!" she howled.

"Mom?" *I asked in disbelief. I was watching my mom, one of the girliest women I'd ever known, sword fight with her father.* "Are you playing 'Alexander and the Persians' with my mom?"

My grandpa smiled proudly. "She loved being Alexander and destroying the evil heathens."

"*You do realize your ancient prejudice could have turned her into an anti-Persian fanatic, right?*"

He shrugged, unconcerned. "*People are people. She knew it was a game.*"

"*Luckily,*" I grumbled, then grinned. "*She looks so happy, so carefree. I've never seen her laugh like that.*"

He nodded solemnly. "*When she and Joe learned they couldn't have children together, it killed something inside her.*" *The heavy emotion in Alexander's voice made me want to hug him. He loved my mom so much, but had abandoned his life as her father because of what he was. And one day, she would grow old and die . . . my mom, but also his daughter. Morosely, I wondered how many children he'd fathered over his two millennia, watching their births, lives, and inevitable deaths. Did he have any Nejeret children, any aunts and uncles with whom I could explore the At?*

With a reluctant sigh, Alexander turned to me. "*There is one last thing I must show you. I apologize, Alexandra . . . it won't be pleasant.*"

"*Okay. What is it? Should I be afraid?*"

"*I can't tell you what it is—that's against the rules, and, well, nobody really knows exactly what it is. And yes, you should be very, very afraid.*" *With those final, ominous words, the swirling colors surrounded us again, fading to utter blackness before the sensation of steadiness returned.*

But it took longer than usual. Even without the rainbow of light flowing in cascading tangles, the inky world heaved and lurched. I heaved and lurched, and eventually I squeezed my eyes shut, wishing the uncomfortable motion would stop. An eternity seemed to pass before it finally did.

"Open your eyes," Alexander said, releasing my hand. When I did, I was surprised to find that I was again sitting at the kitchen table in my cozy apartment.

"I think I'm going to be sick," I proclaimed, rising and lunging toward the garbage can. Sure enough, as soon as I reached the plastic receptacle, I vomited . . . repeatedly.

Alexander handed me a wad of paper towels once I no longer seemed in danger of a heaving relapse. Grateful, I took the offering with shaking hands and wiped my mouth. I tied off the garbage bag and tossed it down the trash chute across the hall from my apartment door.

"Care to explain?" I asked, stomping back into the apartment. "Or is that against the rules too? And whose rules?" I briefly disappeared into my bedroom to retrieve my toothbrush, waving at Grandma Suse as I passed through. She was propped up on the bed, reading.

"Well?" I asked when I returned to the living room seconds later. I shoved my toothbrush into my mouth and started vigorously scrubbing away the taste of sickness.

My grandpa watched me gravely. "At least you're still conscious. I passed out the first time I saw it—the Nothingness. It seemed jerkier this time, though that may have been my imagination." He sighed. "It's the future, Alexandra, and not far off. Come the twenty-first of June, the Nothingness takes over the At."

I stared at him for several long seconds, then spat into the kitchen sink and rinsed my mouth with a handful of water. "What are you saying?" I croaked. "Time stops, or something? Is the world going to end on the summer solstice . . . in six months?"

"Deus, I hope not. We've been working to avert whatever disaster might happen. It could be as simple as us being cut off from the At after the solstice. There is, of course, a prophecy and a potential savior—or destroyer—but it's all very convoluted and likely will end up circumvented and proven irrelevant. Beyond that, I don't think we'll be able to do anything until the twenty-first June. We're not used to operating blind, but this time we have to." He shook his head, obviously frustrated by the situation.

"So . . . the world might be ending, but probably isn't. There might be someone who can save us all, but we don't know. *And that person might destroy us all instead. Great . . .* I love being dependent on such reliable people," I said dryly. In reality, I didn't like being dependent on anyone, reliable or not.

"That's my girl!" Grandma Suse exclaimed softly as she emerged from my bedroom. "I told you she's feisty, Alex. She gets it from my side. She'll be a good addition to your little group of world-savers," she said, sounding like she was talking about something no more serious than a baseball-card-collecting club.

My grandpa acquiesced grudgingly. "Perhaps, but only *after* she's trained."

"Uh . . . do you guys mind not talking about me like I'm not here?" I asked.

Grandma Suse patted my cheek as she shuffled to the table. "Certainly, sweetie, as soon as you serve us dinner."

Snorting, I wondered if Alexander brought out the best or worst in my grandma. I settled on both.

14

DATES & PLANS

"I'm sorry, Lex, but I must have misheard you. What did you just say?" Marcus asked. From the sound of his voice, I knew he'd taken the remarkable effort to swing his desk chair a full one-eighty degrees. Pulling him away from the handwritten journal he'd been examining had been an impossibility all morning. At least, it *had* been, until Dominic asked me why I was so distracted.

For the past four hours, I'd been helping the severe, slightly sullen Project Manager select the excavation field school's final candidates. He and I were crammed together at my desk, shuffling folders around. Much to his chagrin, I'd been touting a view of "if they can manage a trowel and brush without scratching a relief or shattering an artifact, let 'em in" . . . which would have left us with about four hundred participants. We needed to narrow it down to twenty.

I swung my comfy leather chair around to face Marcus. "I said, 'I met my grandpa for the first time last night.' What'd you think I said?"

In true Marcus Bahur style, he ignored the question. "Isn't

155

that a bit odd, meeting one's grandparent in one's"—he paused, examining my face—"mid-twenties?"

You have no idea how odd meeting Alexander really was, I thought.

Marcus wasn't the only one intrigued by my extended family. Dominic had been frozen with shock since I'd first mentioned meeting my grandpa. Suddenly returning to life, he blurted, "I just realized . . . Neffe . . . I forgot to tell her . . ." as he rushed out of the room.

Frowning, I watched him leave before returning my attention to Marcus. "Yes, it's odd. Which is why I'm distracted by it."

Almost imperceptibly, Marcus's eyes narrowed and his mouth puckered. "I see. Would you like to accompany me to lunch, Lex? I thought I might stop by the Burke Café for a bite and coffee."

"Uh . . . sure," I said noncommittally. I had no clue how he'd gone from "What do you mean you just met your grandpa?" to "Let's grab lunch."

"Wonderful," he said, gently closing the leather-bound book on his desk and rising to don his coat. "Shall we?"

Still sitting, I watched him, confused. "Oh! You meant right now? But it's only—" I peeked at my phone. "—a quarter after eleven."

"And yet, I'm famished." He lifted my purple pea coat off the back of my chair and held it out like I was a child getting ready to go play in the snow.

As entertaining as it was to see Marcus standing there like a glorified coat rack, I hardly had a choice. Besides, I was pretty damn hungry, too. I stood and allowed him to settle the coat around my shoulders. I did, however, slap his hands away when he spun me around and tried to button me up, earning a small, secretive smile for the effort.

Our ten-minute stroll to the café was amicable, filled with remarks on the unusually pleasant weather—it wasn't raining for once—and on how different the campus was now that the undergrads had returned from winter break. We were the epitome of friendly colleagues—which is why I was stunned when, just outside the café's door, Marcus reached for my hand and twined his long fingers with mine. The warmth of his hand burned into my palm, climbing up my arm toward my erratically beating heart.

I stopped mid-step. "What are—"

"I would be most appreciative if you would play along, Lex. I'm sure it won't be *too* painful," he said, his black-rimmed amber eyes shimmering in the winter sunlight. Without waiting for a response, he pulled the glass door open and pushed me through ahead of him.

When we reached the end of the short line to order, Marcus released my hand and I was momentarily filled with an unexpected feeling of loss. The arm he draped over my shoulders to pull me snug against his side drove the feeling away, replacing it with astonishment . . . and a pleasant, tingly flutter in my abdomen. *What is going on with me?* I hadn't been so intensely aware of a man in . . . ever. I felt bespelled, like there was some irresistible force drawing me to Marcus, which would have been thrilling if it weren't for the fact that he was my boss. *Off-limits!* I reminded myself, again.

Marcus leaned down, bringing his lips a hair's breadth from my ear. "Really, Lex, I think you can do better . . . you could at least pretend to be enjoying yourself."

As he pulled his taunting mouth away, I snapped my own mouth shut and turned my face to him. Though I wasn't short—just over five foot eight—I still had to tilt my chin up, accounting for our notable height difference. Narrowing my eyes, I glared. His chiseled jaw clenched, making his bone structure more contoured than usual. From inches away, the effect was breathtaking, and my glare faded. So did the mischief lighting his eyes, replaced by something more serious.

Since I'd met Marcus, I'd been embarrassingly unsuccessful

at hiding my attraction, but I was starting to wonder if we were walking down a two-way street. Maybe I wasn't alone on the road. *My turn*, I thought vindictively. We moved forward in the line.

Holding his eyes, I slowly licked my lips, wondering if he could smell the vanilla of my lip balm. As I'd hoped, Marcus took notice. His eyes left mine, lingering on my mouth. When they lifted again, they were on fire with desire.

I rose onto my tiptoes, bringing my face slowly closer to his. I was aching to follow through with the movement, to press my lips against his, but I altered my trajectory at the last minute, aiming for his ear instead. "You'd better have a good explanation for this charade, Marcus. I can't wait to hear it," I purred.

As I dropped my heels back down to the ground, my understanding of Marcus Bahur was confused even further. He was grinning in sheer delight, displaying teeth so straight and white they could have been featured in a toothpaste ad. I'd seen him smile before, but not like that. For once, it reached his eyes.

"Oh Lex, you do surprise me often, and in the *most pleasant* ways. Of course I'll give you *exactly* what you want . . . in private," he said, louder and rougher than necessary. If I hadn't known exactly what I'd said, I would've guessed we'd just agreed on some especially naughty, potentially illegal sexual act. I could only stare at him.

We moved forward again, approaching the counter and its confounded little barista. Cassandra stood opposite us, pressing her lips together so hard they drained of color. She looked like she was either about to throw up, or scream.

"Hello again, Cassandra. I hope you're well," Marcus said to the girl-woman. While he spoke, his arm dropped from my shoulders to wrap possessively around my waist.

I smiled up at him, pretending to be enamored. Well, pretending to pretend.

"Hi, Professor!" Cassandra chirped. She refused to look at me, let alone acknowledge my presence.

"What would you like, my darling?" Marcus asked me, tightening his arm around my waist.

To really be your darling. "Oh, just a latte and a turkey and cheddar sandwich." As an afterthought, I added, "And a raspberry scone." *A well-fed Nejerette is a happy Nejerette*, I justified to myself.

"And I'll have my usual lunch. To go, please," Marcus said, handing Cassandra his card. His usual lunch turned out to be twice as large as mine, but I figured it took a lot of fuel to maintain such a tall, well-honed physique.

Once we had our food and coffees and were out of sight of the café, Marcus let me go. He continued walking for several steps before noticing I'd stopped.

Pausing, he tossed over his shoulder, "Is there a problem, Lex?" He resumed his slow jaunt.

I caught up to him, careful not to spill my latte, and fell in step beside him. "Yes, Marcus, there's a problem. What the hell was that?" Up until the moment he released my hand, I'd thought—just maybe—he and I could overcome the professor-student, boss-underling dilemma. I'd thought he might *want* to, but then he let go and I realized it had all been wishful thinking. I felt used and embarrassed and far angrier than I probably should have.

"I suppose I could ask *you* the same thing."

"Oh, please! You told me to pretend . . . to play along." I was having a hard time keeping my voice at a normal volume. "You owe me an explanation."

He slowed his step and shot me a sidelong glance. "I'm a creature of habit. I dislike having to change my behavior patterns."

"What's that have to do with us pretending to be . . . ?" I

raised my eyebrows and waved my hand in front of me, unable to come up with an appropriate label for our pretense.

"Lovers?" Marcus provided.

I groaned. "God, it sounds so much worse out loud than it did in my head."

"Would it be so unpleasant?" Marcus asked, a chill in his voice.

A laugh of sheer disbelief escaped from my mouth. "Um . . . getting kicked out of my program would be unpleasant. The university has rules against professors and students being together . . . rules with consequences."

"Do you always follow the rules?" he asked, but the chill was gone.

"Yes, as a matter of fact, I do," I said, and it was the truth. I'd never snuck out of my parents' house in high school, I hadn't drunk alcohol until I was twenty-one, and I followed traffic laws as best I could.

Marcus sighed, and to my shock, told me the reason for the scene back at the café. "I'm accustomed to getting my lunch at the Burke Café. Cassandra was becoming a little . . . obsessive. I could no longer sit alone for a quiet break—she'd fill every possible second with mindless chatter. It was getting tiring. I needed to dissuade her," he explained.

"You couldn't just go somewhere else?"

"Like I said, I'm a creature of habit."

I laughed despite my waning exasperation. "You know, Marcus, sometimes change can be a good thing."

"Sometimes. Rarely. Tell me about meeting your grandfather," he said conversationally, like we hadn't just been teetering on a thin, not-okay-to-cross professional boundary.

Carefully, I strung words together into relatively normal sentences. I could hardly say, "He looked like he was thirty, but he's really a little over two thousand years old, and we visited the echo of his childhood home in Herculaneum before the eruption of Mount Vesuvius." Instead, I said, "It was . . . interesting. I'd thought he was dead, so I was more than a little surprised to see him. But after I got over the shock, it was nice. I learned a lot about my family history." *Like, that we're not all human.*

"And did you get along well, you and your newfound grandfather?" Marcus asked, sounding genuinely curious.

I smiled to myself. "Yeah, we really did."

We'd arrived back at Denny Hall and were about to enter through the inconspicuous west door when Marcus stepped ahead of me, blocking the entrance. "Have dinner with me tonight."

"Has anyone ever told you that your transitions are a bit rough?" I asked after overcoming my surprise.

He shrugged. "Have dinner with me tonight."

"Marcus . . . we already talked about this, remember? The rules . . . ?"

"Inconsequential." His eyes burned with such intensity that I had to look away.

"Marcus, I—" *If I pass this up, I'm the biggest idiot ever born.* "I can't."

With a heavy sigh, he turned toward the door.

I grabbed his arm. "Wait. I meant, I can't *tonight.* I already have plans," I explained. "I'm meeting up with Alexa—my grandpa again."

Marcus's arm tensed under my hand, and he said, "Tomorrow night, then. Say yes, Lex."

"Why Marcus," I gasped dramatically. "If I didn't know any better, I'd think you were begging!"

He smiled roguishly, sensing victory. "Trust me. It won't happen again."

"We'll see," I bantered, and his smile widened. "But, fine . . . yes, I'll have dinner with you tomorrow night." *How am I going to wait until then?*

With success secured, Marcus finally allowed me into the building.

The afternoon passed quickly, filled with numerous flirtatious glances between Marcus and me. By the time I left, I'd helped Dominic narrow the list of field school applicants down to the forty we would contact and interview in the coming weeks. I spent the short, lonely walk back to my apartment reading my neglected text messages. While in The Pit, my phone had buzzed at least a half-dozen times, and I hadn't been surprised when I'd seen the name on the call log. Cara. And after each unanswered call, she'd sent a text message.

Hey lady . . . haven't heard from you for a while. Just checking in.

Everything OK? Can you text me back, please?

Annie and I wanted to do dinner with you soon. Tomorrow night? Let me know.

Are you mad at me or something?

You know, it's really not that hard to text someone back.

Okay, I'm officially freaking out. Text me. Or call me. Or stop by.

Are you dead or something? This is getting really old. CALL ME!

Unwilling to face the hour-long interrogation that would undoubtedly result from a phone call, I sent my relentless friend a text: *Sorry Cara. I'm fine. Just been busy with my mom and the excavation prep. Let's definitely do dinner soon.* It wasn't what she wanted to hear, but the words would at least decrease her calling frequency for the night.

When I reached my apartment, Alexander was already waiting in the hallway outside the door. We'd planned to meet up at six o'clock, and I was a few minutes late.

"Sorry! I got held up on campus. Have you been waiting long?" I asked, letting him into my little home.

He smiled kindly. "Not a problem. I brought dinner," he announced, setting a huge bag of Chinese take-out on the kitchen table.

"Alexander, you're a genius! You just might be the best

grandpa ever!" I exclaimed as I retrieved plates and silverware. "What would you like to drink? Beer? Wine?"

"Water is fine. It's unwise to venture into the At while inebriated. When we do, our subconscious starts to take over and it becomes too easy to end up seeing something unintentionally. There are some things you can't unsee, no matter how hard you try," he explained, giving me my first important lesson.

"Okey-dokey, water it is," I said, setting two full glasses on the table. Dinner passed pleasantly, both of us downing generous portions of fried rice, sweet and sour prawns, beef with broccoli, and egg rolls. We swapped stories, me telling Alexander about how I came to love archaeology, and Alexander telling me about his childhood in Herculaneum and his modern life as an explorer of sorts. He'd been traveling around the world, never stopping in one place for more than a year, since he'd left Grandma Suse almost twenty-five years ago. It was nice to learn more about him.

"So, what's on the agenda for tonight? More shocking family revelations? History lessons?" I asked, finally dropping my fork onto my plate with a clink. I was blissfully stuffed.

"Hmm . . . I thought I might answer some of your questions," Alexander said. "If you're anything like me, which I suspect you are, you have hundreds buzzing around in your head."

I straightened, excited by the prospect. *Where to start?* "Is there a limit to how far we can see into the future or past?"

Alexander tensed one side of his mouth. "Well, other than the pesky solstice issue, which prevents anyone from seeing into the At beyond the twenty-first of June, it completely depends on the individual's strength. Only a few years after I manifested, I could see thousands of years behind and several years ahead. The weakest Nejeret I've ever known could only see a few hundred years into the past. Seeing the future has always been the more difficult and rare talent—that's what we call our unique gifts—and those with that talent are called seers."

"I can do it," I said. "I mean, I did it once, but it was only a few days in the future and it definitely wasn't on purpose."

He nodded, apparently expecting no less from a granddaughter of his.

"How many of us are there?" I asked.

Alexander frowned. "I don't know, exactly. Our governing body, the Council of Seven, isn't as well-organized as it once was. The Council used to keep records on all our people, but they haven't been very successful in tracking the births or deaths in a few of the familial lines for at least five hundred years. There could be any number of thousands, maybe even tens of thousands."

"What changed?" I asked, thinking that a people who could literally take a peek into the past shouldn't have too hard of a time with a species-wide census.

"There was a disagreement," Alexander explained. "Half of the members of the Council believed we should force the *prophecy* and bring the savior, the Meswett, into existence." He said "prophecy" like it was a particularly foul obscenity. "The other half believed we should avoid the cursed thing at all costs. After a while, reconciliation was impossible and the Council split."

"Were you on the Council?" I asked, suddenly curious about my grandpa's standing among our people, and through him, my standing.

Shaking his head, Alexander said, "The seven seats on the Council are reserved for the patriarchs of the seven strongest familial lines. There's Heru and Set, though Set disappeared more than a thousand years before I was born, so there are really only six members."

"Did Set die?" At the edge of my mind, I realized that Heru, the man Alexander had set up as my watchdog, was on the

Council of Seven . . . which was crazy. It was like learning the President of the United States had been my bodyguard for who-knew-how-long.

My grandpa shook his head again. "There's also Moshe, Sid, Dedwen, and Shangdi."

I whistled. "Assuming Moshe and Sid are who I think they are"—Moses and Siddhartha, central figures in two of the world's largest modern religions—"that's quite a list of mythical people. Not so good at keeping a low profile, are we?" I asked sardonically.

Alexander laughed. "A fault of our species."

"That was only six, by the way," I informed him.

"Ivan, my father, is the leader of the Council, though they haven't officially met for some time."

I was momentarily stunned—my great-grandpa was the leader of our people. With a dry chuckle, I said, "So I really wasn't far off with the whole 'more shocking family revelations' thing?"

"You seem to be adjusting well to the phenomenon."

I shrugged. "Adapt, or die." I wondered if I was exhibiting some other, hard-to-pinpoint characteristic of our kind—extreme adaptability. It would make sense, considering that our regenerative abilities allowed us to live for thousands of years while the world went through endless changes. *Live for thousands of years . . . me . . . unbelievable.*

I plucked another question out of the miasma. "So, besides some of us being stronger than others, some of us being able to see into the future, and some of us being able to smell in the echoes, are there any other differences between Nejerets?"

"Yes, many." Alexander took a deep breath before diving in. "Some of us are 'tied down,' meaning we have to be physically in the place of the echo we're viewing, and some aren't. For example, if you were tied down and you wanted to see something that happened last year here in this apartment, you'd have to enter the At from this apartment." He paused for a moment. "Some Nejerets can follow an object through the At, viewing all that has or might happen in its presence. Some can do the same in relation to a specific individual. That is called 'finding.' Some can track another Nejeret's projected self, their ba, through the At, following them from echo to echo." Again, he paused. "Some can manipulate the At itself, forever changing what other Nejerets see when viewing a particular echo, or creating false echoes—things that never actually happened. Manipulating is a very dangerous talent—permanently altering the At is forbidden, though on rare occasions we're allowed to create temporary false echoes for training purposes. Related, but not completely forbidden, some can cloak their At-selves or even entire portions of the At containing their past and potential futures. *That* is how Set disappeared; he's created a series of blank spots in the At."

I considered Set and the idea of cloaking in the At. I was fairly certain I'd seen a "cloaked" person in the At before—the man who'd saved me from Mike. With sudden excitement, I wondered if the long-lost Set was my mysterious savior, but my excitement soured almost instantly. The ancient Egyptian god, Set, was often called "Seth" by modern people . . . and "Seth" had been the name attached to the sender of a pretty damning text message on Mike's phone. *Use the lip balm to make her compliant, then complete the mission.* Was Mike's Seth the vanished member of the Council of Seven? Did Mike know about Nejerets . . . about *me*? It seemed like too much of a coincidence.

"That's all I can think of right now," Alexander said, interrupting my wild conjecturing. "I suppose we should write this down in a handbook—it would make training quite a bit easier."

"It's okay," I replied, my head spinning both from the influx of information and my improbable deductions. I didn't know if I could handle anything else at the moment, but I was a staunch believer in the whole "knowledge is power" bit, so I asked another question. "Hmm . . . so if someone alters the At, does it change what actually happened? Like, will the history books suddenly say something different?"

"No. Since we don't actually travel through time, we only view what has been or what could be, only the moment's reflection in the At, its echo, is changed," he said decisively. "Besides, humans would be unaware of the change in the At—only Nejerets would be able to see it, so history would remain the same."

I frowned. "Then why is it such a big deal? If it doesn't actually change anything . . . ?"

A bitter laugh escaped from Alexander. "Nejerets depend on the echoes, and we tend to hold pretty high positions, even in the human world. If *we* base some decision on what we saw in the At, and what we saw was false, then the consequences could be devastating for Nejerets and humans alike."

After a moment of thought, he said, "Someone—we have guesses but we don't know who for sure—manipulated the future At, completely removing all traces of echoes surrounding a certain ambitious member of the Nazi Party. Nejerets in power throughout the world made political decisions based on what they saw in the At, unaware that an entire life had been erased from view. It just so happened that *that* life would prove extremely influential, but because it had been eradicated from the At, Nejeret seers couldn't see the potential horrors it might cause."

Alexander was shaking his head in disbelief. *Was he one of those seers?* I wondered as I took in his state of dejection.

"By the time we noticed the anomaly in the At, it was too late," he continued. "Events had already been set in motion. We did what we could, but . . ." Alexander suddenly looked at me, *into* me. "You must understand that we did what we could. You must," he pleaded. "But the horrors . . . the death . . . those poor humans . . ."

Reaching across the corner of the table, I squeezed his hand. I had no words, but at least I could comfort him with that.

"Whoever manipulated the At . . ." He turned over his hand to grip mine almost painfully. "You study history, Alexandra. You know about power and corruption. Our kind walks a very thin, unsteady line. We may feel like them sometimes, we may even be named for them, but we're *not* gods. Remember that, granddaughter. We. Are. Not. Gods." Alexander's tone was vehement.

Gravely, I said, "I understand." After Alexander nodded, I waited, taking a few contemplative breaths. "So which, um, 'talents' do you have?"

His grip on my hand relented, and I retracted my arm, setting both of my hands in my lap. "Let's see," he said. "I can see very far into the past At and a short way into the future At, and I can smell in echoes, like you. I'm not tied down—I can view any echo within the past several thousand years from anywhere. Though looking further back, tens or hundreds of thousands of years, does require proximity to the echo's place of origin." He leaned toward me as if confessing a secret. "That's why I was in Antarctica for the past few months. I've always wondered what was under all of that ice. Also, I'm a finder—I can search the At focusing on a specific object or individual."

I bit the inside of my lip, digesting his response. "So, on a scale of one to ten, one being the weakest weakling and ten being . . ."

"Nuin?" Alexander supplied.

I shrugged. "Sure. So on that scale, where would you rank in strength?"

"Hmm . . . perhaps a seven. My father would be a nine, certainly, as would the rest of the Council. They are all very powerful, just not to the level of the Great Father."

Too many questions bounced around in my skull, like my head had turned into a pinball game comprised of flesh, bone, and synapses. "Can you teach me how to be a finder?" There were a few people I wanted to follow through the At, but one stood out from the rest in my mind. The mental image of that person glared deadly daggers at the others, commanding them to wait their turn.

"I can try. But it's a rare talent, so I wouldn't get your hopes up," he cautioned.

"Great! Let's do it!" I said with a small bounce in my chair.

"Hang on—one step at a time. First you need to learn how to enter the At at will. How have you done it so far?"

I explained the basics behind my first few unintentional dives into the At, then described how I'd gained some control using my emotions and focusing on what I needed at the moment. I didn't, however, tell him the subjects of the echoes, especially not the one about my criminal father. I needed to know more about that particular element of my nefarious parentage before I shared it with *anyone*. *If* I ever shared it with anyone. It was creepy . . . and weird.

As I spoke, Alexander nodded, sometimes looking surprised and sometimes proud. "You've made a good start of it," he told me after I finished. "If you can gain control over your ability to enter the At while awake this evening, then I'll test you for the finding talent before I leave."

"Okay. So, what do I do?" I asked eagerly.

"Aim for when you opened the door yesterday evening and first met your magnificent grandfather," he said, puffing up jovially as he spoke, which earned a wry laugh from me. He grasped my hand again. "Now, holding that moment in your mind, close your eyes and clear out all other thoughts."

It seemed to be an impossible task, but, I needed it to work . . . I needed to track a very specific person. *Needed.*

"Open your eyes, Alexandra."

When I did, I thought I'd succeeded . . . but then the door burst open. Two unsteady people stumbled into the apartment.

Oh no! No, no, no! *I needed to get away.*

In a flash of colors, the scene shifted to the night with Cara and Annie and the three bottles of wine. The other me was explaining her hesitations about going on the date with Mike, to which Cara and Annie responded with protestations and confusion.

"Damn it!" I hissed. I felt a hand squeeze mine and remembered that Alexander was with me.

"Concentrate, Lex," he encouraged gently. "You're doing fine. Focus on the night you met me."

I remembered opening the door—the stunned moment when incomprehension faded to impossible recognition. The scene flickered.

The other me hurried to the door, obviously excited. She opened it, and seconds later, was lying on the hardwood floor. I'd fainted from the shock of finding my grandpa, alive and young, standing in the hallway.

"There must've been a better way for you and Grandma Suse to have done that," I told Alexander. I was watching the other version of him carry my limp form to the couch.

He shrugged. "At least you didn't hit me." After a pause, he said, "Now, do you remember what you did to get here?"

I nodded, recalling how concentration had surpassed need. I'd felt much more in control.

"Good. Pick out another moment in this apartment, something that happened further back, and take us there."

It was hard to think of anything memorable that hadn't happened in the last month. Part of me felt like my life hadn't really started until that devastating conversation with my mom. Finally, I settled on a moment and concentrated. *The flicker of colors lasted a tiny bit longer than it had the previous time, but it was nothing like the protracted swirl that had surrounded us when we'd viewed Alexander's home in Herculaneum.*

Another version of me was sitting on the couch with a cardboard animal carrier on her lap. The creature inside the carrier emitted a rhythmic string of tiny, frantic meows. The other me opened the box and out popped a softball-sized ball of gray and brown fur.

"*Thora,*" I murmured as I watched the awkward kitten thoroughly sniff first me and then the couch.

"The day you brought your cat home. Good choice. The echoes revolving around our loved ones are both the easiest and hardest to view," he said briskly, shaking me out of my kitten reverie. Baby Thora was stalking a pen that had fallen on the floor, wiggling her little behind clumsily. "Now, I think you're ready for your finder test."

"Really?" I asked, suddenly giddy with excitement.

Alexander nodded. "Pick someone you know of, but you don't know, like a celebrity."

I frowned, squinting my eyes.

"Do you have someone in mind?" Alexander asked.

I nodded, picturing John Jakim, the lead singer of my favorite band, Johnny Stopwatch.

"Good. Now, this time you're going to aim for the When, instead of the Where."

"The When?" I repeated.

"Yes, the When. If we don't know the Where, we must start with the When," he explained. "Open yourself up to the At, thinking only about the world thirty minutes ago. Don't think about a place. Instead, imagine being everywhere in the world at once, at half past nine this evening."

It took nearly twenty minutes to enter the placeless At—the When. For someone used to living in the Where and watching the When go by, readjusting perspectives was unbelievably difficult. My very understanding of time and space had to be melted down and remolded into a more malleable thing.

All of a sudden, I was enmeshed in the targeted When, watching the Where spin around me like a deranged carousel. It was odd to see the colors of the At moving unilaterally, instead of their usual, chaotic swirl.

"Very good, Alexandra!" my grandpa commended. "Now you must find your focal point, your celebrity. He or she is somewhere in this time, but you don't know where, correct?"

"No idea," I said, nodding.

"*Perfect. This part will be easy if you're a finder. Just think about the person, and the At will automatically shift itself around you.*"

I did as he directed, and gasped. *The endless spinning shifted, no longer circling, but instead moving past me like a headwind. When the movement ceased, Alexander and I were standing in a dim, packed bar. In a booth in a dark corner sat John Jakim with the other members of Johnny Stopwatch, a half-empty pint glass in hand.*

"*Is that your focal point?*" *Alexander asked eagerly, pointing to the musician. At my amazed nod, he said, "Wonderful! You're a finder, and to some degree, a seer." His voice was filled to the brim with grandfatherly pride.*

"*Well, you know . . . I get it from my grandpa,*" *I said, bumping his shoulder with my own. I was blushing profusely at his unabashed flattery. "So, should we call it a night? I'm kind of tired after all of this At surfing.*"

"*'At surfing' . . . I like that . . . like channel surfing. But yes, we can be done for today. Would you like to return us, or shall I?*" *he asked politely.*

"Done," I said as the world flickered briefly and we returned to our physical forms. It really wasn't too difficult once I understood the basics. Stretching in my kitchen chair, I asked, "What happens to our bodies while we . . . or, um, our 'ba' is in the At?" According to the ancient Egyptians, the *ba* was one of the three essential pieces comprising a person's soul, and I found it immensely interesting that it was what Nejerets called the part of ourselves that could venture into the At to view what has been and what may be.

Alexander smiled. "I've been waiting for you to ask that. It really is a remarkable thing. When your ba leaves your body, your physical form enters a state of stasis called At-qed"—I recognized the word "qed" as one of the ancient Egyptian words for "sleep"—"where, to observers, we appear to zone out or become lost in thought. More or less, the body's functions slow down and it retains whatever position and expression it held when the ba departed. And, as far as we know, we can remain in At-qed indefinitely."

"So someone could just come in here and do whatever they wanted to our bodies and we wouldn't even notice?" I asked, horrified.

Pressing his lips together, Alexander took a deep breath. "Yes. It's the major downfall to using our gift. We are absolutely vulnerable when our ba enters the At, far more so than when we're simply asleep. That is the very reason you should only enter the At in a safe, private place and not spend too much time viewing echoes . . . either that, or have someone you trust to protect your body while your ba is away."

"Oh. That's . . . interesting," I said, and I meant it, but it came out sounding more like bored disinterest. My head was too full of new information and convoluted concepts: ba, At-qed, the When, the Where, manipulating . . . I needed time to process.

Seeming to read my thoughts, Alexander said, "I should go; you've had a long evening. Same time tomorrow?"

"I can't tomorrow." *I have a date with the most enigmatic and enticing archaeologist on the planet.* "How about Thursday?"

"Very well, my dear. I'll see you then," he said, giving me a brief hug before leaving.

After cleaning up the remnants of our Chinese food feast, I considered turning in for the night. It was nearly midnight and I really was tired, but I wasn't done yet. I wasn't even close.

15

CATCH & TRAP

H e has to be Nejeret, *I thought as, once again, I studied the shadowed man in the echo of the incident with Mike. It was the only way he could've disguised himself in the echo.* But who is he? *Something about him, about that night, had been tugging at my subconscious ever since I woke up in the hospital. I needed to know his identity, desperately . . . even if I didn't understand the reason behind my desperation.*

As I glanced at Mike and registered the absolute terror in his eyes, my need to know the Nejeret's identity became crushing. I was certain there was a way to unmask him, I just had to figure it out. I need more time!

The cloaked Nejeret lurked toward my fallen attacker, spitting vicious, incomprehensible syllables along the way. He beat Mike until his need for violence was expended, and then he returned to the unconscious version of me. He picked her up and carried her out of the apartment.

Again, *I thought, and the echo started over.*

I lost track of how many times I viewed the echo, but eventually I realized I didn't need to keep watching the attack over and over again just to see the shadowed man. Stop, *I thought, and it was as though I'd hit a pause button. The shadowed man was frozen, crouching on his heels with* his hand outstretched toward the other version of me. He was in the middle of brushing a stray lock of hair from her face.

I circled the figure, studying every shadowed inch of him. I could see that the darkness cloaking him was different—set apart from the echo itself. It was like some foreign At had been layered over the original echo, like a palimpsest.

I touched the out-of-place At, and it vibrated. Determined, I grasped the shadowy cloak with both hands and tugged. Nothing happened. I tugged harder, and again, nothing happened.

Apparently I couldn't strip it off . . . but I thought it was possible I could slip between the two layers of At. I was fairly certain that no two particles could occupy the same space at the same time. I only hoped the same rule of matter applied in the At.

Gently, as I'd done the first time, I touched the superimposed At. It vibrated, but I was pretty sure the man underneath remained still. I carefully searched with my fingers, following the increasingly strong vibrations, until I found what felt like an edge. It wasn't an edge in the conventional sense, like the edge of a piece of paper or the hem of a dress. It was more like a sense of something met by a sense of nothing.

I slipped the tips of my fingers under the edge, and then followed with my whole hand. My teeth chattered with the increasingly intense vibrations, but I reached further. When I could finally slip my head between the two layers of At, the vibrations stopped. The cloak, I realized, was gone.

Unfortunately, in my At-splitting, I'd maneuvered myself so that I was crouched in front of the man with my face mere millimeters from his black sweater. I stumbled backward, tripped over the other version of me, and fell on my butt. When I'd finally composed myself enough to stand and look at the man's face, I gasped and dropped back down to the floor.

"Oh my God . . . Marcus!" I exclaimed aloud. Marcus is Nejeret. Marcus is Nejeret! What does this—

"Damn it, Lex!" The growling admonishment filled every open space in the frozen echo. It was Marcus's voice, but the Marcus in the echo, the one I'd just uncloaked and was watching, was still frozen. My stomach dropped as I realized what was going on. Marcus is Nejeret. Marcus, the real Marcus, is *here.*

Gripping my upper arms, he hauled me up off the ground and spun me around. I was staring straight in to the very real, very pissed off face of Marcus Bahur, professor, archaeologist, and undercover Nejeret.

"I was going to explain everything tomorrow night," *he said, articulating each word with exceptional care.*

Instinctively, I punched him in the gut. It was the first time I'd ever really hit another person, and on the whole, it was rather ineffective. He barely flinched.

"How long have you known?" *I shouted.* "I've barely been able to keep my head above the water and you've been sitting by, watching? I thought I was losing my mind!" *I punched him again, hoping for a better reaction. I was let down. So, naturally, I began slapping and hitting every inch of his bare torso. It didn't take me long to tire. I dropped my arms limply to my sides.*

"Are you finished?" *he asked, more than a hint of frost in his tone . . . like, a blizzard's worth.*

I nodded weakly, studying his blue and gray tennis shoes. Marcus never wears tennis shoes. *His bare torso finally registered in the coherent part of my mind. Misbehaving, my eyes raised to the golden brown skin less than a foot away. Hard ridges rippled the perfect flesh, defining muscles I hadn't even known existed.*

I'd seen him shirtless once before—in a dream that had been set in ancient Egypt . . . or what I had thought was a dream. Considering it could have been an echo, I shivered. Marcus would have to be at least three thousand years old.

"Where's your shirt?" *I asked, picking the least terrifying question I could think of.*

"What?" *he asked, surprised. His tone warmed considerably when he continued,* "I was in the middle of a workout when I felt you fumbling with my cloak in this echo. If you wanted to strip off my clothes, all you needed to do was say so." *There was a short pause.* "I must say, Lex, when you blush, it's very becoming." His tone could have melted the polar ice caps.

I realized my eyes were closed when I felt the feather-light touch of his fingertips on the sides of my face. They traced my cheekbones, jawline, and chin, tilting my face up with the faintest pressure.

"You want me," he said. "Admit it."

I shook my head and squeezed my eyes shut more tightly. I was angry —no, pissed—at him. I needed to hold onto that emotion.

"Admit it," he whispered, so close I could feel his breath on my face. My eyes popped open and my heart skipped a beat . . . or three. Not amber, but golden, blazing eyes trapped me. I'd never seen his eyes so light, and I suddenly realized that was what I'd remembered when I first awoke in the hospital—the memory of glorious, golden fire. I must have come to briefly while he'd been transporting me to the hospital and looked into his eyes . . . and felt safe. Staring into those eyes now, I involuntarily wet my lips.

Marcus's fingers slid down my neck to trace my collarbones, then traveled back up to tangle in my hair. A tingling trail burned along my skin, invisibly marking every place he touched. He tightened his grasp, preventing me from turning away. It was unnecessary; I was completely lost, a captive held in the prison of his eyes.

I inhaled softly, my breath catching. One moment, he was staring at me —into me—the next, his lips were parting mine. I gasped at the bruising intensity of the kiss. His tongue delved into my mouth, teasing mine out expertly. His arm dropped to my waist, pulling me against him so ardently that I had to stand on my tiptoes to remain tethered to the ground. Something about the jarring movement shook my brain awake, and I pushed against his bare chest. Until that gesture, I hadn't noticed that my traitorous hands were fondling his muscles. I'm angry, remember! I reminded myself.

"Marcus . . ." I whispered, more than a trace of warning contained in that one word.

As he released his death grip on my hair, I maneuvered myself away from him, retreating through my open bedroom door. I didn't know why or how, but being too close to him tended to cloud my judgment until I could *only make decisions based on the overwhelming desire I felt around him. It was like he naturally emitted an aphrodisiac designed specifically for me, and I craved it when we were apart. But it went beyond lust, beyond desire . . . I felt* good *around him—safe and whole and at peace. I shook my head, trying to dispel my clearly delusional emotions.*

How I'd ever thought he was a plain old human was beyond me. I guess we only see what we want to see . . . what we expect to see . . .

"*Lex—*"

"*I can't trust you,*" *I interrupted.* "*I have no idea who you really are.*" *I spun around. Marcus was standing in the doorway just a few steps away.* "*You're Nejeret, and you've been watching me since before we met at the café, obviously. How long, Marcus? How long have you been spying on me?*"

Anger and frustration flashed across Marcus's face so briefly that I almost missed it. And then, abruptly, his clothes changed. No longer in sneakers and basketball shorts, he wore tailored black trousers and a silver-gray button-down shirt with the sleeves rolled up to reveal toned forearms.

"*Hey! How'd you—*" *I narrowed my eyes.* "*You're not distracting me that easily. How long have you been watching me?*"

He sighed melodramatically, like I was the one being difficult, when in reality, everything was so obviously his fault.

"*Since August,*" *he finally said.*

He's been watching me for five whole months? "*Why?*" *I* spat.

"*Because Alex requested it of me,*" *he responded in kind.* "*Believe me, Lex, I had much better things to do than watch over a woman who was unlikely to even manifest.*"

"*Well, I did manifest, didn't I?*" *I briefly wondered if sticking out my tongue would help get my point across. Then, I remembered where my tongue had just been and blushed.* Damn him!

"*Yes,*" *he purred and stalked toward me, his eyes devouring my every inch.* "*You are manifesting quite nicely.*"

"Stop right there!" I screeched, holding my hand up as I backed away from him.

Marcus stopped, but he didn't look happy about it.

"Alex . . . as in Alexander? My grandpa asked you to keep an eye on me?" I clarified, my voice too high. I'd only known that Alexander had asked Heru, a member of the Council of Seven, to watch over me . . . not Marcus.

"Yes," Marcus said.

A sudden, nauseating thought occurred to me. "And the excavation . . . you didn't really need me to figure out the riddle on the tablet to find the entrance to the temple, did you? You could just look in the At." I took a deep breath, ignoring Marcus's slowly shaking head. "Did you just offer me a position on the excavation because of Alexander, too?"

"No!" he hissed. "We couldn't find the entrance because the At has been manipulated . . . we can't find any of the echoes relating to it. Damn it, Lex, I wanted you on my team because you're good at what you do, unbelievably good for someone so young, but also because"—he shook his head, like he couldn't quite find the words to say what he meant—"you started manifesting. You started manifesting and you know nothing of our people . . . of our customs. Nobody expected you to manifest, so you were never trained in our ways. Other Nejerets will be participating in the excavation. I wanted to give you the chance to interact with others of our kind—to learn all that it means to be Nejeret."

"If you wanted me to learn what it means to be Nejeret, why didn't you just explain what was going on with me?" I sounded so bitchy, I nearly cringed. Instead, I barreled on. "Were you toying with me? Was it fun for you to—"

Marcus turned away abruptly, clenching his hands into fists at his sides. "No, Lex, it wasn't fun for me. Just like it wasn't fun finding that piece of shit forcing himself on you." He spared a moment to glare at Mike's frozen body. "I'd grown somewhat fond of you over the months. I disliked seeing you struggle so much, seeing you in such pain. But it was against the rules for me to tell you of our people, of your heritage. In rare cases like yours, where the Nejeret knows absolutely nothing about his or *her heritage, only the nearest Nejeret in your direct line is allowed to explain. I had to wait for Alex."*

"Rules! Why are we running around following the rules of some 'council' that doesn't even meet anymore?" *Suddenly so exasperated that I had to move, I slipped around Marcus and out of the room. I paced from the bedroom door to the kitchen and back again, over and over.*

"Not the Council's rules—my grandfather's," *Marcus said when he finally emerged from my bedroom.*

I waved my hand dismissively. "And we should follow your grandfather's rules because . . . ?" *That time I did cringe at my snotty, juvenile tone.*

"Because, Little Ivanov, he's the Great Father," *Marcus said quietly from right behind me.*

The Great Father, Nuin, from whom we all descend . . . is Marcus's *grandfather? I halted mid-stride, only a few steps from the fridge. I could hear Marcus's footsteps as he approached behind me.*

"Who are you?" *I whispered to the fridge. I just . . . I couldn't face him.*

"I'm the grandson of Nuin," *he said, his voice hard.* "I'm a member of the Council of Seven, and I'm older than you can imagine." *He was silent for a few moments, the sound of his breathing the only thing I could hear over my pounding heart. Finally, softly, he said,* "I'm also the man who didn't let you die."

Hanging my head in shame, I started to apologize. "Marcus, I'm—" *My words halted in mid-sentence as his second statement registered. I whirled to face him.* "There's no 'Marcus' on the Council."

He took a step closer, and I stepped back. "True. But I have many names," *he explained, his eyes willing me to comprehend.* "You know who I am, Lex. Think about it."

Set. Heru. Moses. Sid. Dedwen. Shangdi. Ivan. *He definitely wasn't Ivan, my great-grandpa . . . not after the kiss.*

Set. Heru. Moses. Sid. Dedwen. Shangdi. *He definitely wasn't Dedwen or Shangdi, based on their mythological descriptions—one was a Nubian god, the other a Chinese deity.*

Set. Heru. Moses. Sid. Marcus Bahur. Marcus Bahur. Marcus. Bahur.

Bahur.

I suddenly felt like the world's biggest idiot.

Marcus took another step toward me, and I backed into the refrigerator. I halted his forward progress with a smile. "Bahur," I said. "'Of Heru.' Clever, Marcus . . . or should I say, Heru?" Heru—commonly known as Horus—was the fierce Egyptian god of kingship and war, whose beautiful eyes had led to one of the most famous ancient Egyptian symbols —the Wedjat, otherwise known as the "Eye of Horus." Marcus, who had kissed me, was Heru. *It was . . . impossible, but then a lot of impossible things had been happening lately.*

When I said his true name, he cringed. Shaking his head, he explained, "I hate the way that name sounds on these lips." He brushed his thumb across my bottom lip for emphasis. "You say 'Heru' like you're talking about a god . . . someone untouchable . . . unknowable. But when you say 'Marcus,' you're talking about a man. A man can be known . . . touched."

With my palms pressed against the cool refrigerator door, I said, "Marcus." I was surprised by the sultriness in my voice.

"Mmm . . . yes, Lex. I do so love the way you say that name . . . my name . . . the way it rises from your tongue," Marcus remarked, raising his arms to press his hands against the freezer door on either side of my head. His arms flexed, and he leaned closer.

"Marcus," I whispered.

He bent his neck, bringing his lips inches from mine. The muscles and tendons of his neck formed thick cords as he hovered, letting his quickened breath mix with mine. It was tantalizing . . . empowering . . . tormenting.

"Marcus . . . I don't . . . I . . . I need . . ." I forced myself to look at Mike and then the wounded version of myself. "I need time." Which was something I doubted a man as tantalizing and intimidating as Marcus would be willing to give me.

"Ah . . . but Lex, we are Nejeret. We have an eternity. By the time our courtship is through, you'll beg me to take you to bed," he whispered near

my ear before leaning back, keeping a hair's breadth between us from head to toe. "And even then, I may make you wait."

Every molecule of air disappeared from my lungs, and all of my blood set a direct route to my groin, spilling heat and tension through my lower abdomen. I was nothing but desire for the man in front of me . . . the god. Without thought, I closed the minuscule distance between us, softly brushing my lips against his. I savored his deliciously spicy scent.

Instantly, Marcus shifted forward, pressing me more firmly against the fridge. "Marcus," I breathed, and it was the last thing I said for several long, glorious seconds.

"Lex, you should know," he said, kissing the sensitive skin beneath my ear, "that what happens in the At isn't real. These aren't our actual bodies. This isn't actually happening . . . and we've never really kissed." I could feel him grin. "I think I'll make you wait for the real thing . . . maybe for days . . . maybe for weeks."

I whimpered.

Gently, he kissed me one last time. He was teasing me. "I'll see you in the morning," he whispered.

In a flicker of color, I was sitting on my couch with Thora curled up in my lap. Leaning the back of my head against the couch, I sighed.

16

DO & DON'T

I shouldn't have been surprised when I found Marcus lounging outside the entrance to my building the following morning . . . shouldn't have been, but was. He leaned with his back against the building's worn bricks, staring up into a sky that was almost perfectly clear. The stark contrast of his very short, very dark hair and long, black eyelashes against the rich golden hues of his skin and eyes was even more striking in the early morning sunlight. As usual, he was impeccably dressed in slate-gray, tailored slacks and a black wool coat, and over it all, he wore confidence like he'd invented it. He embodied what almost every man wanted to be, and who almost every woman wanted to be with.

"Where's the photographer?" I asked as I exited the building.

His enthralling gaze locked onto me, and with the faintest shift in facial muscles, his jaw became more chiseled, his lower lip more luscious. He was so goddamn good at being irresistible, it was preposterous.

Slinking down several concrete steps, I closed the distance between us. I'd dressed carefully, picking out a snug, boat-neck, crimson sweater and my most flattering jeans paired with dark leather boots that nearly reached my knees. With my second-favorite coat, a hip-length, forest-green pea coat, my ensemble emphasized the few curves my slender body actually had.

From the way Marcus's eyes narrowed as I approached, I could tell my clothing choice was having the desired effect. I wanted him to crave me so badly that he'd forgo his ridiculous claim that nothing would happen between us for days, or even weeks. I wanted—no, I needed—his real, physical lips to press against mine, his hands to caress me in a moment of uncontrollable passion. I needed evidence that whatever was happening between us was real. I needed *something* in my life to feel real.

Mimicking his pose, I leaned against the brick wall beside him, our wool sleeves nearly touching.

"The way we look—it's just part of being Nejeret," Marcus said silkily.

I cocked my head, watching him watch me.

"We change more in the year after we manifest than in the rest of our long lives. And then we are forever altered . . . not human . . . *other*." He sounded slightly disgusted. *Does he not like being Nejeret?*

"I don't care," I said, hoping to dispel his suddenly glum mood. "If I were a photographer, I'd beg you to be my model." Admittedly, part of me was trying to provoke him, trying to get him to loosen his rigid control. I was hoping to reduce days or weeks to seconds or minutes.

Rotating abruptly, Marcus planted his hands on either side of me and blocked the outside world with his body. Somehow, not an inch of him was touching me. I wanted to growl in frustration.

"What will change about you, Little Ivanov?" he whispered. Apparently, he'd taken a liking to manipulating my grandfather's surname into his own pet name for me. The cage of flesh and bone was redundant; Marcus's penetrating gaze—again more gold than amber—pinned me in place better than any physical restraints possibly could. "Why can't I keep you just as you are?"

"Maybe I won't change," I said softly.

He chuckled, causing goose bumps to pebble my skin. "You've already started—your eyes have deviated so far from normal human coloring that you'll have to start wearing contacts soon."

"Is that what you do?" I asked. Usually his eyes were a rich, black-rimmed amber color, but today they paled to liquid gold. When he nodded, I said, "But not always."

The corner of his mouth quirked. "No, not always."

I reached my right hand up and traced the sharp contours around his eye, from brow to cheekbone. "I like you better like this . . . au naturel . . ."

He smirked, raising a single eyebrow.

"So, um . . . what were your big changes?" I asked, running my fingers along his jaw. I couldn't imagine a single piece of him different than it was at that moment.

"It's hard to describe . . . maybe I'll take you back sometime, let you decide," he said.

I was about to tell him that I might just peek into the past on my own, that maybe I didn't need him to guide me around the At, but he leaned down, inching his mouth past my lips, chin, jaw. Never touching. Speech evaded me. With his nose barely skimming the skin beneath my ear, he inhaled. The noise he made upon exhaling was rough and animalistic, both satisfied and laden with unfulfilled need. Again, I could feel the blood rushing to my belly and lower, moistening and swelling certain sensitive parts in preparation for what my body wanted . . . for what *I* wanted.

"Time to go, Lex," he said, his voice barely audible, and entwined the fingers of one hand with mine. He pulled me away from the wall, and hand in hand, we headed toward Denny Hall and the work that awaited us.

After hours of phone calls and emails arranging interviews with potential field school students, I finally left The Pit and stepped outside to stretch my legs. I found it slightly amusing that I'd done nothing remotely archaeological for the past two days—not since deciphering the riddle at the end of Senenmut's tablet and possibly discovering the secret temple entrance—and instead was helping Dominic arrange the field school logistics. Interviewing, selecting, and prepping the students who would be the rough equivalent of his slaves for several months was apparently too menial a task for Marcus.

"Help Dom," Marcus had told me as we'd arrived that morning.

"But . . . shouldn't I be using my deciphering skills? What happened to 'your job is to uncover Hatchepsut's many secrets, Ms. Larson'?" I'd asked him, doing a fair job of imitating his confident tone and complex accent.

He'd chuckled. "You've already advanced us greatly with the tablet. *Now* I need you to help Dominic."

"If you say so, *boss*," I'd teased before joining Dominic at the far end of the room. Marcus had disappeared from The Pit shortly thereafter and I hadn't seen him since.

Early in the afternoon, I left the warmth of Denny Hall, intending to take a walk despite the weeping sky. Once outside, I made it about twenty feet. Just as I was nearing the building's southwest corner, the sound of two very angry voices stopped me in my tracks—Marcus and Neffe.

Unabashedly, I slinked closer to the smooth, gray stone wall, inching toward the corner and the argument.

"You are unbelievable!" Neffe shouted in exasperation. "I

cast my lot with you . . . put my trust in you for how many years? And now—*now*—you want to risk it all for some . . . some . . ."

"As I said, *child*, this is none of your concern," Marcus growled.

"Child? Me? *She* is the child! Why her, huh? After so long, why her? At least tell me that!" Neffe yelled.

In a tone so cold I could almost feel the weak rain turning to icy needles, Marcus warned, "You forget yourself, girl."

"I forget *nothing*!" Neffe hissed right before she barreled around the corner . . . straight into me.

"Crap!" I exclaimed. Had I not just been caught eavesdropping on a woman who seemed to despise me and the man I desperately wanted to jump into bed with, Neffe's expression would have been funny. Instead, seeing her perfectly made-up face frozen in shock, seeing her artfully arranged curls out of place, made me cringe. She looked scary as hell.

A normal person would step back and attempt to compose themselves if they ran headlong into someone else. Neffe was far from normal. She leaned in close and whispered, "If you ruin this, I swear—"

Razor-sharp, lyrically beautiful syllables cut her off mid-threat. I had no idea what Marcus had just said, but Neffe's reaction—her features going slack as she stumbled backward—told me he hadn't been talking about fluffy bunnies and milkshakes. She rushed into the building. Or, at least, I think she rushed into the building—my attention had been completely hijacked by the thundercloud of a man approaching me.

"How much did you hear?" he asked, his voice hard.

"Um . . . I'm not sure. It didn't really make sense."

With a frigid laugh, Marcus said, "No, I don't imagine it did."

"Are you two . . . or, were you two, you know . . . involved?" I asked shakily. It *had* sounded like a lovers' spat, and I really wasn't interested in taking on an "other woman" role—not even for Marcus.

His responding laugh shed some of the chill, sounding almost tepid. "No, Lex, definitely not."

I felt a sudden rush of relief. "Oh."

"Neffe won't bother you again, but perhaps you should go home for the day," he suggested.

"Thank you, but, no. I don't know if she thinks this excavation belongs to her, or what, but I won't let her drive me away."

Marcus's lips pursed slightly, like he was trying not to smile. "Very well," he said. "Just don't leave too late. I'll pick you up at seven this evening. Don't forget . . ."

Unwilling to let him tease me into a pile of goo again, I stood up straighter. "I'm going to get back to work."

"I'll walk you up," Marcus said, leading the way to the door and holding it open.

"So . . . what's the plan for tonight? Where are we going?"

"It's a surprise."

For what seemed like the first time in my life, I was ready early. I'd been sitting in my usual kitchen chair, shaking the leather-clad foot of my crossed leg, when the knock sounded at the door. I bounced up and clacked across the hardwood floor in my knee-high boots.

I opened the door and offered a breathy "Hi."

Marcus looked more amazing than usual in an impeccably tailored, charcoal suit and a faintly striped, white dress shirt. The top two buttons were undone, making him look a little relaxed . . . and slightly less intimidating than usual. His golden, tiger eyes scanned me slowly from my toes up, narrowing to predatory slits by the time they reached my face.

"Mmm . . . Lex," he purred. "You look ravishing."

I blushed at the compliment. I was wearing the only remotely acceptable date dress I had. It was a form-fitting, burgundy silk sheath that reached just below mid-thigh. I'd left my hair down, its dark, loose waves reaching the bottom of my shoulder blades.

"You don't look too bad yourself," I mused, watching his eyes glitter at the understated compliment. Marcus, I was sure, was more used to women saying things like "Oh, you're so beautiful, do me right now," or "You're the most handsome man I've ever seen!" Sure, I was thinking both at the moment, but I figured his ego didn't need any additional boosting.

He sighed dramatically. "As much as I hate to say it, I must advise you to cover your . . . *delectable* outfit with a warm coat. It's *snowing*." He said "snowing" like it was a disgusting wad of gum stuck to the bottom of one of his Armani shoes.

"What? Really?" I asked, instantly giddy. Abandoning Marcus in the open doorway, I rushed to the living room window to peer out into the night. Outside of the pools of light coming from the streetlamps, large, fluffy flakes of snow were nearly invisible, making the glowing areas look like conical snow globes.

"Do you always get this excited about snow?" Marcus asked from directly behind me, slipping the sleeves of a black wool trench coat—my third-favorite coat—up my bare arms and over my shoulders.

"No," I said, laughing. "Only in this city—it *never* snows here!"

"I see," he said, reaching around me to fasten the top button of my coat. Unlike the previous time he'd tried to bundle me up, I didn't swat his hands away.

He moved closer, pressing the front of his suit against my

backside from shoulders to mid-thigh. His delicious, spicy scent —like a mixture of cinnamon and nutmeg—enveloped me, along with his arms. Even through the fabric of our clothing, his body felt like layers of powerful, hard-packed muscle. I let my arms dangle, feeling electrically alive with his immense strength wrapped so gently around me. It was like I was a kitten in the lethal clutches of a panther, and I'd never felt more safe.

His wrists lightly skimmed my breasts several times as he fitted the first black disk through its intended slit. With each descending button, an increasingly familiar fluttering amplified in my abdomen. It began like the usual butterflies that burst into life whenever I was around a man I was interested in, but by the third button, located a few inches below my navel, the butterflies had morphed into something larger and more substantial. By the fourth and final button, located directly over my pubic bone, I felt like I had a charm of hummingbirds buzzing around inside me, my whole body thrumming with their frenzied rhythm. Marcus lingered long enough on that lowest enclosure to assure me of his eventual intentions without seeming overtly improprietous. Oh, he definitely seemed improprietous . . . just not *overtly* so.

When he stepped away, my breathing was noticeably quickened and I'd forgotten the snow entirely. Somehow, putting on a heavy winter coat had been the single most erotic experience of my entire life. *Damn . . . I'm in* way *over my head.*

Marcus cleared his throat. "We should go."

I took a moment to compose myself before turning. "Certainly," I said with forced cheerfulness. I didn't want to go anywhere; I wanted to stand in that exact spot while the man before me removed everything I was wearing with the same agonizing attention he'd used to button my coat.

I accepted his outstretched arm, slipping my hand into the crook of his elbow, and we departed my apartment. We left behind most of the sexual tension. Unfortunately, Marcus created the stuff like an industrial fog machine.

"So what kind of car is this, anyway?" I asked as he helped me into the same low coupe he'd driven me home in days before. It was slate-gray, sleek, and a perfect match for its driver.

"An Aston Martin Vantage," Marcus told me, getting into the driver's side.

"Oh, wow," I said, trying not to touch anything unnecessarily. I was about as far as you could get from being a car person, but I wasn't completely clueless. "It's, um . . . really nice."

He laughed, a deep, throaty sound. "I agree. It's my favorite." I couldn't tell if he meant it was his favorite car in the world or his favorite among his own car collection. *He's not just an archaeologist,* I reminded myself. *He's Nejeret and a member of the Council of Seven . . .*

The short drive passed in aching, palpable silence. Though most of my mental power was focused on not jumping the driver, I did manage to spare a few thoughts about where we were going. We skirted the western edge of campus and its many apartment buildings until we reached Ravenna, the adorable neighborhood abutting the university's northern edge. Fraternities and sororities filled the first few blocks with their deceptively beautiful exteriors, slowly giving way to the ivy-covered porches and manicured gardens of a truly residential area. Some of the university's wealthier faculty members and scholars occupied the stately mixture of brick homes and craftsman bungalows.

"Unless there's an unmarked restaurant here, I'm assuming this is your house," I said as we pulled into a narrow gravel driveway. In Ravenna, the presence of any driveway was a sign of luxury, not that the house needed it.

I examined my new surroundings as I emerged from the car. The house was ash-gray with white trim and had an adorable porch spanning the entire front. The centered brick steps leading up to the porch were lined with clay pots brimming with purple, red, and white pansies.

"Welcome to my home away from home," Marcus said as he reached for my hand and led me into the house.

On the walk from entryway to dining room, I peered around at the warm furnishings and tasteful decorations. It was comfy, but nothing I would've expected from Marcus, décor-wise. In the dining room, a square, oak table was set for two with the extravagant complexity and perfection of an Edwardian steward. There were more pieces of silverware than I knew what to do with.

"Why, Marcus," I said, laughing. "Are you making me dinner?"

He chuckled as he held out the chair before the nearest place setting, waiting for me to sit. He sat at the spot on the adjacent side of the table and said, "Definitely not. My culinary repertoire is"—his lips widened to a self-effacing grin—"dated. Breakfast is my strong point." His grin turned wicked, knowing. "What do you prefer in your omelets, Little Ivanov?"

I, of course, blushed furiously at the implication that he would one day be making me breakfast . . . likely after I'd spent the night tangled with him in bed. I'd never been a big blusher, and it was becoming an irritating habit.

Like the flip of a switch, Marcus's face blanked and he explained, "My man, Carlisle, is preparing everything tonight. His food is as good as any I've ever eaten . . . which is saying something. Besides, I thought we'd need the privacy"—his lips quirked, but his face remained expressionless—"for your questions, of course."

I raised my eyebrows at his veiled presumptions. Before I could comment, a man—Carlisle—entered the room carrying two small plates. He definitely wasn't the seasoned, older gentleman I'd expected for someone Marcus regarded as such a talented chef. After Marcus introduced us, Carlisle set the plates in front of us and retreated through a door that I assumed led to the kitchen.

"Carlisle is different than I'd expected," I remarked. I had to admit, the man was exceptionally talented, at least from a presentation standpoint. He'd turned a salad into a minimalistic composition of edible art. Taking a small bite, I noted that the little bundle of color on my plate was at least as delicious as it was beautiful, with sliced heirloom beets, apple, and pickled fennel, all lightly glazed with a tangy vinaigrette.

Marcus chuckled as he chewed. "Don't let his appearance fool you."

"What do you . . . he's Nejeret?"

Marcus nodded.

"And he *serves* you?" I asked doubtfully. "Doesn't he need to do Nejeret things?"

With another chuckle, Marcus clarified, "He *works* for me, Lex. We are *born* Nejeret, like humans are born human or cats are born cats. It's not our occupation. Nejeret is what we are, but *we* decide what we do."

"Oh," I said, a little abashed at my assumption. "So Carlisle is a personal chef?"

Nodding, Marcus finished his bite. "In a way, yes. We all find something we excel at, something we enjoy more than anything else. Call it our . . ." He paused, thinking. "Our passion. For Carlisle, it's the culinary arts . . . and organizing—things, people, you name it, he can whip it into working shape."

I was quiet for a few minutes, contemplating Marcus's words while I finished my salad. "And you?" I finally asked, leaning in with interest. "What's *your* passion?"

Marcus waited for Carlisle to switch out our plates before answering. Instead of a mini salad, I now had two delicately flavored fish tacos, blessedly more substantial than the previous course. I started eating, not-so-patiently waiting for Marcus's response.

"I'm a fighter . . . a warrior," he eventually said. "Lex, you know I'm on the Council. Well, my role there is militaristic. I'm our people's general. It's what I'm good at . . . and what I enjoy." His serious tone implied something graver than his words alone suggested . . . something I had yet to grasp.

Slowly, I shook my head, feeling a crease appear between my eyebrows.

"Damn it, Lex," Marcus said with surprising ferocity, and I flinched imperceptibly. "You *must* understand this!" He held my eyes, his demanding stare boring into me. "Strategy and death, that's what I am. It's what I've been for millennia."

Is he trying to scare me off? He was a fool if he was, and Marcus was no fool. The embodiment of tranquility, I said, "That's very interesting."

"Interesting?" He looked baffled.

"Yeah, Marcus . . . interesting. You hurt people." *Like you hurt Mike*, I thought. "You kill people." I glanced down at my plate, considering how best to say what I felt. "I get it, and, um . . . I'm okay with it." At least I was fairly certain that I was. *How many battles has he fought? How many wars has he been a part of? Were they human wars, or other, unknown-to-me Nejeret wars? How much death has he caused?* "Exactly how old are you, anyway?"

Caught off guard by my question, Marcus's domineering presence evaporated.

While I waited for his response, I ate . . . everything. Carlisle was a genius. Marcus took his time, eating and watching me, not speaking.

"Okay," I said, realizing he wasn't going to answer. "So, Heru . . . Horus. Is the god named after you or you after him?" I asked, using a less direct tactic. It would at least give me an over-under. *Please say you're named after the god*, I thought. *Please tell me you're under five thousand years old.*

"Are you sure you want to know? The truth is the truth, but you cannot unknow it." After reading my silence as acquiescence, he looked into my eyes and answered my question. "I inspired the myths."

My stomach dropped. "Oh my God," I said, at a loss for real, meaningful words.

If he inspired the Heru myths, then he had to be *at least* five thousand years old, give or take a millennia or two. The world had changed so much in that time, civilizations had risen and fallen, thousands of wars had been fought. Had he been involved in most of them? All of them? How could a relationship between us ever work? How could I ever be enough for a man who'd walked the earth for more than five millennia? I shook my head back and forth, staring at him with eyes wide from both shock and awe. "You . . . you're . . . my God . . ."

"Carlisle!" Marcus called out. "Bring wine with the next course."

Numb, I looked down at the suddenly full plate before me. A plump filet of beef tempted me with its promised deliciousness. But . . . *Marcus is older than Alexander, older than the Egyptian civilization. How many people has he killed? How many women has he slept with? How many has he loved? How many children has he fathered? How many . . .*

Marcus said nothing else for a long time, other than telling Carlisle to leave the bottle while I worked through my questions. I demolished the steak and wine with an intensity usually reserved for kneading bread or beating the crap out of someone.

And suddenly, unexpectedly, I decided that it didn't matter. It didn't matter that my life so far had been a blink in comparison to his or that he might grow bored of me in another blink. I wouldn't let my self-doubt get in the way of knowing the man who'd inspired one of ancient Egypt's most beloved and fearsome gods. I wanted to know Heru. I wanted to know Marcus. I wanted to know *him*.

"Okay," I said. "What else?"

For a moment, I thought he might ignore me, staring as he

was at his empty plate. "Josh, Dominic, and Neffe are Nejeret. They know that you are too."

"Okay," I said quietly.

He held his breath for a moment. "And Neffe is my daughter." He sounded resolute in his defeat, like with that statement I would run for the hills, shunning him, his excavation, and our people as I fled.

I thought about Marcus's age and Neffe's status as a Nejerette, and a horrid, cold feeling seeped into my spine. "What's Neffe's full name, Marcus?"

"Neferure."

"Neferure," I repeated. "As in . . ."

"Hatchepsut's daughter, yes," he finished for me.

"Oh my God," I whispered. Neferure, the daughter of the famous female pharaoh, had disappeared from historical record as a young woman. Her mummy had never been found, though a tomb had been constructed for her. *Well, I guess that explains the mystery of the missing princess,* I thought.

Marcus refilled our wine glasses, emptying the bottle between us, but remained quiet.

"The others, are they your kids too?"

"Josh and Dominic?" When I nodded, he said, "No."

"Carlisle?" I asked.

"No. Carlisle is only a few centuries old, and I haven't fathered a child in over a thousand years," Marcus explained.

Our plates were replaced twice more and a second bottle of wine had been brought out while I processed the information.

Finally, Marcus said, "You must have other questions, Lex. Now is the time to ask them." It was the understatement of the century—I had other questions like stray dogs had fleas.

"What are your talents? Obviously you can cloak yourself, or whatever the correct terminology is, but do you have any others?" I asked, genuinely curious.

For the briefest moment, Marcus looked offended, but the

dark emotion quickly melted into amusement. "You should know, Lex, that asking a Nejeret about his talents is akin to asking a woman how many men she's bedded. So, how many men have you bedded?"

I waved his question away. "But Alexander didn't mind," I explained. "I . . . I don't need to know everything . . . it's okay. I'm sorry if that was rude." I looked down at my hands, which were resting on my lap, wondering if there was any way to hide my sudden shame.

"Lex," Marcus said, his tone like honey dripping onto white-hot coals. "I'm not offended. If I were weak or had no talents, I might be, but I am neither of those things. Just be mindful in the future of whom you ask that question, okay?"

After a weak nod, I raised my eyes to meet his.

He smiled genuinely. "My main talents are that I'm a manip-ulator, which includes the cloak you witnessed, and a tracker, so I can follow another's ba as it journeys through the At." His gaze turned sharp, and he said, "Quid pro quo, Little Ivanov . . . have you discovered any talents yet?"

"Yeah. I'm a finder, and to some degree, I'm a seer," I responded nonchalantly. Inside I was bubbling, eager for his approval.

For the first time, Marcus was visibly stunned. "I hope you realize how unusual it is for one of our kind to discover so many talents within a few weeks of manifesting."

"Sure, I guess," I said, when in reality, I hadn't realized it, even with Alexander's proud, grandfatherly reaction to my skills. Taking a sip from my recently refilled wine glass, I bolstered my nerve. I'd overstepped one huge boundary already, so I figured it wouldn't hurt to jump over a few more. "Alexander was able to test me for the finding talent. Can you do the same with me, for manipulating and tracking?"

Marcus looked into my eyes, his black-rimmed gold meeting my sienna, as he silently struggled with something.

He licked his lips before speaking, an unusual display of nerves. "For tracking, yes, but there's no need to test for manipulating."

"Why not? You don't think it's possible?" I asked, feeling slighted. "You know, I might surprise you."

"Evidently." He took a long, deep breath through his nose. "There's no need to test you for the manipulating talent because we already know you can do it."

"What?" I asked, my mouth open in surprise.

Patiently, he explained, "You lifted my cloak in the echo. Only a manipulator—someone who could alter the very fabric of the At—could achieve such a feat."

"Oh. Um . . . sorry for getting snippy," I apologized.

"Don't be. I like you when you're snippy." And with that simple phrase, the business side of our conversation evaporated.

"Do you live here alone?" I asked, glancing around at the un-Marcus-like decor.

"Carlisle stays here, as does Neffe," he replied cautiously, reminding me of his three-thousand-five-hundred-year-old daughter . . . who seemed to despise me.

"Is that normal for you and Neffe? Does she also live with you in Oxford?" Before he could answer, a thought occurred to me and I added, "Are you *really* a visiting professor from Oxford, or is that just a cover for being Nejeret?"

Smiling, Marcus said, "It's not just a cover. I enjoy it, though I rarely actually teach humans. There are quite a few Nejerets at Oxford, and I focus my attention on them . . . helping them get the degrees they need to do what they want to do in the human world. And thankfully, no, I don't usually cohabitate with my daughter. I love her dearly, but after millennia, we'd slaughter each other if we spent too much time together. We're only sharing this little house now because of its convenient location near campus. And truthfully, we almost never occupy it at the same time. My line has another, much larger compound on

Bainbridge Island. Neffe prefers it, and she finds the daily ferry rides calming."

I made a very unladylike snort, thinking Neffe could use a little more calming. Hesitantly, I asked, "Is there, well . . . is there a particular reason why she's so hostile toward me?"

Marcus's slow, silky smile was half the answer. "She's worried I won't be able to focus on my work."

"But it's just an excavation . . . how is that at all interesting when you lived through the time period you're uncovering?"

His raised eyebrows and pursed lips seemed to say, "Come on, Lex, I expected more from you. *Think* about it!"

Several puzzle pieces suddenly snapped into place: Nuin—father of Nejeret-kind—as Nun, Hatchepsut and Marcus, the mention of Set and Nuin on Senenmut's tablet, a Nejeret excavation surrounding a secret temple that had been hidden by someone manipulating the At, the Nothingness in the future At. I slapped my forehead. "Oh my God! How could I be so blind? This whole excavation is about the solstice, isn't it? It's about trying to stop the Nothingness from taking over the possible futures in the At. You think there's something in Senenmut's secret temple that can prevent it?"

Reading the subtle approval in Marcus's eyes, I thought back on the tablet I'd deciphered. Senenmut had written that Nun's power—creation—was locked away in the secret temple. "Marcus!" I exclaimed breathily. "Are you telling me that Nun's—Nuin's—power is a real thing . . . that it's really in there?"

He nodded, one slight, sharp movement.

"Oh, well that's just . . . just . . ."

"Crazy? Impossible? Terrifying?" Marcus offered. "Yes, I quite agree. And what makes it even worse is that we don't really know what this 'power' is. I *knew* him, Lex. I spent time with him, and he never seemed anything but the strongest of us all." He looked around, shaking his head with frustration, or possibly disbelief. "I've spent millennia wondering what his mysterious power might be, and"—he laughed bitterly—"I just don't know."

While I processed Marcus's revelations, Carlisle brought out dessert—two small plates and a tray containing a variety of delicate confections. He added a clear, dainty bottle of Tocay to the table for good measure. Marcus poured a few inches of the dessert wine into each of our glasses. It was the color of golden raisins.

I popped a bite-sized fruit tart—lemon custard contained in flaky, buttery crust and topped with a blueberry, raspberry, and strawberry slice—into my mouth. It was heavenly. Swallowing, I studied my wine glass, then looked at Marcus. "If I didn't know any better, I'd say you were trying to get me drunk for nefarious purposes, Professor Bahur," I said, purposely diverting our conversation to a lighter subject. After all of the delicious food and wine, I was hardly in the best state of mind to contemplate such serious matters as mysterious powers and the impending Nothingness.

Marcus licked a bit of chocolate filling from a tiny cream puff off the tip of his thumb. "But Ms. Larson, what would possibly make you think you know better?"

"Because you won't make it that easy," I said, completely unsure of my words.

"Perhaps," he purred. "And perhaps not." He leaned forward as if he might whisper some forbidden secret, and I suddenly felt his fingertips tracing the top of my boot. His thumb played tenderly with the back of my knee.

Closing my eyes, I shuddered involuntarily. His gentle touch sent bolts of electricity along my nerves. I couldn't believe the sensations he was eliciting simply by touching my knee. Deliberately, he inched his hand up the bare skin of my outer thigh, pausing halfway up. My heart felt like it had been relocated to my groin, and with each pump, like it might explode. My breaths became shorter, quicker, my lungs tightening every time I inhaled.

"But only if you beg," Marcus whispered. His words from when we'd been in the echo together resounded in my head. *By the time our courtship is through, you'll beg me to take you to bed.* "Will you do it now? So soon?" he asked. "So easily?"

My eyes shot open, then narrowed to slits. "You'll have to try harder, Marcus," I said softly.

His smile was roguish as he whispered, "You have no idea how much I wanted to hear you say that." He withdrew his hand.

I rearranged my skirt and crossed my legs, emphasizing my decision. It was possible that, one day, I would beg. But one day, I decided, so would he.

"It's late. I should get you home," Marcus said, taking another sip of the golden dessert wine before standing.

"Can we walk?" I asked, accepting his offered hand. I wanted to extend my time with him, and the cool, night air sounded refreshing.

"It's snowing!" he objected.

"Exactly."

"Can you walk that far in those boots . . . and in the snow?" he asked suspiciously. He led the way back to the front door, collecting my coat from a closet along the way.

"Seriously, Marcus, it's not that far. Besides, I was a ballet dancer growing up—I've done a lot more in *far* less comfortable shoes."

I could feel his eyes examining every inch of my body, devouring my every movement as I shrugged into my coat. "Ballet, hmmm?" One side of his mouth turned up in a sly grin. "That explains so much."

"Like what?"

"Wear these," he said, handing me some fur-lined, black leather gloves and wrapping the softest scarf I'd ever felt around my neck. "The way you walk, the way you move . . . just the way you are. You're graceful . . . it's *very* appealing."

"Hmm . . ." I mused. Finding out what attracted him to me gave me confidence, and equally important, power. Marcus had been using his enigmatic and unavoidable sex appeal to manipulate me since our first unofficial meeting at the bar. The scales were beginning to even out . . . at least a little.

Marcus pulled my hair out from the charcoal-gray scarf and arranged it on my shoulders.

"Whose are these?" I asked, holding up my gloved hands and touching the scarf.

"Neffe's," he informed me.

"Oh . . . maybe I shouldn't wear them." I began to pull the gloves off, but Marcus stopped me.

"She'll never notice they're gone. The girl has more clothing than a department store," he said irritably. *So says the guy with an Aston Martin and a suit for every day of the century.* "Shall we?" he said, opening the front door.

I took his proffered arm, and together, we stepped into the gently falling snow. We took a path through campus, letting the empty streets and brick buildings transport us to an earlier time period.

"You're very tall," I said, breaking the silence halfway through the midnight stroll.

"Correct."

I laughed softly. "No, I meant, how are you so tall? You were born thousands of years ago—you shouldn't be anywhere near as tall as you are."

"Also correct," he said, infuriating me . . . probably on purpose.

"So . . . ?"

He chuckled. "Before I manifested, I was around your height, maybe a bit taller. I *was* tall for the time and among my people. But one of the changes we all experience is the fulfillment of our physical potential. Had I grown up with ideal nutrition and care, I would have reached my current height, but that was impossible then. The changes—the cellular regeneration—it fixes all of that."

"Huh. So, I won't be as tall as you in a year, right?" I asked, seeking confirmation.

"You've grown up in a time and place that provided you with all of the nutrients you needed. So thankfully, no. I was never a big fan of the Amazon mythology. I doubt you'll even gain an inch."

"This is all so strange, you know? It's like a dream I could wake from any moment," I said, my voice hushed.

Marcus's arm tensed in mine. "Would you want to wake up?" He sounded a little sad.

I hugged his arm with both of mine and said, "Not anymore."

When Marcus abruptly stopped, I almost slipped on the slick brick path. With his free hand, he turned me to face him. His cool, leather-clad fingers cupped either side of my face, tilting it up so he could examine my features better in the light of a distant streetlamp. I could feel the faint kiss of each snowflake as it landed on my face.

"What are you, Alexandra Ivanov?" he breathed. "What are you and what are you doing to me?" As his deep, silky voice released each word into the starless night, he leaned closer. Our individual white puffs of breath slowly merged, becoming indistinguishable.

"But—"

"Shhh, Little Ivanov," he murmured, closing the distance between our mouths. His lips touched mine with the faintest possible pressure, brushing first one way, then the other. When I tried to deepen the kiss, he pulled back just enough to maintain the maddening softness.

I slipped my fingertips into his coat pockets, pulling his body closer to mine, and groaned in frustration. I wanted more. I *needed* more.

One of Marcus's arms dropped lower, his palm pressing into my lower back, and he grasped the nape of my neck with his other hand. He'd understood my desire . . . he'd complied. His burning lips worked furiously against mine, and his tongue delved into my mouth, exploring my own with a skill and sensuality I'd never before experienced.

Purposefully, I not-so-gently bit his lower lip, earning a growl. He responded by shifting his hand from my back to the swell of my hips and pulling me even closer to him.

His fervent mouth laid a trail of fire across my cheek and jaw, then down to the tender flesh of my neck. His lips became feather light, perfectly straddling the line between tingle and tickle. "Beg me," he whispered against my skin, making me shiver. "Beg me to take you, right here, right now."

I whimpered. I really, *really* wanted to.

"Beg me, Lex," he repeated, shifting his leg so it pressed against my coat's conveniently placed lowest button.

I moaned brazenly.

"Lex, beg me," he said roughly. I could hear in his voice that nothing less than my desperate pleading would make him take the next step. Oh, I was almost certain that he wanted me just as badly as I wanted him, but I was starting to understand him —this man who'd inspired millennia-old myths, who'd seen the Egyptian, Greek, and Roman civilizations rise and fall. For Marcus, sex was about more than desire; it was also about control.

In the heat of the moment, I almost acquiesced . . . I almost begged him to lift my skirt and take me in the shadows of the abandoned midnight campus. But I wasn't ready to give up the little piece of control I had left in my life.

"No," I whispered, the single word audibly hoarse. Embarrassingly, I was pretty much panting from the way his leg was manipulating that damn button.

With a throaty laugh, Marcus returned his attention to my lips, kissing them tenderly. "You will. Soon."

"I hope you're prepared to wait," I said with a victorious smile. In my head, I was wondering if I would even be able to hold out until the following day.

He kissed me one last time before moving his mouth to my ear and whispering, "However long, Little Ivanov, it will be worth the wait."

SHOW & TELL

"Are you planning to do this every morning?" I asked
Marcus, who currently had his arm draped over my
shoulders as we walked to Denny Hall. It was drizzling, as
usual, but I didn't care.

"Why?" Marcus murmured, glancing down at me.

I shrugged. "I'd just like to know what to expect. I don't like
being disappointed."

"And if I wasn't waiting outside your apartment building to
walk you to a classroom in which we would be spending the day
together, would you be disappointed?" His tone was too unconcerned, too disinterested—he really wanted to know the answer.

"Oh, I don't know . . . hmm . . ." I stopped walking in the
middle of the cement path and rose on tiptoes to plant an undeniably steamy kiss on his lips, unconcerned that other people
were passing around us. "Yes, Marcus," I said, resuming our
meandering pace. "I'd be *very* disappointed."

"Well, then *yes*, I plan to do this every morning," he replied.
"That is, every morning until we wake up together."

"I didn't know you were planning on staying in Seattle for
years," I teased.

"Years," he chortled, like it was the most ridiculous thing he'd ever heard. It *was* the most ridiculous thing *I'd* ever said. But still, he was a cocky bastard.

"Have you spoken to Alexander in the past few days?" I asked.

If Marcus was surprised by the drastic change of subject, he didn't show it. "No, why?"

"So he doesn't know that I know about you and the others?" *And he doesn't know we've been all over each other for the past two days?*

"No," Marcus said. There was something—many things to be sure—he wasn't telling me. But then, there was something I wasn't telling him.

"And the others on the team—they don't know that I know they're Nejeret, do they?"

"No."

"Will you do me a favor?" I asked tentatively.

He narrowed his eyes and looked at me askance. "That would depend on the favor." Oh no, Marcus wasn't on the verge of professing his undying love, to declare he'd do anything for the woman currently holding his attention.

"Just don't let anyone know that I know about you and the others until tomorrow . . . please," I added the last word for good measure. That was phase one of my plan.

I had just set a platter of oven-fried chicken on the table between a serving bowl of mashed potatoes and a gravy boat when Alexander knocked on the door. It was exactly eight o'clock. Pleasantly, I greeted my grandpa, and we headed to the table. Anxiety and excitement flooded my veins as I hurtled into phase two of my plan.

"I'd really like to be able to trust you, Alexander," I began, scooping mashed potatoes onto my plate.

My grandpa looked acceptably confused. "You can trust me," he said, meeting my eyes. I thought I could believe him, and I desperately wanted to.

Lately, my world had been one big tangle of lies and half-truths. Some people lied to protect me, like my parents and Grandma Suse, while others withheld valuable information because it was against "the rules" or for completely unknown reasons, like Marcus, Dr. Isa, and Genevieve. Alexander, too, hadn't given me the full truth, leaving out several important pieces of information, like "your new boss is Nejeret" and "I've had someone spying on you for the past six months." I'd never been one to surround myself with crowds of acquaintances, instead preferring to keep a few true friends—close confidants who I could trust completely. At the moment, I had a grand total of zero true friends. It was time to figure out who I could add to that category.

"I know about Marcus," I told Alexander after I'd finished dishing food onto my plate. At his quizzical head-cocking, I realized he might not know that name, so I clarified, "Heru." *What other names will I use if I end up living as long as Alexander and Marcus?*

Alexander set down his fork with a soft clink. "I see. And what exactly do you know about Heru?"

It was time for the trust test. "Tell me what I *should* know, and I'll tell you if I do." When his mouth pinched and his eyes narrowed, I said, "I'm sorry, Alexander, but I really need you to do this. I need to know I can trust at least one person in my out-of-control life." Desperation resounded in my voice.

Alexander took a deep breath and held it, studying me. Finally, he exhaled. "Heru has been my closest friend for over fifteen hundred years, which is why I asked him to keep an eye on you, just in case you manifested. It was a *very* large favor to ask of him, considering his position on the Council and the unlikelihood of you manifesting . . . but, he owed me. This is delicious, by the way," Alexander said, taking a bite of chicken. "Tastes just like Suse used to make for me, back when she could stand to be in my presence long enough to cook and share a meal."

"Thank you," I said, watching him. I decided he wasn't trying to change the subject, but was just being kind. I dug in, eating while he spoke.

"I'd been watching you for a couple years, since everyone manifests between age eighteen and twenty-five. You were nearing the end of the window, so I was fairly certain it wouldn't happen, but I called in a favor from Heru anyway. He only agreed because he could still plan the big excavation using your university as a hub." Alexander seemed to consider his next words carefully.

"I've been putting off telling you about him because I didn't want you to think being Nejerette was the only reason you were on the excavation. In the process of observing you, Heru—or Marcus, as you know him—discovered that you were a talented ancient linguist. He called me in November, asking my permission to invite you to join the excavation. I wasn't against it, but I let him know I didn't think it was the best idea, considering what could be happening on the solstice and that there would be so many Nejerets present. At that point, you hadn't shown any signs of manifesting, and like I've said before, you manifesting didn't show up in the possible futures at all. There weren't even any possible futures that showed us ever meeting or interacting." He shook his head, clearly confused by the big ol' blank spot in the future At surrounding my Nejerette status.

"Heru is, well, Heru," he said. "He's used to getting what he wants, and since I didn't prohibit it, he asked you to join his little team of Nejeret archaeologists. The last time I spoke with him—in mid-December—he let me know, much to my shock, that you were beginning to manifest. I was planning to return at the end of January. It should have been plenty of time. Unfortunately, your Nejerette traits developed more quickly than expected, and Suse called me in a panic when you started showing that you knew things you could only have learned from an echo, and, well . . ." After a thoughtful moment, he said, "I think that's the gist of it."

"And you two haven't spoken since?"

"Heru and I? No," Alexander said resolutely.

"Why not?"

Alexander glared at the wall. "That, my dear, is between Heru and me."

I pressed my lips together, thinking. Alexander was my grandpa—my blood. He'd helped me understand what I was, and he'd just told me far more than I'd already known about the months leading up to my first journey into the At. If I couldn't trust Alexander, then I couldn't trust anyone.

"Okay," I said simply.

"Okay?"

"Okay," I repeated.

"Okay," he agreed with a nod.

Minutes passed, and we ate in silence. I cleaned my plate and took seconds, while Alexander managed seconds *and* thirds. I wondered what would happen to a Nejeret who didn't receive adequate nutrition, but it was a question for another day.

When both of our plates were clean and we were sitting in contented silence, I decided it was time to initiate phase three of my plan. "There's something I want to show you," I declared. "Are you done?"

Alexander let out a blissful, "Yes."

"Great!" I exclaimed and grabbed his hand. "Hold on."

Taking longer than I was used to when visiting that particular echo, the usual swirl of colors surrounded us before the world resettled in the form of a night-darkened waiting room. Surprisingly, the fertility clinic didn't seem nearly as dark as it had the last time I'd visited this particular echo. Maybe my heightened Nejerette senses are finally kicking in, I considered.

"Would you care to explain our current setting, granddaughter?" Alexander asked curtly, and I wondered if I had yet again breeched some Nejeret social norm.

"We're in the fertility clinic Mom used. It's the night before I'm . . . er . . . conceived," I floundered. "Just watch."

There was a click, and the door separating the clinic from the stairs creaked open. A tall, slender man with pale skin and black hair entered the waiting room.

"And who is this?" Alexander asked, suddenly very curious.

"My father . . . or my biological father. Come on, let's wait for him in here," I said, leading Alexander to the laboratory, where he would be able get a good look at the man whose DNA made up half of mine. I had a theory, but I needed to see Alexander's reaction to know if it was correct.

"What makes you think that criminal is your biological father?"

"Just watch," I repeated.

The man entered the lab and turned on the lights. He headed for the pair of small freezers.

"Deus!" Alexander exclaimed as he stared in horror at the man. He leapt in front of me, gripping my upper arms tightly. "We must leave now, Alexandra." I could feel him attempting to pull me away from the At, but stubbornly, I held us there.

"What? Why?" I asked. In my surprise, I had inadvertently paused the echo.

The man—my father—was frozen with his arm reaching into one of the freezers.

Alexander, realizing I was holding us in the echo, stopped fighting. He studied the man, examining and memorizing every detail of his appearance as well as what he was doing.

"I believe you are right . . . he is your father. But Alexandra, you must release us so we can return to our bodies. It's imperative!" He urged, wrapping me in a tight hug.

I returned us immediately, and once again, we sat at the dinner table with our empty plates in front of us. I let go of Alexander's hand. "What—"

He cut me off. "I've never seen him in person, but we are all forced to memorize his likeness so we know to get as far away from him as possible if we cross his path. He is *very* dangerous." He breathed deeply. "The man in the echo was Set."

"Set?" I asked, astounded. "As in, the Council member who disappeared over three thousand years ago, Set?" I'd thought the man in the echo was Nejeret and had showed him to Alexander to receive confirmation, but Set? *That* I definitely hadn't expected.

"Yes," Alexander said.

"And he's my father?"

"So it would seem," he said carefully. "This discovery is extraordinarily important, but I'll just confuse you if I try to explain why. I should have paid more attention to—" Abruptly, he lifted his fist and brought it back down on the table, hard. "Damn it all to hell!"

I jumped, then leaned back in my chair. "Alexander?" I asked, my voice small. "What's going on?" I was suddenly very frightened. I'd never seen Alexander act like this. I'd never seen *anyone* act like this.

"I'll stay with you tonight and accompany you to work tomorrow morning. Heru and his team are the best in this regard and will help you understand."

"Understand what?" I asked.

"What it means to be of the line of Ivan *and* of the line of Set," he said somberly.

"But—"

"No, Alexandra. You must wait until tomorrow. And whatever you do, do *not* enter the At again tonight. For the sake of your life, please, *do not*."

18

PROPHECIES & PROTECTORS

In his complete and unexplainable paranoia, Alexander had forbidden me access to any mode of communication all night. That, in addition to his interspersed, ominous remarks, had reduced me to a bundle of frayed nerves. By the time we left my building, I was ready to rush into Marcus's arms like a blubbering schoolgirl . . . which was exactly what I did.

"Little Ivanov, what's wrong?" Marcus asked, wrapping his arms around me and resting his chin on top of my head. I knew the exact moment he noticed Alexander because his entire body stiffened. To my surprise, he didn't let go of me. Instead, he tightened his hold.

The complete oddness of dating—if that was what we were doing—a man more than twice as old as my ridiculously ancient grandpa hadn't gone unnoticed by me. Neither had the fact that they were exceptionally close friends. In my many anxious thoughts throughout the long night, I'd worried about the confrontation that was about to happen almost as much as I'd worried about whatever Alexander refused to tell me about Set . . . about my father . . . about *me*.

Hesitantly, Marcus released me until he was holding only my

hand, and then he bowed his head to Alexander. "For my failure, I submit myself to you," he stated, sounding grim and formal.

"I release you, and forgive you . . . not that I should," Alexander said.

"Thank you, my friend. I did what I could . . . I . . . he will never hurt her again," Marcus said.

Are they talking about me . . . and Mike?

"Yes, well, we have more important things to worry about now. Alexandra and I discovered something last night. It's something you and your team will want to hear," Alexander said.

Marcus studied us both before nodding. During the fifteen minute walk to Denny Hall, he maintained a strong, reassuring grip on my hand, even in the face of my grandpa's narrow-eyed glares. Alexander was *not* happy about our familiarity. I thought it was because of the whole ancient-mythical-god-meets-grand-daughter thing, but worried it was something else . . . something worse.

When we burst through the door to The Pit, the three Nejerets already in the room started. Alexander entering with us could only have meant one thing—I knew about the Nejerets. Usually that would've been good news, but from my grandpa's expression, everyone was aware that we were in a bad-news scenario.

"Meeting. Now," Marcus barked.

Josh and Dominic cleared artifacts and books off a long table in the center of the room, and we all settled around it like medieval knights planning for war.

"Welcome to the club," Dominic whispered with a smile. It was the friendliest expression I'd ever seen on his face, but he lost the smile at a glare from Marcus, who was sitting at the head of the table. I was seated to his right, with Alexander directly across from me and Josh by my side. Neffe and Dominic sat beside my grandpa.

"Alex has some important information. Heed his words." Marcus ordered, succinctly passing the ball to my unusually serious grandpa. Under the table, out of the view of the Nejerets, Marcus twined his fingers with mine.

"Last night, Alexandra took me into the At to show me the man she believed to be her biological father," Alexander began.

I could feel Marcus's eyes burning into the side of my face, and I turned my head to meet them.

"She was unfortunately correct. The man she believed to be her father is indeed her father. I am convinced." Alexander paused for a deep breath, suspense piling on the table like centuries of dust. "It's Set."

I would have paid more attention to the three Nejerets on my right who burst into simultaneous, horrified objections if I hadn't been staring into Marcus's black-rimmed, golden irises. His pupils dilated until only a hair-thin line of gold marred the unrelenting black, and under the table, his hand clenched mine painfully.

"Silence!" he ordered. "Alex, are you absolutely certain?"

Alexander nodded and explained what he'd witnessed in the At less than twelve hours earlier. It was decided that I would quickly show Marcus the echo to confirm Set's identity.

Again, it took me longer than usual to enter the echo, almost like the At had thickened and was more difficult to move through. But soon, both Marcus and I were in the echo of the clinic the night before I was conceived.

A string of incomprehensible syllables burst from Marcus's mouth as soon as he saw the man in the lab. I didn't need to be able to understand what he was saying to get the general idea. He was enraged, stalking around the echo of the lab and glaring at Set's frozen form. "I should have known . . . should have seen . . ." he growled, finally speaking in English.

"Marcus, how could you have known? What's the big deal?" I asked, desperately trying to reel him in.

Gently, he held my face between his hands and whispered, "I can see pieces of him in you, now . . . here"—he brushed the pads of his thumbs lightly over my eyelids—"and here." He let his thumbs rest on my high cheekbones. "I'm so sorry, Lex. I am so, unbelievably sorry." He kissed me tenderly, with so much sadness painted across his face that I would have done anything to lift his mood.

"Marcus—"

"Return us," he said gravely, and I did.

"It's true," Marcus confirmed, again sitting to my left at the table in The Pit.

To my complete and utter astonishment, Neffe's eyes were filled with sympathy . . . and she was looking at *me. Oh God . . . if Neffe feels bad for me, then this is worse than I ever could have imagined.*

"How can you be sure?" Dominic asked. "Just because you've seen him—"

"You, of all people, should know *that* is exactly the reason we know it's true," Marcus said, cutting Dominic off. His anger from the echo had changed from hot rage to icy fury, a far more terrifying version of the emotion, and the chill coated his words. "*She* took Alex into one of *Set's* echoes. *She* took me. Only one of *his* blood-line can ever break through his cloaks to catch a glimpse of him in the At. And how many times have you found him, Dom? Twice? Three times? And each of those after thousands of failed attempts. Lex has tried at least three times to see him and succeeded each time. She *is* the daughter of Set." Marcus shifted his intense gaze to Alexander, and his voice broke when he added, "And the great-granddaughter of Ivan." He closed his eyes and bowed his head.

This is so not good . . . Overwhelmed, frustrated, and really scared, I blurted, "Can somebody please explain what's going on? Why is being Set's daughter such a bad thing?"

"It's not all bad, sister," Dominic said. "His bloodline is very powerful."

I gaped at Dominic, absolutely dumbfounded. "I'm sorry, did you just call me *sister?*"

He nodded. "It would seem that we share a father, though I am not also of Ivan's line, so—"

An inhuman hissing—more serpentine than feline—interrupted his statement. It was coming from Neffe. "You will let my father explain!"

I looked back at Marcus in time to catch a heartbreaking play of emotions cross his face before his austere mask slid into place. Something about the development bothered him deeply, beyond whatever he was about to explain. For Marcus, it was personal. *Because he really cares about me? Or because of Set?*

Staring straight ahead, Marcus explained, "Set went rogue a few decades after Nuin's death. When Osiris—my father and the leader of the Council of Seven at the time—was murdered, the Council chose me as his successor over Set, who was also Nuin's grandson but was older. He was furious and power-hungry—probably already somewhat insane at that point, though he hid it well. The day the Council made that decision, Set declared war on all who opposed him, and the Nothingness first appeared. It spread throughout the At, either hiding or destroying the echoes of the distant future. We still don't know what the Nothingness is exactly, just that it is fast approaching and that, starting on the solstice, all future possibilities are hidden from us."

Marcus looked down at the table, then finally met my eyes. "When Nuin died, he sealed his power—what is known as the 'ankh-At'—in an impenetrable chest, which we kept in the Council's vault. Set managed to steal it and hide it from us, even in the At." The corner of his mouth turned down in the barest of frowns. "We don't know how they are connected for certain, but we do know there *is* a connection between the ankh-At, Set, and the Nothingness."

I started to ask, "How—" but Marcus cut me off with a sharp shake of his head.

He took a deep breath, then continued. "There is a prophecy —Nuin's prophecy—which tells of the coming of the only one who can save us. Senenmut's second tablet, the one you haven't seen, is the only record of the prophecy. Nuin uttered the words roughly four thousand years ago, just before he died, but that echo and all others relating to the prophecy were destroyed, as well as all physical record. Only one of Nuin's wives—the only Nejerette wife he ever took—Set, and I were present to hear Nuin make his prophecy, but"—Marcus shook his head—"something I never understood happened, and though I remember being present during the recitation of the prophecy, neither Set nor I could recall Nuin's words—his last words. We searched for his wife, the only other person who had heard it, but she'd vanished. For over a thousand years I searched for her, but I never did find her."

The ghost of a smile touched his lips. "Then, shortly after Neferure was born, a recently manifested Nejeret—Senenmut— came to me with a tablet he'd inscribed. He said the words had just come to him, and that he knew he had to write them down and bring it to me, but he didn't know why. I recognized the words inscribed on the tablet as soon as I laid eyes on them. It was as though a veil had been lifted from my memory. They were Nuin's final words—the prophecy."

And then Marcus started to recite.

She will be the girl-child of Set.
She will be the girl-child of Ivan.
She will acquire the ankh-At or
Mankind will wither under the weight of the Nothingness.
She will obey Set and destroy mankind or
She will defy Set and mankind will prevail.
She will decide and either mankind or Set will be destroyed.

I was shaking. "Obey Set? Defy him how? Make what decision? *Destroy* mankind?" I interrupted. "There must be other descendants of those two lines! This has to be about someone else! You don't even know if it's real!" I exclaimed, but Marcus just continued, shifting his hand so his fingers were again entwined with mine.

The girl-child of Set, the girl-child of Ivan will be born.

Neffe looked at her father sharply, opening her mouth to interject, but the glare Marcus shot her would have silenced even the toughest, bravest, dumbest person.

The girl-child of Set, the girl child of Ivan must be protected.
The girl-child's death will be the death of the world.

"No! This doesn't make any sense!" I declared, looking into the eyes of each of the people seated around the table. "It's wrong! If I die, I die . . . the world won't die with me!" I cried, my voice breaking.

Silently, a tear slid down Neffe's perfect cheek.

"Many have tried to open the chest containing the ankh-At, including Set, but none have succeeded, and since Set hid the chest away, none have been able to even find it . . . until now. The next verse seems to highlight your importance in accessing Nuin's power once we enter the temple," Marcus said coolly, ignoring my outburst.

I, Nuin, make inaccessible my power, the ankh-At.
The ankh-At must be accessed or the world will wither.
No person except for the girl-child shall be able to access the ankh-At.

"And finally," Marcus said, "he leaves a message for you, Lex."

Girl-child, know yourself and you shall know the gods.
Girl-child, trust yourself and you shall trust the gods.

So it ends, from start to finish,
as found in writing.

In the hush that fell over the room, I stood and backed away from the table. Five sets of pitying eyes were trained on me as traitorous tears poured down my cheeks.

Hollow, numb, and nauseated, I wanted to scream. "No . . . it's wrong!" My voice was weak, trembling. "It's a mistake! It's not me! I have a life . . . I have things I want to do, to discover. I have people . . . I have . . . this can't be about me. I'm just . . . I'm just Lex! I'm nobody special!"

Finally feeling the door handle behind me, I twisted it, opened the door, and fled the room. In the empty hallway, the sounds of my panicked flight resonated off the walls like bats flapping in a cavern. I heard footsteps behind me. I had to get away. I made it through the heavy metal door to the stairwell and down one flight of stairs before a body crashed into me from behind, catching me up in an unyielding embrace. I wanted to struggle, to fight my captor off and run away, but he was too strong.

"Calm down, Lex," Marcus whispered near my ear. "No matter what you believe, this is real. You must be protected. Set could come after you at any moment. You *cannot* go wandering around on your own." He paused, breathing heavily. "The future of humanity—of our people—depends on your safety."

No, no, no! I thought, but I had no choice but to comply. Marcus was too strong, and if he was right about Nuin's prophecy, about me . . . "Okay," I breathed under his constricting hold. With that single word, he released me.

Gasping, I staggered forward and rested my forehead against the wall while I caught my breath. I could feel myself shutting down mentally, blocking out everything—thoughts, emotions—so I didn't have to face what might be real.

"You're going home, and I'm coming with you," Marcus stated.

"Alexander?" I asked hollowly.

"Alex is going to visit Ivan. The others need to know the prophecy has been enacted. Come on," Marcus said, taking my elbow and pulling me away from the wall.

In a numb fog, I let Marcus guide me outside, settle me into his car, and safely and swiftly deliver me to my apartment. Thora greeted our entrance with the utmost seriousness, meowing somberly and rubbing against our legs. I would have stayed standing in the middle of the apartment, focusing on the normalcy of my cat's body twining around my ankles, if Marcus hadn't led me to the couch and forced me to sit. He made food, though I had no idea what, and I ate it—it tasted like cardboard. Lobster would have tasted like cardboard.

"I don't understand," I said, watching Marcus remove the empty plate from my lap and carry it to the sink. It was the first time I'd spoken since we left Denny Hall.

Marcus washed the plates and set them on the drying rack, the perfect image of domesticity. I would have smiled if I'd remembered how.

"I know," he said. He was standing in front of me, looking down with the fierce expression of a man who had once been believed to be a god. "How could you understand? You are so incredibly young . . . so innocent . . . so naïve." He sighed. "We've been working on circumventing Nuin's prophecy for thousands of years, but in the end, everything falls into the hands of a relative child. I still think there may be a way to nullify it altogether . . . but you don't need to worry about that right now. You need to rest."

On the very edge of my numb mind, faint traces of annoyance danced. True as they were, his words were also demeaning. He'd called me a child.

Regardless, I let him pull me up by my hands and walk me into my bedroom like I was his puppet to manipulate. He guided me to the bed, helped me lay down, then tucked the covers around me. He turned to leave.

"Wait," I whispered, surprised by the speed with which my hand struck out to grab his wrist. "Stay with me, please," I pleaded. The unquenchable longing coursing through my body permeated my voice.

Marcus's eyes widened, and he frowned. "Lex, I don't think—"

"Stay with me, Marcus. Just . . . just stay. Please," I said. The unreality of the world threatened to wash me away—I needed something to tether me to what was real. I needed Marcus.

Silently, he struggled for a few seconds before removing his shoes and belt and joining me between the sheets. With assured strength, he embraced me, wrapping an arm around my middle and pulling my body back against his. I was asleep within minutes.

"Lex," Marcus hissed, his arms tightening painfully around my ribs. "Wake up!"

I did, instantly. "Marcus," I whispered, "wha—"

"Shhh . . ." he breathed almost inaudibly. In a smooth, silent motion he had me out of bed and cradled in his arms like a small child. Setting me down on the cold bathroom tile, he whispered, "Stay in here." And then he was gone.

What? I slunk back out into the bedroom and cracked open the door, peeking into the living room. *What's going on?*

Two black-clad men entered the apartment and were struck solidly in the neck by small, silver knives before they'd taken more than a few steps—knives that Marcus had thrown.

Who walks around with knives hidden in their clothes? And where was he hiding them? And in the furthest reaches of my mind, I thought, *I just watched him kill two people.*

Two more knives replaced the originals in Marcus's hands as four more men rushed into my small living space. Like a comic book hero, Marcus leapt at the lead man, flawlessly flinging his left knife into the eye socket of the next intruder. He sliced the first man's neck cleanly while the second was still falling to the floor. The third and fourth men, one tall and one short, lunged in unison, dodging Marcus's blade as they danced gracefully around him. Marcus stood still as stone, simultaneously looking like he might never move again and like he might strike at any second. He was, I truly realized for the first time, a *very* dangerous man.

The shorter intruder feinted a kick, but Marcus remained still. The taller intruder pretended to slowly circle behind Marcus, attempting to divide his attention. With a cobra-like strike, Marcus slashed his remaining knife across the taller intruder's throat. The instant Marcus moved, the shorter intruder lunged, only to have Marcus wrap his arm around his neck and twist it until it snapped a fraction of a second later. Marcus fought with the grace of a dancer, making the whole minute-long fight beautifully macabre.

"You are hiding yourself from me in the future At," said a velvety, male voice. It had an aristocratic British accent. When the owner of the voice stepped into the glow of streetlamps streaming through the blinds, I nearly gasped. It was Set . . . my father. "You've been keeping secrets, cousin. I didn't know you had the talent to cloak future echoes."

"I don't," Marcus admitted. He stood in a relaxed position, looking about as harmless as a tiger.

"You *lie*," Set hissed. "I couldn't see this possibility . . . I couldn't see my daughter. You hid her!" He came momentarily unhinged, exposing the maniacal, power-maddened man he truly was.

The image of self-possession, Marcus replied, "I do not, and I did not. I'm disappointed in you, old friend. Six men? For me? And not one carrying a gun. I would have expected more from someone so . . . paranoid."

"You weren't supposed to be here!"

"And yet, here I am."

Set's countenance changed abruptly, becoming mild and pleasant. "Where is my daughter? In the bedroom, perhaps? Were you in there with her, helping the prophecy—*my* prophecy—along? I wouldn't have expected to find you wearing so—"

"Enough!" Marcus barked. "It's not *your* prophecy."

Set laughed joyously. "It's as much mine as it is yours. Or *hers*. Remember that, Heru." He stepped further into the apartment, looking around the living room with apt interest. "Does she know about you? I'm sure you'll tell her everything you can to paint me the evil monster, if you haven't already. But try not to omit your own morbid colors—red and black, blood and death—that's what you are, cousin. It's what you'll always be."

"I am what I've always been," Marcus said coldly. "And if you'd just accept what you are, we could be out of this mess. You can end this, cousin, just give up your god delusions."

"*They are not delusions!*" Set roared.

I cringed—there was no way the neighbors wouldn't call the cops after hearing that. I glanced at one of the bodies on the floor by Marcus, a puddle of blood slowly expanding around him, and swallowed a sudden rush of bile. *I will* not *throw up!* My breath started coming faster, and I choked on a sob. *Calm down, damn it!* But the bodies were still out there, as was Set. *What will he do to me if he gets through Marcus?*

Set turned and marched toward the front door. "I know you, cousin. You're still trying to find a way to sidestep the prophecy. It *will* happen. She *will* choose and, one way or another, she *will* obey. Now, I must depart before those pesky little law enforcers arrive, as I'm certain they will. I'm sure that once they leave, you can find some pleasant diversion to occupy your . . . minds . . . and to help *my* prophecy along. Goodnight, Heru." He raised his voice and called toward the bedroom, "Goodnight, Daughter!"

After Set had been gone for at least a minute, Marcus said, "You can come out, Lex. I know you watched . . . and listened."

He studied me closely as I emerged from the bedroom. I wasn't sure if he was waiting for me to run screaming, to faint, or to throw up, but he seemed surprised by what he saw.

"I've never seen a real dead person before," I said numbly. I stopped as my feet reached the nearest one and gazed down at him. It was the short man with his grossly twisted neck.

Marcus moved closer to me, but halted when I held up my hand. "No. I need a moment."

His hands—his lethal, sensual hands—rose in a momentary display of supplication before falling to his sides. Would I finally understand him, understand what he was, like he'd demanded on our date? Would I understand him, and toss him away in disgust?

When I finally spoke, my voice sounded hollow, as though the inside of my body had been carved into a living cavern. "Who were they? Did they have families? Wives? Children? Did you just destroy dozens of people's lives?" It was the wrong thing to say.

Moving more quickly than a regular human, Marcus rushed me from behind and forced me to my knees with him. My bones banged onto the wood floor, and I knew I would bruise, at least for a few hours.

"Wha—"

"Turn his head. Look at the back of his neck, Lex," Marcus ordered angrily.

"No! I don't want to touch him!" I tried to rise, but Marcus's strength far surpassed mine and his hold on my arms was absolute.

"Do it," he growled.

I started to shake, one of my tell-tale precursors to ugly, heaving sobs.

"Before the police arrive, preferably," Marcus urged, tightening his grip. "I doubt they'd take kindly to you messing with their crime scene."

My throat clenched involuntarily as I reached toward the man's unnaturally bent neck. I had to adjust his head to a more normal position in order to see the tattoo. In thick, black ink, the back of the man's neck was marked with the pointy-eared, forked-tailed Set-animal. I pulled away like I'd been burned. Mike . . . he'd had the same tattoo . . . in the same place. With a chilly wash of realization, I knew with absolute certainty that Set, my father, *had* been the man urging Mike to drug me . . . to rape me. *But, why?*

"These men were from Set's cult," Marcus explained, releasing me so I could stand. I didn't.

Marcus had just fought six men devoted to my psychopathic father, and defeated them easily. I had no idea what methods Set would use to ensure my obedience, but considering my stubbornness, I doubted the process would be pleasant. I did not doubt, however, that Set could find some way to force me to obey. I had no romantic delusions about my ability to withstand physical torture.

I leaned back against Marcus, finally noticing how entangled we were. My knees were between his, my socked feet between his ankles. He wrapped his arms around my middle, holding me tightly against him. Unexpectedly, a sob bubbled up from my chest, closely followed by another, and another. *I don't want this life. I don't want dead bodies in my home, or a psychotic father. I don't want to decide the fate of humanity.* Tears streamed down my face as tremors racked my body. *I can't do this. I'm not strong enough. I want things to go back to the way they were. I don't want this . . . I don't want this . . . I don't want this!*

"I know, Lex . . . I know," Marcus said, and I realized I'd been repeating my final thought aloud. He still held me, reminding me that I wasn't alone. "We have to go. We can't stay here . . . the police will be here soon."

I nodded, still sniffling and shaking, and Marcus helped me up to my feet. "Thora," I managed to mumble.

Miraculously, Marcus understood. Within minutes, we had my cat tucked into her plastic carrier, I'd thrown a few essential items into my messenger bag with my computer, and we were hustling down the stairwell. In the distance, sirens wailed. We were out the back door and disappearing down the street just as they pulled up to my building.

Am I a criminal now? Will they think I killed those men? Should I go to the police station? It wasn't like I'd done anything wrong, but Marcus . . . I couldn't tell the police that Marcus had killed six people to protect me from my insane, inhuman—as in, of a different species—father. *Should I call someone?* But there was no one I could call, not really. *Is this my life now?*

As we sped away, I watched the red and blue police lights fade into the distance in the side mirror. All I could think was, *only the guilty run.*

19

THERE & GONE

L ife, I was quickly learning, is very similar to war. The
latter, it has been said, is filled with years and years of
relentless boredom, routine, and monotony, interspersed with
brief moments of sheer terror. In the case of life, the boredom is
broken up by spikes of excitement morphing from joy to despair,
hatred to love, and from passion to disgust. I had been in the
boredom phase for the first twenty-four years of my life. I wasn't
anymore.

Unfortunately, life and war decided to converge and throw
everything they had at me all at once. I had more excitement
than I knew what to do with. My father was a psychotic, evil
megalomaniac, an ancient prophecy placed the fate of humans
and Nejerets in my hands, and I was falling for an ancient and
volatile god-inspiring man. The life I'd worked so hard for was
disintegrating all around me. I didn't think things could get any
worse.

"So . . . am I right in assuming this is the place you
mentioned at dinner the other night? Your line's, um,
compound?" I asked. My voice felt appropriately unused—

neither Marcus nor I had broken the thick silence since leaving my apartment, and we'd been in the car together for over two hours.

"Yes." Unlike mine, his voice was perfect—smooth as silk and deep as the ocean.

I watched classically constructed stone and brick buildings pass by my window. If I hadn't known better, I would have thought we'd entered a nearly abandoned, Ivy League college campus. "And we're here because . . . ?"

"You'll be staying here until we leave for the excavation."

"You want me to stay here for . . . for *four months?*" I spluttered. "I don't have a car . . . the university's two hours and a ferry ride away . . . how will I get there? How will I help with the excavation prep? And Jesus, Marcus . . . don't we need to talk to the police about what happened in my apartment?"

"I'll take care of it."

I made a rough sound, part snort, part laugh. "What about *my life?*"

Marcus stopped the car in the roundabout driveway of an enormous, chateau-like building constructed from pale gray stone. "This is your life now," he told me.

"And if I don't want it to be?" I asked through gritted teeth as I glared out the window. I was acting like a bratty teenager— something that had been happening way too often lately—but I didn't care. I figured the prophesied messiah of an entire species deserved a little leeway.

Marcus reached out and clenched my jaw in his hand, turning my face toward him. "Grow up, Lex. You don't have the luxury of an independent life anymore. *You* are our only chance. *You* are the future of our people. *You* are so much more than this childish façade." His touch softened, turning tender, but his eyes retained their fierce golden glow. "I've seen what's inside you . . . when you work, when you flirt, when you kiss . . . you're a woman with the ferocity and cunning of a lioness. We need you to be *that* woman . . . *that* Lex."

Wide-eyed, I stared at him.

"Now, you may be happy to hear we're moving The Pit to one of the meeting rooms in the main house. You'll still be an active participant in the excavation and its planning, but you won't have to dodge assassination and kidnapping attempts like you would on campus."

My eyes narrowed. "Assassination attempts? Who—"

"There is a small offshoot of our kind that believes Nuin's prophecy could be averted by ending your life."

"I guess they skipped the part of the prophecy where my death is the death of the world," I grumbled.

"So it would seem," he agreed. Marcus exited the car and joined me on the passenger side to help me out. "Come. Carlisle's staff will take your cat and bag up to your suite. There are some matters we must attend to before—" He seemed to catch himself.

"Before what?"

"Nothing," he said, dismissing my question. "It's unimportant." But I recognized the look in his eyes as he turned away—pain, sorrow. He was lying to me; whatever he was withholding was *very* important.

Swallowing my desperate urge to badger Marcus until he enlightened me, I walked beside him into the exquisite building. For once, he didn't hold my hand.

After we walked down a wide hallway, we entered an expansive, modernly furnished room in the back corner of the enormous home. The couches and chairs were all upholstered in various shades of black, gray, and white, and the square coffee table appeared to be a solid slab of polished granite. Black and white prints of people's faces and other, more sensual body parts decorated the walls, and there was an elaborate fireplace carved from some white-veined, black stone on the far wall. Carlisle, Dominic, Josh, and Neffe awaited us in the room, along with two pairs of unfamiliar men and women. All eight people rose and instantly fell to their knees with bowed heads. "I live to serve, Meswett. My life is yours, Meswett, may you live forever," they intoned as one.

Meswett . . . girl-child, I translated in my head. It was from Nuin's prophecy—*the girl-child of Set, the girl-child of Ivan.* Even Neffe was kneeling in submission. My mouth grew instantly parched, my cheeks heated. *What am I supposed to do?*

Marcus leaned in close to me and whispered, "I accept your life and service, Nejerets. May I prove worthy. Rise."

I repeated his words with numb clarity, sounding cold and resolute. All eight Nejerets rose when I commanded it, and watched me with guarded expressions. "Please, sit," I said upon realizing why they were still standing. They did, though they didn't stop staring at me. I shot a furious glare at Marcus. *He should have warned me!*

He smiled, a sad twist of his lips, and spoke to the group. "As you all know, the Meswett, Alexandra, will be staying here until we depart for Kemet," he said, using the ancient Egyptians' name for their homeland in lieu of the western world's modern label.

After all eight Nejeret nodded in acquiescence, Marcus faced me. "This group constitutes the core of your guard."

"My . . . guard?" I repeated, astonished. And then, when I didn't think my world could revert any further into an archaic, fantastical realm, Marcus explained each guardsman's role.

"Each Nejeret present is of my line, more or less. I trust them above all others, and they will protect you with their lives. On that, you have my word." Marcus held his hand out toward the man and woman seated furthest left in the room, on a charcoal suede couch. "Heimdall and Saga," he said, apparently telling me their names. Both were tall and slender with crystal-blue eyes and fair coloring. I would've wagered my trivial savings account balance that they were siblings, if not twins. "They are two of the most talented seers alive. At least one of them will be scouring your potential futures for danger at all times." He paused and divided a sharp, agitated look between them. "Which one of you should be doing right now. Why is neither of you in the At?"

Heimdall bowed his head in deference. "Apologies, Father . . . apologies, Meswett. We have been having difficulty—"

"—finding her future in the At," Saga said, finishing his explanation fluidly. "It's being hidden by someone . . . perhaps her father?"

"No," Marcus said thoughtfully. "It's not Set. She was hidden from him as well. Lex"—he looked at me—"you aren't, by any chance, concealing your future in the At, are you?"

Baffled, I shook my head. "Not that I know of." After a hesitant pause, I said, "But . . . is it possible to conceal myself without meaning to?"

"Damn it, Lex," Marcus growled, earning a chorus of hisses from the women and an admonishing "Heru!" from Dominic. Appeasing them, Marcus modified his statement, though his eyes sparkled with irritation. "*Meswett*, if anyone could do such a thing, I have no doubt it would be you. You might just bring Nuin back from the dead and save us all the trouble of dealing with his inconvenient prophecy." He took a deep breath.

"Heimdall and Saga will work with you on removing whatever kind of cloak you've created. Vali and Sandra," Marcus said, motioning toward a muscular man and svelte woman on the opposite side of the room from Heimdall and Saga, "will take turns heading your bodyguards. Don't let Sandra's size fool you—she's as vicious and clever a warrior as ever has lived."

"Thank you, Grandfather," the slight woman said. Pale, dark-haired, and pretty, she had a childlike quality to her features.

"When I'm away, Carlisle runs the entire Heru compound, including the guards covering the perimeter and grounds. If you intend to leave this building, you *must* let him know." Marcus stepped in front of me, holding my stubborn gaze with his own. "I mean it, Le—*Meswett*. You may leave the main house and explore the grounds and other buildings as you wish, but you *will* tell Carlisle first. Do you understand?"

"Yes, *Heru*," I said, and he flinched.

His eyes seemed to plead with me to understand . . . to forgive. "Neffe and Josh will remain in your vicinity whenever their excavation duties allow. Dominic has volunteered to be your chief bodyguard and attendant. He will keep a room adjoining yours and remain near you at all times. Anything you need, you can get through him."

It was utterly insane . . . all of it. I was overwhelmed with the sudden significance of my existence and my position among my people. I didn't ask for it. I didn't *want* it. Two weeks earlier, I had been Alexandra Larson, archaeologist, sperm donor baby, and possible lunatic. Two days earlier, I'd been Alexandra Larson Ivanov, archaeologist, Nejerette, and Marcus Bahur's potential love interest. But those had all been eclipsed by my current identity—Alexandra, Meswett, prophesied savior of the Nejerets. Who would I become next? *What* would I become?

"And you?" I asked the tall, striking man who held my heart in his deadly hand. "What's your role?"

"I am Heru," he stated simply, his three words squeezing my heart until it ruptured.

"Are you?" Overwhelming bitterness and disappointment colored my next words. "My apologies, I mistook you for someone else—for a *man*. I won't make the same mistake again, *Heru*." With each syllable, traces of my Marcus chipped away, revealing the arrogance and coldness—the blood and death—of Heru. I could no longer tell if my Marcus had ever really existed.

I cleared my throat, a vain attempt to shove away my heartbreak—my desire to cry—and turned away from him. Blinking away tears, I said, "I thank you all for your service, and I look forward to getting to know each of you better. Now, if it's not too much trouble, I'd like to rest for a few hours. It's been a long night."

Dominic earned my instant and immutable love when he rushed to my side, saying, "I'll show you to your suite, Meswett." He draped a comforting arm around my shoulders and hustled me from the room. I wasn't far enough away, or they didn't speak quietly enough, when the argument started.

"What the hell are you doing?" Neffe hissed.

"What must be done," came Marcus's reply.

"You are trying to go around it . . . to void it with your idiocy! You cannot stop it from happening! You cannot prevent her from being the Meswett by pretending!" she yelled. "It's too late!" The last was a shriek worthy of a banshee.

Marcus's cold voice responded like a whiplash, "Remember your place, Daughter!"

"And *you* remember *yours*, Father! She is already too far gone for what you're about to do. It won't work! And you—I've never seen you so . . . so . . . affected. You're in deeper than she is! For her sake, if not for yours, don't do this! Mark my words, *Heru*," Neffe said, spitting her father's name like a curse, "you will ruin us all if you persist with this charade."

Their argument continued, but Dominic and I were finally far enough away that only the muffled sounds of angry voices reached my ears. I reveled in the release from their harsh words. I didn't know why Marcus was behaving so coldly toward me, and I was hurt enough that, at the moment, I didn't want to find out.

Dominic tightened his hold. "Don't worry, sister. Everything will work out in the end. I know it."

An incessant, rhythmic vibration on the bedside table woke me from dreamless sleep. Dominic had settled me in an enormous, unfamiliar bed and given me some water and a small, orange pill, promising it would bring true rest rather than the fitful half-echoes that frequently plagued our kind's dreams.

I fumbled for my buzzing cell phone and tried several times to touch the screen's answer button before succeeding. "Hello?" I croaked. Coughing softly, I cleared my throat.

"Lex? Is it really you?"

I groaned. "Hi, Cara. Yes, it's me."

"Oh my God! I feel like I haven't talked to you in *forever!* How are you? Are you okay?" *Did she hear about the dead bodies in my apartment? Was it on the news?*

"I'm . . ." . . . *horrible, lost, brokenhearted, pissed off, scared, worried, overwhelmed.* "I'm fine. How are you?"

"Uh, good, I guess. Worried about you. What's been going on with you? I haven't been able to get ahold of you since the . . . since New Year's," Cara whined.

"Oh yeah, sorry." *I guess she hasn't heard about the dead men . . .* "With my mom here and then the quarter starting, it's just been kind of crazy," I explained, repeating the excuses I'd given her days ago and withholding pretty much everything else. *Great— I'm becoming just like my parents, Grandma Suse, Alexander, and Marcus . . .* Picturing Marcus, I squeezed my eyes shut, willing away my sudden, roiling despair.

"Okay, well . . . I'm glad you're okay."

"Thanks." I rolled over at the sound of a door opening and waved at Dominic. He was standing in the open doorway joining our two bedrooms. "I'm fine," I mouthed and he slipped back into his space, leaving the door ajar. Privacy, I noted, was quickly becoming a thing of the past. I really, *really* missed it.

"So, could we meet up for lunch or something . . . soon?" she asked. "I miss you, Lex."

No . . . but I wish we could. "Cara, it's only been two weeks. We've gone way longer than this without speaking or seeing each other before."

"Yeah, well, we've never gone so long after one of us almost died!" she screeched.

"I'm fine, I swear," I told her.

She scoffed. I was quickly wearing down her thin veneer of patience. "Come on, Lex. When can we get together? Annie's worried about you, too."

Frantically, I tried to think of an excuse. I could hardly tell her the truth—that I was being held captive for my own good because I was the subject of a millennia-old prophecy. "I don't know . . . it's complicated. I'm out of town for the excavation for a while."

"For how long?"

"A while," I repeated.

"Which is?"

"A while?" I offered, again.

"Nice try, sugar lips. What's going on, really?"

"I'm out of town for the excavation for a while."

"Is it a guy?" she asked. Sometimes, I could've sworn she was part bloodhound.

"Cara! I'm. Out. Of. Town."

"Geesh! Repeat much? So when are you back?" she asked.

"Honestly, I don't know. The director is kind of a dick," I explained. I heard Dominic snort loudly in his room, and I smiled.

"Oh . . . well, do you think it'd be possible to get my dress back?"

The dress I was almost date-raped in? Who wouldn't want that? "Sure. It's at the dry cleaner's." I hadn't had the balls to pick it up.

"Oh, which one?"

"College Suds on the Ave. It should be ready by now," I told her.

"Great! Thanks! I have a date next week with this totally hot younger guy. He's a personal trainer . . . a.k.a. *yummy*."

"That sounds awesome, Cara." I tried to sound enthusiastic, but the emotion refused to form to back my words.

"You sure you're okay?" Cara asked suspiciously.

"Yeah," I replied. "Just tired."

"Oh, well, I'll let you go then." *She's definitely getting pissed.*

"Okay, thanks."

"But you have to promise to call me soon and tell me everything that's going on in your crazy Egyptologist life!" *Maybe not too pissed . . .*

I laughed, "Okay, I promise."

"Good. Bye, Lex."

"Bye," I mumbled as the line disconnected. I stretched, wondering if I could fall back asleep. A knock at the door to the sitting room adjacent to what was now my bedroom ruined my plans. Marcus hadn't been joking when he'd said I would have my own suite. My cluster of rooms consisted of a sitting room, which also had the only door out to the second-floor hallway, a bedroom with an adjoining full bathroom, and a smaller bedroom—Dominic's room—with doors to both my bedroom and the sitting room. It was all very medieval.

I heard the door in the sitting room open and Dominic say, "I don't know if it's best to tell her about this right now."

A few seconds later, Sandra followed Neffe into my new, lavish bedroom. The curvaceous beauty waved the smaller, deadlier woman away. "She'll be fine with me, my dear, I promise. Though you may remain if the Meswett wishes." Neffe looked to me for my opinion. When I shook my head, my petite bodyguard left the room.

"My niece is diligent, but can be a bit overzealous at times,"

Neffe said as she approached my bedside. She shot an irritated glance at Dominic's open door, but dismissed it with a roll of her luminous, amber eyes. Darker, but so much like Marcus's. I sighed. *Not Marcus . . . Heru.*

"Please sit, Neffe. What is it?" I asked, propping myself up with pillows. I wasn't used to receiving guests in bed, but I considered it one of the issues accordant with being a messiah. It was annoying—I didn't want to be a messiah.

"It's my father," she said, pulling a burnt-orange suede armchair nearer to the bed. "He's being unreasonable—more so than usual—and you deserve to know what's going on."

"Okay, what's going on?"

"Don't get me wrong, it's not like I like you or anything," she told me bluntly.

I took a slow, deep breath. "Right, so . . . ?"

"But I do love my father, even if we tend to fight each other like scorpions, and he's done something that will hurt you both . . . and I really don't think it's necessary."

"Neffe, just tell me."

"He left," she explained, without explaining anything.

"Marcus left? Where? When? How long will he be gone?" I asked. *Was it me? Did I drive him away?* I'd only intended to give as much cold bitchiness as I got—and it had been coming off Marcus in waves—but I now feared I'd gone too far.

"Precisely," Neffe said, sounding so much like her father that my heart ached. "He's being an idiot, by the way. He's been focused on Nuin's prophecy for so long that the real world rose up and bit him in the ass without warning . . . except it wasn't the real world . . . it was you and his precious prophecy. I should have realized what was going on earlier! How was I so blind?"

"Neffe . . . you know I have absolutely no idea what you're talking about."

"I know!" she exclaimed. "I think that's why I find you so

infuriating. You weren't raised like us, and you don't know our customs, so why are *you* the Meswett?"

"Because Set decided to impregnate my mom?" I offered dryly.

"I suppose you are correct—it's not really your fault. I know," she said, looking sort of ashamed. "But my father, he's going to ruin everything."

Right, that explains so much. I was getting the impression that Nejeret minds worked quite a bit differently from that of regular Homo sapiens. I sighed, not doing a very good job of hiding my exasperation. "And how exactly is he going to 'ruin everything'?" I asked.

"You must understand him . . . his past. He's been trying to work around Nuin's prophecy for thousands of years. His vehemence that it could be avoided . . . it's started wars . . . it split the Council down the middle . . ."

"And he left *now*, because . . . ?" I urged.

"Because of the part of Nuin's prophecy that he left out when he was explaining it to you," Neffe said sadly. She started reciting.

Heru will look after the girl-child and
She will trust him.
Heru will set his heart on the girl-child and
She will trust him above all others.
Heru will make her his she-falcon and
She will bind herself to him.

"What does it mean by 'she-falcon'?" I asked.

"According to my father and everyone else who knew him, Nuin was quite the wordsmith. By 'she-falcon,' he was referring to Heru's match—the woman who would bring him to heel and force him to remember certain, deeper pleasures . . . not just sex, but companionship and love. In modern terms, I suppose it would be called his 'soul mate.' I was just a little girl, but I remember my father being furious when he read the prophecy on Senenmut's tablet for the first time." She shook her head, her dark-as-night waves brushing back and forth over her shoulders. "Perhaps it was because he loathed the idea of being bound to anyone. For so long he's been arrogant, cold, and frustrating." Her amber gaze sharpened. "But with you, he's so vibrantly alive, so completely engaged. It was unexpected. I'm sure you can understand why I was so upset the day you overheard our argument."

"Yes, I understand," I said, in truth, understanding very little. "And now he's gone away?"

Neffe looked down at her hands, which were clasped discreetly in her lap. "Yes, Meswett. He thought going away would dampen the feelings between the two of you, prevent the binding, and nullify Nuin's prophecy. Without one verse, how could the others be true?" She shrugged gracefully. "At least, that's how he's looking at it."

I turned away from her too-familiar eyes. I understood why he'd left—it was an ingenious plan. Rather, it would have been an ingenious plan if I hadn't already fallen for him. A silent tear leaked from the corner of my eye and trailed down my cheek.

"He wasn't trying to hurt you, Meswett, I know it!" Neffe proclaimed desperately. "My father didn't *want* to leave. He lov—"

"That's enough, Neffe," Dominic said, placing a hand on her shoulder. "She needs rest, not troublesome thoughts. Leave us."

Fury flashed across her face, but she responded, "Yes, *Milord*." To me she pleaded, "Don't forsake him. He already has his heart set on you, whether or not he realizes it." Swiftly, she swept out of the room.

"I feel like I'm being shredded into a million little pieces," I said to the ceiling. My voice was high and wobbly.

Dominic sat in the same chair in which Neffe had been sitting, directly beside the bed. "I know, Lex."

"How do I make it stop?"

"You don't," he said quietly, grasping my hand. I curled into a ball around his arm and began to cry.

PART II

The Heru Compound
Bainbridge Island, Washington

20

ENEMIES & FRIENDS

Sandwiched between Dominic and Josh at the Plaintiff's table in a courtroom on the eighth floor of the King County Courthouse, I waited anxiously for the jury to emerge and share their verdict. Marcus had been gone for nearly two months, and though every minute of every day had been filled with learning how to be the Meswett to my people, honing my Nejerette skills, preparing for the excavation, and attempting to get Mike an extended stay behind bars, I never stopped thinking about him . . . missing him . . . hating him . . . possibly even loving him.

It was the twelfth day of the trial, and I couldn't wait for it to be over, regardless of the verdict. The entire time, it had been impossible to ignore one particularly sharp gaze digging into the back of my skull. Set was sitting in the front row on Mike's side of the courtroom, and I refused to look at him. Not that it had been brought up during the trial, but *he*—my own biological father—had been the one who sent Mike the text ordering him to use the drugged lip balm. I consoled myself by thinking that Mike, who had entered the courtroom every day using a cane and walking with an obvious limp, wouldn't be at peak raping performance for a long time. Unfortunately, his miserable-looking physical state seemed to earn him sympathetic looks from jury members throughout the trial.

"You're positive that last witness is your friend?" Dominic asked, referring to Cara. I thought back on her testimony and scowled.

The defending lawyer, with the black lines of a conspicuous Set-animal peeking out above the back of his collar, had asked her, "And you're certain the Plaintiff was excited about the date with the Defendant?"

"Yes, very," Cara had responded. She'd refused to look in my direction.

"Did the Plaintiff talk about having sexual relations with the Defendant?"

"Yes, she was excited and nervous."

"Why was she nervous?"

"Because she hadn't been with anyone for a long time," Cara had explained helpfully. I'd never wanted to disappear more in my life—my parents, Jenny, and Grandma Suse were sitting less than a dozen feet behind me.

"Is there any additional reason she was nervous?"

Cara had bit her lip before answering. "Yes. She had a dream that the date ended in rape." The audience gasped. Her words had been like sharp, invisible daggers stabbing into my back. *Why would she ever volunteer that information? Why?* I'd wondered, feeling unbearably betrayed.

"And do you think it's possible that the Plaintiff wanted her disturbed fantasy to play out?"

"I don't . . . no! Nobody would want that!" Cara had seemed to suddenly wake up from the spell of disloyalty that had her in its thrall.

"The Plaintiff went to a great effort to entice the Defendant, did she not?" the attorney had asked.

Cara had sounded defeated when she'd replied, "Yes."

"What did she do to entice him?"

"She, um . . . she borrowed a dress from me, and our other friend helped her do her hair," Cara had answered.

"No further questions, Your Honor," Mike's lawyer had said, shooting me a smug grin as he'd returned to his seat.

I shook my head, dispelling the disturbing memory of Cara's testimony. "I used to think she was one of my best friends, but I don't know anymore," I told Dominic.

"Had you been considering confiding the truth of your nature to any humans, might I suggest avoiding her?" he whispered.

"Thanks for the tip," I whispered back. Some of the heightened Nejeret ears in the audience had heard us, and Set barked a laugh.

Dominic, Josh, and I shared an irritated look. Alexander had called in additional bodyguards from our familial line as soon as my deranged father appeared on the first day of the trial. Filled with slightly too large and undeniably "perfect" people, the courtroom looked like the setting for a cheesy, prime-time legal drama.

"Has anyone been able to get ahold of him?" I asked Dominic, referring to my absentee patron and the breaker of my heart.

Dominic shook his head and corners of his thin lips turned down. "He's ignoring us. At least before this farce started"—he waved his hand, indicating the courtroom—"we knew he was alive. Every day included a dozen emails, calls, and texts checking up on you. Are you sure you want to get involved with him? He's proving to be a bit obsessive."

"Dom . . ." I warned. Ever since Marcus abandoned me in his secure compound, my half-brother had been slipping in little criticisms of his behavior whenever possible. It had been two months and the reminders of Marcus's flaws were beyond getting old—they were mummified. But, Dominic was also the one who comforted me every time I broke down . . . which, I was ashamed to admit, happened on a daily basis. Sometimes it was about Marcus, sometimes it was about being the Meswett, and sometimes it was just about feeling completely and utterly lost in what had become of my life.

"Right, apologies," Dominic said, letting his French accent deepen and flashing his killer smile. "Just don't let him off too easy when he finally realizes his mistake and returns."

"Not a chance," I agreed.

Josh whispered, "Would you guys mind saving this private conversation for somewhere a little more *private?*" He hitched his head toward the rows of Nejerets with exceptional hearing packed into the courtroom. They were all sitting quietly, intently focused on something . . . on us.

Heightened senses, it turned out, was just another genetic trait coded into our Nejeret DNA. My hearing and sight had been improving noticeably, though neither had yet developed the sensitivity of a fully manifested Nejeret, and it was proving to be less of a perk than I'd expected. Falling asleep was not as easy as it used to be, especially not when I could hear almost everything people were saying or doing in the nearby rooms.

I opened my mouth to respond at the exact moment the door to the jury room opened, announcing the return of the jury. The twelve men and women filed back to their seats. None looked at me as the jury announced its verdict of "Not Guilty" to a half-outraged, half-ecstatic courtroom.

I bowed my head to hide an inappropriate smile. I'd been doing something I wasn't supposed to do: peering into the possible futures to find out when Marcus might return. After the first time I'd done it, Saga and Heimdall had explained to me that not only was it against Nejeret law to look into the future At without Council approval, it was also a major faux pas. With our heightened senses and ability to peek into the past, we had little enough privacy, and looking into someone's future uninvited was a serious invasion of that precious commodity. Heeding their advice, I had continued searching for Marcus's return but had stopped telling them about it. What I'd learned in the At was the cause for my smile. In all of the futures I viewed, losing the trial signaled Marcus's immediate return.

"Come on, Lex, let's get you out of here. The press is going to become more and more voracious the longer they have to wait," Dominic said.

How my date-rape case against Mike had piqued the interest of the mainstream media baffled me, but I suspected Set's meddlesome hands were pulling the strings. Anything to make my life harder seemed to tickle him pink. I *really* didn't like him.

"I'm *not* talking to the press," I told Dominic vehemently.

Josh had signaled for Sandra, Vali, and five of my largest bodyguards to meet me in the aisle. After quick words, Sandra hustled away, corralling several dozen more Nejeret bodyguards with her.

"Nobody wants to talk to the press," Dominic said, guiding me toward the aisle. "But *they* want to talk to you. We'll get you through the crowd as quickly as possible. The car's already waiting."

Sadly, I nodded, and then I turned to my waiting family.

"Oh sweetie, we're so sorry that—that cretin is getting away with—with what he did to you," my Mom said between sobs. I gave her a hug, unable to tell her that Nejeret justice would take over since the human version had failed, and Nejeret justice was far harsher.

"It's okay, Mom, I'm just glad it's over," I told her, and I meant it. Reliving the awful experience in the At was one thing, but recounting every detail, repeatedly, before a packed courtroom was another entirely. Besides, I was tired of all of the character-bashing and victim-blame.

My father wrapped his arms around us both. "Someday, Lelee, that little shit will pay for what he did."

I really didn't like the note of promise in his voice. "I know, Dad, someday he *will* pay. Just don't do anything stupid . . ."

. . . like personally getting revenge on your daughter's attempted rapist.

"Meswett," Dominic whispered, loud enough for me to hear, but too quiet for my parents' human ears to pick up. It was time to go.

"I'm really sorry Mom, Dad"—I peeked over their shoulders to offer a tight smile to Jenny and Grandma Suse—"but I absolutely have to get back to work. I'm lucky the director didn't kick me off the team for taking so much time with the trial," I said, squeezing them one last time.

"I'm proud of you for taking this so well, sweetie," my mom said tearfully. "You've had such a rough few months . . ." She was referring not only to her revelation about my parentage, but also to what Seattle police had deemed a "freak gang showdown" that had taken place in my apartment while I'd been out—I definitely didn't feel the need to correct *that* mistaken assumption—and, of course, the trial.

I pulled away, my motions hesitant. I really did miss my family. "I'll talk to you soon, okay," I promised.

"Of course, sweetie," my mom said, closely followed by my father's "We love you, Lex."

Turning away, I willed myself not to cry. As Dominic sprang to my side and six bodyguards encircled us, I wondered for the thousandth time how odd my entourage must've looked to my parents. How were they justifying the scene in their minds? They hadn't mentioned anything about it to me. Perhaps they thought the excavation director was a paranoid billionaire concerned with losing his ancient languages specialist? Or maybe they thought he was simply a billionaire who had become enamored with their little girl?

"Lex! I'm sorry, Lex!" Cara shouted from outside my cocoon of muscle. "Lex? Please say you'll forgive me!"

I ignored her and continued out of the courtroom, across a

wide, marble hallway to the elevators, and down to the waiting throng of reporters. *Stupid Set . . .*

To my immense relief, Sandra and dozens of Nejeret guards had managed to create a pathway from the courthouse door to my waiting car. I wouldn't have to speak into single microphone about the injustice of the verdict. I wouldn't have to listen politely as a reporter badgered me into an emotional reaction or shocking revelation. I wanted to crow with delight or possibly kiss the small woman. She was a tactical genius and a killer chess player—I'd yet to beat her, and we played almost every evening. It was my favorite part of Meswett training—learning how to think strategically via chess.

Dominic opened the black sedan's rear door, helped me into the backseat, and then took his own place in the front passenger seat. Neffe was already sitting in the backseat, grinning knowingly.

"Neffe, you know that's not the appropriate reaction to losing a trial, right?" I asked her suspiciously. The more I'd gotten to know her, the more I'd grown to appreciate her oddities . . . and she had many of them.

She raised a single, arched eyebrow and said, "He's back. He's waiting for you at the compound."

Relief flooded my body, and I finally felt like I could breathe. "It's about time."

21

HELLO & GOODBYE

The two-hour trip back to the Heru compound on Bainbridge Island had been torturous, as was the walk through the house and up the stairs to my suite, where I knew Marcus awaited me. Dominic was by my side as usual, while Neffe kept pace on my left. Vali led our silent procession, and Sandra brought up the rear. Even with all the people around me, I felt completely alone.

Vali pushed through the door to my sitting room, and I waited the usual thirty seconds for the all-clear, a four-toned whistle. It put a serious dent in my day when I had to wait for my guards to search and approve *every* room I intended to enter. I missed being a nobody. I missed being able to relax, drink wine, eat cheese and popcorn, and watch comic book movies with Cara and Annie. *Not like that'll ever happen again*, I thought bitterly.

Vali whistled. I took a deep breath, then another, and walked through the doorway.

Marcus stood at the center window on the opposite side of the room, looking down on the immaculately manicured grounds. He was a king surveying his realm, a god observing his creation. At the sight of him in his impeccable charcoal suit, my chest exploded with joy. He clashed with the sitting room's warm decor—soft greens, oranges, and creams accented the oak furniture and papered the walls. I loved my rooms, felt comfortable in them, and Marcus didn't seem to belong. I didn't like that.

"Leave us," he ordered quietly.

Vali looked to me, and at my nod, ushered everyone back out to the hallway . . . everyone except Dominic, who refused to leave.

Dominic had become extremely attached to me, as I'd become to him. His constant presence soothed me when little else would ease my perpetual heartache. He would tell me stories of his early childhood in the Loire Valley, of his many exciting adventures across Europe over the centuries, and what it was like to watch the world change around him while he remained, more or less, the same.

I touched his arm, saying, "Dom, I'll be fine. *He* won't hurt me."

Dominic peered down at me with sad eyes. "He already has," he said softly, though the glare he shot Marcus was diamond-hard.

Marcus watched Dominic leave, irritation tightening the skin around his eyes. "You two seem to have become quite close," he observed.

I marched between a pale-green sofa and a glass-topped coffee table straight toward Marcus and slapped his perfect face as hard as I could. "Ow!" I howled immediately after, shaking my stinging palm.

He didn't even have the decency to pretend it had hurt.

"You are such an asshole, *Heru!*" I screeched, hitting him in the chest with my open hands. "And an idiot!" I hit him again. "And a coward!" Again. "And a—"

He reached up and caught my wrists in an iron grip. "I've

been called many things, Little Ivanov, but never a coward. And I'd appreciate it if you wouldn't use *that* name."

"What name?" I spat. His hold on me was unbreakable. No matter how hard I tugged, I couldn't pull my wrists free.

"Heru," he said with disgust.

That caught me off guard, and I stopped struggling. "But it's your name. You made that very clear the last time I saw you." I didn't tell him that, to me, he would always be Marcus.

His tiger eyes flashed with anger. "I told you once before that I preferred for *you* to call me Marcus. That preference has not changed."

I raised my eyebrows. "What? So everyone else can call you by your real name, but I get stuck with your most recent pseudonym?"

His grip tightened, and he raked his eyes over my face, shoulders, and chest. The anger lighting his gaze transformed into heat of another kind—desire. I didn't know what he found so exciting, dressed as I was in a cream silk blouse and tailored black blazer. "I have no desire for everyone else to see me as I would have you see me."

"And that would be as what?" I fumed.

He answered without hesitation. "The first thing you think of upon waking and the last upon falling asleep. The man you call out to in times of unbearable pain and desperate pleasure, and the man who will do anything to keep you alive," he professed, his black-rimmed gold eyes burning through my anger.

"Oh," I said softly.

"I tried for two months, but I . . . I had to return," he said, sounding desperate. Marcus was evidently unused to being ruled by emotion. How had I sauntered into his world and ripped apart his rigid control and unfailing logic? What made *me* so special? I honestly didn't understand why I had such an effect on him. But, I was glad I did.

"Heru will set his heart on her," I said quietly, quoting Nuin's prophecy.

Marcus released me, bowing his head and turning away to face the window once more. "So they told you. I made them swear not to. Who disobeyed me?"

"Does it really matter . . . if they did it for me? The person responsible is sworn to *me* now, not just you," I reminded him, hoping to spare Neffe whatever punishment her father might want to dole out.

Grudgingly, Marcus said, "Fine. It is done."

I hesitated, then spoke, picking my words carefully. "I understand why you left, Marcus, I really do. It was a clever idea. Idiotic, but clever."

"What are you saying?" he asked, his voice rough. He continued to stare out the window.

"Just that I understand why you did it . . . why you tried to work around Nuin's prophecy. But you need to understand something." I glared at the back of his head. "You hurt me!" At my words, or maybe at the harsh anger laced through them, he bowed his head lower. "The way you spoke to me in front of the others," I continued, "and then you left and I . . . it felt like you took a part of me with you . . . an essential part."

Without warning, he turned and knelt before me.

I said nothing, unable to form any sounds when faced with such a proud man kneeling at my feet. I desperately wanted to touch him, and I had to consciously stop my hands from reaching out.

Holding my gaze with eyes blazing like golden suns, Marcus spoke. "I live to serve, Meswett. My life is yours, Meswett, may you live forever."

I inhaled sharply. I'd heard those words dozens of times from all my guards and had accepted every offering, but hearing them from Marcus disgusted me.

Falling to my knees, I stared at him—his eyes were liquid,

molten, and challenging. "I do *not* accept your service or your life, Nejeret. I refuse to be the Meswett to you."

He gazed at me, an unfathomable mixture of emotions altering his expression—widening his eyes, tensing his jaw, parting his lips. Heat and desire burned in his eyes, and I thought he might ravish me right then and there. I wanted him to. I wanted an excuse to experience every carnal thing he'd learned in his thousands of years, and beyond that, to be as close to him as possible, both physically and emotionally. Desperately, I wanted him to take the decision out of my hands. But Marcus was a master of control and desire . . . and antic-ipation.

He rose and moved away so quickly that I almost fell forward. When I regained my balance, he was once again staring out the window.

Holding my head high, I stood but didn't approach him. "Why return now?" I asked. *Why did losing the trial bring you back to me?*

Fists clenching, he explained, "That little piece of shit had his hands all over you . . . he had his tongue shoved in your mouth, his hand up your skirt. I can't stand the idea of him getting near you again. Just knowing he has those memories, that he can recall the feel of your most intimate parts at will, makes me want to rip out his throat." He paused, then added, "Which I may still do."

I approached him cautiously, hoping to avoid triggering the rage that boiled just beneath his surface. Gently touching his shoulder, I swallowed my pride and said, "Marcus . . . I'm glad you're back."

Marcus sighed, regaining his control. "As am I."

I let my hand slip down his arm and rest in the crook of his elbow. "Come on, there's a huge banquet downstairs to cele-brate the end of the trial. I think they're all just happy we don't have to go out in public en masse for a while. We really do draw the attention of the humans . . . they must think we're a pack of day-walking vampires or something . . ."

Shaking his head, Marcus almost smiled. "Yes, I'll come down to your little feast. I have news to share with everyone. Besides"—he gazed down at me in a way that made me want to melt into his arms—"I'll use any excuse to touch you for a few more minutes." He was studying me intently. "You've changed," he said, a note of sadness in his voice.

"Not where it matters," I told him softly, earning a faint smile.

Arms linked, we made our way downstairs, acquiring Vali and two more bodyguards along the way. When we entered the dining hall—what could easily have been classified as the most tasteful of ballrooms—the Nejerets filling it slowly fell into an eerie hush.

Marcus gazed around the room, his expression haughty. He was Heru, the falcon god, patriarch of one of the most powerful Nejeret familial lines. When he entered any room he commanded the attention of everyone present, and like a celestial body, his gravitational pull required everyone to remain aware of him hours later. Over a hundred pairs of Nejeret eyes were locked on him, riveted.

Releasing his arm, I stepped back a few paces.

"My family and friends, I greet you! And I thank you from the bottom of my heart"—he touched his right hand to his chest —"for taking such good care of the Meswett in my absence. I assure you, it is my intention to never leave her side again."

Echoing the emotion in my chest, an enthusiastic cheer roared throughout the room for a few moments. They all knew the prophecy, and they knew what it meant for Marcus to make such a claim.

"I have news to share with all of you. My time away was split

257

between Kemet and Firenze," he stated, earning hushed speculation from nearly everyone. That he'd spent time in Kemet, the ancient name for Egypt, indicated he'd been doing something related to the upcoming excavation. Firenze—Florence, Italy— I'd recently learned, was the auspicious location of Ivan's headquarters and therefore the international center for his familial line—for *my* ancestral line. *Was Marcus visiting Ivan?*

"I met with many officials in our ancient homeland," Marcus continued, "and am pleased to announce that the excavation has been moved up. We will depart on the twenty-second of March."

I glanced at Dominic and Neffe just in time to see them exchange a look of shared angst and frustration. Everything, from the field school participants to the housing and travel arrangements, was set up for a departure date roughly two months later than the one just announced. Marcus, who didn't care to dirty himself with such menial tasks, would no doubt leave the tireless job of logistical rearrangement to Dominic and Neffe. They were going to be a *joy* to work with for the next week.

"My second piece of news," Marcus said to the quieting crowd, "regards this most recent unpleasantness. The six remaining members of the Council of Seven have met to pass sentence on the Set-cult member, Mike Hernandez. As you can all imagine, Ivan was quite distraught about the human's actions toward the Meswett, his great-granddaughter. He felt the human justice system would likely fail our most important sister in her time of need. In anticipation of their failure, we found him guilty and sentenced him—"

"The tyranny of the Council and their false prophecy will end with the Meswett's death!" a man shouted from the back of the room.

Gasps erupted throughout the cavernous space as men and women turned to search the back of the dining hall for the speaker.

Marcus's body slammed into mine, knocking me to the marble floor, just as three explosive cracks sounded in quick succession. I lay on my back, something warm and wet spreading across my torso. *Is it blood? Am I bleeding?* Marcus's ashen face was inches from mine, his black pupils constricting until his eyes were more golden than I'd ever seen them.

"I've got him!" a woman shouted in the erupting cacophony. She sounded distant and hollow, like she was speaking through a tin can phone.

"Will you accept . . . my life now, Little Ivanov?" Marcus rasped through bloodstained lips. "I give it . . . to you . . . gladly." He rested his head on my shoulder and fell still.

"No!" I shrieked. "NO! I won't accept it! I don't want it! NO! Take it back!" I shouted, repeating variations of the same words over and over again. *Why didn't I tell him how I felt? Why am I so stubborn? I'm always so stupidly stubborn!*

Is he dying? Is he dead? NO!

Hands were on me, gentle and firm, and four pairs of concerned eyes stared down at me from familiar faces . . . alive faces. But none of them was the right face. Why wasn't Marcus looking at me the way they were? Why wasn't he looking at me at all? Why was he just lying on top of me, unmoving?

Dominic asked me something, but his words didn't make any sense. They were meaningless . . . everything was meaningless without *him*. *Why isn't he moving?*

At my blank stare, Dominic growled, "Was she hit? Neffe! Did any bullets hit her?!"

"I don't know! There's so much blood . . . I think it's all from my father. We need to move him," she replied. "Now!"

Marcus's body was rolled off mine and Neffe's precise hands began examining every inch of my body. I stared at Marcus's blood-smeared face, at his vacant eyes, while Neffe searched me for bullet holes that weren't there. She was focusing on the wrong body—she needed to be working on *him*—a realization that snapped me out of my shock.

I pushed her hands away. "I'm fine! Help him! HELP HIM! If he dies . . . If he dies . . ."

Somehow, Neffe read the desperation in my eyes, a desperation verging on insanity. Her resolve hardened, and she spun on her knees. "Vali! Pick him up—carefully!" she ordered, pressing a wad of cloth napkins against her father's punctured, bleeding chest while the huge, blond man lifted him off the floor.

I followed as they took Marcus's body to a nearby room, one I'd yet to explore. I was surprised to find a well-stocked home clinic. I might have wondered what the hell it was doing in the main house of the Heru compound, but all I could think about was Marcus. *He can't die. He's lived for thousands of years . . . he can't die!*

"Carlisle, find the three oldest Nejerets here and begin drawing their blood," Neffe ordered. "We need to transfuse."

"Take mine, please," I begged.

Quietly, Dominic explained, "His body needs stronger blood . . . more mature blood. The older the Nejeret, the more developed their regenerative abilities. I'm sorry, Lex, but you can't help him." Until Dominic spoke, I hadn't noticed his arm around my waist keeping me standing.

"Don't we need a doctor?" I asked, watching Neffe cut off her father's shirt.

"Neffe has more medical degrees than any other living being, Nejeret or otherwise. She's the best," Dominic informed me.

I watched Carlisle herd in his three chosen, ancient blood donors, one of which was Sandra. I hadn't known she was among the oldest of Marcus's line. "What about their blood types? What if they have the wrong kind?" I asked, panic and fear thick in my voice. "We might kill him!"

"Start the transfusion," Neffe told another Nejerette I didn't recognize. "He's AB positive—a universal receiver," she explained as she cut an impossibly deep incision down the center of Marcus's chest. Blood, thick and incredibly dark, welled up and over the edges of the incision, and not once did Marcus flinch.

Because Marcus was dead.

22

AGE & WISDOM

Neffe revived Marcus three times before he finally stabilized. One of the bullets had pierced his heart, the other two his left lung—it had taken her fifteen minutes to repair the wounds enough that his vital organs would mend themselves properly. Once she'd cracked his sternum open, I had to look away.

"He'll live, I'm positive," Neffe told me as she shamelessly peeled off her bloody clothes in the center of the home clinic. I hit Dominic's arm with the back of my hand for his equally shameless ogling.

"What? I've seen it all before . . . several times," he replied, his thin lips curling up into a sly, close-mouthed smile.

Neffe rolled her eyes and shrugged. "Sometimes I get lonely." She motioned for me to follow her into the attached bathroom, where she stepped into the shower. Marcus's blood was all over her, even in her hair. I, on the other hand, only had it on my shirt.

Shutting the door, I asked, "So, what happens now?" I hopped up and perched beside the sink on the white tile counter.

From beyond a fogged glass door, Neffe explained, "Now he regenerates. It could take him up to twenty-four hours to heal enough to regain consciousness. All of his body's energy is currently going toward repairing his vital organs. We'll move him up to his suite, and if you'd like, you can stay with him there. I just assumed that once he returned, the two of you would start sharing a bed . . ."

"Neffe . . . he's your dad!" I exclaimed. "How can you even think about that?"

She laughed, and the sound reverberated in the increasingly steamy, confined space. "You should ask around about his reputation." She paused. "Actually, maybe you shouldn't. Anyway, he'll look different for a while—noticeably thinner and possibly sickly or older. His body will be focused entirely on healing what it needs to survive, not on remaining young or robust," she explained. "But don't worry, he'll be the old Heru—Marcus—in no time. One of the perks of being so ridiculously ancient."

After my mini-coma, I'd lost weight and appeared sickly, and I'd only been out for a handful of hours. Marcus, on the other, had actually died . . . several times. *How different will he look?*

After listening to the shower run for a long moment, I asked the question that had been troubling me since I became certain of Marcus's recovery. "Neffe, what about the guy who shot him?"

"Ah, yes. He is, by his own stupid announcement, guilty of attempting to assassinate the Meswett *and* nearly murdering a member of the Council of Seven. We don't kill our kind easily, but he'll be executed . . . after he's interrogated, of course. We must discover the other traitors behind the attack. Do you approve?"

"Yes," I hissed, surprised by the venom the single word could contain. I wanted to tear the shooter apart with my bare hands.

"Wonderful," Neffe said, shutting off the water and stepping out of the shower. I tried to ignore her perfect, curvaceous body while she toweled off, but it wasn't easy. I frowned, knowing I would never have curves like hers.

Unhurried, Neffe slipped into a soft white robe. "Now, I have many things to do for the excavation if we truly are to leave next Friday. You should go upstairs and change, then go to my father. Sit with him. Your presence will bring him comfort."

I did as she suggested, winding my way through hallways, stairwells, and corridors, Vali leading and Sandra trailing behind me. I stopped by my own rooms just long enough to exchange my bloody silk blouse for a plain black T-shirt and to wipe the crusted blood off my stomach before heading to the suite next door—Marcus's suite. The two guards at the door instantly let me inside, offering supportive smiles.

Thanking them, I slipped through Marcus's sitting room without a single glance around me—I needed to see Marcus, not what he owned. But, holy crap, I was terrified. *Will I even recognize him?*

"How is he?" I asked Dominic, who was standing in the doorway between the sitting room and the bedroom.

"He's healing," my half-brother said, giving my shoulder a squeeze. "He's . . . did Neffe explain that he would look different for a while?"

"Yeah. Thanks, by the way, for everything you did. I probably would have collapsed if you hadn't kept me standing."

Dominic lifted his hand, and with gentle fingers, tilted my face up so he could see it better. "It was nothing." A faint smile softened his sharp, pale features. "Someday I'll tell you of our father. I'll tell you of his treatment of my mother and of me. Then, I think, you'll understand why I would do anything for you, the one prophesied to cause his destruction." *Or the world's.* Dominic's eyes shone with unshed tears, but before I could voice my doubts, he dropped his hand and said, "I'll leave you two to your happy reunion." He left me in the doorway and sat in the furthest armchair.

With an apprehensive sigh, I walked into Marcus's bedroom. It took me several breaths to fully comprehend that the middle-aged man lying under the covers in the enormous, four-poster bed was Marcus.

As I approached the bed, I took note of all the little changes to his face. His hair was salt and pepper instead of jet black, and there were faint wrinkles on his brow, at the corners of his eyes, and around his mouth. Some of the precision of his bone structure had been softened. I let out a shaky laugh, thinking it was so typical of Marcus that he would look like a dapper older gentleman instead of someone suffering from a chronic illness, which had been my body's reaction to using regeneration to heal.

I grasped his nearest hand, wrapping both of mine around it. "I will *never* accept your life in exchange for mine," I whispered vehemently. "Do you understand me, Marcus? I *refuse* to live in a world where you don't exist."

I laid my forehead on the bed between my arms. To an observer I probably looked like a woman deep in prayer. If I were, it was to a very old, very proud man, who had once been considered a god. There, lying in supplication to Marcus or Heru —whoever he was—I fell asleep. Thankfully, I didn't dream.

"Wake up, Little Ivanov," murmured a quiet, masculine voice. It was the sweetest sound I'd ever heard. The hand I'd been holding when I'd fallen asleep was gone from my grasp— instead his fingers were gently stroking my mess of mahogany hair. I smiled into the comforter before raising my head.

Though he was still the middle-aged version of himself, the sight that greeted me was breathtaking. Marcus was awake . . . smiling . . . alive.

"Come here," he said softly, patting the comforter on the opposite side of his body.

I yearned to cuddle with him, to feel his warm, solid body next to mine, but I shook my head. "I don't want to hurt you."

"Come here," he repeated, demanding.

I bit my lower lip in hesitation, but the yearning in his eyes won me over. I walked around the bed and carefully slid closer to him.

"I'll recover, Lex," he murmured, and a rush of relief filled my chest. Part of me hadn't believed that he really was okay until that moment.

I curled up against him, and voice wobbly, said, "I'm counting on it."

He sighed and tightened his arm around my waist.

I breathed in, eager for his spicy scent, but I was disappointed. "Why do you smell different? I mean, you don't smell *bad*, just . . . different."

His thumb began caressing my ribs as he spoke. "Well . . . as far as I could tell, I was shot in the heart. Am I correct?"

I nodded against his shoulder, attempting to keep my breathing steady. The skin he was stroking burned with a pleasant fire.

"Then I must have been given blood from another Nejeret—possibly several. Until my own blood cells replace it, I'll smell a little bit like each of them. You're developing heightened senses rapidly, Little Ivanov, if you could smell the difference. Did you know that in the most powerful of us, our sensation of touch is heightened as well? I am one of those . . . are you?" He chuckled as his thumb continued its gentle stroking.

"Marcus," I finally growled between uneven breaths. It just

so happened that all of my senses *had* been slowly becoming more sensitive, including touch.

"Ah . . . very well," Marcus said, ceasing his tactile ministrations. Lightly, he pressed his lips to my forehead, the hint of his stubble a pleasant scratchiness.

"Pardon the interruption, Meswett," Carlisle said from the doorway. "But Heru should really eat now that he's awake. It'll hasten his healing process. There's a tray of food for you as well in the sitting room," he said as he wheeled in a multi-level food cart heaped with a variety of dishes.

Sitting up, I gaped. "That's *all* for him?"

"Regeneration brings on a hearty appetite," was Carlisle's response. It made sense; I recalled my own increased appetite after waking from the coma.

"Why's my food out there?" I pointed my thumb over my shoulder toward the sitting room. "I'll eat in here with him."

"Meswett, I'm not sure you want to watch him eating just yet. After recovery from such a fatal injury, the first few meals can be . . . unpleasant," Carlisle warned. I tried to picture polite and proper Marcus shoving handfuls of food into his mouth, but couldn't.

I clenched my teeth and stated, "I'm staying."

"Lex . . ." Marcus said, his voice laden with warning.

"Marcus."

He sighed at my mulishness, and followed up with a groan as Carlisle rearranged pillows and propped him up into a sitting position. "If you let me eat my first five meals alone, I'll tell you the truth behind the Contendings of Heru and Set myth."

A glimpse into Marcus's past, a chance to see the man who'd inspired one of the most famous Egyptian myths, was almost too much to pass up . . . almost. "Three," I countered.

He narrowed his eyes. "Five."

"Four."

"Five."

I snorted in exasperation. "Fine, five meals. But you'd better let me know as soon as he finishes," I told Carlisle. I really didn't want to leave Marcus's side, but I didn't want to make him uncomfortable, either.

"Of course, Meswett," Carlisle said with a bow and minutely shaking shoulders. I was pretty sure he was laughing at me.

I left the bedroom and quickly ate my own food—lemon and herb-roasted chicken, mashed potatoes and gravy, and glazed heirloom carrots, paired with a small carafe of a light white wine —at a small, granite-topped dining table set in front of a picture window. Staring out at the tree-lined horizon, I sighed. *He really is okay.*

"Daydreaming?" Dominic asked in his smooth, French accent. I'd been so lost in thought, I hadn't heard him enter the room.

"Sort of," I said, turning to look at him. He was sitting in an oversized, steel-gray armchair on the opposite side of the room. His chin-length, nearly black hair was slicked back as usual, but it looked wet. I figured he'd taken a break from chaperoning me to get cleaned up. Last I'd seen him, his clothes had been stained with nearly as much blood as mine had been, but his current attire—black-on-black pinstriped suit pants and a midnight blue dress shirt—was immaculate. "You're very sneaky, you know."

Amusement touched his handsome features, curving his thin lips and making his coal-black eyes sparkle. "Precisely the reason your Marcus frequently employs me as a spy," he told me. "And I prefer the term 'stealthy.'"

"Alright . . . stealthy," I agreed.

For the first time, I had a chance to examine the décor in Marcus's personal space. His house in Ravenna had been deco-rated generically, reflecting none of his actual taste, but his sitting room screamed "MARCUS" as loudly as if he'd stamped his name on every chair, table, and trinket in bold, garish letters. Gray and black, the two colors that dominated his wardrobe, seemed to govern his home décor tastes as well. Every piece of furniture was sleek and elegant, somehow managing a level of subtle sensuality.

Strewn about the room on shelves and tables were little bits of bright blue, orange, red, and violet, all in the form of priceless antiques. And they weren't corner-shop-in-a-quaint-town antiques, but million-dollar, personal-invitation-to-a-silent-auction antiques. They were black market with a capital B.

"You can return, Meswett," Carlisle said, making me jump. I was glad I'd refrained from picking up any of the irreplaceable statuettes or vases—otherwise one might've been in pieces on the floor.

"Thank you." To Dominic, I said, "Maybe you should ask Neffe to come up and keep you company, if you plan to hang around."

My comment earned a bark of laughter from the bedroom.

"I think not," was Dominic's reply. "Go to him. Saga and Sandra will join me here soon enough."

I nodded, thanking him silently for releasing me from the guilt of abandoning him. I hurried into the bedroom and shut the door.

"I expected you to look different," I told Marcus as I crawled toward him on the bed.

Locked on me, his irises bled from gold to black in an instant before his eyes narrowed, and he groaned.

"What? What is it? Does something hurt?" I asked frantically, my hands fluttering around him.

He squeezed his eyes shut. "No, definitely not. Definitely, definitely not."

"Okay . . . will you tell me your tale now or do I have to actually wait until you've consumed all five of the agreed-upon meals?" I asked as I cuddled against him.

"After I rest," he said, pulling me closer.

With my head laid on his shoulder, I warned, "You'd better not back out of our deal." When he didn't respond, I looked up at his face. He was already asleep.

Sometime during the next morning, I woke and adjourned to my suite to brush my teeth and shower. When I returned to Marcus's bedroom, he was already awake and sitting up in bed. I gasped when I saw him.

"Marcus! You look ten years younger!" I exclaimed. He didn't look his usual late-twenties or early-thirties, but he was getting there.

"Do I?" he asked, unconcerned.

"Are you going to tell me about the myth now?" I settled in the large cushy chair at his bedside, dropping a leather tote stuffed with books and my laptop on the floor.

"No," he said, smiling mysteriously. "I must eat again, and then rest. I hope you don't mind." His eyes twinkled. He was toying with me, seeing how far he could push me.

We danced that little routine at least a dozen times over the next several days, me asking for the true story behind the myth, him denying me and then eating and falling asleep. I would sit at his bedside and watch him breathe, or I would read or hold quiet discussions with other Nejerets in his sitting room. It was simple and domestic—an easy routine to fall into.

On the fifth evening after the shooting, while I was sleeping in my own bed for once, my ba found its way into the At of its own accord.

I was watching five-year-old me play lackadaisically on the swings in my parents' backyard. A dark-haired and golden-skinned man dressed in a colorful, belted robe was approaching the little-girl version of me. Turning, he sat on the next swing over, and I inhaled sharply.

For a long moment, I thought the man was Marcus—he bore a striking resemblance in both coloring and bone structure, but there were subtle differences. Marcus was slightly shorter, making his musculature seem bulkier, and he carried himself differently, more like a modern man. The familiar stranger had an alien grace, his movements too smooth, too quick, too fluid. Who is he?

Five-year-old me giggled joyfully, like the tinkling of a dozen bells. "You're dressed funny!"

The man smiled back at her, but said nothing.

I knew I was in an echo of something that happened when I was a little girl, but I would have sworn the interaction I was watching never actually happened. I couldn't remember ever meeting this Marcus lookalike.

"I'm Alexandra," the little girl version of me announced, her swinging newly enthused.

The man who wasn't Marcus inclined his head and repeated in a foreign, ancient accent, "Alexandra." It sounded like "Ah-leek-saaandrah." He pressed the fingertips of his right hand to his chest and said, "Nuin."

"No way!" I exclaimed, my voice hushed. "No freaking way!" Nuin, the Great Father, the man who had started our species, visited me when I was a little girl. *It wasn't possible—he was supposed to be dead . . . like, thousands of years dead. Marcus saw him die.*

"Alexandra."

At hearing my name, I swiveled my head to the left and found another version of the same man standing only feet away. Shocked, I accosted him with words. "You're Nuin! But everyone thinks you're dead! Can you help us? Can you help me? The prophecy . . . your prophecy . . . *it must be wrong! Why did you choose me?"*

Nuin shook his head and said something incomprehensible, his words ancient and alien. I had to remind myself that, despite the resemblance, the man standing beside me was not Marcus. Nuin pointed to another part of the yard, a place young me couldn't see. A now-familiar and very pissed-off man was lurking behind a tree. It would have been comical, like a scene taken from an old Sunday morning cartoon, but for the identity of the man—Set.

"No! He might hurt her!" I exclaimed. I realized the statement was moronic as soon as I voiced it. I hadn't been hurt by Set as a child. In fact, I'd never even seen Set until the first time I entered the echo in the fertility clinic.

Nuin, ancient and radiating some otherworldly power, raised his hand to touch his first two fingers to my forehead. Instantly, I remembered . . . everything.

I remembered waking up to find Nuin sitting in a chair in the corner of my room, watching over me as I slept . . . protecting me.

I remembered catching sight of Nuin in the distance while I rounded the turn of a slide at the park.

I remembered repeating and practicing unfamiliar sounds as Nuin taught me his language during long, sleepless nights.

I remembered Nuin—dressed in modern clothes—sitting side-by-side in the bleachers with hundreds of parents and high school students at the homecoming game during my junior year of high school, watching me watch the game.

I remembered the feeling of Nuin's lips pressed gently against mine as tears dried on my cheeks. I'd been sixteen, horribly ashamed that a boy had yet to kiss me, and had just learned that my best friend was dating my crush.

I remembered smiling down at Nuin, who was clapping enthusiastically from the front row at my final ballet performance.

I remembered Nuin holding my hand during the entire fifteen-hour plane ride from Seattle to Minneapolis to Rome. It had been my first time flying internationally, and I'd been all alone.

Thousands of memories bombarded me, exploding into and merging with my own, redefining my identity. In a young, naïve way, I'd loved Nuin deeply . . . I probably always would. I wondered if Nuin had been the reason that so few boys, or as I grew older, men, had interested me. None could compare, in looks or substance, to the glorious enigma that was Nuin . . . my Nuin. Well, none until Marcus.

In his ancient language—a predecessor to Old Egyptian—I asked, "Will you take them away again?" Every time Nuin visited me, he left by sealing my memories, only to unseal them again on his next visit.

"No, my Alexandra," he said sadly, a tear sliding down his chiseled face.

"What's wrong?" Without hesitation, I closed the distance between us and wrapped my arms around his neck, standing on tiptoes to bury my face against his collar.

"I am weary. I have lived for too long in this body and my time is coming to an end," Nuin whispered into my hair. "I have done the best I could . . . kept you safe from he-who-would-use-you until my grandson, Heru, could take over. He will protect you now."

I pulled away and gazed into his color-changing eyes. Remotely, I realized that they resembled the swirling colors in the At. "Heru?" I asked, my mind taking longer than usual to register that he was talking about Marcus.

Nuin nodded solemnly. "I hope to see you once more, but I will miss you, my Alexandra," he remarked, kissing me lightly on the forehead.

"I don't understand," I admitted.

With a humorless laugh, he said, "I know. If everything works out properly, you will understand soon. Sooner than you'd like."

"You're going away . . . possibly forever," I stated, making sense of his forlorn looks and cryptic words. "That's why I get to keep my memories of you, isn't it?"

"Yes." Before I could wallow in the sorrow of losing him, a hidden constant in my life, he asked, "Do you love him?"

"Do I love him? Who?"

"Heru."

I frowned and glanced down at the grass. "I don't know . . . I think so, but I barely know him."

"Oh, my sweet Alexandra. Love isn't about knowing, love is about feeling."

I thought about his words and about Marcus. I knew I loved Nuin, but my feelings for Marcus were different—searingly raw. Nuin had been my comforting, wise companion while Marcus was rage and intelligence, strength and sex, all wrapped up in an enticing, black and golden package. In the past few months, Marcus had made me feel more alive than I'd ever felt before. I craved taking the next physical steps with him like a drug addict looking for a more powerful hit. Around Marcus, my emotions were unusually volatile—anger, lust, joy, and frustration all waiting eagerly for the chance to explode. So, do I love him?

"I admit, he is young and inconceivably proud and ruthless, but I believe time may temper his rougher qualities. I must pass your care into the hands of another, and there is no better man." Nuin looked around momentarily, as though he could hear something that I couldn't, and briefly smiled. *"I must leave you now, my Alexandra. I have a guest awaiting my attention."*

"But—"

"All will work out—I'm certain of that now." He looked around thoughtfully, and then his gaze sharpened, focusing on me. *"There are three things you must do to survive what's coming: no matter what, do not trust your father, never say his name in the At, and keep your younger sister nearby at all times."*

"Jenny?" I asked, surprised at the mention of my sister. "Why?"

"Not Jenny."

"But—"

"I will see you again," he promised and kissed me lightly before disappearing. It was the chaste kiss of a cherished friend. Other than a healthy scattering of gentle pecks and a few hotter, heavier kisses at my more needy moments, my relationship with Nuin had been mostly platonic. Nuin was, and would always be, my first love. But those feelings had been grossly eclipsed by more mature, ferocious versions . . . for Marcus.

I watched the past version of Nuin hover protectively around my five-year-old self for a while, wondering who Nuin could have possibly meant *by my "younger sister," if not Jenny. Eventually, regular, restful dreams replaced the echo.*

The following morning, I entered Marcus's bedroom feeling anxious and a little ill. I had no idea how to tell him about seeing Nuin in the At . . . about everything I now remembered. I started to laugh, a shrill, slightly hysterical sound as I approached Marcus. He was seated at a small, round ebony table by the window on the left side of his bed, watching me. He looked himself, if still a little thinner than usual. His face was carefully composed—expressionless—but there was a pitiless glint to his eyes. *Is he mad about something? Oh God . . . does he already know about my history with Nuin? How?*

Stopping behind the chair opposite him, I opened my mouth, then closed it again. How was I supposed to start? *With the truth,* I told myself. I took a deep breath, then said, "Marcus, I think—"

He held up his hand, stopping my words. "Sit, Lex." It wasn't a request.

Hands shaking, I pulled out the chair and sat. Seconds passed, and still, Marcus simply watched me. I cleared my throat, preparing to try again.

He beat me to it. "I owe you a story . . . *my* story." He looked away, focusing on something beyond the window pane. "*One* of my stories," he said, correcting himself. "It's not a happy tale, and I don't enjoy telling it, so you'll have to forgive my shortness."

His story . . . he's going to tell me about him and Set. That's what's putting him in such a bad mood. I almost laughed with relief, but managed to contain myself. I crossed my legs and waited, recalling what I knew of the myth.

The Contendings of Heru and Set is one of the more well-known Egyptian myths, and like many ancient stories, it sounds a little odd to modern ears. It chronicles the struggle between the two gods to decide who would be Osiris's successor and rule over all of Egypt and her deities. Since some of the gods favored Heru and some favored Set, the two were required to engage in a series of contests. At one point, Heru's mother, Aset—commonly known as Isis—attempted to aid Heru, but she backed out in the end, unwilling to hurt Set. This apparently enraged Heru, and he cut off her head. As punishment, Set gouged out one of Heru's eyes, though another goddess replaced it. The competition between the two gods finally came to a head when Set tricked Heru into having intercourse with him. He believed that if he could prove he'd planted his seed inside Heru, the other gods would see him as the dominant of the two and name him as Osiris's successor. Heru, however, was even more clever than the duplicitous Set. When Set ejaculated, Heru caught his semen and later fed it to him disguised as food. The other gods ruled in favor of Heru as the rightful king of Egypt and her deities, and he became a symbol of the divine right to rule.

Finally, Marcus began telling me *his* version of the myth—the true version. "My father, Osiris, ruled the Council of Seven for decades, from Nuin's death until his own," he said in his silk and stone voice. "He was the last son of Nuin, so the succession of his throne fell to the grandsons. Set and I were the two oldest and most powerful among them. Most of the Council thought I deserved to take over because my father had been the last ruler, but Set and one other member of the Council believed he was the rightful successor. He argued that he'd been the patriarch of his line for many years and knew how to lead. I argued that my father had groomed me for the position, and that because of his guidance, I already knew everything required of the position." Marcus gave a sad laugh and shook his head.

"The Council ruled in my favor—unlike in the myth, there were no trials or contests—and I became the rightful ruler of our people. However, two days after my coronation, Set approached me, claiming false friendship. He attacked me and gouged my eyes, rendering me blind for a time. He said he wanted me to die slowly, losing my life piece by piece until everything was taken from me, like it had been taken from him. I didn't understand this change in him—I still don't. Before my father's death, we'd been the closest of friends. Sometimes we'd even shared lovers." He watched me, searching for some sort of a reaction. Inside, I felt queasy; outside, I was granite.

"We became enemies unlike any the world had ever known. Aset—who was my sister, not my mother as the mythology claims—found us fighting, or rather, me dying slowly and blind. She launched herself at Set, distracting him long enough for her servants to carry me away. I'd loved her dearly for hundreds of years, and he killed her, not me—the myth has that wrong as well. I would never have hurt Aset. I wanted her beside me for eternity." He sighed, deep and heavy with longing.

"My eyes healed and I regained my sight the following day, and then I resumed leadership of the Netjer-At. I moved my court and the Council to Hierakonopolis and ruled for many peaceful centuries. The humans knew of us in those days, and considered us gods for our 'immortality' and abilities to know the past and to predict the future. They worshiped us, just as some still believe they should. And that is the truth behind the myth." Marcus fell silent, letting me digest his words.

"I'm sort of surprised by the accuracy of the myth—fighting over Osiris's throne, Aset dying, your eyes . . ." I said. "Thank you for telling me."

He nodded. "Sometimes the humans get it right, or mostly right. Though I never understood why they cast Aset as my mother," he pondered aloud. "Maybe it made her seem a more sympathetic character?"

"I have to tell you something," I blurted, before he distracted me with another tale or before I lost my nerve.

Marcus blinked several times, then raised a single, arched eyebrow.

I took a deep breath. "I, um . . . I'm pretty sure Nuin could actually travel through time, not just enter the At," I said with one eye squeezed shut and the other barely open to observe his reaction.

"Pray tell, Lex, what makes you think this?"

I started to babble. "Because he visited me when I was five years old . . . and then again . . . and again . . . thousands of times as I grew up. He blocked my memories every time he left so I couldn't recall anything about him when he wasn't there. Obviously a little bit slipped through . . . you know, with my obsession with ancient Egypt and all. He taught me his language, which is probably why I'm so good at deciphering ancient texts, and he used to keep me safe from Set when he would come after me . . . probably trying to kidnap me. I think Set wanted to raise me as his perfect little obedient daughter, and not have me grow up to be, well, this," I said, pointing to myself.

"Anyway, Nuin visited me in an echo while I was sleeping last night. He released his memory block, and now I remember everything." I fell silent, holding my breath for a long moment before releasing it. "Please, say something."

"This is bad," he said, his voice cold and level.

"I'm sorry," I whispered.

"No," he said. "It's not your fault that Nuin—" Abruptly, he laughed, a harsh, humorless sound. "Gods, Lex, you probably know him better than I do. He was never an easy man to know."

I frowned, wondering if we were really talking about the same man. The Nuin I knew was kind, wise, and gentle.

"What's bad," Marcus continued, "is what's locked in that temple. *Now* we know why Set wants the ankh-At so badly." His tiger eyes flashed with rage, or possibly fear. "He wants the power to travel through time."

"Oh my God," I whispered. "Then he could change anything."

23

MOTHER & CHILD

Breaking just about every traffic law possible, we sped along the freeway into Seattle and through her soggy streets. Jenny, as it turned out, wasn't my only younger sister. That title also belonged to none other than Genevieve's daughter, Kat, who was my half-sister through Set. Traffic was predictably heavy as we made our way toward Genevieve's shop, the Goddess's Blessing, further darkening Marcus's stormy mood. He wasn't happy that I hadn't told him about Nuin as soon as I woke up that morning.

"Why don't we just not go to Egypt?" I asked for the umpteenth time. He'd yet to grant me a response more verbose than a grunt and a shaking of his head. "If I don't go . . . I don't have to choose to obey or defy him. If 'nobody but the girl-child can access the ankh-At,' then Set needs *me* to be *there* to get to Nuin's time-travel power. So . . . just take me out of the equation!"

"That's exactly what the man who shot me said during his interrogation. 'Kill the Meswett—take her out of the equation.' I killed him for those words," Marcus told me, his tone cold.

"What? When did you see the prisoner? He's already been killed? By you?" I asked, aghast.

Snickering, Marcus mocked, "Poor Little Ivanov . . . still feeling squeamish about killing?"

"I wanted to be there," I said, gritting my teeth. *I watched you die.*

Marcus's hands tightened visibly on the steering wheel, blanching the skin covering his knuckles, but he said nothing. Neither of us spoke for the rest of the drive.

Marcus easily parallel parked the car in a spot I was sure would prove too small. With the engine still running, he unbuckled his seatbelt and lunged over the low center console, pressing me back against the passenger seat.

Hot and urgent, his lips found mine. He invaded my mouth with his tongue, and when I tried to reciprocate, he tightly gripped the back of my neck and growled. The kiss was about more than lust or passion, it was about possession—about Marcus's need to make me his. In that moment, with each thrust and caress of his tongue, he owned me . . . and I liked it.

"I'm beginning to understand the meaning behind 'she-falcon,'" Marcus whispered against my cheek. "Would you have killed the gunman yourself for what he did, Little Ivanov? Do you think you could have?"

Unable to form the words, I nodded, earning a rough, animalistic sound from the man pinning me against the seatback.

"Nuin's prophecy says nothing about his power being what destroys the world, either in the case of your death or your obedience to Set, only that his power—the ankh-At—must be accessed and that you obeying Set is the end of mankind," he said, finally answering my question. "Set's had enough time to acquire weapons of mass destruction, be they nuclear, biological, or other, and is psychotic enough to hold the world hostage with them. I guarantee that he will do something along those lines if you don't continue, especially since you are his only chance at accessing Nuin's power. We *must* proceed with the excavation, enter the hidden temple, access the ankh-At, and get it out of Set's reach. There are *no* other options."

With a huge, resigned breath, I nodded against his cheekbone, and only then did he pull away.

Marcus had turned off the car, exited, and was around to open my door in a matter seconds. He extended his hand and helped me out. "Shall we continue on our business, then?"

I laughed, adjusting my coat. "You are unbelievable. Just like that"—I snapped my fingers—"you're all business again."

He leaned into me, pressing me against the car, and whispered, "Not *all* business."

I could feel the hard length of him nudge against my hip. *Damn* . . . "You should really do something about that," I purred.

He chuckled, a low, rough sound, but didn't say anything.

After another moment of smoothing and adjusting clothing, we were making our way up the block to the magic shop, Marcus's arm latched possessively around my waist. His mood had lightened considerably.

Tinkling bells announced our entrance into Genevieve's magic shop, earning a "Be right out!" from the back room. While we waited, Marcus followed me from shelf to shelf, from table to table, as I examined the many curiosities. He stood far too close behind me, making my hands shake with the anticipation of his touch.

"Jittery, Little Ivanov?" he whispered, his lips almost touching my hair. He seemed to savor the affect his proximity had on me.

Turning my head, I looked up into the black-rimmed gold of his eyes from inches away. "I must just be *excited* about our business," I said pointedly. "Are you still *excited?*"

"When I'm around carmine-eyed temptresses," he said,

daring me to close the distance between our mouths, "I'm nearly *overcome* with excitement."

Just as I was leaning into him, Genevieve's husky voice intervened. "How can I help you?" she asked, pulling a dolly stacked high with boxes through the beaded curtain.

Marcus barely brushed his lips across mine before pulling away. "Ah, Gen, I thought we were closer than that," he said warmly. "'How can I help you?' is a little impersonal, is it not?"

Genevieve immediately let go of the cart, standing noticeably straighter. "Marcus!" she exclaimed, facing us with a joyous smile. "And . . . I'm sorry, but I don't recall your name," she added, letting the curve of her mouth turn faintly bitter as she addressed me.

"Lex," I supplied.

She nodded. "Welcome back to the Goddess's Blessing, Lex. I hope you found your answers. What brings you back so soon, Marcus? Why, it was just a few weeks ago that you were here!"

Eyes narrowed to slits, I studied Marcus. If he'd visited the shop a few weeks ago, that meant he'd been in town *before* he'd met up with me after the trial. How long had he been back? How long had he been avoiding me?

Marcus stared back, unblinking, though the corner of his mouth rose infinitesimally. Something about my reaction pleased him.

I took a deep, calming breath. "Are you going to explain what brings you back so soon, Marcus, or shall I?" I asked, only the tiniest edge of frustration apparent. If anything, the corner of his mouth rose further.

Genevieve, whose smile had returned to its original exuberance during our exchange, seemed to deflate when Marcus said, "No, my darling, I can take care of it." She looked like she'd just sunk her teeth into a furry, rotten lemon.

After quickly locking the shop's door, Marcus gave Genevieve a brief update on my entrance into and involvement with the

Nejerets over the past few months. "It's time, Gen, and we have to make sure Kat's safe. She's an easy target for Set," he told her. What he didn't say was that *I* needed to keep Kat close because Nuin had traveled through time to tell me so.

"But she's only a teenager! It's her senior year, she—" Genevieve started wringing her hands. "Why would he come after her? Why now?"

Marcus stepped closer to her and squeezed her upper arms. "Gen . . . he's unpredictable. You know that as well as anyone. He'll use any tool he can get his hands on, and he'll see Kat as a valuable tool because he knows I care about her, and about you."

She looked up at him with hope-filled eyes, and I had to turn away. Even though it was clear that she had feelings for Marcus, I didn't like watching anyone's hopes being dashed. I stared through the glass door at the outlines of the two bodyguards who'd positioned themselves outside, pitying Genevieve.

"Gather what things you both need from upstairs. There's a van out front that will take you to pick up Kat from school and then bring you both to my compound. Do you understand me, Gen? You must do this!" Marcus urged, his voice vehement.

While Genevieve packed the bare necessities for her daughter and herself, Marcus and I waited in the shop, standing close to each other but not talking. I was feeling too pensive for casual conversation. *Why didn't he come back to the Heru compound as soon as he was back in town? Why did he visit Genevieve?* Again, I wondered if there had ever been something more than friendship between Marcus and the sultry shop owner. Kat had denied it months ago, but a mother wouldn't tell her daughter about her sex life. *What if . . .*

As Marcus escorted Genevieve to the waiting van, I stayed with the guards. Marcus swiftly returned and walked me to his car, again offering silence and letting me lose myself in thought. It wasn't until we were on the ferry back to Bainbridge Island, standing on the starboard deck, that he broke the silence. He was behind me, his arms wrapped around me to insulate me from some of the chill carried by the brisk sea air. "Tell me your thoughts," he said, and I could feel his jaw move against the side of my head.

I didn't want to ask the one thing that kept dancing through my mind. I'd never been a jealous person, and I didn't like that my relationship with Marcus was bringing the ugly emotion out. But I also wasn't interested in a relationship based on lies or half-truths, so I asked, "Were you ever involved with her?"

"Jealous?"

What do you think? "Should I be?"

Marcus sighed and held me more tightly. "Gen and I have been involved since she discovered she was pregnant with Kat and Set left her. I looked out for them, assuring they had everything they needed. I told you all of this earlier," he reminded me.

"So . . . ?" *Was that a 'no'?*

"If I said yes? If I told you that Gen and I had shared a bed many years ago . . . or merely months ago, would it matter?"

I squeezed my eyes shut, willing myself not to cry over something as mundane as past lovers, because Marcus sure as hell had *plenty* of those.

Marcus seemed to read my mind, and though his words stung, his voice was soft. "And what about the hundreds—thousands—of women I've had over my long life? Do they matter? Do *they* change anything?"

Thousands? How can I possibly compete against thousands *of women?* Throat parched, I said, "No. I just . . ."

"Just what?" he persisted.

"I hate them," I said, feeling pathetic.

"And there it is." He sighed. "You are no virgin, correct?"

Discomfited, I replied, "Um . . . yeah. I mean, no . . . I'm not . . ."

"I don't care how many men you've . . . been with" —*Four . . . and not one was worth it*—"I'd gladly cut the balls off of each and every one," Marcus proclaimed with more vicious chill than I'd ever heard in his voice. "But no," he added, "I've never been intimate with Gen."

I felt like a thousand-pound dumbbell had been lifted off my chest. I hated thinking that Marcus had slept with her, and then brought me to her shop and flirted with me in front of her. It would have been remarkably cruel. He was serious and severe and very lethal, but I didn't think he was cruel.

"Thank you for telling me," I said into the wind. Below, the choppy gray-blue water of the Puget Sound undulated and foamed, and a little ways off, a seagull flapped and coasted, flapped and coasted, almost keeping up with the ferry. "Have you looked after all of Set's abandoned women and children so well?" I asked with genuine curiosity. *How many half-siblings do I have?*

"No," Marcus said, and the single word rang with finality. "We're getting close."

I let him take my hand and lead me back down a narrow staircase to our car. I didn't know why, but I'd just banged on a closed, dead-bolted, and padlocked door. Marcus really didn't want to tell me something, and I was getting the feeling it was extremely important. It was deal-breaker important. I needed to break through that door. I needed to find a battering ram.

24

STRUGGLE & SURVIVE

"You have to decide," Neffe told her father in her haughtiest voice. "Cancel the field school, or don't, but I need to know ASAP. I mean, we're leaving in the morning!"

Along with Marcus, Neffe, and me, Dominic, Vali, and Alexander had spent the past three hours in one of two conference rooms on the ground floor of the main house, discussing the varying details of the excavation. Undergrad field school students weren't scheduled to arrive until late May, and since it was too late to rearrange their course schedules with their various universities, Neffe and Dominic had arranged for several dozen Nejerets to join in their stead until they arrived. Now we just had to decide whether the field school students, who were humans, would be joining the excavation at all. Would they still be necessary? Would it be too risky to mix such a large group of Nejerets with humans? Having the small horde of Nejerets accompany me to the courthouse during the trial was one thing, but actually living together for months—the humans were bound to notice, and talk, and possibly do something unwise like try to expose the apparently superhuman humanoids living among them to the rest of the world.

"Cancel it," Marcus said. "The humans are no longer necessary. They'll just get in the way."

"Or," I interjected, "we could have them arrive as scheduled in May, but keep them in a separate 'field school camp,' away from the Nejerets." I snorted softly. "We all know Deir el-Bahri is plenty large enough for two camps, and it's not fair to the students to cancel the field school . . . they're counting on this."

Under the table, Marcus's fingers cinched on my thigh. "Do as the Meswett wishes," he told Neffe.

"Finally!" Neffe exclaimed. "At least *someone* can make a reasonable decision. Thanks, Lex."

Neffe, you're so not helping me, I thought, momentarily squeezing my eyes shut. "So are we finished then?" I asked, and again, Marcus tightened his grip on my leg. Since I was the Meswett and Marcus was the head of his familial line and the leader of the excavation to locate the ankh-At—Nuin's time-travel power—we both were consulted regarding all important decisions. Marcus, who was used to being the sole decision-maker, developed acute stick-up-ass every time I influenced said decisions, even by doing something as small as attempting to end a meeting. Apparently he didn't like to share control.

"For the most part," Neffe said. "We have our Nejeret workers, field school students, transportation and accommodation arrangements, permits, and bribes taken care of. We may have to do some last-minute rearranging of personnel, but don't worry, I'm sure Dom and I can take care of that—like we've done with everything else," she said pointedly.

"Which you've both done very well," I said with a warm smile.

Before I could speak, Marcus said, "Yes. Now, I would appreciate it if you could all leave me with the Meswett to discuss a few final matters."

Chairs rolled on hardwood, people mumbled, and in a matter of seconds, everyone had left.

"What?" I asked wearily. We hadn't had much time alone since Marcus's return, and I had the anxious feeling that we weren't about to have a sweet little tête-à-tête followed by a kiss and cuddle.

"You undermined my command," he said softly, dangerously. "Don't do it again."

I straightened, holding my head high. "These people swore their lives to me—at your direction, I might add. What'd you expect, Marcus? Would you prefer they didn't respect me . . . didn't listen to me? Now that you've returned, am I just supposed to step back like a good little Nejerette and let almighty Heru take charge?"

Marcus's lips spread into a razor-sharp grin and he said, "Most women enjoy it when I take charge."

Suddenly exhausted, I ran my fingers through my loose hair and sighed. "I can't do this right now, Marcus. I just can't." There was too much on my mind—too much worry about Set and the Nothingness and ankh-At—to waste energy on a power struggle with Marcus.

I rose and left the room, not stopping until I reached my bedroom. Needing to be alone, I locked the doors and started pacing. I felt physically ill, and it infuriated me that an unresolved dispute with Marcus could affect me so. *Is this what a relationship with him will be like, just one long power struggle? Why did I think I could handle him?* We were too dissimilar, products of vastly different times. Could I live with being what he apparently wanted me to be—his possession?

Absolutely not.

Could I live without him?

Yeah, but I really don't want to.

A heavy, domineering knock rattled the door from the sitting room, and I heard the handle jiggle. "Lex," Marcus called through the door. "Let me in."

I approached the door and rested my hand against its

surface, as though I could feel Marcus's frustration through the solid oak.

"Lex, I'm . . . damn it!" His final word was emphasized with hard slap against the door. After minutes of silence, I decided he'd left.

I retreated to the oversized bed and curled into a ball in the center . . . and cried. I was sick of crying, sick of feeling weak. How many tears had Marcus coaxed from my tired eyes? How had he taken control of my emotions so completely? Why had I let him? I didn't want to give him up, but I couldn't be with him if he didn't accept me as his equal. I couldn't change him—make him less—and I didn't want to, but maybe I could change how he saw *me*.

Curled up on the bed, I resolved to show Marcus that I truly was his she-falcon, a woman worthy of his respect as well as his emotional and physical attentions. With my heart settled, my head was free to spiral out of control. I'd been wrong in thinking Marcus was the cause of my current distress. He was only the tip of the iceberg.

Who am I? Alice and Joe Larson's little girl? Daughter of Set? Great-granddaughter of Ivan, leader of the Nejeret? Marcus's . . . something? Meswett, prophesied girl-child and savior of two species, one of which is oblivious to my existence? Destroyer of the world?

Who am I? What happened to Lex, the archaeologist? I liked her. She didn't date much, but she was content with her place in the world. She had friends who cared about her . . .

Did they really?

. . . and a loving family. Her life wasn't full of secrets . . .

Wasn't it? Who am I kidding? This is how it's always been . . . I just didn't know. Which was the real problem, what was really bothering me—if I could return to my happy life, to my ignorant state of mind, would I?

No way in hell.

So who am I?

Lex.

Some time later, I heard the click of a lock, the opening of a door, and familiar, stealthy footsteps approaching the bed. Dominic.

"You didn't give him the key?" I asked quietly.

Dominic sat behind me on the edge of the bed. "He didn't ask. But had he, I would have refused."

I rolled onto my back and reached out. Dominic grasped my hand and stretched out beside me. On the fluffy white comforter, we looked like a couple of oversized kids preparing to make a conjoined snow angel.

"Everything's going to change tomorrow," I said.

"Hasn't it already?"

A soft laugh escaped from me. "Sometimes I feel like I've known you forever, Dom. I wish I had."

"My forever, or yours?" he asked, notes of pain evident in his voice.

Turning my head, I examined his profile for evidence of whatever troubled him. Like all Nejerets, his features had been honed to perfection when he'd manifested. His pale skin and midnight hair stood in stark contrast around sharp, elfin bone structure. He and I shared the same high cheekbones and slightly pointy chin, but it was our father—Set—who he really resembled. I wondered how I hadn't noticed the resemblance when we first met in Denny Hall.

"Both," I said. "Will you tell me what Set did to you?"

Dominic's facial muscles tensed. "I don't . . . it's not pleasant."

Squeezing his hand, I said, "I'm not sure what our *dear father* will do to make me obey him, but I'm pretty damn sure it'll be worse than anything I can think of. Why should I hate him? Why should I want to destroy him *at all costs*? I need to know, Dom. I need ammo. Please, tell me."

Dominic shut his eyes tightly, like he was trying to hide from something, except whatever he was trying to hide from was already inside his head. After a few seconds, his eyelids snapped open, and he stared at the molded plaster ceiling.

Finally, he said, "I was born in a small village in the Loire Valley in the late sixteenth century. My mother had been a great beauty at court, and like most of her peers, had been enamored with a handsome Russian diplomat—Set's cover at the time. He wooed his way into her bed, but unlike the rest of the courtiers, she was cunning, and mistrustful by nature. While their affair proceeded, she spied on him and discovered she was one of dozens. You see, Set wanted to build an army, so he spent hundreds of years bouncing from court to court, impregnating as many high-born women as possible. Carriers of the Nejeret genes are more prevalent in the upper class—probably because we naturally seek positions of power and our human offspring tend to benefit from that in both status and means.

"After several months, my mother learned she was pregnant and fled to a small village, where she hid and I was eventually born. Set didn't try to follow her, but I've often wondered if he knew where we were the whole time, because when I manifested, he came after us immediately. He imprisoned my mother in one of his fortresses and cared for her only for the sake of keeping her alive, because alive, she could be used as leverage against me. He threatened to hurt her if I didn't follow his wishes. On multiple occasions, he did hurt her, until I finally learned to obey.

"He made me into his hunter—his assassin—and set me on the track of Ivan's line. At that time, he'd only been focused on preventing his prophesied destruction, and to do that, he planned to wipe out Ivan and his descendants completely. It was the same reason he forced Senenmut to build the hidden temple in the first place—to lock the ankh-At away forever. It wasn't until the nineteenth century that he realized the girl-child would be his key to ruling the world." Dominic shook his head, messing up his usually smooth hair. "I did horrible things at his command . . . but I managed to do some good, too. I helped some of your brethren escape and go into hiding." Dominic paused and looked at me with a sad smile.

"On the night my mother died from an impromptu, excessive beating, I vowed to kill Set. As I made my way to his bedchamber, I was accosted by a man who'd been hidden in the shadows. In my time serving as Set's personal assassin, I'd become highly skilled in the darker arts—lock-picking, breaking and entering, hand-to-hand combat, and of course, killing. But even I was no match for this man. I held my own against him for a few seconds, but he quickly had me weaponless and pinned on the ground.

"He asked me, 'Are you ready to die, traitor?' I nodded, but requested that he might hold off on my execution until after I'd killed Set. And he laughed! He told me that perhaps he wouldn't kill me just yet—that he might have a use for me—and we fled the fortress together. He showed me the truth, and I learned of Nuin's prophecy and that killing Set would destroy the easiest path to all of his offspring—possible harbingers of the doom predicted in the prophecy."

I wasn't quite sure what he meant, but unable to hold in my curiosity, I asked, "Who was he? The man who stopped you, I mean."

Dominic looked at me quizzically. "Heru, of course."

"And you've been working for him ever since?"

"With him, yes," he said. "Fighting the good fight, and all that."

"Thank you for telling me, Dom. I can't believe what Set did to you and your mom . . . he . . . I'll . . ."

"I know, Lex. For the first time since my mother's death, I have family again," he told me somberly. "Just try not to destroy yourself in the process of destroying him."

"Do you think he'll try to use my family against me, like he did with you and your mom?"

Dominic sat up abruptly. "I can't imagine him *not* trying that. I'm sorry, Lex . . . I should have thought of it sooner."

"Oh my God!" I exclaimed and launched off the bed. "I need to talk to Marcus."

In seconds, I'd unlocked the door to the sitting room, opened it, and almost run straight into a six-and-a-half-foot wall of hard muscle covered in expensive, exquisitely tailored fabric.

I took a step backward. "Have you been standing here the whole time?" I asked, avoiding his eyes.

"No," Marcus replied with a voice like silk. "I listened as you wept and then as you fell silent. When I heard nothing for nearly two hours, I left briefly to search for Dom and asked him to check on you."

He listened to me cry? He stood out there for hours? "Oh, um, thanks." I finally raised my eyes to his, but he wasn't looking at me. Instead, he was glaring at Dominic, who was still sitting on the bed.

"Dom," Marcus said, his voice low with warning.

Dominic instantly stood, and I would have been curious about what he'd done to set off Marcus—this time—but there were far more important matters on my mind.

"Marcus . . . my family," I said, worry straining the words.

"Ah, yes . . . I think it's time for another little meeting."

Promptly, the three of us, along with four bodyguards, returned to the meeting room downstairs and waited for the others. Carlisle, Josh, Neffe, and Alexander all appeared within ten minutes of our own arrival.

After a long discussion, I made a list of everyone Set could possibly use against me as he'd used Dominic's mother against him. It wasn't a long list, consisting of my immediate family, my few aunts, uncles, and cousins, Grandma Suse, a half-dozen friends, Dr. Ramirez, and my cat. I hesitated only a moment before adding Cara to the list. After all, she had only spoken the truth on the witness stand.

"Are you sure that's everyone?" Alexander asked.

I scanned the list. "Yep."

"There must be more people you care about," he insisted. "We need to know *every single one*, otherwise we won't be able to protect them."

"That's it," I said, growing self-conscious. I reexamined the short list of people, of the handful of meaningful relationships I'd accumulated over the first twenty-four years of my life. It wasn't a very impressive list. *Why so few? Have I always known I was different? Could others tell?*

"But this is barely—"

"Let it go, Alex," Marcus said quietly.

At his friend's words, Alexander closed his mouth and studied me. Whatever he found troubled him, creasing his brow and pulling down the corners of his mouth.

"Carlisle," Marcus said, "set up teams to monitor each person on this list. Dispatch them immediately. They are to report back as soon as they make indirect contact. Under only one circumstance are they to engage with their charge—direct threat from Set or his followers."

"Yes, Sir," Carlisle said as he pulled out his cell phone and began texting ferociously.

We spent the rest of the evening brainstorming the possible threats and acts Set might use to coerce my obedience. Until that night, I'd had no idea how many ways a person could be physically, mentally, and emotionally tortured. I felt like I was halfway to cracking under the pressure already, and Set was nowhere in sight.

"Lex, did you hear me?" Marcus asked, squeezing my knee.

"No," I said, feeling empty. I had the vague impression that everyone was staring at me.

"I know you're tired, but you can sleep on the plane. This is important. You need to focus," Marcus urged. I felt him give my knee a shake.

"I . . . I . . . it's . . ." I couldn't seem to form a complete thought, couldn't get a grip on reality. I was stuck in my head, imagining my fingernails being torn out with pliers, or being forced to watch my mom being raped.

"Leave us," Marcus said quietly, and I heard the sounds of the others exiting the room.

When we were alone, Marcus spun my chair so I faced him. Slowly, his hands slid up my thighs and gripped the swell of my hips, pulling my butt to the edge of the seat. He knelt on the hardwood floor before me, parting my knees and fitting himself between my legs. All numbness—mental and physical—immediately vanished. I became hyper-aware of every part of my body, and his.

"I don't think I can do this," I said quietly.

He leaned his forehead against mine and whispered, "Of course you can. You're my she-falcon."

I smiled faintly, and he mirrored the expression.

"This is very important, Lex," he said softly, his voice somber. "If it comes down to physical torture, you must leave your body and enter the At. You won't feel the pain there."

"But what about my body?" My voice was small, childlike.

"It will heal."

"It will heal if I stay, too."

"Yes," he agreed. "But your mind might not."

"Oh."

Chastely, he touched his lips to mine. "You are the daughter of two of the most powerful Nejeret lines. You are the Meswett. But most importantly, you are *mine*."

Tears welled in my eyes, overflowing at the corners.

With more tenderness than I'd thought possible, Marcus kissed away each salty droplet. "You are mine, and I command you to survive this," he whispered.

I shook with soft laughter. "There you go again, ordering me around."

Marcus touched his lips to mine, but all of the chasteness of his previous kiss was gone. "Contrary to what you think, I don't want to control you," he said as he pulled away, reclaiming his seat.

I scooted back in my own chair and crossed my legs. "Why do I feel like there's a 'but' coming?"

Marcus raised an eyebrow. "But . . . I'd really appreciate it if you didn't let other men lie on your bed. I don't want to smell them when I'm in it with you. It should just be the scent of you and me . . . together."

My cheeks flushed. "But it was just Dom. He's my—"

Shaking his head, Marcus took a deep breath. "Sibling relationships are different among our kind, Lex."

At his implication, I gagged. "Are you saying that brothers and sisters . . . that Nejerets are incestuous?" I asked Marcus, appalled.

Marcus replied with a question. "Is there incest when the female half of the species cannot procreate? Surely you must have considered that my grandfather—"

"Don't say it," I warned, standing and taking several steps away from Marcus.

"—is your great-grandfather through Set—"

I clapped my hands over my ears and closed my eyes, chanting, "Stop it! Stop it! Stop it!"

"—and the same, only a little further removed, through your mother. Why, that would make us—"

Turning around, I blurted, "Okay! I get it . . . loud and clear." *I think I'm going to be sick.*

"I don't think you do," Marcus said, stalking toward me. I stood my ground. How had he gone from tender and caring to such a vicious creature in a matter of seconds? "You're disgusted. You want me, but now you're conflicted. You're concerned with human social norms. Well guess what, Lex? You're *not* human. You're Nejerette. Get used to it and keep Dominic off your bed."

"Fine," I agreed, and he actually looked surprised. "But you have to stop ordering me around."

Raising his hand, Marcus gently stroked the side of my face with the backs of his fingers. Before I could lean into his touch, he clamped his hand around my jaw and clenched his own. "Fine."

25

DO & DAMN

I grew up in a middle-class, apple-pie-with-vanilla-ice-cream, American home. On Christmas, a holiday that had no religious significance to my family aside from the worship of one exceptionally jolly, exceptionally fat man, our tree always sheltered a moderately generous cache of presents. Frosty and Max, our family cats, would play with any ornaments they could reach, adding new scratches to those left over from years past. We didn't buy new, perfect, and shiny baubles to decorate the tree every year, and we didn't give each other everything we could ever want. We couldn't afford to. And in a sense, it was something I appreciated—not being handed every little thing I wanted gave me something to work toward.

I was sitting alone on an unbelievably soft, beige leather couch on one of Marcus's huge, super-luxurious private jets. Marcus had abandoned me to pace while he carried on a heated phone conversation with somebody important, not that I knew who.

While staying at the Heru compound, I'd managed to trick myself into thinking of the chateau and its outbuildings more like a resort than a private residence. But I couldn't ignore

Marcus's obscene wealth when it was shaped like a metal tube and was hurtling me through the air at breakneck speeds. One of the few things seers were always allowed to look for in the future At was a means to make money. Playing the stock market, investing in business ventures, gambling—it was all Council-approved so long as it bettered Nejeret-kind.

Briefly, I wondered if Alexander was anywhere near as well-off as Marcus, and if he was, why Grandma Suse didn't live in some opulent mansion. Unless . . . maybe she didn't want to? Grandma Suse was a proud, honest woman—a *human* woman— and I could easily imagine her rejecting Alexander's money as soon as she'd learned the truth about him and how he gained it . . . however he *had* gained it. *She probably considered it cheating . . . an unfair advantage over "normal folks" or something like that.*

"I'm sorry I woke you," Marcus said as he settled beside me, draping his arm over my shoulders.

I rested my head against his chest. "It's okay." After a moment, I said, "I didn't know you could use cell phones on airplanes."

"Ah . . . our plane is different."

When he didn't explain further, I glanced up at his face—his lips were pressed into an unusually thin line. "What's wrong?"

He sighed. "All of the people on your list are accounted for and are being monitored . . . except one."

"Who?" I asked. I could feel Alexander's eyes on me from a dozen feet away.

"Your sister."

I glanced at Kat, who was sitting beside Alexander. "Jenny's missing?" My brain instantly tried to come up with possible explanations. "She could be . . . maybe she's just—"

Marcus held me more tightly against his side. "We have finders looking for her current location in the At. We're doing our best to figure out where she is and if something has happened to her."

"Something . . . ? Like, if she's been hurt . . . or . . . or *killed?*" I asked, horrified.

He exhaled bitterly. "*That* is unlikely. She's useless to Set dead."

My chest felt like it had been pulverized by a meat tenderizer from the inside out. "He has her, doesn't he?"

After kissing the top of my head, Marcus released me and I sat up straight. "I think so. Otherwise we would have been able to find her in the At by now."

"Can I use your phone?" I asked, holding out my hand.

"No, but you can use *your* phone," he said, placing a shiny new iPhone in my waiting palm. "It's already programmed with all of our people as well as everyone on your list."

I didn't need pre-programmed contacts to call Jenny, but my hands were shaking so badly that I had to dial her number four times before I got it right. It went straight to voicemail.

"Shit!" I hissed before the beep. "Jenny, call me back as soon as you get this. It's important, like life-or-death important. There are some things about you and me that I have to tell you. I love you, J."

As soon as I hit "end" I was dialing another number.

"Hello?"

"Mom—"

"Hi, sweetie!" my mom exclaimed. My chin began trembling at the sound of her voice—an involuntary reaction from all the times she'd comforted me growing up.

"Hey Mom, do—"

"I thought you were flying out today," she interrupted. "Are you already in Egypt?"

"Uh, yeah, just landed," I lied. "But—"

"How was it? I always hate those long flights. My legs get so achy."

"Yeah, it was . . . long. I'd love to talk, but I really need to know how to get ahold of Jenny. I promise I'll call you back when I'm settled in."

"Oh, of course, sweetie. Are you going to try to meet up with her?"

"What?" I asked, instantly confused.

"Jenny. You know, since she's in the same neighborhood as you?"

What? "Yeah . . ."

"I bet she's having the time of her life cruising around the Mediterranean with that new boyfriend of hers."

Something in my chest clenched. *Please let her new boyfriend not be who I think he might be,* I thought frantically. "Yep, sounds awesome," I said. "But, uh, she forgot to give me a way to reach her." *Liar, liar, pants on fire . . .*

"Oh good! You girls will have so much fun together. It's just what you need to mend things. Now let's see . . . I know it's around here . . . hmm . . . did I put it . . . ah, here it is. Are you ready?"

"Yeah, Mom," I said, accepting a pen and small notebook from Marcus. I jotted down the numbers and then repeated them back for confirmation. "Thanks, Mom. I'll call you soon. Be safe."

"That's my line," she said, laughing softly. "Be safe, Lex. And have fun!"

"Love you, Mom." I didn't want to end the call; I wanted to keep talking to her forever.

"I love you too, sweetie. Bye."

"Bye," I said and listened as my mom fumbled with the phone, trying to disconnect the call on her end.

Taking a long, deep breath, I dialed the unfamiliar combination of numbers. It seemed to take hours to connect, but finally it rang once . . . twice . . .

"Hello, my darling girl." It was the last voice I wanted to hear. I'd suspected, all the while hoping desperately to be wrong, that Jenny was with Set . . . her new boyfriend. *That is so wrong . . .*

"Where's my sister?" I asked icily.

Set chuckled. "She's a pretty little thing, isn't she? She lacks some of your . . . hmmm . . . severity. I wonder if Heru is so drawn to you because your eyes are the color of his favorite thing."

Marcus was as still as a statue beside me, and Alexander joined us, sitting on my opposite side.

"And that would be . . . ?" I asked.

I could hear the smile in his voice as he said, "Blood, as it thickens and dries. Do you really know so little about him, daughter? Perhaps I'll enlighten you when I see you next."

Ignoring his taunts, I repeated, "Where's my sister? If you've hurt her . . ."

"We need not be enemies, my—"

"Oh, I think we need be," I said, cutting him off. "Where's Jenny?"

"Sunning on the deck," he answered pleasantly. "And if you call again or try to contact her in any other way, I'll cut her throat." He hung up.

I dropped the phone on the floor and stood. Numbly, I hurried past a handful of Nejerets to the large bathroom in the rear of the jet, locking myself inside. As soon as I looked at the toilet, I fell to my knees and vomited. My stomach heaved until it was empty, and then dry-heaved a few more times for good measure.

Still crumpled on my knees, I flushed the toilet, trying to get rid of the smell, then searched the drawers and compartments in the bathroom until I found what I needed.

I took my time, brushing my hair, rinsing my face with cold water, and cleaning my teeth with enthusiasm. I remembered the thousands of times I'd gone through similar morning and nighttime routines, shoulder to shoulder with Jenny as we shared the sink in our bathroom. We'd been so close when we were little girls. *How did we let ourselves drift so far apart?*

Suddenly, I felt overwhelming determination to find my sister . . . to save her from Set. I had begun mending things with her over the holidays, and I wouldn't let her die without finishing what I'd started. She was *my* sister—if Set hurt her, I would do my damndest to make him pay.

I emerged from the lavatory with a plan. Marcus was waiting for me just outside, leaning against the opposite wall. I blinked in surprise, then grabbed his hand and pulled him into the rear bedroom cabin and closed the door, shutting out dozens of sets of prying eyes. I led him to the foot of the bed, then sat down. He followed suit.

Reaching behind me, he began rubbing my neck, somehow knowing I was developing a monster of a headache. I slouched, letting his fingers work their temporary magic and murmuring, "Mmm . . ."

Minutes later, I gathered my courage and pulled Marcus's hand away from my neck. I held it to my lips, kissing each fingertip softly. "Thank you," I whispered, pressing my lips against his palm. Impulsively, I met his gaze at the exact moment that I gently bit the meaty part of his palm and watched his eyes burn gold and black with desire.

I had no idea why fortune had favored me with this aphrodisiacal power over such an imposing and undeniably desirable man, but I relished it. It was intoxicating—his responses drove me wild with lust. The fates, it seemed, believed in fair play, because his power over me was equally potent.

"I'm going into the At," I said against his palm before releasing it, "to look for my sister. If she's really with Set, then I may be the only one who can find her, and I *have* to find her. He'll use her against me, threaten her again, and"—my chin quivered—"Marcus, I don't know if I can resist."

Jaw clenched, Marcus said, "Going into the At is unwise. If Set finds your ba while it's in an echo . . ."

I stood and started pacing in the small space. "I know. He could hurt me . . . maybe even trap me. It's really stupid. But"—I turned to face him, wrapping my arms around my middle —"I'm doing it anyway. I have to."

Something in my eyes convinced Marcus that I couldn't be dissuaded. "Then I'm going with you."

I shook my head, sincerely wishing he could accompany me. "It was harder to enter the echo at the fertility clinic when I had you or Alexander tagging along, and I knew that echo. I think the only way I can find Jenny is if I'm alone."

In an instant, Marcus was standing before me and his hands were on me, caressing my face, my neck, my shoulders, my hair. "Don't do this, Lex. We'll find another way . . ."

Pressing my lips against his, I kissed him long and tenderly. "I'm going," I whispered. "The only question left is—will you watch over my body while I'm gone?"

"Of course." His voice was rough.

I smiled a weak, miserable smile. "Thanks."

I stood, surrounded by the horizontal whirl of colors, amazed at how much easier it had been to enter the placeless When—as opposed to the timeless Where—of the At than it had been during my finder test with Alexander. I focused on the time of my phone call with Set, the only concrete hold I had on him. But instead of Set, I focused on Jenny, searching the recent past for her.

The colors shifted, flying by like they were stars and I was in a spaceship in hyperdrive. Abruptly, the motionless shifting of the At ceased. Glaringly bright, the sun shown down on sparkling, sapphire water, and *gulls squawked overhead. An arrhythmic tap-thud-slap, tap-thud-slap, tap-thud-slap repeated endlessly. I was on Set's yacht.*

It was beautiful, though in a totally different way than Marcus's private jets. Marcus preferred tasteful and reserved décor, usually of grays or blacks, while Set veered toward gaudy and extravagant. He wanted to shove everyone's face in his wealth and power. The disparity between the two men intrigued me, considering how close they had once been.

I recalled Marcus's admission that they had even "shared lovers." What the hell does that even mean? *Had they participated in a bunch of ménage-a-trois . . . or ménage-a-more-than-trois?*

Shaking my head, I focused on my fear for Jenny . . . on my devastation at the thought of losing her forever. If I let my mind stray, it would be too easy to accidentally relocate myself in the At and end up watching one of the ménage-a-whatevers, which I really *didn't want to do. Finding Jenny was what was important.*

I turned away from the gemstone ocean and scanned the deck. Sure enough, Jenny was sprawled lazily in a purple bikini near the bow of the boat, and no matter how badly I wanted to warn her of the danger she was in with Set, she wouldn't hear me. I was viewing the past, and she wasn't really there.

Strong hands settled on my shoulders and began a slow, deep massage.

Smiling, I admonished, "I thought I told you to stay . . ." I trailed off, realizing the person behind me didn't smell a thing like Marcus. Instead of exotic and sweet spices, I was surrounded by a subtle, cool mint, almost like a mojito. "Set!" I hissed.

"I wondered if you would come . . . though I thought it would take you longer," Set said, smooth-voiced. "You don't waste time. Has my dear cousin benefited from this element of your character?"

"What I do with him is none of your business," I snapped, acutely aware that this was the first time I'd spoken to Set face-to-face, so to speak.

He spun me around to face him. "On the contrary, daughter. What Heru does with my property is every bit my business."

His property? *"Fuck you!" I spat.*

Set smiled—a simple baring of teeth—and scoured my body with his eyes. "It's a little unconventional, even for Nejerets, but if that's what would sway you to my side, I'm sure I could oblige."

"Ugh! No! What's wrong with you?" I tried to shove off his hold, but he was far stronger than me.

"Hmmm . . ." He cocked his head to the side. "I don't want us to be enemies, Daughter. What can I say to ease your antagonism toward me?"

"Nothing. Your actions have spoken loud enough."

"What evil deeds have you assigned to your loving father?" he asked pleasantly.

"Joe Larson is my loving father and he's done nothing evil," I said, verbally slapping Set. "You, on the other hand, stalked me throughout my life—probably hoping to kidnap me—assigned a man to drug and rape me, broke into my apartment with a group of your cult followers, and then kidnapped my sister and threatened to kill her." I glared, trying to stab him with my eyeballs. "Don't you think that's enough?"

Set's grasp on my shoulders tightened painfully, but I didn't do anything to indicate my discomfort. I was too worried it would please him.

"I am your father. Without me, you wouldn't exist. Don't forget that, girl. And did you consider that perhaps I was just watching you as you grew to keep you safe? And that idiot, Mike, kept lathering on the drug-laced lip balm until you nearly overdosed. He was supposed to use it to lower your inhibitions only enough that you'd willingly share his bed. And pretty Jenny came with me willingly. She thinks she's in love with Seth McDougal," he explained, puffing up.

His excuses were crap and I told him so. "What about the men who broke into my apartment?" I asked, and he shrugged.

"Like I said, actions speak." I watched as something darker than the inky black of his irises—possibly his sanity—slid around in his eyes, sometimes filling them, other times leaving them wild and vacant. Holy crap, I thought, terrified of the man before me. He really is insane.

"How about these actions," Set said softly. "Your beautiful Heru spent over two millennia hunting down and killing my offspring. The *blood of my children—your siblings—pours from his hands, but you would damn me for merely threatening the life of your sister. You should be damned him!"*

"You lie!" I cried and kneed him in the groin as hard as I could. As he crumpled to the ground, I fled back into my body.

I was lying on my back on the bed in Marcus's private jet. Opening my eyes, I raised my head and stared at his broad shoulders, at the corded tendons and muscles snaking up his neck and the line where night-dark hair met golden-honey skin. He sat in the same position he'd been in when I first closed my eyes, just beyond my feet at the end of the bed.

"I found her," I said quietly, but Marcus didn't turn. I sat up.

"And . . . ?"

"She's with him, but she's not hurt. He said she's in love with him." I watched closely for a reaction.

Marcus's shoulders tensed. "So he showed up. I figured he would."

"Don't you want to know what else he told me?"

"I can guess," Marcus said, hanging his head. "Was it something along the lines of 'Heru spent thousands of years killing your siblings'?"

"It's true?" I whispered, wanting him to deny it. He didn't, and I felt like the world was being ripped out from under my feet and I was falling endlessly into oblivion. My half-siblings, like Dominic and Kat, had been hunted down and killed by Marcus? *Why?*

"It's part of the truth," Marcus said quietly. He stood and walked to the door. "When you decide you want to know the rest, let me know."

"Marcus," I said, but he was already gone.

PART III

Deir el-Bahri
Luxor, Egypt

26

CLAIM & BOND

As demonstrated by the brevity of my "people I care about" list, I'd never been one to hand out affection like candy on Halloween. But, on the rare occasion that I let someone in, they had a chance to become a cornerstone in my life. Of the people on my list, only my parents, Grandma Suse, Jenny, Annie, and Cara were cornerstones. Once I'd laid them in my foundation, it took a lot to remove them. Even Cara's honest betrayal on the stand hadn't done it, though her stability had been dramatically loosened. But, once they were gone, ripped from the recess that had been finely hewn to fit only them, they were gone for good. It was something hammered into the very fiber of my being.

Set's words haunted me. *"Heru spent over two millennia hunting down and killing my offspring. The blood of my children—your siblings—pours from his hands . . ."*

I couldn't fathom any reason to hunt and kill people simply because they had the misfortune of being fathered by a psychotic, evil man. Even if that father was prophesied to potentially lead one of his children to destroy the world, it just didn't make sense . . . they were still their own people. Just because

Set fathered them didn't mean he owned their minds. And I wondered, *had I been born a hundred years earlier, would Marcus have hunted down and killed me too?*

Like Set's, Marcus's words echoed in my mind. *"When you decide you want to know the rest, let me know."* He had uttered the emotionless syllables earlier that morning, before we'd even touched down on the sun-drenched runway at Luxor International Airport. It had only taken me the afternoon to decide—I wanted to know the rest. I wanted Marcus as a corner-stone. Especially with Jenny still in Set's hands and the impending Nothingness on the horizon, I needed someone . . . I needed Marcus.

I emerged from the ten-by-twenty-foot canvas tent that would be my home for the next several months, taking a moment to stare in wonder at Djeser-Djeseru—Hatchepsut's mortuary temple—about a half-mile to the west. Its three tiers of columned promenades were lit up for the night, making the enormous temple glow majestically and casting eerie, jagged shadows against the limestone cliffs towering behind it. Tomorrow, I would finally walk up the two gradual limestone ramps to Djeser-Djeseru's third level and begin searching the upper Anubis chapel for the hidden entrance to Senenmut's underground temple.

Sighing, I turned away and headed for Marcus's tent. It was a duplicate of mine, a rectangular canvas structure divided into two rooms—a ten-by-ten-foot "office," and beyond that, personal living quarters of the same dimensions—and had been erected only a handful of paces from my own tent. Together, our two canvas homes comprised the center of a tent town. Dozens of smaller tents had been set up around ours in a very neat grid pattern, with a main thoroughfare running east and west, directly between Marcus's and my tents. Beyond the west edge of the mini-city of canvas and sand, an expansive canopy had been set up over several dozen collapsible picnic tables, and two long restroom trailers had been parked beyond the east edge of camp. The entire temple complex had been shut down to tourists and would remain so until August, leaving us free to conduct our work away from prying eyes.

As I crossed the sandy "main street" to Marcus's tent, my two bodyguards followed, positioned like splayed wings behind me. I stopped when I reached the curtain-like door, trying to work up the nerve to push through and step inside. A soft, feminine laugh sounded within.

I scurried around the corner of the tent, motioning frantically for my guards to return to my own tent. Whether or not they would have obeyed didn't matter, because a slender, caramel-complexioned woman emerged from Marcus's tent saying, ". . . want me to stay." She stuck out her lower lip in a sultry pout. "I haven't been able to think about anything else for weeks." There was no mistaking what she was talking about—sex . . . with Marcus.

Weeks? Why would she say that . . . unless . . . I choked on a scream. Had Marcus been with her—slept with her—during our two months of estrangement? *He did say he was in Egypt . . .* Jealousy unlike anything I'd ever felt before washed through me, setting me aflame with rage. My emotions where Marcus was concerned tended toward volatility, but this was getting ridiculous. I hated that woman. I wanted to hurt her. I wanted to erase her and whatever carnal experiences Marcus had shared with her from his mind.

"Hello, boys," the woman mused, looking each of my guards up and down admiringly. She wasn't Nejerette; she lacked the finely hewn perfection I'd come to recognize as a tell-tale sign, but she was striking nonetheless. Her bold features were just feminine enough for beauty, but too masculine for anonymity. I watched as she sauntered slowly away, toward the enormous parking lot east of the tent town.

"What are you doing, Lex?" Marcus asked in my general direction, his voice bland.

I stepped out from the shadows and into the moonlight. "Who is she?" I asked with nod toward the woman.

"Sara," he said, his expression carefully blank.

"She's human," I said, which was noteworthy considering we'd agreed to keep the Nejeret camp human-free, aside from Genevieve. "What's she doing here?"

Marcus opened his mouth to speak, but apparently thought better of whatever he'd been about to say and closed it again.

Without thinking, I turned on my heel and stalked after the willowy woman. "Hey! Hey, Sara!" I called after her, and she halted.

"Yes?" she asked with genuine curiosity. She turned gracefully, examined me from head to toe, and said, "I'm sorry, you seem to have me at a disadvantage. You are . . . ?" Her accent was upper-crust British, full of education and class.

"Lex," I replied. "What were you doing in Marcus's tent?" Accusation clouded the air, as did a growing crowd of Nejerets. *Oh look, the Meswett is having a breakdown—let's watch!* I had no idea what I was doing, or why—other than feeling an overwhelming need to claim Marcus as my own.

Sara gave me a knowing look that seemed to say, *"Oh, honey, don't even bother with him. He needs a real woman."* Out loud, she said, "Why don't you ask him?"

"Because I'm asking *you*," I said evenly.

"We had a few drinks," she purred.

"And . . . ?"

"Lex, come on. Let the woman go," Dominic said as he carefully approached me from the left.

I thrust my hand toward him and growled, "I love you, Dom, but I swear if you touch me right now I'll kick you in the balls so hard they'll pop out of your mouth."

More than a few Nejerets chuckled, and Dominic's lips pursed and twitched. He didn't, however, come any closer.

"And . . . ?" I prompted Sara again.

As she'd watched the exchange between me and Dominic, concern had formed a faint line between her eyebrows. She was starting to understand—I wasn't just some young archaeologist with a crush on the excavation director.

"And we talked," she said primly.

"About . . . ?"

Concerned or not, she was affronted. "About old times, if you must know," she said haughtily. *Old times.* It was the wrong thing to say. *Old times* that had been spent in bed together? Maybe they'd been reliving *old times*?

A growing murmur was coming from the crowd of Nejerets. A quick glance around told me pretty much everyone in the camp was watching us.

What am I doing? Get a hold of yourself, Lex! Unable to stop myself, I stepped closer to Sara, and she stepped back. It was like there was an invisible force field between us. It amused some instinctual Nejerette part of me, so I did it again. Sara took another step back. *She's afraid of me,* I thought, and though I didn't know why, the realization gave me pleasure.

"Don't move," I told her, and cocked my head. "I won't hurt you . . . if you don't move."

As I approached her, Sara's wide, wild, chocolate-brown eyes burned into mine, pleading silently. She was an inch or two taller than me, but nothing could give her an edge over my all-encompassing fury. I was starting to wonder if heightened emotions accompanied the other intensified sensations afflicting my kind.

"Oh dear God, your eyes," Sara whispered, once I was only a few inches away. The reaction had become normal from regular humans, and annoying enough that I'd started to wear brown contact lenses when the need for discretion arose. "Somebody get her away from me!" Sara screeched, looking around at the crowd. "She's . . . she's . . . possessed or something! Won't anyone help me? Marcus?"

Nobody made a move to step in and rescue the terrified woman. This—whatever it was—was between the Meswett, a member of the Council of Seven, and some woman . . . some *human* woman. Nobody had the right to interfere, and nobody would.

I smiled, enjoying her fear. But, I needed to find out if she deserved worse than fear. I took another step toward her, and leaned in close like I might lay a soft kiss upon her full lips. She shivered as I breathed in through my nose. *What the hell am I doing?* I thought as I bent my neck to sniff both sides of hers and then her hair with long, deep breaths. There was no scent of Marcus's tantalizing spice, only her subtle floral perfume— expensive and delicate—Scotch, and fear. Marcus hadn't touched her, at least not enough to mark her.

"Leave now," I whispered into her ear. "Don't come back. Got it?"

I felt the air shift between our cheeks as she nodded.

"Good. Leave."

As I watched her hurry away, I wondered why my jealous rage wasn't dissipating. I'd taken care of the threat, but I still felt drunk with it.

"Don't," I told Dominic as he again started to approach me. At only a few strides away, I could see something in his eyes that looked like sadness mixed with admiration, or maybe envy. I couldn't believe it. *Does he think I handled that well? Was that some instinctive Nejeret thing?*

The truth behind Marcus's many claims that we weren't human finally sunk in. In my recent identity crisis, I'd been asking the wrong question. I shouldn't have been focused on the who, but on the what. *What am I?*

Not human.

Wrapping my wild emotions around me, I approached Marcus. The crowd parted for me obediently, each Nejeret head bowing as I passed. It had the feeling of ritual.

Marcus still stood just outside the door to his tent, arms crossed and watching me. He hadn't moved a muscle to rescue Sara.

I stopped a few feet in front of him, watching him . . . waiting. His face was a thin mask of unconcern barely concealing some unidentifiable, intense emotion.

"Back to your tents," he called over my head to the crowd before reaching behind him to hold open the flap covering the entrance to his tent.

I ducked under his arm and entered his temporary home. It was the first time I'd actually set foot in his tent. There was a small wooden desk, several folding chairs, and a few trunks set against the canvas wall. An electric lantern hanging at the apex of the ceiling was the only source of light. With a deep inhale, I assured myself that the interior didn't smell like sex. *What the hell is up with me and sniffing?* I wondered remotely.

Marcus followed close behind me. The temperature had been in the mid-nineties earlier that day, but it had dropped drastically when the sun went down a short while ago. It was Marcus's heat that seeped into me now.

"Satisfied?" he asked roughly.

I took several steps away from him, toward the doorway to his "bedroom," and peered over my shoulder. "Satisfied? I definitely wouldn't describe myself as satisfied at the moment."

His chest rumbled, and his expression turned predatory.

Not human, I reminded myself.

"Would you like me to remedy that?" he asked quietly.

Looking away, I stepped out of my sandals and let the warm sand beneath the canvas floor mold to my feet. "Tell me why you killed my siblings."

From the sound of Marcus's exhale, he hadn't moved. "I

killed them because it was my job. I killed them because the majority of the Council decreed it and because they refused to forswear their bloodline and swear loyalty to the Council. I *killed* them because they followed Set blindly."

I faced him, surprised by his answer. I'd been under the mistaken impression that he'd hunted Set's offspring, killing any and all he could get his hands on.

"Ah . . . I see it in your eyes. You thought the worst. Did you think I killed them as babes in their cradles? Or maybe tore them from their mothers' breasts? Or, perhaps I just killed the pregnant mothers? No. They were grown. They had a choice. They chose wrong."

As a silent, shameful tear slid down my cheek, I asked, "Why didn't you just tell me the truth on the plane? I imagined such awful things about you."

He chuckled, but the sound held no amusement. "You thought the worst, and yet you were still willing to claim me as yours. You are unbelievable."

I shifted my feet and frowned. "Claim you as mine?" I remembered thinking something similar, but I had no clue where the urge had come from. *Who claims another person?*

Shaking his head, Marcus said, "And you don't even know what you did. I forget sometimes that you weren't raised among us, that you don't know our ways. But, it would seem that your instincts have a way of making up for your missing knowledge." He hitched his head toward the direction of my confrontation with Sara. "What you just did—that was one of several types of claiming ceremonies. In the old ways, you just declared me yours."

"I did? But I didn't mean to."

"Too late. It's done." He took a small step toward me, then another. "Do you know what comes next?"

Swallowing, I shook my head.

"Once the Nejeret, or Nejerette in this case, claims her

intended, it's up to the claimed to complete the ceremony by either rejecting or accepting the Nejerette," he explained.

Looking at his boots, I asked, "How would the claimed reject the Nejerette?"

"By publicly vowing never to speak to her, touch her, or look upon her again. It's the reason claiming is not very common."

My eyes flew up to his, searching his face for any hint of his intentions. *Will he reject me?* After what I'd thought of him, I feared it was a distinct possibility.

"And how would the claimed accept the Nejerette?" I asked softly.

A slow, wolfish smile spread across Marcus's face, and his golden eyes darkened with desire.

"Oh," I breathed. My belly tightened, and my groin throbbed in rhythm with my suddenly speeding heartbeat.

"Would the Nejerette like her claimed to accept?" Marcus took another small step, leaving only a few feet between us.

Unable to look away from his eyes, I nodded. Short, quick breaths prevented me from speaking.

"Tell me you want me to accept." His deep voice, with its complex accent, curled around me, enticing, encouraging. "Tell me what you want." Not "beg me to accept," or even "ask me to accept." He wanted me to tell him. He was giving me the control, setting me up as his equal.

He took one last step, closing the distance between us.

"I want you to accept," I said, and miraculously, both my gaze and voice were steady.

"Finally," he growled, picking me up by the waist and setting me on the desk. Just like that, he took back control.

By the time his lips touched mine, he was between my legs, grinding against me. I let out a throaty groan and grasped his firm backside, increasing the friction between us.

Marcus kissed me like I was air and he'd been underwater for years. His jaw forced mine open, allowing his tongue entry to explore. I thought I'd experienced the glories of his mouth before, of his lips and tongue, but I'd been wrong.

While he kissed me, his hands traveled over my white linen dress, from my hips to my waist, searing along my ribcage and breasts, until they reached the thin straps at my shoulders. One at a time I removed my hands from their hold on his rhythmically clenching glutes so he could slip the strips of fabric over my shoulders and down my arms.

Only then did he break our kiss. As each part of me was revealed, he worshiped it like I was a goddess . . . his goddess . . . his she-falcon. First my breasts, then my rib cage, waist, and hips received his mouth's devoted attention until, finally, he reached my lower abdomen.

He began at my left hip, laying a line of feather-light kisses along the top of my pale-blue lace panties until he reached the other side. Lips still pressed against my oh-so-sensitive flesh, he looked up, locking our gazes. His eyes were black wells of desire, his pupils dilated completely. He looked high out of his mind. I *felt* high out of my mind and wondered if my eyes were as black as his. The heightened emotions he stirred within me— the jealousy and desire, and above all, something that could only be described as love, except love wasn't strong enough, didn't encompass the enormity of what I felt for him—they were addictive. I craved him and the emotions he stoked so desperately that I felt I might die if I didn't get another, stronger fix. It felt unnatural and possibly unhealthy, and I didn't care. I needed him . . . more of him . . . *all* of him, body, mind, and soul.

Momentarily lifting my butt off the desk, Marcus inched my dress and underwear over the curve of my hips. He knelt, sliding the fabric down until he'd uncovered every part of me and a small pile of white linen and light blue lace lay on the floor at his knees.

He was utterly transfixed by his examination of my body. Tenderly, greedily, he kissed my inner thighs, leaving a trail of pleasurable, electric fire as he moved higher. Brazen moans escaped my throat, growing desperate the closer he came to the junction between my thighs. I'd become so incredibly aroused during the process that as soon as his mouth closed over my most sensitive of places, as soon as his tongue caressed me, pleasure exploded in my core. An intense, electric sensation throbbed outward toward my nerve endings, making me gasp and groan as I shuddered.

"Mmm . . ." Marcus rumbled, giving me a long, languorous lick.

"Marcus," I gasped, tugging at the shoulders of his shirt to bring him back up to my level. He stood, catching his breath when I found the hard length of him and rubbed it through his pants. "I need you inside me . . . please . . . now. Marcus . . ." I begged. He'd said I would beg, and he'd been right. Something was happening inside of me, something wild and terrifying, and I seriously feared for my sanity—and possibly for my life—if I didn't join with him immediately.

"You have no idea how many times I've imagined hearing you say those words," he said, stepping back to pull his shirt over his head.

Oh. My. God. His pants were suddenly on the ground and he was absolutely, wonderfully naked. My eyes feasted on his pristine masculinity. The lines of his muscles all flowed together in a pattern that screamed of savagery, strength, and sex.

I wasn't allowed to stare for long. He resumed his position between my legs, rubbing himself against me and kissing me deeply. "What do you want?" he asked against my mouth.

"You," I breathed.

"Where?"

"Inside me," I said. My pulse was erratic, my need for him all-encompassing. To continue living, to continue breathing, I needed to be one with him. It was the only thing that mattered.

With one hand between my shoulder blades and the other

pressed against my lower back, he lifted me off the desk and sank himself into my core.

"Marcus!" I exclaimed. Finally he was inside me, joined with me, where he belonged. I'd been aching for him so intensely that it both satiated and stoked an infinite hunger—feasting on Marcus only made me want more . . . *need* more.

Still joined, he lowered me to the ground until my back touched canvas. Watching my face with unrivaled intensity, he slowly moved within me. His eyes scoured my features like he was memorizing me, preparing to immortalize my every expression in stone. He continued the achingly slow pace until I made a noise of frustration—a groan mixed with a growl. I wanted more. I needed more.

"Ah . . . that's what I was waiting for," he said roughly and brushed his lips against mine. He pulled away just in time to hold my eyes for his first, powerful thrust. I nearly screamed.

Moving with the precision of a calligrapher and the focus of hunter stalking prey, Marcus was the embodiment of raw, unbridled sexuality. His intensity only increased, and he became the center of my world . . . he became my world. Nothing existed outside of him and the way he felt . . . tasted . . . sounded. With my enhanced Nejerette senses, I experienced sensations unlike anything I'd ever felt. But, there was something else . . . something more . . . something different.

As I cried out and dug my nails into his back, climaxing unexpectedly, Marcus roared above me, his whole body tensing with the strength of his own release. I thought he was finished. I was so wonderfully wrong.

Flipping me over onto hands and knees, Marcus reentered me. Strong and solid, his arms wrapped around me, one at my middle and the other reaching higher so he could wrap a gentle hand around my neck. He held me against him, kissing my shoulder and the side of my neck as he resumed his relentless thrusting.

Abruptly, he reached a second, more intense crescendo, driving into me as deeply as possible and holding me against him in a crushing embrace. He touched me with his fingers as he filled me, dragging me with him over the edge and into an abyss of white-hot pleasure.

I gasped, oblivious to everything but him. "Marcus! Oh God, Marcus!" Even after the spasms subsided, my pulse throbbed under the hand he still held against my pubic bone. I let out a shaky breath. *Is it possible to die from too much pleasure?*

"Fuck, woman . . ." Marcus groaned.

"Hmmm . . . mmm . . ." I mumbled lazily.

Hours later, I was straddling his hips as he lay on his cot. He was once again hard and sheathed inside me, but we remained still. We both enjoyed the sensation of being joined, motionless, like we were one being. Elbows on his chest, I was resting my chin on my hands and watching him as he studied me with an unfathomable expression.

"Is it always like this?" I asked.

He traced my lips with his thumb before sliding both of his hands down my body, grazing over my breasts, belly, and hips. "What do you mean?"

"I've never felt anything like this . . . I don't think I could have felt anything like this before," I explained. "When two Nejerets are together, is it always so intense?"

Inhaling deeply, he grasped my hips and ground his pubic bone against mine, pushing himself deeper within me. An involuntary groan escaped from my throat, and he smiled lazily. I loved when he smiled like that. It seemed to temporarily wash away all the pain and inhumanity that had built up over his thousands of years.

"No," he said. "Definitely not."

"But how do you—" I let the words die unspoken at his wary expression. "Never mind. I don't want to know."

"No, you don't," he agreed. His voice had deepened, grown rougher, and I felt him throb inside me. After another slow grind and my answering moan, he said, "Whatever genetic mutation enabled us to enter the At also altered us significantly from humans in other ways. Regeneration, sensory enhancement . . . you know about those changes. But there are other, more subtle differences. Some of our people have been researching a pheromone we release when we're particularly enamored with someone. We seem to have specific receptors that become, for lack of a better word, addicted to a specific Nejeret or Nejerette's pheromone. We call it 'bonding.'"

Nuin's prophecy mentioned bonding—*Heru will make her his she-falcon and she will bind herself to him.* Was it referring to an actual, physiological phenomenon? I'd thought it was figurative, but I'd been wrong about so many other things, it was feasible that I was wrong about that as well.

Marcus's expression filled with amazement as he continued, "I didn't expect it to be so intense, but it's the only explanation for . . ." He closed his eyes momentarily and took a deep, blissful breath. "It's the only explanation for this." His fingers dug into the soft swell of my hips as he pushed deeper into me once again.

"Oh!" I exclaimed, trembling. I sat up and ran my hands over his tensed abdomen. "So you're not usually such a repeat offender?" I teased, shifting my hips in a slow, circular motion. He'd already reached completion three times in the past few hours—a feat I hadn't known was possible for a man in a single night, at least, not a human man. But human was something Marcus had never truly been.

Groaning, he closed his eyes and tilted his head back as I continued to move on top of him, so incredibly slowly. He was practically panting, and I couldn't tear my eyes away from the enraptured expression on his face. "No, Lex . . . I'm not. At least . . . not with . . . quite so . . . many . . . repeats."

Convulsively, his hands clenched on my hips, and his breathing turned erratic. He made a guttural noise and raised his head, his blackened-gold irises locking onto their red-brown counterparts. I could feel his abs flexing rhythmically under my hands.

"Lex," he whispered, letting his head fall back. "Lex . . ."

I leaned down and kissed the shallow valley between his pectorals, darting out my tongue to taste his damp, salty skin. When I raised my eyes, I found him watching me. Without breaking eye contact, I again touched my lips to his skin and whispered a single word. "Mine."

27

SEX & BLOOD

"Do you think they know?" I asked, peeking through the door of Marcus's tent. The sun had just risen, bringing our sprawling canvas town to life. I should have been exhausted from sleeping only a few hours, but I wasn't. I was exhilarated.

Chuckling, Marcus wrapped his arms around my waist and buried his face in my neck. "Little Ivanov . . . they *heard*." I groaned, and Marcus's chuckle turned into a full-blown laugh. His breath tickled my skin as he inhaled and exhaled deeply. "We need to shower—you smell like you just had marathon sex."

"Funny . . . I wonder if that's because I just *had* marathon sex." I leaned against him, already wanting him again. The hyperaware, hypersensitive bonding thing would take some getting used to—everywhere he touched me felt infinitely more sensitive than it had the previous day, and I couldn't resist touching him at every possible opportunity.

"It just may be," he said, nibbling the curve between my shoulder and neck. "But I don't want anyone else smelling you like this." He inhaled again. "Mmm . . . *this* is mine."

"There's a slight problem, then," I told him.

"Hmm?" His attentions to my neck continued, giving me goose bumps.

"We have to pass pretty much everyone on the way to the showers, and they all have noses, so . . ."

He smiled against my skin before letting me go and poking his head out of the tent to bark some orders to my guards. Minutes later, we stepped out into the bright light of the new day; the camp appeared empty aside from my guards, who were standing about ten tents away. Marcus had cleared us a path.

We stopped by my neighboring tent so I could grab some clean clothes and toiletries, and then we headed to the shower trailer beyond the west edge of camp. We showered together in the large, handicapped stall, washing each other liberally. We were nearly finished when Marcus slipped his hand between my legs.

"Marcus! You're defeating the purpose," I gasped as his fingers found my most sensitive place.

"Apologies, Little Ivanov, but seeing you like this—" He removed his hand, and within seconds, had my back against the wall, my legs wrapped around his hips. "—I . . . just . . . can't . . . resist."

We agreed to wash our own bodies after that, "to prevent wasting all the water," Marcus had said. I'd laughed.

Finally, hand in hand, Marcus and I emerged from the trailer, clean and fully clothed. I wasn't prepared for the dozens of Nejerets who offered us generous bows and congratulations as we walked back up the main drag to our tents. Marcus, on the other hand, accepted them graciously, almost as though he'd expected the reaction.

"I've never had so many people excited about my sex life," I murmured, hoping only Marcus was close enough to hear.

He shot me a look that told me I was being unbelievably dense.

"Oh." I blushed, realizing my folly. Apparently I was still

thinking like a human. "It's because I claimed you, and you accepted, isn't it? So . . . what does *that* mean?"

"In human terms, we're married," he explained, stopping at the entrance to my tent.

I gaped up at him. Like having children, I had pretty much given up on the idea of ever getting married, instead opting to gallivant around the Mediterranean, searching for remnants of the ancient, forgotten past. Besides, Marcus was pushing at least five thousand, while I was pushing only twenty-five. And we were *married? Oh my God . . . what are my parents going to say?*

He kissed me on the cheek and whispered, "I'll have some of the guards move your things into my tent along with a larger cot. Tonight we can further explore the more personal details of our marriage . . . if you'd like."

Regardless of my mental woes, I smiled, feeling my body tighten in anticipation. "I'd like," I said quietly. I was pretty sure the whole "marriage" thing had yet to really sink in.

Marcus pulled away, his eyes burning with promise. "Gather what you need for the day. I'll meet you here in five minutes." He walked toward his tent with purpose.

Ducking inside my own canvas home, I took a few humongous breaths. Much had changed since I'd left the previous night, and I couldn't help but lose myself in the unbelievably pleasant memories.

"Lex!" Marcus called from outside. "Hurry up! I'm famished!"

Laughing at myself for getting lost in daydreams, I picked up my excavation bag and hurried out into the warm desert air.

"We thought maybe—" Neffe began, but she was silenced by

a sharp sound from her father. "It's her choice," she snapped in response. She was sitting across from me at one of the green fold-out picnic tables underneath the canopy at the west edge of camp. Dominic sat beside her, and Marcus beside me while we ate a breakfast of oatmeal and fruit salad.

"*What* is my choice?" I asked, shooting Marcus a suspicious glance. He needed to learn that he couldn't run my life by omitting certain significant pieces of information, mythic Egyptian god or not.

Ignoring her father's furious glare, Neffe explained, "When I was growing up, shortly after Senenmut presented him with the tablet containing Nuin's lost prophecy, he"—she pointed her chin at Marcus—"left my mother and me because Set threatened to take my life if he stayed. He didn't know why Set made the threat, but he knew Set would carry it out because of what happened with Aset—Isis—and he knew Set would hold his word and not kill me if he left." Her full lips curved down in a frown. "Set does have a sense of honor, twisted as his mind is. Anyway, my mother was furious—maybe because having Heru as her husband was part of what kept her in power as the mighty pharaoh Hatchepsut—so she took up with Set instead. My father made Senenmut stay behind to watch over for me and keep me safe in his absence, but my mother coerced him into obeying Set, if only to ensure that Set would stay with her so she could retain her power."

God, she sounds like a real gem of a mother, I thought sarcastically.

Sighing, Neffe continued, "In the guise of my mother's stepson, Set forced Senenmut to work as his own personal architect, designing and constructing a handful of projects throughout the land. We now know that one is the very temple we're searching for, though nobody but Set, Senenmut, and the workers knew about it at the time, and Set cloaked all echoes relating to the temple long ago, before anyone knew to look for it in the At . . . not to mention he killed all of the workers upon its completion, including Senenmut." A deep sadness stirred in Neffe's eyes, and I instantly knew that she had cared deeply for the ancient architect.

"It wasn't until we found Senenmut's second tablet in his mother's coffin that we had some idea of where Set had hidden the chest containing the ankh-At." Squinting, Neffe looked up at the expanse of tan canvas sheltering us from the morning sun. "And that was maybe . . . around fifty years ago that we found the tablet." She shook her head, swishing her thick black pony-tail. "The point is, none of us can break through his cloak, but *you* can because you share his DNA *and* you're a manipulator. None of his other children, at least not the ones on our side, can manipulate the At. But, if you can slip through his cloak and learn the exact location of the entrance in the upper Anubis chapel, it would save us from having to tear the whole thing apart in our search."

I wanted to help, but I was scared. As the Meswett, I was supposed to be strong. I was supposed to save my people—and the world—but memories of Set and his poisonous words plagued me. *And* he had Jenny. What if I did something to anger him, and he took his rage out on my sister? But . . . what if we managed to find the hidden entrance, enter the temple, and somehow open the chest containing the ankh-At—Nuin's power—and gain control of that power before Set could coerce it from me? Surely, once I'd accessed Nuin's power over time, defeating Set would be easy. No Set, no Nothingness, safe world. It was ideal and oh so close I could almost reach out and touch it.

"I'll do it," I said, determined. Marcus's hand clenched my thigh, but he let my decision stand. "When?" I asked.

Neffe's eyes darted back and forth between us. "How about now?" she suggested.

"Now? Here?" Marcus spat. Turning all of his attention on me, he murmured, "You can do this later, Lex. We have time."

I leaned in, giving him a very steamy kiss, and whispered, "Be back in a few."

And then I was gone, enmeshed in the absolutely when-less Where for the first time. It intrigued me that the At's kaleidoscope colors flowed ceaselessly up and down, as opposed to the round and round of the where-less When I'd grown so familiar with. Shifting my focus slightly to the upper Anubis Chapel, I thought about Set . . . really, really hard . . . and eventually the world slammed into place.

I stumbled forward several steps, listening as the ground didn't *crunch beneath my feet. When I finally righted myself, I noticed two robed men standing before me, one pale-skinned—Set—the other tan.*

Set tapped on a limestone wall, speaking in what sounded like the same beautifully sibilant language I'd heard Marcus use several times— Middle Egyptian. It was so similar to Nuin's language . . . just not quite the same, like Spanish versus Italian.

"You should know better than this by now," Set said from behind me. I knew it was the real Set—his ba—not the echo of a past version of himself like the Set I was watching interact with a man I assumed was Senenmut.

I groaned. He's right. I really should know better. *I did* know *better . . . but people were depending on me.*

"I'm looking for the entrance. I thought you wanted me to find it so I can access the ankh-At," I said. "That way you can try to command me and all . . ."

Set laughed. "I want you to find it in the right state of mind. Are you in the right state of mind, Daughter?"

I refused to turn around.

"Be my daughter, my true daughter. Join my family in purpose as well as blood. You and I, we can do great things together," he cooed.

"No," I said. "We really can't."

"Join me. Obtain the ankh-At for me. Obey me," he urged.

"Never going to happen," I told him as I watched the other Set, the one from millennia past, argue with the golden-skinned man.

"*I'll destroy your precious state of Washington,*" Set said.

"*And then I'll never obey you. Not ever. I'll have nothing left to lose,*" *I told him.* Oh God . . . what if he really does it?

His hand latched around the back of my neck, squeezing so hard he forced my spine to arch. "*You think that? I am not so sure.*"

Suddenly, Set was in front of me. He backhanded me, hitting the left side of my face, and I sprawled onto the ground on hands and knees, spitting blood and saliva. I'd never been hit before, not really. The shock almost overwhelmed the pain . . . for about a second.

Kicking me in the gut, he said, "*Take a look, Daughter. See exactly what it is you have to lose.*"

I was suddenly crouched on hands and knees in my canvas tent, gasping for breath. The world was dead silent around me . . . too silent.

Did Set sent me back to my body? How'd I get back to my tent? *I groaned.* God, I hurt . . . *Taking a deep, painful breath, I called out,* "*Marcus? Dom? Vali? Sandra?*"

Dead silence.

I pushed myself up to my feet and swiped my swelling mouth with the back of my hand. It came away smeared with blood.

"*Hello! Anyone?*" *I called, passing through the wide-open doorway and into the dry heat of Deir el-Bahri.*

In the glaring midday sun, I hadn't noticed the debris piled on the ground in front of my little doorway. I tripped, stumbling several steps before sprawling out on hands and knees again. My palms were quickly becoming badly scraped, with sharp little rocks slicing into my flesh.

"*Damn it,*" *I grumbled, looking behind me to see what I'd tripped over. It was Dominic. My Dominic.*

"*Oh no! No, no no! Dom? Dom!*" *I scrambled the few feet to his motionless body.* "*Help!*" *I yelled.* "*Someone! HELP!*"

Even if the greatest doctor who'd ever lived had heard, it wouldn't have mattered. Dominic's open eyes were vacant, his face white and bloodless. I reached out, but snatched my hand back almost instantly. I couldn't bear to touch him.

Jerkily, I crawled to Marcus's tent. But after a quick peek through the open doorway, I knew it was empty.

Slowing down my panicked brain, I forced myself to remember where I'd been before I'd entered the At . . . before I'd encountered Set. At the tables under the canopy, eating breakfast with Marcus, Dominic, and Neffe.

Standing, I raced through the middle of camp. When I reached the west edge and saw what lay just beyond one of the tents along the perimeter, I skidded to a halt. It was another person. Familiar chestnut-brown hair fanned over the fine bones of a feminine, middle-aged face. Her arm was outstretched, fingers reaching toward the crumpled body of a stocky man.

Crouching at the woman's side, I extended a shaking hand toward her to brush the hair from her face, but stopped short. There was no question. I thought maybe I'd been wrong. Maybe it just looked like her. Maybe it was someone else, some other nameless woman. Someone else's mom. Not mine.

"NOOOOO!" I wailed, pounding the earth with my bloodied palms. I reached for her, needing to feel her in my arms. I had to let her know I was there for her, even if it was too late, but my hands were stopped short . . . by something . . . by nothing . . . by At.

The realization that I was in an echo hit me soundly in the chest. I sat back, taking in my surroundings. Questions swarmed my brain, buzzing, humming, flapping. Is it real? What kind of echo is it? Is it the past? Did something awful happen right after I entered the At? Or is it the future? But why would my parents be here? *I remembered Alexander once telling me that temporary, false echoes were allowed for training purposes.* Is it a false echo? Did Set fabricate this place? Can he even do that? *Marcus had told me that Set was the most talented manipulator of At, so I figured if anyone could create such a detailed, horrific false echo, it was him.*

Terrified, I fled from the echo . . . or I tried to. After a brief jarring sensation, I ended up right back where I'd been—on the ground before my dead mother. I couldn't leave the echo. Somehow, Set was keeping me there. I was in a cage composed of At . . . his cage.

"Lex? There you are! Are you all right?" *I spun on my knees at Marcus's voice.* Marcus. Sanctuary. Haven.

"Marcus! Thank—"

My words were cut short by the splattering of warm wetness on my face. Blood welled out of a hole in Marcus's forehead, and he fell to his knees.

All realization that I was in a fabricated echo evaporated. Marcus, my Marcus, lay dead in front of me. His blood was pooling on the ground, inching toward my splayed fingers.

"NO!" *I screamed. Keening, ancient and instinctual, I rocked on my knees beside the body of the man I loved. My essence simmered down to one thing—despair.*

Anything but him. Anyone but him.

"Ah, daughter, I should have known," *Set said with satisfaction, then winked.* "Got you."

Minutes, hours, days later, I trembled beside another bloodied, dead Marcus. How many? Why?

"Just do what I say. Obey me, and I won't kill him again," *Set explained for the hundredth, thousandth, millionth time.* "Why is that so hard for you to understand?"

Because if I obey you, mankind will be destroyed, you bastard! *My perpetually bloody mouth opened in a grim smile, and I spat out some pinkish saliva. Splatters landed on his designer shoes.* "Maybe I just like the sound of your voice when you're pissy," *I cooed.*

"You little whore," *he howled, kicking me in the abdomen. I curled into the fetal position, but it didn't stop him. Aiming for my back and legs, Set kicked me until I could no longer think. There was only pain.*

Sometime later, I heard the voice of an angel. "Lex . . . why are you on the ground?" It was Marcus, again.

I needed him . . . to hold me . . . to tell me everything would be okay . . . to remind me to survive. I needed him to remind me why I should want to survive.

"Don't look at him," Set commanded.

Right, *I thought.* If I look at him, he dies. If I disobey you, he dies. *Against my every instinct, my every desire, I squeezed my eyes shut.*

"Lex . . . Little Ivanov, come here," Marcus said, sounding worried.

"Tell him you hate him. Tell him he means nothing to you," Set *ordered.*

But I love him . . . he means everything to me. *"NO!"*

A gunshot. The heavy sound of a body hitting the ground. Both had become so familiar that they were like my heartbeat and the whoosh of air slipping in and out of my lungs.

Again.

And again.

And again. Forever.

"Lex . . . why won't you look at me?" Marcus asked, sounding heartbroken.

Because I can't. Because you'll die. I can't watch you die, not again.

"Please Lex, tell me what's wrong. I'll do anything . . . I love you!" Marcus exclaimed.

"Tell him you hate him. Tell him he means nothing to you," Set *ordered.*

With a deep, horrified breath, I croaked, "Marcus, I hate you. You mean nothing to me."

"Now look at him," Set directed.

I turned, and nearly fell to my knees. Marcus, in all of his masculine glory, was weeping.

"Why, Lex?" Marcus asked, his golden eyes burning accusation into mine.

"I . . . I . . . can't," I gasped.

"Touching, really," Set said urbanely. "Now come give Daddy a kiss. And make it count."

"Never!" I hissed and watched a bullet tunnel through Marcus's skull.

Closing my eyes, I bowed my head at the death of my latest Marcus. I never wanted to watch him die again. I would trade the world for him. It was what Set wanted, for me to be willing to trade something for the world . . . for there to be some price high enough to buy my obedience . . . for me to make that decision on instinct, every time. He'd succeeded.

"I'll give you some time to think," Set said before vanishing.

But I didn't need time to think—he'd broken me. He'd won. Anything for Marcus. The world for Marcus.

I would obey.

28

MARCUS

If anyone even mentioned the solstice or the Nothingness again, Marcus was going to lose it. He gripped the edge of his desk with both hands, waiting for his daughter or one of the men sitting on either side of her to speak. His head was throbbing, and his hands would have been shaking if not for their death grip on the desk. Bonding withdrawals. If he didn't get them under control soon, the withdrawals would be the death of him. Literally.

Neffe opened her mouth, took a deep breath, and exhaled loudly. "This is ridiculous! The solstice is in a w—"

"I don't care!" Marcus shouted, flipping his desk over as his rage and pain converged within him, erupting outward. Various pens, papers, and books went flying. He was sick of talking about things that didn't matter. Finding her ba was all that mattered.

Marcus didn't care that his refusal to leave his tent and its priceless occupant for more than a few minutes forced his people to come to him whenever they needed to speak with him. He was used to people coming to him. He didn't care that everyone treated him like he had lost most of his mental facul-

337

ties. He didn't care about the excavation or the Nothingness or the destruction of the goddamn world.

Nothing mattered but the woman lying in At-qed on his cot —*their* cot. She'd been like that for nearly three months. He'd never heard of anyone remaining in the suspended physical state for so long, and he couldn't help but imagine every passing second damaging her body. Theoretically, she could survive for years in At-qed without food or water. Theoretically, to her body, only a few hours had passed. Theoretically, if she woke at that moment, she would feel like she'd taken a several-hour nap. Theoretically.

Apparently unperturbed by his outburst, Neffe brushed a few stray papers off her lap. "We have to do something," she grumbled, looking to Alexander and Dominic for support.

Marcus glared at her for a long time before looking away, unable to bear the weight of her pitying expression. He couldn't stand to look at *anyone* for more than a few seconds—they all felt sorry for him, and he hated them for it. They were wasting their energy worrying about him when they should have been finding a way to help her. Lex.

"Find her," he growled. "That's doing something."

"And if she's not anywhere? If she can't be found? If she's just *gone?*" Neffe asked, and Alexander and Dominic held their breath. Marcus's volatility became more dangerous each day that passed without Lex's ba returning to her body.

It was the pain, and not just emotional devastation at the possibility of losing her forever, but the tormenting, ever-increasing physical pain of bonding withdrawals. Unlike kicking a regular addiction, Marcus's need—his craving—for her bonding pheromones would only get worse. Only two things could stop the pain—Lex returning to her body and becoming one with him in the most intimate of acts, or his death.

Standing, Marcus strode the few paces into the tent's second room and sat beside Lex on the edge of the wide cot. She lay on her back, slender and pale and, as far as his eyes could tell, healthy. Neffe examined her every day to make sure nothing was amiss, and he washed her every night so she would be comfortable.

Gazing down at her, Marcus ran his fingers along the silken strands of mahogany hair that splayed across the off-white pillowcase. She looked so peaceful with her eyes closed and lips barely parted . . . so unlike her usual, focused expression. Marcus imagined her face with a faint line between her eyebrows and her eyes narrowed in thought . . . or accusation . . . or determination. He closed his eyes for a long moment, swallowing his rising despair.

Gently, he brushed his thumb across her soft, rosy lips, again trying to press them together, but she refused to keep her mouth closed. He traced his fingers over her chin, down the steep slope to her slender neck, and lower, until his palm rested over her heart . . . and he waited. A minute. Two. Three. Thud-THUMP.

He tried to speak twice before he could form the words. His mouth was too dry, his throat constricted. "If she's gone," he said hoarsely, "then nothing matters anymore."

Marcus heard a rustle of fabric as Neffe stood. "Father—"

"Leave me," he said quietly. "Dom, you stay."

He didn't look behind him to watch Neffe and Alexander's hasty exit, but the scuffle of shoe soles on canvas and the brief burst of less stagnant air told him that they had left. It would be . . . difficult, what he was about to do . . . difficult and cruel, but also necessary.

"Come here," Marcus said to the only other conscious person in the tent. Dom had been his right hand, functioning as his protégé for centuries, and Marcus trusted few above him. What he was about to do might destroy everything between them.

The Frenchman moved instantly, stopping at the head of the

cot. He stared down at Lex's porcelain face, his pale, sharp features etched with longing.

Slowly, Marcus slid his hand down the shallow valley between her black linen-covered breasts, letting it settle in the curve of her waist. "She's perfect, is she not?"

The choking sound that escaped from Dominic's throat confirmed his suspicions—Dominic was in love with Lex . . . with *his* Lex. It was the last thing he wanted to hear, but it was what he needed to hear. "What would you do to bring her back?" Marcus asked, deceptively calm.

"Anything," Dominic whispered, his accent heavier than usual.

"Why can't you find her?"

"I've told you—"

"Tell me again," Marcus ordered.

Exhaling his frustration, Dominic explained, "Every time I get a sense of where he's holding her in the At, it's as though I'm blocked by a wall. I can't get through. I can't even see what's on the other side. I'm just not strong enough."

"So what would make you stronger?" Marcus asked.

"More of Set in my veins—sharing half of his DNA just isn't enough" Dominic said caustically. "It's like there's a scale I can't quite tip enough in my favor to break through."

Marcus turned his head abruptly, focusing on the man standing beside him. "And if I could increase it? If you entered the At joined with someone who could tip the ratio of Set DNA in your favor?"

"Hypotheticals get us nowhere," Dominic responded.

"It's not hypothetical."

Dominic shook his head slowly. "But that would mean . . . *Dieu!* Set reproduced with his own human offspring?" His severe features twisted in disgust.

Marcus nodded, equally appalled. It was one of the most horrific crimes their people could commit, but for once, he was glad of his ancient, misguided friend's heinous faults. Set having reproduced with his own carrier daughter might very well save Lex.

"Only once, that I know of," Marcus said.

Dominic was suddenly alert, displaying the razor-sharp intensity that had drawn Marcus to him when they first met centuries ago. "Who? Where?"

Marcus looked back down at Lex, flexing his fingers into her tantalizingly soft flesh. "She's here," he rasped. "With her mother."

"With her *mother*?" Dominic asked, clearly surprised. Only the very young still had mothers, since Nejerettes couldn't bear children. Every Nejeret's mother was a human carrier. "What aren't you telling me?"

"She hasn't manifested yet."

"You would force her?" Dominic asked, horrified.

"Without an ounce of hesitation or remorse. But the question is, will you?" Marcus asked.

It was a horrible, dreadful thing to ask of Dominic. Forcing any Nejeret to manifest by thrusting them into the At essentially froze the Nejeret's body at its current state of physical maturity. If the Nejeret or Nejerette were too young, he or she would die. If the Nejeret or Nejerette survived, his or her body would remain perpetually on the cusp of adulthood. In terms of Nejeret crimes, forcing someone to manifest was second only to incestuous procreation with your own human offspring —but it wasn't *as* bad. It was acceptable—it had to be. For Lex.

Dominic only hesitated for a moment before answering. "Yes, I'll do it . . . for Lex. How old is the girl?"

"Eighteen."

"You're certain she'll manifest . . . that she's truly Nejerette?" Dominic asked. If she weren't, attempting to force manifestation would be a death sentence.

Marcus nodded. "She's already showing the signs of pre-manifestation."

"Who?"

"Katarina Dubois, Gen's daughter."

"*Merde!* I didn't realize Gen was . . . how did you discover she's Set's daughter?" Dominic asked with morbid curiosity.

"I had her DNA tested as soon as I learned Set had impregnated her. Had to know if she was an Ivanov," Marcus said. "She wasn't."

"I see. Get the child to agree, and I'll do it." Dominic looked nauseated as he spoke. "Get her to agree, and we can find Lex."

"Done," Marcus said, rising from the cot. "Wait here." He strode from the tent with an undeniable purpose. The ache in his head spread throughout his body as he walked. It was always worse when he moved.

"Sir?" a man chirped from Marcus's right as he marched through the camp.

"No."

"But—"

Marcus thrust his arm out, effectively clotheslining the Nejeret. Less than a minute later, he reached Genevieve and Kat's tent and ducked through the small doorway.

"Marcus!" Genevieve exclaimed, rising from her seat. The desk in front of her was filled with empty and half-empty bottles. She'd continued her role as purveyor of the mystical and occult—mostly rubbish—as soon as they'd set up camp. "I still haven't found anything that can draw her back to her body," she said.

Marcus doubted she'd put much effort into her search. "Where's Kat?"

"Kat? Why?"

"I need to ask her a question."

Genevieve narrowed her eyes. "Which would be . . . ?"

Marcus took a deep, calming breath. He had neither the time

nor the patience for this. "I'd like to ask her if she would be interested in taking up a position on the excavation."

Genevieve's dark eyes had always reminded him of Set, but he'd frequently wondered if he saw what he expected rather than what was really there. Those midnight pools slanted hotly. "Doing what, exactly? And don't you dare say 'excavating.'"

Purposely, Marcus let his emotional restraint break. He could use it. He could use Genevieve—she was a woman, and he'd always been able to manipulate women. "I need her help, Gen. With Lex."

"How could my daughter possibly help you with your *woman?*"

"If Dominic brings Kat into the At, they can break through Set's barrier and get to Lex. It's the only way," Marcus said, letting his voice hitch.

"But Kat's not ready. She's too young. She can't even do it yet!"

"If she lets Dom take her into the At, he can make it work," Marcus explained.

She inhaled sharply. "No! I know what you're talking about —*forcing*. You won't do that to my daughter!"

Marcus clouded his voice with as much genuine emotion as he could muster. "Gen, I need you. You and Kat, you're the only ones who can help me. I—I'll die without your help."

Her anger wavered, but it quickly reformed under the strength of motherly protectiveness. "Absolutely no—"

"Will *she* die without my help?" Kat asked from behind Marcus. Unbelievably, she'd eavesdropped on their conversation without Marcus noticing.

Marcus turned slowly, settling his desperate gaze on Kat. "Eventually, yes."

"Am I *really* the only one who can help?" she asked.

Genevieve began, "Kat, go back to—"

"No, Mom! This is *my* business, not yours." She ignored her spluttering mother and addressed Marcus. "Well, am I?"

"Yes. I would be forever in your—"

"Oh, please." Kat rolled her eyes. "Get over yourself already. I don't want you to be forever in my anything. I'll do it—for Lex. I like her. She's strong. She doesn't let you push her around with all your 'I'm such a hottie stud god' crap. Plus, she's my sister. I'd like to have her around again."

It took Marcus a few seconds to wade through her language, but eventually he stared at her, awestruck. "You'll do it?"

"Seriously? Didn't I just say that? I thought you guys were big on, like, verbal agreements or whatever."

At a loss for words, Marcus closed the short distance between himself and the teenage girl and hugged her. She was slender, like Lex, and easy to lift until her feet dangled uselessly.

"Thank you!" he said fiercely before setting her back down.

Breathily, Kat said, "You can totally do that anytime you want."

"Kat!" her mother screeched. "I forbid you fro—"

"You can't stop me, Mom. Marcus won't let you," she told her mother. The girl was as fierce as a wildcat.

Genevieve turned her dark, furious eyes on Marcus. "If this harms her in any way, I swear to you . . ."

"I know," Marcus said. "Kat, Dominic awaits us in my tent. Come."

"Now?" Kat asked. Her eyes were wide, making her look younger, but not afraid.

"Was I unclear? Yes, now."

"Fine. Don't get your tighty whities in a bunch!" Kat stated hotly. "I don't know how she puts up with you . . . she deserves, like, a medal or something for messiah girlfriend of the year. You'd better treat her well!"

She swept out of the tent with Marcus and Genevieve close behind her.

29

LOST & FOUND

Standing at the edge of the illusory camp, I stared out at Hatchepsut's unreachable mortuary temple. Set had made the impenetrable perimeter of my prison large enough for a variety of death scenes, but cramped enough to taunt me with views of places I couldn't reach. The temple ruins and surrounding cliffs glowed an eerie orange under a perpetual sunrise.

I hugged myself, holding completely still and silent. How long have I been trapped in here? *It felt like years.*

At the sudden, abrasive crunch of footsteps, I squeezed my eyes shut and held my breath. Soon Set would strike, belittle, or command me. The order was unpredictable, though all three were inevitable.

"Dieu!" an unexpected male voice exclaimed, quickly followed by the softer, shaky words of a woman. "Oh. Em. Gee. Is it always like that? It was like an acid trip. Not that I've done acid or anything. Where are—holy shit! How many . . . are all of those bodies Marcus's? Oh . . . I think I'm gonna puke."

I wrapped my arms around myself more tightly, taking slow, deep breaths and trying to ignore the new, confusing twist to Set's torture. Dominic hadn't been present for at least several hundred death cycles. I wished Set would just show himself, so I could let him know he'd won, that he'd broken me to the point of obedience, and the torment could stop.

"Lex?" the false Dominic said, only feet behind me.

I hunched in on myself. Why Dom? Why now?

"Are you okay? Lex?" Dominic asked, concern lacing his words.

"What's wrong with her?" I heard the female voice—Kat, I realized —ask in front of me, but I refused to open my eyes.

Dominic, his sensuous accent inflaming my turmoil, joined Kat in front of me. "Lex? Why won't you answer? Look at me, Lex. Open your eyes."

"No. You're not real," I whimpered.

"Oh, Lex," he whispered. "What did he do to you? Your face . . ."

"It's not just her face," Kat said. "Look at her arms, her legs . . ."

"Oh, Dieu . . ." Dominic groaned.

"He's not real," I reminded myself out loud, trying to ignore the mental image of the man who had quickly tunneled his way into my heart, becoming my closest friend. "He's not real . . . he's not real . . ."

"D'you think she's broken?" Kat asked.

"I don't know . . . Lex?" Dominic said again, and my eyes flashed open when I felt his gentle fingers on my elbows.

I stumbled backward, gaping. "You can't . . . you're not real. You can't touch me!" Shock, more than anything else, made my eyes widen and dart around franticly. Where is he? He's here, I know it!

Dominic approached me again, wrapping his long, graceful fingers around the hand I'd flung out as a shield. "Feel me, Lex. I'm real."

Trembling, I let him pull me in close and wrap his arms around me. His lean body hummed with tension like a live wire.

"Dom?" My voice was breathy and too high. "Are you really here?"

"Yes. I promise." He held me tighter, trapping my hands against his chest. I balled the soft cotton of his shirt in my fists and succumbed to violent, uncontrollable sobs. Had his arms not been around me, I would have collapsed to the ground, a broken heap of the woman I'd once been.

"Um . . . guys?" Kat said from inches behind me. "I hate to interrupt *this lovefest, but shouldn't we, you know, get the hell outta here? 'Cause, if this was a movie, the evil dude would totally show up right now."*

"Well put, Katarina."

My body went rigid at the sound of Set's voice, smooth and contemptuous, and I groaned against Dominic's shoulder.

"Merde!" Dominic hissed. At feeling one of his arms release me, I held onto his shirt more tightly.

Set chuckled. "My three favorite children visiting all at once . . . now, tell me how you broke through my—NO!"

His wail echoed as the world melted around us, dissolving into a frenzy of erratic colors that blinked in and out of existence. The At felt dangerously unstable as it swirled, as though we'd been caught in an endless, violent wave.

Abruptly, the disorienting motion ceased, and one blessed realization overtook my entire consciousness—the absence of pain. For once, my body felt whole. My ribs and abdomen didn't ache. My hands weren't sliced with a thousand cuts. Amazingly, my mouth neither tasted of blood nor felt swollen.

Eyes still closed, I smelled the spicy, alluring scent surrounding me, and my pulse sped. That was something Set had gotten wrong; he hadn't been able to recreate Marcus's enticing aroma, nor his electric presence. I felt Marcus squeeze my hand, his warm, real fingers sending a thrill of sensation up my arm.

"Lex?" Marcus whispered and I moaned at hearing the richness of his voice. "Lex? Can you hear me?" He sounded anxious . . . eager . . . desperate.

"Mmmm . . . Marcus . . . you smell good," I murmured.

"Are—are you alright?" He gently ran his finger along my forearm as he waited for my response.

Smiling, I whispered, "You're here," and opened my eyes. It was bright—too bright to focus right away. "Why wouldn't I be alr—" My question cut off as soon as my vision cleared and

Marcus's concerned face came into view. He was leaning over me, his beautiful, blazing eyes searing into mine. My entire body tensed, and I sat up, ripping my hand out of his grasp. I instantly turned away from him and pulled my legs up, hugging them to my chest. A low keening tickled my ears, and I realized, belatedly, that it was mine. The sound rose and fell with my rhythmic rocking motion.

"Lex—what's wrong? Why won't you look at me?" Marcus asked.

"*Don't look at him,*" Set's voice replayed in my head.

"No," I whimpered. "I won't."

"Please, Lex, tell me what's wrong. Tell me what he did to you. Just look at me!" Marcus ordered, his words increasingly frantic.

"*Tell him you hate him. Tell him he means nothing to you.*"

"No!" I wailed, rocking with increased intensity. "You'll die! He'll kill you! You'll die!"

Hands were on my shoulders, stilling me, and I knew they were Marcus's from the pleasant thrum their touch invoked in my blood.

"So she really is broken," Kat said. "Should we, like, slap her or something?"

"Absolutely not!" Dominic nearly shouted. "She's been beaten enough already!"

"Set beat you?" Marcus asked, hoarse. Nobody but me seemed to hear him.

"Fine, fine, whatever. Don't Hulk out on me, dude! I'm just saying, maybe Marcus should back off. Seems to me he's the one driving her batshit . . ."

"You should probably stop talking now," Dominic advised.

"Well, *he* should probably leave her alone! He's making her worse!" she huffed.

"Dear *little* sister, this is quickly becoming none of your business. Perhaps you should take your leave," Dominic suggested, his voice cold.

"Screw you! And you too, Marcus!" Kat screeched. "I totally made a flippin' huge sacrifice for her—my boobs are *never* getting any bigger! Of course she's gonna freak out at the sight of him—there was a mountain of dead Marcuses in that echo prison thing. So, if you two could take a break from the ultimate douchebag competition for a few minutes and let me have some girl time with Lex, maybe she'll calm down!"

Marcus's hands withdrew from my shoulders, but I remained still, staring at the tan, canvas wall of Marcus's tent. "What do you mean, 'mountain of dead Marcuses'?" he asked, sounding shaken.

Dominic spoke defensively, "I was going to tell you as soon as—"

"Kat?" I said softly. My single word cut through the explosive atmosphere, diffusing it immediately.

"Yeah, Lex?" The girl's voice had utterly transformed from that of a pissed off teenager to that of a caring friend.

When I spoke, it was to the tent wall. "What are you talking about? What huge sacrifice?"

Kat sat on the cot beside me, facing the opposite direction, her hip flush with mine. "Um . . . they needed me to go with Dom into the At. It was the only way to break through the barrier to get to you."

Turning my head, I rested my cheek on my knee and met her rich brown, almond-shaped eyes. "But you're too young."

"I know. It's called 'forcing.' Now I'll go through all the usual manifestation crap like you've been dealing with, just a little earlier than expected."

"What's that have to do with your boobs?" I asked, feeling like I wasn't seeing the whole picture.

"I'm frozen . . . like this. Sure, I'll get all the healing

awesomeness and be über-glam and whatever, but I'll always look eighteen."

"Oh, Kat," I said, reaching for her slim hand and giving it a gentle squeeze. "I'm so sorry."

She nudged my knees with her shoulder and rolled her eyes. "Seriously, don't worry about it. I'm gonna be one of a kind—a superhot teen chick for thousands of years," she preened.

I wondered if she'd have to deal with the shitty adolescent mood swings forever. It would pave the way for an exciting life, if nothing else, but it was a high price to pay.

"Thank you," I said, trying to hold back the guilt and self-loathing that were suddenly coursing through me. *Did she sacrifice her maturity for nothing? Were they too late?*

"Hey . . . Lex . . ." she soothed, misreading the cause of my souring mood. "It's okay, really. It was my choice."

"I'm in your debt, okay? Whatever happens, I owe you . . . big time," I told her. "Deal?"

She gave me a genuine grin and agreed, "Deal."

"Wonderful," Marcus said, his voice deep, smooth, and razor-sharp. "Now, someone tell me what the hell happened to Lex over the last three months and why she can't stand to look at me. That is, if it's not too much trouble . . ."

Three months? What . . . how is that possible? I felt like I'd just woken up from a nap, not from a three-month coma. I had no feeding tube, no catheter—I gave my shoulder a sniff—I didn't smell different than I usually did, and my mouth didn't taste like anything had crawled inside and died, so . . . *what's the deal?*

Taking a deep breath, I released Kat's hand and slowly rotated on the cot, noting how surprisingly normal my muscles felt. I wasn't weak or stiff. I just felt like me. I dangled my legs over the edge of the cot next to Kat's, facing the center of the tent. I was looking at the canvas floor, at two pairs of men's work boots, one set of reddish black leather, the other light brown. They belonged to two of the people I cared about most in the world, and I was terrified to look at either of them.

"He killed you," I said hollowly, studying their khaki trousers. "He killed everyone I . . . everyone I love . . . at first. My mom, Dom, you, everyone. And then he focused on you, Marcus. He'd switch it up every once in a while, tossing in Jenny or Grandma Suse or Alexander or . . . anyone. But after a while, it was just you. Over and over and over. It felt like forever. If I didn't do what he said, he'd shoot you in the head. If I looked at you without his permission, he'd kill you. If I said the wrong thing, you were dead. If . . ."

"What was the *right* thing? What did he make you say to me?"

"I had to tell you that I"—I stifled a sob—"that I hated you and that you meant nothing to me. I told you I was disgusted by your touch and that you should go be with other women. And I told you I never wanted to see you again. Hundreds of times . . . maybe thousands." I lifted one shoulder in a weak shrug. "If he didn't believe it, he'd shoot you. You always ended up dead. I couldn't . . . I've never been a good liar."

Tears streamed down my face as I waited, staring at their legs. Silence, thick and palpable, filled the tent.

Marcus was the one who finally broke it. "Dom, Kat . . . leave us."

"Why? What are you gonna do to her?" Kat screeched, scooting closer to wrap a protective arm around my shoulders. "You can't be mad at her . . . she didn't mean it!"

"I'm not. I just need to talk to her. Alone." As Marcus spoke, it became evident that his patience had waned to a fragile thread.

"Come along, Kat. I'm sure your mother will want to know you're back and not . . . damaged." The darker shoes— Dominic's—stepped forward, and he reached his hand out for Kat, latching onto her wrist. He pulled her up and dragged her toward the exit. Before leaving, he said, "Can I speak with you for a moment? Outside?" I assumed he wasn't talking to me.

"I'll be in my mom's tent if you need me, Lex!" Kat called from outside. She and Dominic were closely followed by Marcus.

Staying as silent as possible, I focused on my heightened sense of hearing. I hoped Marcus and Dominic didn't move too far away from the tent, so I could catch whatever it was that Dominic wanted to say to Marcus . . . that he wouldn't say in front of me.

"Just give her time," Dominic said quietly. "She seems more or less okay. She'll probably come around eventually."

"Probably? You mean 'might not.' You'd like that, I'm sure, but I can't accept that." Though his voice was also quiet, Marcus sounded strained.

"If she's not ready to be around you, that's all there is to it. You can't make her be the way she was before."

"No, you don't understand," Marcus growled. "I *have* to get rid of her aversion—for her sake as much as mine. She's been in At-qed so the effects have been slowed for her, but if she goes much longer, she's going to start having withdrawal pains, and then . . ."

There was a choking sound, and when Dominic spoke, his voice sounded tight, like he might be sick. "Are you saying—you and she—you've *bonded*?"

"Yes."

"But it's been months. You must be in agony. People have died from the withdrawals!"

"All true," Marcus said.

"Well, that explains a lot. You've been acting—"

"I'm fully aware of my behavior. Are we done?"

"Uh . . . yes," Dominic said, though he sounded hesitant.

"Did you listen?" Marcus asked as he reentered the tent. I

watched his boots as he moved closer, stopping with their toes inches from my bare, dangling feet.

"Yes."

Kneeling on the canvas floor, he took my hands in his. "I won't force you to do anything, Little Ivanov, but if you can't even look at me, in a few hours you're going to be in unimaginable pain."

"Why?"

He exhaled heavily. "Not much is known about bonding . . . at least not scientifically. There are no fully bonded couples living today, only some partials. But one thing is certain—bonding withdrawals are both painful and deadly. If one half of a bonded couple dies, the other follows shortly after."

"You said you've been in pain? For months?"

"Since the day you didn't come back from the At."

"Marcus, I don't—" My words ended abruptly when I raised my eyes to his. Simultaneously, I fought the instinct to look away and was drawn to the raw pain tightening his facial muscles. Every possible feature seemed pinched and strained, and his golden eyes glowed feverishly. "I don't know how to make it stop!" I wailed. "God, Marcus, I feel like a dog slobbering at a bell. I don't want to be afraid to look at you, and I hate hurting you, but I . . . I . . . ."

As I drank in the masculine perfection of Marcus's tensed face, I realized that Set had given me the one Pavlovian response I needed to overcome his adverse psychological training. I felt the need to look away from Marcus because I didn't want to hurt him. For months, looking at him without permission had meant his death. But that aversion would hurt him, too. It *was* hurting him. He was, as Dominic had said, in agony, but I had the ability to take the pain away. That knowledge was the most effective and welcome aversion override I could have wished for.

"I love you, but . . . are you sure you want this . . . to be bound forever? It might not be too late to stop . . . I mean . . . I don't want to make you do it just because of the pain," I said, feeling suddenly self-conscious.

"Too late or not, pain or not . . . I want this—you—more than I've ever wanted anything," Marcus said, his voice huskier than before.

His words filled my chest with a warm, joyous glow and shot electricity straight to my core. It was the only confirmation I needed. Scooting to the edge of the cot, I parted my knees and hooked my fingers through Marcus's belt loops, pulling him between my legs.

"Lex, I—"

"Let me help you," I whispered, running my hands up over the front of his button-down shirt. The thin fabric did little to conceal the hard ridges of muscle shaping his torso.

With wide eyes and parted lips, Marcus raised his hands to my shoulders. He slid his fingertips over the sensitive skin along my collarbone. "Lex—"

"Let me make the pain stop," I begged softly. My nimble fingers were undoing the buttons on his shirt from the top down.

"Woman," he rumbled in his silky bass. "Let me speak!" His cross tone warred with the combination of passion and pain burning in his eyes.

I winced, pausing on the last button. "Sorry."

Holding my gaze, he said, "I love you, Lex." He filled his words with countless layers of meaning, and my lips spread into a warm smile.

He looked flabbergasted. "That's it? A smile?"

Laughing softly, I glanced down to finish unbuttoning his shirt. "Don't worry . . . you're getting more than a smile. It's not like it's the first time you've told me."

Marcus's hands, lightning quick, shifted to the sides of my head and tilted my face back up. "Yes, Little Ivanov, it is."

"No, Marcus, it's . . . oh." I closed my eyes to hold back the sudden and furious welling of tears. It was the first time the *real* Marcus had told me he loved me. Set had taken something invaluable from us—the right to express our feelings in our own time. It was something that could never be replaced and I hated him that much more for stealing it.

"Lex?"

"Hmmm?"

Feather-light, his lips brushed across first one cheekbone, then the other. "Little Ivanov?"

"Yeah?" I whispered, my furious sorrow diminishing immediately.

Burying one hand in my hair, Marcus turned my head so his breath came close against the skin between my ear and jaw. Each time his mouth barely touched me, tendrils of fiery pleasure burst to life beneath my skin. The thumb of his other hand skimmed my lips, and my breath came out noticeably shaky.

"I love you." His thumb slipped between my lips, tasting faintly of salt as he wet it with saliva from my tongue. The damp fingertip ran softly from one corner of my lower lip to the other, and back. "And only you."

Tightening his grip on my hair, he tilted my head back, giving him easier access to my neck. He inhaled deeply as he nibbled an electric line to my right collarbone. He licked along the graceful arc of bone in one smooth motion, from shoulder inward, ending by kissing the hollow at the base of my throat. A delicious ache was building within me, and a soft moan escaped from my parted lips.

"I want you," he said. The fingers of his free hand mirrored his tongue's path, eventually trailing down to my breastbone and slipping under the low neck of my dress. I whimpered when he ignored my breasts, instead pressing his palm against the center of my chest and smiling against my neck. "Only you," he whispered.

He raised his head from my throat, removed his hand from

my chest, and released my hair. Holding my eyes, he lowered his hands to my knees and slid them up under my dress. The intense hunger in his eyes did as much to prepare me for him as his touch.

There was a tearing sound—Marcus had literally ripped my underwear off. As soon as they were out of the way, I heard the metallic clang of his belt and the sound of his zipper.

"And all of you," he finished. Gripping my hips firmly, he pulled me off the cot and onto him, both of us grunting as we joined.

While the initial, intense sensation of holding him within me still pulsed from my core, Marcus embraced me tightly and sat back on his heels. So urgent was our need for one another that his quick, rough pace brought me to my peak remarkably soon. And when he buried his face in my neck and groaned, embracing me desperately, I flew away. Throbbing fire exploded in my belly and spread outward with nearly unbearable force. I was falling . . . soaring . . . unraveling. I lost myself and became someone else—the impossible combination of two souls, two minds, two bodies, but one being. I bound myself to Marcus, wholly and completely.

Slowly, as conscious thought returned, I became aware of Marcus's soft words. He rocked me gently, murmuring ancient, beautiful words that I couldn't understand. Pulling away enough to see his face, to read it for lingering signs of agony, I found only peace.

"Better?" I asked.

Lazily, Marcus smiled, his eyes like molten gold, and he let out a deep, satisfied hum.

Slipping my hands under the shirt he still partially wore, I ran my fingertips up and down his back, savoring the way he shivered with my touch. "I love you, Marcus."

He chuckled and brushed his lips softly against mine.

"Marcus?"

"Hmm?"

I took a deep breath. "You said I was trapped in the At for months? What's the date?"

He tensed, turning to stone even as he held me, and dread took root in my chest.

Leaning back, I asked, "How many days do we have left?"

His jaw clenched, once, twice. "The solstice is in a week."

My heart felt like it stopped beating entirely.

A week until the solstice.

A week until the Nothingness takes over the At.

Sometime between then and now, I decide the fate of the world. Not good.

3 0

ENTER & UNLOCK

"I can't wait to see the chest," I said, pulling on some olive-green cargo shorts I'd found in one of the trunks set along the wall opposite the cot. Marcus, still half-naked and lounging on the floor, watched intently as they slid up my long legs. Luckily, Marcus had moved my things into his tent while I'd been trapped in the At, so I had everything I needed at my fingertips. I found my favorite black bra deeper in the trunk and slipped it on. "Is it big? Gold? Covered in jewels?"

Marcus stood, shed the remainder of his clothes, and stretched his toned body, graceful as a cat. I was really enjoying the view. "The chest is . . . hard to describe. You'll see."

"Not if you don't put some clothes on," I said, giving him a pointed look. "Or are you planning on giving everyone up at the temple a show?"

Smirking, Marcus quickly dressed his lower half in thin, camel-colored trousers. As he shrugged into a white linen shirt, his face turned serious. "Promise me something, Little Ivanov?"

I raised my eyebrows.

"Take it slow once we get in there? The Nothingness doesn't

take over the At for another week—we don't have to rush opening the chest."

I recited part of the first verse of Nuin's prophecy aloud.

She will acquire the ankh-At or
Mankind will wither under the weight of the Nothingness.

"Sooner's better than later," I said, and my mood suddenly soured. "You know, I can't believe Set's my father. He's such an evil dick," I huffed, yanking on a black tank top over my head.

Marcus finished buttoning his shirt, leaving the top two buttons undone, and reached for his boots. "He wasn't always like that. He was a good man once."

I shrugged while tying my own dark hiking boots. Silently, I recited the next part of the prophecy.

She will obey Set and destroy mankind or
She will defy Set and mankind will prevail.
She will decide and either mankind or Set will be destroyed.

The world's screwed, I thought and scowled.

Sighing, Marcus finished with his laces and closed the distance between us, wrapping me in his protective arms.

Breathing in his delicious, spicy scent, I tried to forget about Set, the prophecy, the ankh-At, and the Nothingness for few seconds. "I just want to stay with you, in here, forever," I whispered.

Marcus pulled away slightly, then lowered his face to mine, kissing me tenderly on the lips. "Come on, Little Ivanov, the others are waiting."

He threaded his fingers through mine and led me out into the dry heat of the late afternoon.

As we neared the western boundary of camp, Sandra and Vali trailing close behind, I asked, "So . . . how'd you guys find the super-secret entrance?" I frowned. "And what about the other one—the main entrance your geologic studies found?"

"Decoy. As for the—"

Upon reaching the perimeter that had functioned as my prison wall in Set's fabricated echo of the camp, I hesitated.

"Lex? What's wrong?" Concern coated Marcus's deeply melodic voice.

"It . . . it's just that . . ." Taking a deep breath, I raised my foot and crossed the invisible line, breaking down another of the barriers Set had constructed in my mind. "It's nothing."

Marcus's eyes tightened with worry, but he didn't speak. He knew Set well enough that he could probably deduce the causes of any odd behavior I displayed after being held captive.

"I'm fine," I said, comforted by his concern. I tugged him along, and we continued the half-mile trek across superheated sand toward Djeser-Djeseru.

After a few minutes, I said, "Marcus?"

He glanced at me quizzically.

"Why don't I feel worse? I mean, why don't I feel like I've been comatose for three months?"

"Didn't anyone explain At-qed to you?"

I shrugged. "Only briefly."

Sighing, Marcus said, "At-qed decreases the body's metabolic rate to a near stop. All functions—cardiovascular, respiratory, digestive—slow drastically. You don't require food or water for many months, maybe even years. *You* were in the At for months, but your heart beat about as many times as it normally would in a couple of hours."

"Huh," I said, thinking it was just another unbelievable item to add to the list of insanity that had become my life.

As we stepped over a short, crumbling limestone wall and into the lower terrace of the temple complex, I took a deep breath, slowly releasing it with contentment. I'd yet to actually enter Hatchepsut's mortuary temple, and the thrill of approaching such a majestic structure rushed through me in waves. Blessedly empty of tourists, the temple, with its three levels of columned porticoes and terraces, looked like a giant, prize-winning sandcastle . . . or an enormous, beige wedding cake.

"You know, it's always going to be crazy to me that you were Hatchepsut's consort. I mean, she was a pharaoh . . . one of the most famous . . . and you had a kid together . . ." I glanced at him, wondering if she'd given him more than one child. *I can never do that.*

He squeezed my hand. "It was a long, long time ago. She was an *interesting* woman. She grew quite obese during the second half of her life, or so I heard. I was already gone by then . . ."

"It must've killed you to leave," I said, recalling Neffe's story of how Set had forced Marcus to leave his family.

Marcus smiled bitterly. "It was painful. I was very attached to Neffe . . . she was a firecracker of a young girl, as I'm sure you can imagine."

"But not Hatchepsut? You weren't really attached to her?"

"Our arrangement was more political than romantic."

I chewed on my lower lip for a moment. "Well, at least you've had many, many, *many* years to make up for lost time with Neffe."

"True." The single word sounded hollow, and I knew Marcus's mind had traveled to times long past. How many years would it take for the familiar structures of my life to devolve into ruins and be hidden by time's relentless efforts? How would I deal with my contemporary time becoming the distant, ancient past, as Marcus's already had?

I bumped Marcus's shoulder with my own. "So . . . you never did tell me how you guys found the hidden entrance."

Marcus laughed, and the genuine amusement it contained made me smile. "I wish you'd seen it. It was . . . unintentional. Dom, Alex, and Neffe were arguing in the sanctuary of the upper Anubis chapel. Dom said something about your capture being Neffe's fault, and she shoved him—into a three-thousand-five-hundred-year-old wall. Its decoration crumpled to the ground, revealing a solid limestone doorway."

"So was there a secret latch to open it, or something?"

Marcus looked at me askance. "I thought you were a professional—a *real* archaeologist."

"Oh, shut up."

"It would seem you've watched too many movies," he teased dryly.

"Well, how'd you get the huge slab of stone out, then?"

"Very carefully, Little Ivanov."

"Okay . . ." I said, equally irritated and amused by his useless evasion. "I wonder why Set didn't just tell us how to get into the temple. I mean, he wants me to open the chest and get the ankh-At for him, right?"

Shaking his head, Marcus said, "After the Council chose me as their leader over him, Set changed . . . his mind no longer works like yours or mine. His logic is impossible to understand. Why did he choose to hide the ankh-At here, in the heart of our homeland? Why not far away? Why did he change his mind from wanting to prevent the prophecy—prevent your birth—to actively working toward it?" Shaking his head, Marcus said, "So why didn't he draw us a map leading to the temple entrance? Maybe he wanted it to be just you and him, not to have other Nejerets surrounding you—Nejerets who would help you defy him."

Pursing my lips, I pondered his words, rolling them around in my head. I was certain of one thing: Set's unpredictability made him a whole lot scarier. I shivered.

As we walked up the centralized ramp leading to the temple's third level, I could see a handful of people mingling among the square columns and the few remaining statues of Hatchepsut. Neffe, Dominic, and Alexander were among them, along with at least a dozen more Nejerets. I was moderately surprised to find Kat standing beside Dominic, bouncing excitedly on the balls of her feet.

The mortuary temple's expansive, sand-colored portico reminded me of the wide front porch on a southern plantation home. Or it would have, if any plantation home had ever been built entirely out of limestone in a dusty desert with lumpy tan cliffs jutting up behind it. It was a bit of a stretch, but I'd always had an active imagination.

I was eager to greet my friends, especially my youthful grandpa. But I was equally as uncomfortable, fully aware that they knew I'd been back for well over an hour and had spent most of that time in Marcus's tent. The fate of the world was hanging in the balance, but we had to take a sex break while everyone else waited for us. No really, we *had* to.

Leaning in close, Marcus whispered, "Dom will have told them what you've been through and about the bonding—they'll understand."

I looked at him sharply. "What? Are you a mind reader now?" The confirmation that they knew what we'd been doing only amped up my chagrin.

Inches from my ear, Marcus chuckled, sending shocks of remembered pleasure dancing along my skin. "Hardly. You were just being exceptionally expressive."

"Oh." I could feel my cheeks growing hot. Damn, being bound to him made the most benign interactions feel like foreplay.

Softly, Marcus pressed his lips against my cheek, feeling cool against my flushed skin. "Alex might throttle me if I don't hand you over within the next five seconds . . ."

Letting go of Marcus's hand, I approached Alexander. He stood beside one of the seven remaining, mostly intact statues of Hatchepsut still decorating the fronts of the columns, looking equally as regal, though the statue was easily twice his height.

He wore a solemn expression as I neared, and closed the distance between us in two large strides. His arms enfolded me in a sturdy, comforting hug.

"Dear granddaughter, I'm so sorry for what Set has done to you. Ivan and the rest of the Council have sworn to forsake the swift release of death in his case. He will suffer for a very, very long time."

While part of my mind danced a merry jig at the thought of Set suffering an eternity of torture, I wondered if it would ever come to pass. Likely as not, the rest of us would end up being the victims of a hell inflicted by my father. And it all depended on me. *Oh joy.* I *really* hated him.

"Thanks, Alexander," I said, giving my grandpa a final squeeze. "I really appreciate the . . . er . . . sentiment."

After we broke apart, I received greetings and hugs from the others, including a promise from Kat to "kick that phony god's pretty ass" if he ever stepped out of line. She hadn't been talking about Set.

"Can we show her now?" Neffe asked, breaking through the good-humored reunion.

When Marcus nodded, Neffe reached for me and clasped her hand around my wrist, tugging me out of the cluster of Nejerets. Setting a quicker pace than I'd expected with her shorter legs, she dragged me through the blocky entryway to the upper court-yard and immediately turned right, following a tall, limestone wall. Multiple rows of polygonal columns were arranged evenly near the perimeter of the rectangular courtyard, broken off at various heights. Some still held vestiges of their ancient decorations, haphazard chunks emblazoned with faded amber hiero-glyphs and depictions of the ancient gods.

Freeing my wrist from Neffe's sharp-nailed grasp, I stopped with a slight stumble. "Thanks, Neffe, but I can walk on my own."

"Sorry," she said, shooting a wary look over my shoulder. I

knew what she was watching, or rather, who; I could feel Marcus's proximity even before his arm slipped around my waist. "I'm just a little excited."

"A little?" Dominic said, sneering as he passed her.

Neffe jogged for a few steps to reclaim her position as guide, and we followed. "You see, Lex, for weeks we haven't been able to make any progress because we needed you," she called over her shoulder. "We've explored every part of the temple and have found the chest containing the ankh-At—it's pretty hard to miss, really—but, like Nuin's prophecy says, *'No person except for the Meswett shall be able to access the ankh-At.'* You're the only Meswett there is, and with you here, we'll finally be able to open the chest and get to the ankh-At. I just can't believe it's all finally happening!" she exclaimed excitedly. *I guess she's not worried that I'll cave in, obey Set, and destroy the world . . .*

She led us through a small doorway leading into an open-air chamber. In its center stood what had once been a sun altar, a large square platform of decaying limestone. In singles and pairs, we followed Neffe diagonally across the debris-strewn ground to an even smaller opening in the opposite wall. My heart sped in anticipation of finally being able to enter Senenmut's secret temple. Begrudgingly, I admitted it was equally Set's secret temple.

Our clustered train of Nejerets narrowed to a single-file line so we could all pass through the slim doorway into the enclosed sanctuary of the upper Anubis Chapel. Vibrant colors covered the walls of the long room as well as its smaller annex, which was accessible by a petite doorway near the back left corner of the sanctuary. The sight of them sent a thrill through me. Seeing them in the modern time, thousands of years after they were first created, was totally different than seeing their pristine perfection in the At. For me, the beauty and magic of being an archaeologist was in uncovering what was hidden, in being the first to see or touch something in thousands of years.

Dominic stood aside at the end of the sanctuary, allowing me to enter the annex directly behind Neffe. A piece of my archaeologist soul shattered when I saw the long wall on the right—its decoration completely destroyed. However, the cavernous rectangle of glowing light in the center of the ruined wall more than made up for it. It was the entrance into the hidden temple.

"Archaeology is a destructive process," my Archy 101 professor's voice echoed in my head. I could almost see him standing on the raised dais, explaining that the world's beloved Pompeii would be completely destroyed the next time Mt. Vesuvius erupted, all because we'd uncovered it, exposing it to the world. *But it's worth it, right?*

While we waited for Neffe to unlock an iron gate blocking the previously hidden opening, I looked behind me at Marcus. One glance at the Nejerets packed into the sanctuary behind him and unexpected claustrophobia bloomed inside me. Even with the clear ropes of LED lights strung along the ground and only three of us actually standing in the annex, I was feeling suddenly, uncomfortably trapped.

Picking up on my distress, Marcus ordered, "Everyone back to camp but Dom, Alex, and Neffe." As they shuffled out, he added, "I want guards on the chapel entrance."

Seconds later, Marcus's eyes fell on Kat's slender, tan figure —she was still standing in the sanctuary. "Why are you still here, girl?"

"Because Dom promised I could come with you guys, *man.*" She sounded every bit the sullen teen, but a diamond-hard vein ran through her words. *She's got backbone, that's for sure.*

"Dom should be careful of what he promises." Marcus's jaw was clenched, and he was staring straight at Dominic. "But, if he's up to babysitting"—he turned back to Kat—"accompany us, by all means."

I rolled my eyes, exasperated that he'd entered his bossy, former-god state of mind. "Cut it out, Marcus—this is neither the time nor the place for a pissing contest." Given half the chance in his current state of mind, he would argue the most unimportant matters to the ground.

I flinched at seeing the cold look he turned on me, watching as its iciness thawed, and with narrowed eyes, heated to inappropriate levels. "This isn't the time or place for *that*, either!" I hissed, feeling exceptionally uncomfortable about the four sets of eyes watching us.

"The . . . um . . . gate's unlocked. So . . . shall we enter?" Neffe asked tentatively.

"Yes," I breathed, utterly thankful for her interruption. "Please."

Where ground met wall on either side, more LED ropes lined the passageway, illuminating everything surprisingly well. The persistent white light seemed eerily out of place within the rough-hewn corridor. There were chisel marks covering the walls, running from the ceiling down to the floor like streaming water. Passing through the entrance behind Neffe, I could easily touch both walls and the ceiling without extending my arms completely. My heartbeat sped up with a mixture of anticipation and anxiety as we burrowed further into Deir el-Bahri's limestone cliffs.

"This is totally better than air conditioning," Kat whispered. The temperature was dropping noticeably—an immense relief. The sound of her soft words bounced off the walls until they faded out of existence. Somebody, likely Dominic, shushed her.

Reaching behind me, I found Marcus's hand and gave it a quick squeeze, hoping he would hold his tongue. Neither patience nor tolerance was among the skills he'd honed during his long life.

After several minutes of moving at our slow pace, we reached a point in the passageway where it abruptly branched into four separate corridors. Two were perpendicular to the main passageway while two more evenly split the way going forward, creating a crisp corner straight ahead.

"This is odd," I said quietly as Neffe stopped at the intersection. She turned around and nodded sedately, clasping her hands in front of her.

Without further direction, I wandered down the passageway on my left, running my fingers along the walls as I went. The chisel marks were different there, running horizontally instead of vertically. I estimated the offshoot to be half as long as the main corridor—maybe fifty meters—and was intrigued to find that my arms were far more outstretched when I neared the end than they had been at the beginning. In the light from the LED ropes, I could see that a niche was cut into the wall at the end of the passage, twice as tall as it was wide. Reaching out, I traced the two-foot-tall ankh carved into the limestone at its center. My fingers started at the bottom, followed the straight stem of the symbol up until it split into an upside-down teardrop, worked their way around the curve, and ended by tracing the perpendicular line crossing the symbol at its midpoint.

"Life," I whispered. It was beautiful in its simplicity, both in shape and meaning.

Looking behind me, I was surprised to find that Marcus hadn't followed. Instead, he was locked in a hushed, extremely intense conversation with his daughter . . . in Middle Egyptian. I headed back up the passage, rejoining the fiercely whispering pair. They cut their words short as I neared them.

"Something wrong?" I asked quietly.

Neither Neffe nor Marcus said anything, and I figured Marcus was trying to hide something from me—again. Frustrated, I brushed past them, heading down the nearest corridor —one of the middle passageways. The limestone walls of the faintly curving passage had been polished completely smooth, making them seem impossibly modern. With the pale, artificial light from the LED ropes, I easily could have been in an elegant hotel or a contemporary monument.

When I paused and looked over my shoulder, I found that I was far enough down the corridor for its curvature to hide me from the five-way intersection. Footsteps, quick and determined, preceded Marcus as he came into view. Upon seeing him, I turned and continued down the passageway.

Sooner than I'd expected, he clamped his fingers around my upper arm, stopping me mid-step. "What exactly is the problem, Lex?"

"That you're hurting my arm," I told him. In the unnerving white light, his golden features appeared pale . . . gray. I must have looked ghostly.

Face blank, Marcus watched me. He didn't loosen his grip. He didn't glower. He just stared, passive.

I looked down at the floor, noticing it was just as smooth as the walls. "You're hiding something from me. Last time you did that, you left. And before that, I had to discover what I am on my own. So, what is it?" I asked, my voice small. I raised my eyes to his.

Finally, he released my arm. "Whether or not you should be allowed to open the chest today. Neffe thinks you should. I don't."

"Why not?"

He sighed, and reached out a hand to brush the backs of his fingers across my cheek. "I just got you back . . . and we don't know what opening the chest will do."

"I see," I said, frowning. "But you don't have a problem with me seeing it, do you?"

Shaking his head, Marcus took hold of my hand and pulled me back into motion. His mood instantly shifted to that of a little boy approaching the shimmering, present-strewn tree on Christmas morning. He led me down the passageway, the curve growing increasingly severe the further we walked. My mental blueprints of the temple were developing into an exciting, familiar shape.

"Does this corridor meet up with the other?" I asked eagerly.

"Yes."

So it's shaped like an ankh! "Then where's the . . ." On the outer wall a short way ahead, a spot of light brighter than that of the LED ropes came into view. It was oddly shaped, reaching from floor to ceiling, and symmetrical with irregular waves and points on either side. And it was warmer than the harsh white luminescence of the LEDs. After a brief moment, I realized it was the reflection of light through a doorway into a more brightly lit area. My pace slowed as I savored the delicious anticipation.

Six steps nearer, huge carved shapes took form on the inner wall. At first I thought it was a column, one of two framing the doorway, with its relatively featureless length and jutting protrusion a foot from the ceiling.

Four more steps and the base of the column started to look less like a base and more like a huge paw with finger-length claws. Another step and my eyes traveled up a five-foot-long foreleg to a strong, canine shoulder, sinuous neck, and long, downward curving muzzle.

After five final steps, I was standing before the monstrous statue, horrified. It was an enormous Set-animal, like the tattoo on the backs of the necks of Set's human followers. One of a pair, it was seated, looking like a gigantic greyhound with the snout of an anteater. With its partner five feet beyond, it seemed to hold sentry over the doorway—or what was beyond.

I briefly glanced through the doorway. At least, the glance was intended to be brief. "Oh my God," I whispered, stepping between the statues and into a breathtaking chamber.

Vibrant, almost violent swirls of color covered the walls and ceiling of the cavernous space. As I traced the line of the nearest wall all the way around the room and then overhead, I realized it was one continuous surface. The chamber was, in fact, a dome. With a floor that looked to be around forty meters in diameter, and curved proportions that I would've wagered measured into a flawless, geometric half-sphere, it was the least Egyptian and most architecturally astounding site I'd ever seen. How Senenmut had hollowed out a twenty-meter-high dome in the heart of the limestone cliffs with Middle Kingdom technology was beyond me. *Maybe he cheated by peeking into the future for help.*

"Eat your heart out, Brunelleschi," I whispered as I drew closer to the wall near the entrance. "And Michelangelo," I added, observing the fine detail of the seamless mural. Inlayed into the millennia-old paint, adding delightful chaos to the decoration, were colored stones, gems, and glass beads. Each matched the color in which it was set, but stood out by shimmering in the warm glow of the modern bulbs that had been placed evenly around the chamber. I was actually a little surprised that the floor wasn't decorated as well, though the highly polished limestone did a good job of reflecting the dizzying colors.

"It's just like in the At." My reverent words drew Marcus into the chamber.

"Yes," he whispered, stopping close behind me. "Senenmut was far beyond his time, even for a Nejeret. Set did our kind a great disservice by killing him." A little louder, he said, "Neffe, you may join us now."

I reached out my hand, but before my fingers could brush what looked like a very large, irregularly wispy strip of gold inlay in the brightly colored wall, Marcus caught my wrist. "I wouldn't," he said softly. His breath tickled the back of my neck, and I shivered. "It's quite fragile. The only reason it didn't crumble off a thousand years ago is that there was no air flow and no real temperature or moisture fluctuation. But now—"

"I really hate that, you know. We're destroying it just by being here," I said, sounding wistful and a little despondent.

"You wanted to be an archaeologist, Little Ivanov. You have to take the good with the bad." Marcus's voice changed as he moved away, toward the center of the floor. "Would you rather beautiful, ancient things remain hidden, or share their glory with the world? Or would you prefer to just see them in the At? You must remember that nothing lasts forever—not even us."

I pondered his words but said nothing.

"It's beautiful, is it not?" Neffe remarked as she entered the domed chamber. "Josh has come up with a very interesting preservation idea. He plans to use a specially prepared spray adhesive to glaze and protect the dome."

"Aren't we just sealing the entrance back up?" I asked, turning to her.

She nodded. "But the damage, I fear, is done."

Frowning, I turned toward the center of the chamber . . . toward Marcus and what I'd been ignoring. A three-foot-high circular dais had been left by the workers when they carved the chamber into the solid limestone. Resting on the raised platform was the object that could be nothing other than the chest containing the ankh-At.

The thing was a study of opposites—ancient Egyptian and modern, clear and opaque, moving and still, always and a single moment. It looked like somebody had taken a beautifully carved Old Kingdom chest, set it on fire, and then frozen time and transformed the entire jumble into crystal. It was hypnotizing and disturbing and the single most beautiful thing I'd ever seen. In its presence, I completely forgot the stunning dome overhead.

"Oh . . . oh, wow." My voice was hushed, awed.

Marcus turned away from the chest and watched me, his expression expectant. Because he was looking at me, he couldn't see what happened to the chest as I moved closer.

It began to glow.

"Oh . . ." I said, but lost the capacity for words as the chest's internal light shone brighter, extending to the upward-reaching tendrils. It called to me, almost hummed, sending a hair-raising tingling sensation all over my body.

Seeing the glow reflected on my skin, Marcus murmured, "What the—"

"It's never—" Neffe said at the same time that Alexander exclaimed, "Deus! It's glowing!"

Marcus grabbed my forearm. "Lex? I don't think you should do that."

Faintly, I heard him, and the hand I'd been reaching out to touch the glorious monstrosity paused inches from its surface. I felt like I was locked in a bubble of frozen time. I could hear and see everything going on around me, but I couldn't join. I was set apart . . . but I'd always been separate, apart from the rest of the world. I just hadn't known. I just hadn't remembered. And at the moment, I just couldn't speak.

A long moment of silence was broken by a muffled crack, and then another. Marcus released my wrist and turned away, probably to look for the source of the noise, but he didn't account for the freedom letting go would give me, and I didn't have the self-restraint to stop myself. My fingers inched forward and brushed the surface of the iridescent, glowing chest.

Instantly, the temple disappeared from my muted awareness, and the unbearably beautiful glow became everything. It was every*where* . . . every*when*. Nothing existed outside of it. I was it, and it was me.

Encapsulated in its warmth and comfort, I never wanted to leave. Finally, for the first time in my life, I was at peace.

31

ONCE & AGAIN

"My dear Alexandra," the richest, most melodious voice said in a language I only understood because Nuin had taken the effort to teach me years ago. "I see it is time. But then, it has always been time. Always and never."

"Nuin?" I asked, and though my voice was hushed, it echoed all around me. I spun in place, taking in the crystalline beauty of everything. It was as though I was in a small cavern fashioned entirely from quartz, the barely opaque walls resembling the frozen stream of a waterfall. Stepping toward the nearest surface, I watched in awe as everything within the chamber shifted with me, like it was an exoskeleton.

"Nuin? Where are you?" I asked in his language. Glancing up at the ceiling, I was almost surprised not to find any stalactites. I added, "Where am I? The At?"

"Why, dear Alexandra, you are in a time of my own creation. While only your ba can enter the At, your entire being is *here*."

I spun again, facing the direction his voice had come from, but Nuin was nowhere in sight. "How did I get here?" I asked into empty space.

"By my power, of course," Nuin's disembodied voice

answered. "I left the tiniest sliver buried deep within you the first time I visited you, when I solidified your role as the Meswett. It awakened when you touched the chest."

To my complete and utter shock, Nuin stepped out of the wall. He didn't step through the wall, as if it were composed of nothing more substantial than smoke, but seemed to emerge from it. It was almost like he was made from the wall, his shape taking on form and color as he broke free from its hold.

Hundreds of questions whirled in my mind, but Nuin's presence made them impossible to grasp. He stood several steps away, resplendent in exotic, ancient robes of white, gold, and teal. He was naked of jewelry, but then, beside the brilliant colors swirling around in his eyes, any precious metals or gemstones would lose their splendor. As he moved closer to me, I couldn't help but notice that, unlike me, he wasn't anchored to the chamber. He moved, and the walls stayed put.

"I didn't know if I'd ever see you again," I said, sounding teary. *My God, I forgot how much he looks like Marcus!*

Nuin reached out and cupped the side of my face with his hand. "I didn't know until a few moments ago . . . I just left you in the At, watching yourself play as a child. It was never certain you would make it this far. Indeed, it was not the most likely outcome."

Leaning into his hand, I frowned. "But the prophecy—*your* prophecy—it said I would get into the chest."

"No, dear Alexandra; it says that you, and only you, *could* get into the chest, not that you would." As I lost myself in his luminous, multicolored eyes, he continued, "There were other routes I could have taken, other bloodlines I could have pursued that would have produced a Meswett with slightly higher odds of making it this far."

"What?" I asked, pulling away from his hand. Suddenly, I felt cold and alone. "So it didn't have to be me? You could have chosen to dump all of this torture and pain and danger on someone else?"

Nuin watched and, smiling, nodded. "Yes. That is precisely what I'm telling you. And though I gave you a life with pain and danger, I also led you down a path toward the purest, strongest connection possible between two sentient beings. Very few have experienced such intense, beautiful emotions. Most would tear the world apart just to feel such a thing for a few moments. You and Heru may have it for eternity."

"May," I repeated. "Set will kill him if I don't hand over your power. And then what? Then I have nothing . . . then I die too."

"Ah—but that is precisely why I chose you over all the other possible Meswetts. There may have been others who were more likely to make it this far, but few had any real chance of successfully navigating what comes next," he explained cryptically.

"This doesn't make any sense. I have absolutely no idea what you're talking about."

"Yes," he said calmly. "You have some idea."

I fidgeted, shifting from foot to foot, and watched the cavern move with me. "You mean the choice from the prophecy—to obey Set or to defy him. Is that what you're talking about?"

Nuin nodded. "That's part of it."

Wrapping my arms around my middle, I turned away from him and hung my head. "If you're counting on me to reject Set's demands at all costs, you bet on the wrong horse," I said softly.

"I did *not* make an unwise wager. Everything that has happened between my time and yours has happened to bring you and Heru together. You had to be created—his perfect match—to ensure the strongest bonding possible. The two of you are essential to the past, present, and future. Of all the possible Nejeret–Nejerette pairings, only the two of you have a chance at succeeding." He paused his confounding explanation and rested a hand on my shoulder. "I know what you fear, Alexandra."

I turned my head to look into his kaleidoscope eyes, and he squeezed my shoulder. "You are not afraid that Set will threaten Heru's life. You expect it. What you fear is that you may lose him, no matter your choice."

Breathing in a slow, deep breath, I bowed my head. *How did he know?* Even if I agreed to hand the ankh-At to Set, there was no reason to believe my father wouldn't just kill Marcus anyway. Once he had Nuin's power, he could travel to any time and take out anybody he pleased by simply ensuring that person was never born. What would prevent him from doing that to Marcus? And then there was the actual power transfer to think about. Was the ankh-At something physical, a talisman of sorts, that contained the power? Or was it the power itself? Would Nuin give me a power-containing object, or would he imbue me with it directly? How would I pass it on to Set? Would he have to kill me to take the power, thus killing Marcus, too?

"What's going to happen?" I asked, my voice small and childlike.

"I only know all possible futures, not which one will truly come to pass." Nuin's resignation and hints of sadness worried me.

"At least . . . can you tell me . . ." I began, but had to take several heaving breaths before I could finish the thought. "Is there a chance that everything will work out okay? That the good guys will win and we'll all live happily ever after?"

Nuin said nothing for a while, and I thought I had my answer. Finally, he spoke. "If you weren't the best possible chance for everything to work out the way I need it to, I would not have chosen you."

"You mean—"

"I mean exactly what I said," Nuin interrupted. "In truth, I wish I could tell you more. I'm sorry, Alexandra, but doing so ruins your chances of succeeding. Here." He pulled an object out from the neck of his robes and held it up before me.

About the size and shape of a sand dollar, a brilliantly glowing pendant hung from a long, silver chain. It shone with wispy, ever-changing swirls of every color, just like Nuin's eyes always had. I quickly glanced up into his eyes, and though they were a remarkably luminous shade of amber, they were now just normal eyes.

"I thought silver fitting for your coloring," he said with uncommon reserve.

Letting my hands drop to my sides, I breathed, "Is that—"

"The ankh-At? My power? Yes. You must take it and return to your time. The medallion is fashioned from the essence of the At. It will feel odd when you touch it," he warned, draping the power-filled amulet around my neck.

"What do you mean—oh!" I said as soon as he tucked the dangling disk into the neck of my tank top. I was suddenly overwhelmed by a rush of softly tingling electricity. "What . . . what . . . ?"

"It's the power. It's entering you," he explained.

"But what if I don't want it?" I screeched, frantic and uncomfortable.

"Irrelevant. You need it. Are you ready to return to Heru?" he asked.

"I don't know how," I told him, fearing I would be stuck in the quartz prison for eternity.

"Just walk into the wall."

"I can't . . . it won't let me," I said, remembering the way the chamber had moved with me.

"It will now," Nuin said, giving me a gentle push toward the wall. To my utter amazement, the cavern stayed in place as I moved.

"What did you do?"

"Nothing. You must return to Heru now, my Alexandra. You're still anchored to your own timeline, and events there are reaching a critical point." He moved me even closer to the wall and I noticed that it glowed with a soft iridescence.

"Will I see you again?" I asked as my fingers pressed into the warm, comforting substance.

"If everything works out, you will," Nuin said, pushing me further into the malleable wall. As my entire body was enveloped in the iridescent glow, once again, the overwhelming feeling of peace settled over me, mixing with the tingling feeling of Nuin's power.

Distantly, I heard Nuin say, "When you return to your time, you must give the amulet to Heru so he can absorb the male half of my power."

I floated in a state of baffled calm for what felt like eternity. And then, suddenly, everything changed. The peaceful, iridescent glow gave way to artificially lit, bright colors. The gentle warmth gave way to cool, dry air. The soft hum gave way to angry voices . . . to yelling.

"WHERE DID SHE TAKE IT?" shouted the man nearest me. Set. He stood on the other side of the now-blackened chest, his back to me. He was pointing two pistols . . . at two different people.

A young woman was huddled on the ground near his feet. She was shaking with silent sobs, her face frozen in terror as she stared down the barrel of one gun. *Oh my God, Jenny!*

Several paces beyond Set, Marcus stood with his hands outstretched, placating my enraged father. The second gun was aimed at his forehead. Nejerets can recover from many things, but a gunshot to the head wasn't one of them.

Neffe, Alexander, Dominic, and Kat were all being restrained by black-clad men. Knowing that few humans could match a Nejeret in speed, strength, and skill, I assumed the men were Nejerets as well. *This is just swell . . .*

Miraculously, nobody had noticed my abrupt arrival. I removed my hands from the chest's apparently charred surface, and for the first time in all the chaos, noticed that the tingling had stopped. *Is the power transfer complete? Shouldn't I feel different? Did it even work?*

I yanked the amulet out of my tank top by its chain and stared. It still swirled with luminous colors, but lacked the reds, yellows, and oranges it had once contained. *Interesting . . .*

"If you don't tell me where she went, I'll kill her sister. And if you still refuse to answer, I'll kill your daughter," Set said, boiling with raging hysteria.

"I'd really prefer it if you didn't," I said, my voice strong, resonant. It had the desired effect.

Every set of eyes snapped to me. I latched onto Set's, black as onyx, holding them without fear.

"You want Nuin's power?" I pulled the chain over my head, held the glowing amulet in my hand, and raised my arm. "Catch."

Set's expression changed from shock to excitement as I spoke, and then to pure, unbridled fury as he saw the trajectory of the amulet . . . of Nuin's power. It arced over him and landed with a faint thump in Marcus's hand.

"NO!" Set screamed. "You little bitch! How dare you! Traitorous . . . ungrateful whore! That's mine!" Before I knew what was happening, he raised his left hand, which had drooped, and shot Marcus directly between the eyes.

It was my turn to scream. But I didn't. I just stood, numb with shock, as Marcus's body went limp and crumpled to the floor. Far slower than I expected, his blood spilled out and pooled on the polished limestone, glossy and thick.

But Nuin said . . . Nuin said . . . Nuin told me to give it to Marcus . . .

Marcus can't be . . . Marcus isn't . . . how can he be . . . dead?

"Now it's mine," Set's poisonous voice broke through my shock.

Marcus is dead?

I watched Set stroll over to Marcus's limp body and exchange one of his guns for the shining amulet, plucking it from Marcus's limp hand. His face turned rapturous as the other half of Nuin's power oozed into him—the male half.

Marcus is dead.

Screaming, I launched myself at my father. My rage and sorrow were so great that I no longer had room for anything else. I had one purpose—to destroy him.

He didn't see me coming. He couldn't see me coming. One second, I was standing next to the chest, screaming. In the same second, at the exact same moment, I was in front of him tearing the remaining pistol from his grasp. It was impossible, how I'd moved, but it didn't matter, not when I carried Nuin's power in my body. Tendrils of the fabric of the At swirled around me like smoke, a part of me.

"How—?"

Set didn't have time to finish the question. I shoved his gun against the side of his head and pulled the trigger. I didn't even watch him fall, I just yanked the amulet from his hand and turned.

Suddenly, in another flash of rainbow smoke, I was kneeling beside Marcus. I'd moved too fast again, going directly from one place to another, completely skipping everything in between.

Marcus . . . my Marcus . . . he can't be dead!

Keening, I rocked beside his body. I felt hollow. Numb. Wrong. Broken. It was familiar. I'd done this thousands of times before. But he wouldn't come back this time. No other version of Marcus would suddenly appear. Marcus was gone.

I won't let him be dead!

I needed him. I couldn't live without him. My body would

literally die, deprived of his bonding pheromone. But beyond that, I didn't want to live without him. The sorrow was too much. I was drowning in the missing. Death would be a relief. I would prefer death.

Staring at his body, hearing my moaning wail, I realized I was wrong. I would prefer life with Marcus to death without him. I had to do something else. I had to do *something*. Lucky for me, I *could* do something else.

I screamed.

Like ripples on the surface of a pond, time wavered around me, and stilled.

I screamed again.

Everything shivered. Slowly, in flashes, the scene changed. The people around me acted out the past thirty seconds in reverse. They were jerky, like the unnatural movements of a reanimated corpse.

Set stood. *Marcus is still dead.*

Set replaced the amulet in Marcus's hand. *Marcus is still dead.*

Marcus regained his feet, his face surprised as he stared at the amulet in his hand. *Marcus is alive!*

That was when things had been going well. *That* was the perfect moment.

With a shiver, time halted again. I spared a moment to stare at Marcus, to watch his features once again alight with life, before dealing with the pressing issue—Set's pistols.

I had to do it right. I didn't know how I was controlling the power, or if I could even do it again. If I only had one chance, I couldn't waste it.

Tentatively, I approached Set's immobile form. His arms had drooped from their earlier positions when he thought I was tossing him the ankh-At; one pistol was at his side, the other aimed at the floor in front of him. Trying to remove the weapons was futile. They were locked in his time-frozen grasp.

Attempting to shove Marcus out of the bullet's future trajectory proved equally impossible.

I glanced back at myself—or where I should have been, behind the shrine—and was momentarily stunned. I was gone. Had I displaced myself in the timeline? Could only one of me occupy a specific time at once? But then, amidst the confounding thoughts, an idea flickered into existence.

Once time restarted, everyone would expect me to be there, by the shrine. Exactly as I had been after I'd tossed the amulet to Marcus. But, if I stood in front of Set and knocked the gun out of his hand before he processed my change in position, I might be able to save Marcus . . . to change the future.

Standing in front of my father, I wrapped my hands around his wrist and pushed down.

When I released my hold on time, the world resumed. Set was definitely surprised. His hand only raised partially. Unfortunately, he still pulled the trigger; he just didn't shoot Marcus in the head.

The crack of the gun firing shocked me so much that I barely felt it . . . at first. I took a single breath, and let it out with a horrible wail as lightning bolts of pain shot through my abdomen.

"Lex!" Marcus shouted, lunging toward us in time to catch me on my way to the polished limestone floor.

"I'll take that," Set said, but I couldn't spare a thought to figure out what the hell he was talking about. Marcus had torn off his shirt and was holding it against my stomach, making the pain more intense. Around us, the domed chamber was full of harsh voices and rushing bodies. People were fighting and shouting out in pain.

"LET'S GO!" Set yelled. "Jenny, come!"

"No!" my sister shouted. "Fuck you, you bastard! Lex!"

"Jenny," I gasped between clenched teeth. I refused to look at my middle, which felt like it was on fire. I couldn't let Set steal my sister again.

"Shhh . . ." Marcus murmured, hovering over me.

I heard Set mutter, "Not worth the trouble," then shout, "Move, you imbeciles!" just before Jenny scooted to my side.

"Oh God, Lex!" my sister exclaimed, touching my face and leaning close. She looked up at Marcus. "Is she going to be okay?"

A soft clink barely registered as I stared into Jenny's frightened eyes. The second clink caught my attention enough to draw my eyes away. As my gaze flitted around the huge chamber, I noticed little pieces of the dome's beautiful decoration raining to the floor. They were followed by larger pieces of what looked like very ancient, very hard plaster. The shouting and gunshots had disrupted the stability of the dome.

"Marcus," I rasped, but he didn't turn his attention to me. He was watching something I couldn't see. "Marcus!" That time, he did look. "We need to leave. Now." A large, heavy-sounding chunk crashed on the floor a few feet away, spraying the three of us with dust and debris. Marcus got the point.

He scooped me up and shouted, "Dom, get the others out of here! This place is coming down!" Without looking back to make sure his order was followed, Marcus sprinted out of the chamber and along the curving, ankh-shaped passageway. He didn't stop when we made it to the chapel.

The ground trembled with what I assumed was the collapse of the entire dome. Whatever Senenmut had used in his grand creation had been pretty damn heavy.

Marcus and I made it out into the evening air only seconds before the rest of our crew, and they were followed closely by a groaning rumble and a thick poof of dust.

"Dom, Alex—check if Vali and the others are alive and bring them back to camp. Neffe, come with me," Marcus ordered before he started jogging, me still cradled in his arms.

I was woozy and in a whole lot of pain. "Where's the amulet?" I managed to ask between shallow breaths. "Did you bring it out?"

"No," Marcus said. "Set took it."

Crap! "Was it still glowing when he took it?"

"Yes."

"But the power . . . some of it went into you, didn't it?" I asked.

"I think so."

Flooded with relief, I passed out.

PART IV

Council Headquarters
Florence, Italy

3 2

INTRODUCTIONS & CELEBRATIONS

Turning my head on a pillow, I groaned. My skull felt like it was stuffed with cotton candy—the kind that's a fluffy swirl of pink and blue with hard little chunks of sugar that didn't quite make it all the way to the 'cotton' stage. Because of the cottony confection seemingly filling my head, it took me several long moments to realize my abdomen didn't hurt at all. *God I love regeneration*, I thought lazily.

Cracking one eyelid open, I peeked at my surroundings. Everything in the room was gilded or flowery or carved in an extravagant manner. And, everything was compact. It was like the maker of each piece of furniture had been trying to make up for its petite size by adding an overabundance of decoration.

I rolled over, half-expecting to find Marcus asleep beside me. I was more than a little disappointed to find the other side of the bed empty and tidily made. *Where's Marcus? Where am I?*

Sitting up, I shook my head to clear the webs of cotton candy. I twisted, dangling my legs over the side of the bed so the balls of my feet brushed a soft, crimson and gold Persian rug. I slipped my bare feet into grey, velvety slippers and found a floor-length silk robe draped over a chair by the window. It was a monochromatic crimson so deep it almost looked purple. As I donned and tied the robe over a long, black satin nightgown that most certainly did *not* belong to me, I peered through a crack in the gold brocade curtains. The view gave no hint as to my current whereabouts. I was looking down upon a beautifully manicured garden that could've been in upstate New York just as easily as in England or France. Of one thing I was certain—I was *not* in Egypt.

Walking around the room, I searched for hotel stationary or any other sign of my current location. There was nothing. I would have started panicking, but I saw several of Marcus's elegant suitcases in the corner on the opposite side of the bed. *Marcus is with me. Marcus is safe.*

Marcus is alive.

Stop it! It never happened! I shook my head, forcing away the images of Marcus, the real Marcus, dead with a bloody hole in his head. I buried them in an imaginary titanium time capsule in my head, along with the memory of shooting my father, which also hadn't happened, at least not in *this* timeline. *No, not my father—Set.*

With a deep breath, I forced a smile and opened the bedroom door. My lips pursed when I heard the sound of cheerful voices drifting down a long, dimly lit hallway. The voices carried with them the sound of clinking dishes, silverware, and glasses, along with the most delicious smells. Basil and oregano mixed with tomatoes, bread, and cheeses in an unmistakable blend—Italian food! *Am I in Italy?*

My stomach growled loudly, pulling me down the lavishly decorated hallway toward a curving stairwell and the promise of food. My robe was several inches too long, pooling on the floor when I paused and fluttering around my feet when I walked. I felt elegant in it, almost like a noble woman in a medieval King's court.

All thoughts of clothes and anything else disappeared when I heard *his* voice: "—hope that it's all over. And if it's not, we will hunt him down until it is."

Marcus. Alive.

Soft cheers rose and glasses clinked and people laughed as I started down the stairs. When I reached the bottom, I froze.

Due to the curvature to stairway, the view through the wide doorway leading into the dining room had been hidden. In fact, it wasn't a dining room at all, but an enormous banquet hall filled with long, extravagantly set tables seating several hundred people. Based on the diners' sleek beauty, it looked like they were all Nejerets. They were also all suddenly staring at me. I recognized almost nobody in the crowd.

"Hi?" I croaked, coloring as I realized I was wearing nothing but a nightgown, robe, and slippers while they were all dressed in evening finery.

At the far end of the room a man stood from what was undoubtedly the head table. It took me only a moment to recognize him as Marcus. But it was a Marcus I had never seen, wearing a pale gray tuxedo of the finest cut and emitting an air of irrefutable authority.

He rounded his long table and slowly strode between the others like a jungle cat. His keen eyes were locked on me, glinting slyly to match his quirked mouth, and he walked with undeniable confidence. He drew most of the attention away from me—not a single woman was glancing my way by the time he reached the center of the room.

I was starting to wonder if Marcus purposely toned down his charisma when he was around me, so I wouldn't feel overwhelmed. At the moment, he wasn't putting an ounce of effort in that direction.

Crap—did the regeneration make me look sickly again? I ran fingers through my hair, wishing I'd at least put it in a ponytail before leaving the room, but resigned to let it hang in loose, tangled waves.

With narrowed eyes and pursed lips, Marcus reached me. He walked a slow circle around me, examining my every inch. Pausing with his back to the crowd, he murmured, "In that delectably thin robe and with bed-mussed hair, you put the rest of these Nejerettes to shame, Little Ivanov. I'm of half a mind to take you back upstairs and act out some of the *very* inappropriate things I'm imagining . . . but I'll save that for later." He smirked wickedly and raised a single eyebrow. "Are you ready to meet your admirers?"

Based on the catty glares being thrown in my direction by most of the women, I thought 'admirers' was a gross overstatement of the crowd's opinion of me.

"Now?" I whispered, fully aware that every single person was staring at us and that bailing was pretty much useless.

Marcus's smirk widened into a grin.

"Okay, I guess," I said, unsure.

He took a step closer and leaned in. I thought he was going to kiss me, there, in front of everyone. He didn't. Instead, he veered to the left, finding my ear. "Do you feel alright? I can have food sent up to the room if you don't feel up to this. You've only been out for eight or nine hours . . . we didn't expect you up yet."

I shivered at feeling his breath rustle my hair. "I'm fine," I whispered.

"Good," he said, pulling away. To my surprise, he did pause to lightly brush his lips against mine, chuckling when he heard me squeak.

The room was filled with a hushed murmur as he pulled away. Men and women alike were whispering to each other behind their hands. Apparently, claiming and bonding in a small camp was one thing, but such a small public display of affection before a formal assembly of Nejerets was another.

Marcus took my arm, placing my hand on his forearm, and presented me to the room. Staring out at the vast array of exquisitely dressed, gorgeous people, I felt completely inadequate.

"May I present to you all the Meswett, Alexandra Ivanov, great-granddaughter of Ivan and daughter of Set," he boomed.

I half-expected the crowd to explode into applause and cheers, though for what, I don't know. It didn't. It was so quiet, I was pretty sure every person could hear my stomach growling as Marcus led me down the center of the room toward the head table. We took the same path he had used in his approach, and by the time we reached the table, an additional, intricate place setting had been laid out between Marcus and Neffe's plates.

Sitting in the chair Marcus pulled out for me, I tried to ignore the scrutinizing eyes prodding me from every direction. I made a valiant attempt to focus on Neffe's words as she explained that I'd only missed the first course and that my hair didn't really look too bad and that the regeneration hadn't made me look too sick and that my sister was fine—resting upstairs—but my stupid Nejerette hearing perked up as various women throughout the hall made audible judgments.

"She's pretty enough, I guess, but she still looks human-ish."

"Did you see her eyes? Blood-red is fitting for one of Set's line."

"It's just her ancestors that make her the Meswett—I'm sure there's actually nothing special about her."

"Wasn't she just shot in the stomach this morning? That's pretty quick to be completely healed, and she doesn't really look like she just regenerated."

"Poor Heru, having to train such a child in the delicate arts," said a husky French voice. "When I was with him, I always gave him something new and exciting. Whatever he wanted, I did, along with some things he didn't know he wanted until I did them to him. He will never be satisfied with a girl like her. Eventually, he will come back to my bed." She laughed suggestively, and I found her in the crowd, staring at Marcus with so much heat it looked like she was trying to set him aflame with her eyes alone.

Marcus, I discovered irately, was returning the stare. Albeit, devoid of the excessive lust hers held, but still . . .

My blood boiled. Who was this woman to declare such a thing loud enough for the large gathering of Nejerets to hear every word? *How dare she! I ought to—*

Without warning, I winked out of time and space in a swirl of smoky colors and reappeared before the spiteful hussy. Shouts of surprise and gasps followed my abrupt change of position.

While tendrils of At were still floating around me, making me look like some sort of furious rainbow fairy, I slammed my hands on the pale yellow tablecloth in front of the woman and hissed, "Listen up, you French whore. You may have been with him in the past, and you may have had to practice bedroom Olympics because without amazing feats of wonder, being with you is just too damn boring." Taking in her beautiful, silver-blonde hair, pale blue eyes, and creamy skin, I sneered. "But that's the thing with bonding . . . with me. Just the touch of my fingertips on his skin is better than anything you might have done to him. You're a forgotten memory." I licked my lips and added, "Enjoy your dinner."

Straightening, I tried to flash back to my seat at the head table. Nothing happened. I tried again. Nothing happened, again.

So, I smiled at the people sitting on either side of the scandalized French Nejerette and turned to glide back up to my table. I was more than a little relieved to find Dominic approaching, several paces away.

"Might I escort you back to your seat, Meswett?" he asked, doing a valiant job of hiding his amusement.

My plastered-on smile melted into something genuine, and I nodded. "I'd like that, Dom. Thanks."

He took my arm and led me away, smiling and nodding at certain people as we passed. Low enough that only I heard, he whispered, "If there's one thing we can be certain of, it's that we'll never be short on entertainment when you're around."

"Ha. Ha. Very funny."

Letting his French accent grow heavier, he murmured, "I was being completely serious."

Grinning, I settled back into my seat. "Thanks, Dom."

"Rescuing you is quickly becoming my calling."

Marcus cleared his throat. Dominic had been there to save my sanity when Marcus left, and it had been Dominic who'd rescued me from Set, not Marcus. For some reason, a new tension had developed between the two men, and it seemed to be increasing.

Dominic slipped away, graceful as a dancer and deadly as a viper, to his seat on the other side of Neffe.

Leaning in, Marcus whispered, "I love it when you do that."

"What? Embarrass myself in front of hundreds of people?"

"No," he said. "I love watching you assert your claim on me. The second time was just as good as the first. Maybe better. It makes my hunger for you fathomless, every time." He reached for my hand and guided it under the tablecloth to his groin so I could feel the evidence of his hunger.

I blushed and withdrew my hand before we caused a scene. "Oh . . . well, that's what every girl wants to hear."

"Mmm . . . but you're not every girl, are you?" There was a slight, unexpected edge to his tone. "I think you just showed us all that."

Cringing, I thought about how I'd just inadvertently used Nuin's power to shift from one place to another, as I'd done in the temple . . . when Marcus had died. "Right, about that . . ."

"Yes, Lex, let's talk about *that*." He shifted in his chair, letting the server place a bowl of creamy yellow soup in front of each of us, and demanded, "Tell me everything that happened in the temple." I raised my eyebrows at the haughtiness in his words, and he added a delightfully sensual, "Please?"

So I told him . . . almost everything, leaving out the part about tweaking the timeline . . . about him dying . . . about killing Set. I whispered as quietly as possible, hoping only those nearest to us could overhear.

"It doesn't quite make sense," Marcus said after I finished. "If Nuin held all the power himself, why did it need to be split into male and female halves when he passed it on?"

"I know!" I agreed. "And why did he have to pass it on in the first place? He looked perfectly healthy at first, but near the end he seemed a little, I don't know . . . wane. It was like getting rid of his power made him weak. You were there . . . how'd he die?"

Frowning, Marcus said, "It took some time, but he gradually weakened until he died. There was a woman—the Nejerette wife I told you about before—she took care of him until he drew his final breath. Some believed she somehow caused his death . . . maybe poisoned him. I don't remember much about her, other than that she was his only Nejerette wife and that I knew she hadn't harmed him—that she had loved him as we all had. Nobody knew how old he really was, so I just thought his wasting sickness might be what happens once Nejerets reach a certain age."

"I think . . . do you think he might have died because he gave up his power?" I blinked rapidly at the welling of tears in my eyes. "Did giving me his power kill him? Did *I* kill him?"

Marcus shook his head. "He gave *us* his power, Lex. *Us.* And Nuin never did anything without a very good reason, so if he gave us his power and that killed him, it was what had to be done."

Some of my worry eased as I stared into his golden, tiger eyes. And then I registered his words. "Us? Are you saying you definitely have the male half? But you said the amulet was still glowing when Set took it."

"It *was* still glowing," he interrupted. "But it was faint. I'm certain I absorbed some of the male half, though I have no idea how much or what that really means."

"So Set at least has some of the power, too." I frowned, thinking. "Has anyone checked on the Nothingness?"

He nodded. "It's still there, but a little less . . . dense. Like a fog that has thinned."

"Damn," I said with a sigh. "Maybe controlling the Nothingness is part of Nuin's power? Maybe that's the part that Set absorbed?"

Marcus snorted. "I honestly haven't the slightest idea."

"Do you think Set knows about the two halves? That I have half of Nuin's power roiling inside me?" I asked.

"Probably. He did see you do your disappearing act in the temple." He squeezed my thigh under the table before picking up his spoon. "Eat. You must be famished."

I was hungry, but not starved like I'd been the last time I'd used my regenerative abilities to heal. "I'm surprised I don't look like I'm eighty years old," I joked. When he said nothing, I became suddenly worried and asked, "I don't look eighty, do I?"

He laughed, "No, Little Ivanov. You just look tired . . . and hungry. Eat."

I took a spoonful of soup, and then another . . . and then another. "Oh, wow. This is amazing!"

"Enjoy it. We've got thirteen more courses of amazing," he told me, and my eyes widened.

Out of nowhere, I laughed. It was bubbly and throaty and full of happiness.

"Care to share?" Marcus asked, glancing at me sideways.

"I just realized something—we have more than half of Nuin's power. Set has less than us." I grinned, my eyes full of wonder. "We're going to be okay, aren't we?"

Marcus brushed a stray strand of hair out of my eyes. "Yes, my darling, I think so."

EPILOGUE

Set

Heru thinks he knows. He runs around with my daughter. *Mine!* And he thinks he knows how this will all turn out. But Heru has always thought just a little too highly of himself. Where he captures power through strength and charisma, I use knowledge. He thinks he knows everything he needs to know, so he doesn't seek.

I seek . . . listen . . . learn . . . *know.*

I know about her. I know about him. I know about the power. And I know about Nuin, what he is and what he's planning. *I* know, so *I* have the power.

GLOSSARY

- **At** Ancient Egyptian, "moment, instant, time"; The *At* is the actual fabric of time.
- **ankh** Ancient Egyptian, "life".
- **ankh-At** Nuin's power. Includes (at least) the power to travel through time, to create and remove memory blocks, and to fashion objects from the At.
- **Anubis** Ancient Egyptian god (Anapa) associated with cemeteries, embalming, and the afterlife. Anubis is often portrayed as a jackal or jackal-headed.
- **Aset (Isis)** Nejerette. Heru's sister. Aset was worshipped as a goddess associated with motherhood, magic, and nature by the ancient Egyptians.
- **At-qed** State of stasis a Nejeret's body enters when his or her ba departs for the At.
- **ba** Considered one of the three essential parts of the soul by the ancient Egyptians. In regards to Nejerets, the ba is the part of a person that can enter the At.
- **Bahur** Arabic, "of Horus" or "of Heru".
- **Council of Seven** The body of leadership that governs the Nejerets. The Council is headed by the

patriarchs of the seven strongest Nejeret families: Ivan, Heru, Set, Sid, Moshe, Dedwen, and Shangdi.

- **Dedwen** A member of the Council of Seven. Dedwen was worshipped as a god associated with prosperity, wealth, and fire by the ancient Nubians.
- **Deir el-Bahri** Located on the west side of the Nile, just across the river from Luxor in Upper (southern) Egypt. Several mortuary temples and tombs are located in Deir el-Bahri, including Djeser-Djeseru, Queen Hatchepsut's mortuary temple.
- **Djeser-Djeseru** Ancient Egyptian, "Holy of Holies". Queen Hatchepsut's mortuary temple in Deir el-Bahri.
- **Firenze** Florence, Italy.
- **Hatchepsut** (ruled 1479—1457 BCE) Female Pharaoh during the Middle Kingdom of ancient Egypt.
- **Hathor** Ancient Egyptian goddess associated with love, fertility, sexuality, music, and dance. According to the Contendings of Heru and Set myth, Hathor is the goddess who healed Heru's eye. She is often depicted as a cow or a woman with cow ears or horns, and a sun disk is frequently cradled by the horns.
- **Hatnofer** Carrier. Mother of Senenmut.
- **Heru (Horus)** Nejeret. Osiris's son, Nuin's grandson, Aset's brother, and former leader of the Council of Seven. Heru stepped down from his role as leader to function as the Council's general and assassin, when necessary. Heru was worshipped as the god of the sky, kingship, and authority by the ancient Egyptians. He is often depicted as a falcon or falcon-headed.
- **Ivan** Nejeret. Leader of the Council of Seven. Alexander's father and Lex's great-grandfather.
- **Kemet** Ancient Egyptian, "Black Land". Kemet is one of the names ancient Egyptians called their homeland.

- **Middle Kingdom** Period of Egyptian history from 2055—1650 BCE.
- **Meswett** Ancient Egyptian (mswtt), "girl-child". The Meswett is the prophesied savior/destroyer of the Nejerets, as foretold by Nuin upon his deathbed.
- **Moshe (Moses)** Nejeret. Member of the Council of Seven. Central figure in most western religions.
- **Neferure** Nejerette. Daughter of Hatchepsut and Heru.
- **Nejeret (male)/Nejerette (female)/Nejerets (plural)** Modern term for the Netjer-At.
- **Netjer-At** Ancient Egyptian, "Gods of Time".
- **Nuin (Nun)** Nejeret. Also known as the "Great Father", Nuin was the original Nejeret and the father of all Nejeret-kind. Nuin was worshipped as a god associated with the primordial waters and creation by the ancient Egyptians.
- **Old Kingdom** Period of Egyptian history from 2686 —2181 BCE.
- **Osiris** Nejeret. Heru and Aset's father and leader of the Council of Seven until his murder a few decades after Nuin's death. Osiris was worshipped as a god associated with death, the afterlife, fertility, and agriculture by the ancient Egyptians.
- **Senenmut** Nejeret. Scribe of Nuin's prophecy and architect of the underground temple housing the ankh-At at Deir el-Bahri. Senenmut was the "high steward of the king" to Queen Hatchepsut as well as Neferure's tutor. Senenmut was killed by Set after the completion of the underground temple.
- **Set (Seth)** Nejeret. Nuin's grandson, father of Dom, Genevieve, Kat, and Lex, and member of the Council of Seven. Set went rogue when the Council of Seven chose Heru as their leader after Osiris's death around

4,000 years ago. Set is determined to secure the ankh-At as his own to wield.

- **Shangdi** Nejerette. Member of the Council of Seven. Shangdi is worshipped as the supreme sky deity in the traditional Chinese religion.
- **Sid (Siddhartha Gautama)** Nejeret. More commonly known as "Buddha" to humans.
- **Wedjat (Eye of Horus)** Ancient Egyptian symbol of protection, healing, strength, and perfection.

CAN'T GET ENOUGH?

NEWSLETTER: www.lindseyfairleigh.com/join-newsletter
WEBSITE: www.lindseyfairleigh.com
FACEBOOK: Lindsey Fairleigh
INSTAGRAM: @LindseyFairleigh
PINTEREST: LindsFairleigh
PATREON: www.patreon.com/lindseyfairleigh

Reviews are always appreciated. They help indie authors like me sell books (and keep writing them!).

ALSO BY LINDSEY FAIRLEIGH

ECHO TRILOGY

Echo in Time

Resonance

Time Anomaly

Dissonance

Ricochet Through Time

KAT DUBOIS CHRONICLES

Ink Witch

Outcast

Underground

Soul Eater

Judgement

Afterlife

ATLANTIS LEGACY

Sacrifice of the Sinners

Legacy of the Lost

Fate of the Fallen

Dreams of the Damned

Song of the Soulless

THE ENDING SERIES

Beginnings: The Ending Series Origin Stories

After The Ending

Into The Fire

Out Of The Ashes

Before The Dawn

World Before

World After

FOR MORE INFORMATION ON LINDSEY FAIRLEIGH & THE ECHO TRILOGY:

www.lindseyfairleigh.com

Reviews are always appreciated. They help indie authors like me sell books (and keep writing them!).

ABOUT THE AUTHOR

Lindsey Fairleigh a bestselling
Science Fiction and Fantasy author
who lives her life with one foot in
a book—so long as that book
transports her to a magical world
or bends the rules of science. Her
novels, from Post-apocalyptic to
Time Travel Romance, always offer
up a hearty dose of unreality,
along with plenty of history, mystery, adventure, and romance.
When she's not working on her next novel, Lindsey spends her
time walking around the foothills surrounding her home with
her son, playing video games, and trying out new recipes in the
kitchen. She lives in the Pacific Northwest with her family and
their small pack of dogs and cats.

www.lindseyfairleigh.com